Pre-Publication Praise

"Rosalee Jaeger traces Edie Stern's eventful journey from the constricted straits of a 1940's Detroit Jewish neighborhood and lesser child status ("the girl") to an ever-widening world of unlimited possibilities. She dreams and dares to develop her own skills, find her own loves, make her own friends, as millions of her age, kind, class, and ethnicity have. Failing at one aspiration, she seeks another: concert pianist, writer, and finally, restaurateur. With no less abandon, she pursues love: Jack, Stanley, Zola, Mike, Ken. The constants in her adult life are her three children, and her friend, Janet-Gianna, a Holocaust-haunted Italian Jew; the one, who despite seemingly insurmountable differences, always returns. Written in a simple, straightforward style, women who have engaged in a similar search for selfhood and love will rejoice and weep with Jaeger's characters. Readers who have lived and suffered with these peripatic pathfinders, may view them with more compassion-even pride."

Harriet Rochlin,
Social Historian and Novelist

"Edie and Janet's journey through life is a powerful tale. Read and enjoy this compelling novel."

Richard Krevolin,
Author of *Screenwriting From the Soul*, and, *How to Adapt Anything Into A Screenplay*; Adjunct Professor of Screenwriting at USC School of Cinema/TV and at UCLA School of Theater, Film and TV.

Love
and
Other Passions

~Rosalee Mandell Jaeger~

Llumina Press

Requests for permission to make copies of any part of this work should be mailed to Permissions Department, Llumina Press, P.O. Box 772246, Coral Springs, Florida 33077-2246.

ISBN: 1-932047-94-8.

Printed in the United States of America.

Acknowledgments

I would like to thank all of the people who helped me in the writing and publishing of this novel, including:

Daisy Miller, dear friend and confidant, and Inge and Franco Servi who know all things Italian; Anna Mae Haas, Mimi Hoffman, Bea Mandell, Amy Kussro, and Mitchell Ross for their excellent input and editing; Marlene Chessler, my computer whiz; Mark Harris, renowned author and teacher, for his encouragement; Nancy Silverton, world-famous pastry chef and co-owner of Campanile Restaurant in Los Angeles; Angelo Auriana, chef extraordinaire of Valentino's Restaurant in Santa Monica, CA, and Robert Ravi, partner in the wonderful Alessio Restaurant in Northridge, CA, for their expertise; the late Alan Seager, Anne Hockensmith and Robert Kirsch, my illustrious creative writing teachers for believing in me; my husband, Martin Jaeger, for his unequivocal love and support; my family: Stuart, Karen, Zachary, Evan, and Alan Jaeger; Sue, Doug, Hanna, and Harrison Turner; and Lee Mandell for their love and inspiration.

To Marty, who makes all things possible.

Chapter One
Detroit, Michigan

The first boy Edith Stern ever loved was her brother, Frank. Frank was four years older than Edie, and she followed him about like a pesky fly. Sometimes he would shoo her off, but mostly he was nice to her.

Edie, Frank and their parents, Ben and Lilly, lived in a red-brick duplex on Pasadena Avenue. They occupied the downstairs flat and rented out the upstairs flat to a widow lady named Mrs. Belinsky. Their neighborhood was completely Jewish. On the Jewish High Holidays, the elementary school could have closed, and at Christmas-time, there was not a Christmas tree in sight.

For the first five years of Edie's life, she slept in Frank's bedroom. Their flat had only three bedrooms, so when Edie's father opened his own insurance agency, Edie's parents had to rent out the third bedroom to a boarder to help pay Ben's rent. The boarder's name was Mr. Ratner. Edie thought he looked like a rat, with his impish body and small white teeth, and was sure he ate cheese at every meal.

By the time Edie started kindergarten, Ben was selling so much insurance that they no longer needed a border. So on December 14, seven days after the Japanese bombed Pearl Harbor, Mr. Ratner moved out of the third bedroom and Edie moved in. Her mother bought her a new bed, a pink bedspread, pink curtains, and a brown veneer bookcase. Edie was most thrilled with the new bookcase, because now she had a place to put all her precious books.

Eight years later, when Edie was 13, her mother, Lilly, came to her with a proposal. Her mother was, as usual, on her way out to a meeting. Today it was the Pioneer Women. She was all dressed up in a navy blue suit and navy blue high heels, her brown hair teased out a mile, and her nails polished a bright red. "Edie, I have a big favor to ask of you. Dad wants to buy a television set, and if I put it in the living room, it'll ruin my furniture, you know, with the eating and all. Would you mind terribly if we turned your bedroom into a den?"

"But where will I sleep?" Edie asked, a little disconcerted.

"Oh, we'll buy you a sofa-bed."

Edie thought it over a moment. She didn't really want to give up her bedroom, but then again, she really did want a television set. "Okay, mom."

"I knew you'd do it," her mother said, glee written all over her face.

So out went the bed, the pink bedspread, the pink curtains, and in came the new beige sofa-bed, beige curtains, and a brand new 13-inch black and white Philco television set.

By the time Edie was 16, she had been on a few dates and kissed a few boys at "spin the bottle" parties, but she had never had a boyfriend, and she was beginning to wonder if she ever would. Her mother had told her on more than one occasion that she wasn't "the prettiest girl in the world." But now that she had lost 20 pounds, and all the pimples on her face had disappeared (except for an occasional "shiner" as her mother called them), she thought she looked okay. Maybe not pretty, but cute. She was 5 foot 6, slim, with blue eyes, and light brown hair. She tried to wear her hair in a page boy, but it had a mind of its own, and instead of turning under, went every which way. She didn't care though, because fortunately, it had enough curl so she didn't have to put it in pink rollers every night, like most of her friends did. She didn't wear much makeup, just a little powder and lipstick, because she didn't want to look like her mother. Her mother poured it on, the eye shadow, the mascara, and especially the bright pink rouge on her cheeks. Her mother also went to the beauty parlor every Friday to get her hair done. She was always perfectly coifed and stylishly dressed. If this is what it took to get a boyfriend, Edie knew she would never have one.

And then she met Jack Shine.

She met Jack her first year at Cass Technical High School. She went to Cass, the downtown school in the heart of the Negro ghetto, instead of Central High, the neighborhood "Jewish" school, because she wanted to be a concert pianist, and Cass offered a music program. When Edie's mother heard that Edie had decided to go to Cass, she had a fit.

"I can't understand why you would want to travel 40 minutes on the bus each way to go to school with a bunch of "schvartzas" (the Jewish word for "Negroes").

"Because I want to be a concert pianist, and don't call them 'schvartzas'". Edie was always getting into arguments with her parents about their attitude toward Negroes. She couldn't understand how they could be so upset about anti-semitism, and then call Negroes "schvartzas" and tell mean jokes about them. Especially since they adored Mrs. Giles, their Negro cleaning lady, who came in every week to give the house a good scrubbing. They felt sorry for her, and gave her extra money, even though she was dumb enough to get pregnant three times out of wedlock.

Edie's mother wasn't only upset about Edie attending Cass, but that she *wasn't* going to Central. How was she ever going to meet a nice Jewish boy and get married? And worse yet, what if she fell in love with a Negro? God forbid a million times! "Honestly, Edie, I'll never understand you. Why can't you be like the other girls?"

"Because I don't want to be like the other girls." By "other" girls, Edie's mother meant those girls who were only interested in boys, clothes, being popular, and how many cashmere sweaters they could accumulate. Edie was interested in those things too, except for the cashmere sweaters, but she wanted something more out of life than to get married, have kids, and live and die in Detroit, Michigan. She wanted to lead an exciting life. She wanted to be the heroine of every book she read. Like Dominique in *The Fountainhead*. *The Fountainhead* was her bible and Howard Roark was her hero. As soon as she was old enough, she wanted to move to New York, get a penthouse apartment, and find a man who was just like Howard Roark. In fact, on the night of graduation from junior high, she had talked her two best friends, Sandy Stahler and Naomi Parker, into signing a pact in blood, each girl pricking her finger, that if they weren't married by the time they were 18, they would move to New York with her.

For her final comment, her mother said, "I would never have given you piano lessons if I knew it would end like this!" And she stomped out of the room.

Edie met Jack Shine in her music theory class. Of the forty students in the class, only five were white, and Jack was one of them. She knew she was spending too much time looking at him instead of the blackboard, but she couldn't help it. Unlike his name, Jack Shine was not bright and sunny, but morose and brooding, with dark eyes and straight black hair. He wore a white dress shirt to school every day, and always had a serious expression on his face. When he did smile, his lips barely parted, as if it was painful to smile. Edie knew he was Jewish and that he played the violin. Perhaps he thought violinists were supposed to be dark, moody, and never smile.

It was about five weeks into the semester when Jack came up to her after class and asked if she'd like to play duets with him sometime. She was flustered, but flattered. "Sure," she said.

Without hesitating, he said, "How about Saturday afternoon?" She wondered if he was asking her out on a date, or did he really just want to come over and play duets. "Sure," she said, "That'd be great."

Saturday afternoon was a perfect autumn day. The sun high in a blue sky, a cool breeze blowing, and thousands of red, orange, and yellow leaves floating to earth from every tree on the block.

At one o'clock, Jack's mother dropped him off at Edie's house. He was wearing a light blue shirt, and carrying his violin in one hand and a stack of sheet music in the other.

They played an Elgar sonata, then a Brahms sonata. Jack's playing was a little ragged, but still it was fun. When they finished the Brahms, Edie led Jack out of the living room (where they didn't qualify as company and therefore couldn't sit) into her bedroom-den.

Edie was still wondering if this was a date or not, when Jack turned to her with those wistful black eyes and said, "You know, you're the prettiest girl at Cass." She felt prickles on her skin. It *was* a date. He liked her. He thought she was pretty! Could this be it? Was she finally going to have a boyfriend? He took her hand in his and they sat on her sofa-bed holding hands and talking until his mother came to pick him up.

After that Saturday, Edie and Jack began seeing each other as often as possible. Unfortunately, Edie didn't have much free time. In addition to doing her homework, she practiced the piano two hours a day, played piano at a ballet school Tuesday and Thursday nights, accompanied several singing groups at school, and gave piano lessons to seven little kids in her neighborhood for a dollar an hour. Still, she saw Jack every day at school, and on the weekends, and sometimes during the week. When they were together, they'd go to a movie, play ping-pong in Edie's basement, play duets, or if they were alone in the house, they'd go into Edie's bedroom-den and kiss. Edie loved kissing Jack. His lips were soft and gentle. She felt emotions she had never felt before. She thought it must be love, so one Sunday afternoon, when he asked her to go steady, she gladly accepted.

A week later, when Jack had his wisdom tooth pulled, he drilled a hole in it, put it on a silver chain from Kresge's Five and Dime and gave it to her. "I want you to have a part of me with you all the time."

She thought it a little weird, but touching. "I'll wear it every day," she told him, fastening it around her neck.

In December, Edie's best friend, Sandy Stahler, was going to have a sweet sixteen party. Sandy, a pretty girl with red hair and freckles, had lived next door to Edie from the time Edie was seven until she was 15. They had gone back and forth across the driveway between their houses a thousand times. They were constantly together, sharing secrets, listening to records, dreaming about meeting the man of their dreams. When they entered Durfee Junior High, they and six of their closest friends formed a club. All the girls at Durfee belonged to a club, except for the very least popular ones. The only purpose of the clubs was to meet boys. Every Friday night the clubs would have an open house, and boys would travel from club to club meeting girls. The girls in Edie's club weren't the most popular at school, so they didn't attract the best boys. But some of them did get dates from the Friday night open houses, including Naomi Parker, who was now in love with Harvey Cohen, and Beverly Schwartz, who was now going steady with Marvin Goodman.

Edie was the only girl in her club who went to Cass instead of Central, but she was still friends with the other girls, especially Sandy Stahler and Naomi Parker. She was very excited about going to the party. It would be the first party she'd ever gone to with a boyfriend!

But on the Monday evening before the Saturday night party, Jack called. "I have some bad news," he said. "My parents think I'm spending too much time with you, that you're distracting me from my practicing. From now on, they said I can only see you on Sunday afternoons."

She felt her heart sink. "But what about the party?"

"Obviously," he said, "I can't go."

"But surely you can convince your parents to make this one exception. We won't see each other for two Sundays, but please get them to let you go to this party."

"They won't listen," he said with annoyance in his voice.

"How do you know if you don't try?"

"I know my parents," he said. "Once they make up their mind, they won't budge."

Edie was furious. Not just at Jack's parents, but at Jack. Where was his fight, his determination? If he really cared about her, he would find a way to go. He could lie to his parents. Tell them he was going to a friend's. Lock his bedroom door and climb out the window. If he really cared about her.

As if reading her thoughts, he said. "It's just a party. One party."

She wanted to say, "But it's the first party I've ever gone to with a boyfriend." Instead she said, "I suppose I could ask one of my friends to fix me up."

"No," he said, "I don't want that. I'll tell you what, I have a friend. A friend I trust. His name is Stanley Rader. I'll ask him tonight if he'll take you to the party, and I'll tell you in school tomorrow what he said. I have to hang up now."

Edie hung up the phone feeling totally dejected. Not just about the party, but about Jack. She couldn't believe that he wouldn't even ask his parents. That he wouldn't even try to go. Maybe he wasn't the person she thought he was.

Now what to do? Take a chance on Jack's friend? Ask one of her friends to fix her up? Go by herself, or not go at all.

She went to Frank with her dilemma. She still idolized Frank. Didn't everyone? Especially her parents. Whenever they spoke about him, it was in reverent tones. Frank could do no wrong, he knew everything about everything, and of course, he was going to be a doctor. He was also good looking, medium height, medium build, with curly brown hair, and his ever-present horn-rimmed glasses. But Edie didn't resent Frank's status in the family. She only wanted to be worthy of his affection, to be the kind of girl he would want to marry. She knew Frank admired her for her piano playing and good marks in school, and she didn't want to ruin her reputation with her anxiety over this sweet sixteen party. But she needed his advice. She knocked on his bedroom door. He was always studying, either sitting at his desk or lying on his bed. "Come in," he called. This afternoon, he was sitting at his desk. "What's up?" he asked.

She told him her story, and when she was finished, he made his pronouncement, "It's obvious that you should go by yourself. What do you care what anyone thinks? You have a boyfriend; he couldn't make it, and that's that."

She wanted to say, "But Frank--you don't understand how humiliating it is to be the only girl without a date." But she didn't say that. She didn't want Frank to think her weak or vain.

In school the next day, Jack told her that Stanley had agreed to take her to the party.

"You're sure there's no way you can get your parents to let you go?"

"I'm sure," he said, with an irritating edge to his voice.

"All right," she said, "then I'll go with Stanley. By the way, what does he look like?"

Jack annoyed, "I don't know."

"Well, is he tall or short?"

Then spit out all in one breath, "He's tall and blond and he's 19 and he goes to college and he has his own car."

Edie was impressed. Not that he had a car, but that he was 19 and in college. "Okay then, tell him to pick me up at 6:30 Saturday night."

All day Saturday, Edie was a nervous wreck.

She practiced the piano for three hours, hoping the music would get her mind off the coming event. But it didn't work. If only she knew what Stanley was like. He could be awful, but then again, he could be great. If she knew he was horrible, and she was going to be humiliated and embarrassed, she could adjust. But what if he was handsome, intelligent? What if he turned out to be the man of her dreams? She went back and forth in her mind. If only she knew which way it was going to go, she could stop thinking about it. It was the "not knowing" that was killing her.

Just before he was to arrive, Edie, in a complete state of anxiety, was in her bedroom-den putting on lipstick, when her mother appeared at the door. Her mother was wearing a red dress, red shoes, and a bouffant hairdo that had so much hairspray on it, not a hair could move if it wanted to. Her parents were going to their Saturday night poker game. They also had a Tuesday night poker game, and a Thursday night canasta game. Ben loved to play cards, and Lilly loved being with her friends. They played for a penny, two, and three, but now and then the men would play for a nickel, dime, and quarter. Lilly frowned on that. She considered it gambling, not a thing a Jewish person should do.

"I'm glad you're going out with someone besides that Jack Shine," her mother said.

Immediately Edie's back arched, "What's wrong with Jack Shine?"

Her mother backed off, "Nothing. It's just that you should be going out with lots of boys."

"In case you haven't noticed, 'lots of boys' haven't asked me."

"That's because you stuck yourself away in that music school. How are you going to meet anyone decent there?"

"I met Jack Shine."

"Exactly my point," her mother said.

"Please, mom," Edie said, "would you mind leaving me alone. I'm trying to get ready." Edie was nervous enough without her mother undermining her confidence.

Just then, Edie's father popped into the room. In looks, her father was an older version of her brother Frank: slightly taller, much broader, but with the same brown eyes and the same curly brown hair, now speckled with gray and thinning at the temples. In personality, however, her dad was completely different from Frank; he was always smiling, always with a joke to tell, always with a pat on the back, and a twinkle in his eyes. No wonder he was kept busy day and night selling insurance.

"Well, don't you look spiffy," he said to Edie.

How Edie loved him. "Thanks, dad."

Edie was wearing a black dress, tight fitting in the bodice, with a long flowing skirt; her hair, of course, would not cooperate, and her page boy was out, instead of under. She had given in to wearing a hint of rouge on her cheeks, and a touch of blue on her eyelids to bring out the blue of her eyes.

"You do look very pretty tonight," her mother said, with some warmth in her tone.

"Thanks, mom."

And then the doorbell rang.

"I've got to go," Edie said, picking up her little black purse, and kissing both parents on the cheek.

When she got to the door, her insides were churning. She put her hand on the knob, the lady or the tiger, and then pulled the door open, and there standing before her was Stanley Rader, the most handsome boy she'd ever met. He was tall, with the front of his wavy blond hair in a perfect pompadour, and gray-green eyes that must have been the exact color of Howard Roark's.

"Hi," he said, holding out his hand.

"Hi," she said taking it.

As the evening progressed, she discovered that not only did Stanley Rader have a car, a 1948 green Plymouth, but that he was in college, in pre-med. In some of the same classes as Frank! How could she be so lucky? He had only one flaw. As the evening progressed, his left eyelid began to droop. However, Edie didn't focus on his eye, but on the words he spoke.

All the girls at the party were very impressed with Stanley, and girls who hadn't spoken to Edie in years came over to say, "Hi, how've you been?" Edie felt like Cinderella at the Ball, only she didn't have to be home by midnight.

After the party, Stanley drove her to Palmer Park, an outlying neighborhood of Detroit, with spacious lawns, large homes, and this time of year, decorated Christmas trees that you could see through the front glass windows. Stanley and Edie sat shivering in Stanley's green Plymouth, the engine turned off, the windows steamy from the cold, and talked.

"I had a wonderful time tonight," Stanley said.

"So did I," she said, getting colder by the minute, but willing to freeze to death to have this night go on forever.

"I was so worried after I told Jack I'd do it. I didn't know what you'd be like."

"I know," she said. "I felt the same way."

"It's amazing," he said. "I feel so comfortable with you."

"Have you dated many girls?" she asked.

"A few," he said. "How about you?"

"Jack is my first boyfriend. But it isn't that serious between us."

"That's not what he said."

"What did he say?"

"He said you were going steady."

"Well, we were."

She looked at him. He looked at her, and then they just kind of came together, and he was kissing her. It was nothing like kissing Jack. It was deep and moving and sad.

When he pulled back, he said, "We can't see each other again."

She felt like Kathy in *Wuthering Heights*. She had found the great passion of her life, but uncontrollable circumstances were keeping them apart. "I've got to see you again," she said. "I'm going to break up with Jack."

"I can't allow that," Stanley said, perhaps acting out his own tragic novel. "He's my friend. He trusted me. I can't do this to him."

"I'm going to stop seeing him anyway."

"Then maybe later. After you've broken up. I don't want him to think I was the cause of it."

"I'm going to tell him tomorrow."

"I don't know," he said. "I feel terrible." But not so terrible that he didn't kiss her again and again, long, soulful kisses. She put her hands inside his coat to keep warm, and he put his inside hers for the same reason. Finally, he said, "I'm freezing. Aren't you?"

"It is a little cold," she said through chattering teeth, envisioning tomorrow's headlines: "Couple found frozen to death in Palmer Park."

He drove her home and walked her to the door. "I'll call you," he said. He kissed her once again, and then hurried down the steps back to his car.

Once inside the house, Edie pulled off her shoes and began rubbing her toes. She hoped she wouldn't lose all of them to frostbite, but even if she did, it would have been worth it. It was worth anything to have met Stanley Rader, to have been kissed by him, to have been held by him. And he was in some of Frank's classes! Wouldn't Frank be impressed with that? One thing was clear, she would have to break up with Jack as soon as possible. She could see now how immature he was, how childish. Especially compared to Stanley Rader. If only she could think of a way to break up with him without hurting him. She unhooked his chain and put it on the dresser. She would never wear it again. Then she undressed, opened her sofa bed, put on her pillows and blanket, and crawled in. She didn't want to tell Jack the truth, but she didn't want to lie to him, either. Lying there under her warm blanket, she thought, "I'll think about it tomorrow at Tara, for tonight I only want to think about Stanley Rader."

The next day, Sunday, Jack's mother dropped him off at her house. "I can only stay an hour," he told her.

They went into her bedroom-den and he wanted to kiss.

She was more nervous than before her date with Stanley.

"Jack," her voice was cracking, "there's something I have to tell you."

He sat on her sofa-bed. "What?"

She summoned her courage, "I don't want to go steady anymore."

His face turned crimson. "It's Stanley, isn't it?" He stood up. "I knew I shouldn't have trusted him. That dirty rat!"

"Please," she said. "It wasn't his fault."

"If I never fixed you up with him, this wouldn't have happened."

What could she say? It was true.

"Give me back my tooth," he said.

She walked over to the dresser and handed it to him. He took the tooth off the chain and threw the chain on the floor. "You can keep that!" he said and slammed out of the house.

She began to shake. She felt horrible. She hadn't wanted to hurt Jack. She didn't want to hurt anyone. But what choice did she have? She couldn't continue seeing Jack when she was so enamored with Stanley Rader. She picked up the chain that was lying on the carpet, and put it in her drawer. She didn't have the heart to throw it away.

Now she waited for Stanley to call. She moped around the house each evening, waiting for the phone to ring. "I'll call you," he had said, but she remembered a story she had read in English class where the boy said, "I'll call you" and never did. The last lines of the story went, "and now she knew what the stars knew all along, he'll never call, never." Was it to be this way with Stanley?

"Don't look so gloomy," her mother said. "He'll call, and if he doesn't, there's plenty of fish in the ocean."

Of course her mother would think that. Her mother had no idea of what Edie was going through. Her mother had always been popular and could have had any man she wanted. She had told Edie enough times about all the men who wanted to marry her. "There was Moishe, the doctor, and Hymie, the CPA, and Sam who worked at Dun and Bradstreet. I had a millionaire after me, you know, Aunt Esther's cousin, Abie, poor guy, he died from cancer when he was thirty. I could have married any of them, but I fell in love with your dad, a poor greenie from Poland. Let me tell you, Edie, that's the most important thing in life. Love. Without love, life is nothing."

Edie sat down at the piano and began to play a Chopin Etude. For once, her mother was right: love was everything. If Stanley didn't call, Edie would throw herself under a train like Anna Karennina.

A week passed, and then on a Thursday night, after supper, he called.

"Hello, Edie?" there was no mistaking his voice, "it's Stanley."

Frank had told her that if Stanley called, she shouldn't sound too eager; she should play hard-to-get; boys liked that. But when she heard his voice, she couldn't hold back her excitement, "Oh Stanley, I'm so happy you called. I was so afraid you wouldn't."

"I wanted to call you sooner, but I didn't have the nerve to call Jack until tonight. Boy is he mad."

"I know. He's still not speaking to me."

"Would you like to go for a ride?"

"You mean now?"

"Yes."

"Yes."

She hung up the phone. Oh God. He called. She ran to Frank's bedroom where he was sitting at his desk studying. "Frank, he called!"

"Good for you," he said.

She saw Stanley that night and the next night, but not again until the following Friday night.

He didn't have much time for her because he was busy with school and studying and working in his father's auto parts store, but he saw her whenever he could.

He would usually call at the last minute and they would go out to the show, or for a hamburger or just drive somewhere and sit kissing for hours in his green car. Or he'd come over to her house, and they'd play ping-pong in the basement, and then, after the rest of the family was asleep, they'd lie on her bedroom-den floor, kissing and caressing each other until 1 or 2 o'clock in the morning. Neither of them thought of going all the way. It wasn't something that nice girls did. And Edie considered herself a nice girl. She was determined to be a virgin when she got married--or at least until she was 22, which she decided was long enough to wait to experience life's most touted pleasure.

She was still working at the ballet school on Tuesday and Thursday nights, taking two streetcars to get there and two home, and occasionally Stanley would come by to pick her up. Each time she emerged from the studio, she prayed she would see his green Plymouth parked out front, and if it was there, her heart would leap with joy. Not just because she wouldn't have to take the two streetcars home, but, because, by now, she was totally, completely in love with him.

But did he love her? He had made it clear from the beginning that he was in no position to go steady or get serious. He was a poor boy from a poor family, and his number one priority was to go to medical school. And while he seemed to love her at times, other times she might not hear from him for several weeks while he was off dating some other girl. But somehow he kept returning to Edie, and every time he did, she was glad to have him back. He told her that she should date other boys, that it made him feel guilty to have her waiting for him. But how could she date anyone else, when she was in love with Stanley?

Each time he came back to her, it was as if they'd never been apart. She told him everything. He told her everything. Perhaps most touching was the night he told her how embarrassed he was about his eye.

"I don't even notice it," she said.

They had just finished playing ping-pong in the basement, Edie winning two out of three games in spite of Frank's admonition, "Never beat a boy at ping-pong."

"Yes, but you noticed it the first time we met."

"Maybe the first time we met."

"It seems to happen most when I'm tired or nervous. And now I have to go on these interviews for medical school and I'm scared they'll turn me down because of it."

"No, they won't," Edie said, trying to sound like Frank. "Just go in there like you own the world, and they won't even notice it."

"I hope you're right," he said and pulled her to him. "No wonder I keep coming back to you," he said.

And her reply was lost in a kiss.

During her junior year, Edie began writing short stories. Her English teacher, Mr. Dow, who had given her an "A" on every paper she had written for English class, suggested it. "You have a bit of talent," he said, in his droll way. He was a nice looking middle-aged man, soft spoken, always in brown tweed jackets that smelled of pipe tobacco.

So Edie gave it a try. She might pick on any incident that happened at school, or at the grocery store or bakery, or just passing someone on the street, and build a story around it. She didn't make them too long, because she first hand-wrote them, and then had to type them on her brother's Underwood, which took a long time.

Mr. Dow would have her stories read by the next day, and usually made suggestions on how to make them better. But sometimes he would say, "Quite an impressive piece of work."

By her senior year, Edie realized that she enjoyed writing short stories as much as she liked playing the piano. She still wanted to be a concert pianist, but it was getting more and more difficult to put in those two hours of practicing every single day. In any event, the day of judgment was at hand. Each semester, a senior was chosen to play a piano concerto with the Cass Tech Symphony Orchestra. If she really was to become a concert pianist, then she had better win this competition.

The closer the date came, the more Edie wanted to win. There were only two people to fear: Eleanor Plotkin and Carol Hicks. They were both working on Chopin's 1st; Edie was working on Beethoven's 2nd. Edie increased her practice time from two to three hours a day, which meant canceling the lessons she was giving to her now 13 students, and cutting out one night at the ballet school. She knew she should cut out both nights, but she couldn't bring herself to practice one more minute than she was already practicing.

The try-outs went on for three days, and Edie was scheduled to play at 10 o'clock on Wednesday, the third day. Frank and Stanley drove over together, both cutting an important class in quantitative analysis to attend. And her dad was there, but her mother had a nominating committee meeting of Hadassah that she just could not miss. "But don't worry, honey, if you win the contest, I'll be at the concert for sure." Edie wasn't surprised. Since her mother's friends and her mother's clubs had always come first in her mother's life, why should today be different? Still, Edie was disappointed that just this once, her mother couldn't put Edie first. But Edie couldn't afford to dwell on that now, she had to concentrate on her performance.

As Edie's name was called and she stepped onto the stage, her body turned to ice. She had played for people all her life, in her home, at other people's houses, in combos, accompanying singers and violinists at school, and at the ballet school, but now, on this stage, before these three judges and the smattering of people in the audience, she was terrified. She forced herself to the piano bench. If only she had practiced more, if only she had gone over the cadenza one more time. Would she remember the notes? Would she be able to play at all? She stared at the black and white keys before her; they were like strangers she had never met.

Edie's teacher, Miss Good, sat at the piano across from Edie and began playing the orchestra part. When it was time for Edie to come in, Miss Good nodded at her. Edie began to play, amazed that her fingers knew what to do, that they remembered all the notes. Gradually she began to hear the music, to feel it, and finally to get lost in it.

When she finished, she felt exhilarated. She knew she had played well. She sat a moment, gathering herself, then stood. The people in the audience and the members of the jury applauded and she bowed to them and to her teacher.

Off stage in the wings, Miss Good embraced her. "That was marvelous, Edie. I hope you win."

Edie couldn't wait to get the results. At this moment, nothing mattered more, not Stanley, not her schoolwork, not her friends, nothing but winning this competition.

Two days later, on Friday morning, the results were posted. Eleanor Plotkin would play Chopin's Piano Concerto No. 1. If she were unable, Carol Hicks would play Chopin's Piano Concerto No. l. If those two were unable, then Edith Stern would play Beethoven's Piano Concerto No. 2.

Edie was shattered. She wanted to run home, to hide, to lock herself in her room and never come out. She was embarrassed to face her classmates, her friends, her family. But she stayed at school, attending every class, close to tears with every, "Sorry, Edie," and "You should have won, Edie," and Jack Shine's first words to her since their breakup, "I was rooting for you, Edie." And finally, in her last class of the day, breaking out in tears when a myriad of black arms enveloped her, "We don't care about no damn contest, you're the best!"

Her last stop before going home was to see Mr. Dow. "Maybe you ought to become an English teacher," he said.

"Never," she said. "Remember what you told me, 'Those who can, do. Those who can't, teach.' I want to 'do'."

"Then how about being a writer? You've written some pretty good stories."

"I don't know what I want to do at this point."

"Don't be too tough on yourself, Edie. Life doesn't always turn out the way you expect it to."

"I think I already figured that out, Mr. Dow."

By the time she got home, she was feeling a little better, but now came the next trauma, facing her family.

She found her mother in the kitchen, browning pieces of meat in a frying pan. Tins of salt, pepper and paprika stood on the counter, and her mother's hands stained by the paprika were almost as red as the rouge on her cheeks. Her mother was wearing pink slippers and a pink print housedress.

"You're home early," Edie said.

"I decided to make a stew tonight and it takes a good two hours to cook the meat."

Better to get it over with, just blurt it out. "I lost," Edie said.

"You lost?" her mother repeated, looking somewhat bewildered.

Something so important to Edie, and her mother didn't even remember it. "The competition."

"Oh," her mother said, her face turning redder than it had been before. "Oh Edie, I'm truly sorry."

"I came in third, behind Eleanor Plotkin and Carol Hicks."

"Well, third's not so bad," her mother said, turning the meat with a metal spoon. Then trying to sound sympathetic, "Maybe it's for the best. It's not a good life for a woman, being a concert pianist. You should be something else."

"But I wanted to be a concert pianist," Edie said, and fighting to hold in her tears, turned and ran off to her bedroom-den. She shut the door, and stood by the window, looking out. The sky was already beginning to darken and she could just barely make out the stars coming to light. "Now I know what the stars knew all along," she thought, "I'll never be a concert pianist, never."

She walked away from the window and sat on her sofa-bed, looking at the blank screen of the television set. Perhaps if she had practiced more, but at this stage of her life, there were too many other things she wanted to do. If she was going to be totally honest with herself, she would have to face the fact that she didn't really have what it takes to be a concert pianist. Not the talent, not the dedication, and certainly not the single-mindedness.

So now what was she going to do? Going off to New York with Sandy Stahler and Naomi Parker was out. Naomi Parker was going to marry Harvey Cohen and Sandy Stahler had already enrolled at the University of Michigan. Maybe that's what she should do, go to Michigan with Sandy Stahler. Become a writer like Mr. Dow had suggested. She had always loved to read, she enjoyed writing, and Mr. Dow said she had talent, so why not? She felt an excitement building in her. She could be like Jo in *Little Women*. She ran to the phone in the hallway, and called Sandy Stahler.

That night Stanley came by to console her. "I'm really sorry," he said.

"It's okay," she said. "I'm through with the piano."

"Just like that?"

"Just like that."

It was 11 o'clock. The rest of the family was already asleep, and she and Stanley were alone in her bedroom-den.

"You're being too hard on yourself. You shouldn't let a little thing like a high school competition ruin your life."

"But that's the point. All it was was a little high school competition and I couldn't even win that." And then taking a deep breath, did she trust him enough to bare her soul, "The truth is I didn't deserve to win."

"But I heard you myself. You played beautifully."

"Not as beautifully as Eleanor and Carol. Not as beautifully as if I had practiced six hours a day for the last 10 years."

"Who could do that?"

"People who become concert pianists."

"So now what?"

"I think I'd like to be a writer."

"A writer! Where'd you come up with that?"

"This afternoon. And I want to go to Michigan. With Sandy Stahler. I already talked to her and we're going to be room-mates."

"You don't waste a minute, do you?"

"I had to do something."

He thought for a moment. "You know if you go to Michigan I'll hardly see you."

"You hardly see me now."

"But if you go to Michigan, it'll be even less."

"You can come up and visit me."

"It wouldn't be the same."

She suddenly felt light-headed. Was he trying to tell her something? Was he finally ready to make a commitment, to tell her he loved her, to ask her to marry him? She could barely get the question out, "Do you want me to stay Stanley? Because if you do, I won't go."

She held her breath, ready to explode with joy.

"No," he said, "I think you should go."

The letdown was almost as bad as losing the competition this morning. She felt like a boxer who'd been punched all day and now taken the knockout blow. So that was it. She was not going to be a concert pianist and she was not going to marry Stanley Rader.

"Don't look so glum," he said. "Nothing's changed between us. I just want what's best for you."

"Of course," she said.

And in the warmth of his lips, Edie forgot what a terrible day it had been.

The next morning, Edie told her mother she wanted to go to Michigan.

"Michigan!" her mother said. "Where did you come up with that idea?"

"Sandy's going and I thought I'd go, too."

"And what are you planning to study?"

"Writing. I'm going to be a writer."

"Since when?"

"Since yesterday."

"Honestly, Edie," her mother said, "I don't know where you get these crazy ideas."

"From Mr. Dow, my English teacher."

"Well, you don't need to go to Michigan for that. You don't need to go to college at all."

"Frank's going to college."

"That's different. He's a boy," and then spoken in the reverent tone, "and he's going to become a doctor."

"So I can't go to college because I'm a girl."

"That's right. You don't need to go to college to learn how to change dirty diapers." Then, seeing the forlorn look on her daughter's face, Lilly said, "If you insist on going to college, then you can go to Wayne. If it's good enough for Frank, it's good enough for you."

"But I don't want to go to Wayne. I want to go to Michigan."

"You're not going to Michigan, and that's final," her mother said.

Edie was fuming. If Frank had wanted to go to Michigan, her mother would have consented in a minute. Edie retreated to her bedroom-den and took out her bankbook. She had saved almost $400 from playing piano in the ballet school and giving piano lessons, not even enough to pay for one semester of tuition and living expenses. But she had to find a way. She would shrivel up and die if she had to go to Wayne. It would be like going back to high school, no worse, like going back to junior high school--locked up for the next four years with the same people she had tried to escape by going to Cass. She made up her mind; if her mother wouldn't let her go to Michigan, then she'd move to New York by herself. She had enough money to get there, and probably enough to pay for one month's rent. She'd get an apartment in Greenwich Village, work as a pianist if she could, or a waitress if she couldn't, and write short stories in her spare time. She'd let her hair grow down to her waist, wear long dangley earrings and brown leather sandals. She'd show her mother.

But before making a train reservation, she went to Frank for help. She knew her dad would be on her side, but her dad didn't have any clout with her mother. Frank did. She explained to him what she wanted to do, and then added, "Please Frank, you've got to help me. You've got to talk mom into letting me go to Michigan. I'll die if I have to go to Wayne."

"Don't be so dramatic," Frank said. But he took off his horn-rimmed glasses, set them on his desk, and went to find their mother who was reading the newspaper at the kitchen table.

Edie stood behind him as he spoke, as if he were her shield. "Mom, I think you should let Edie go to Michigan."

"Oh, so she's talked to you. Well she doesn't need to go to Michigan, or anywhere else. She's just going to get too smart and then nobody's going to want to marry her. She should get a job, get married, and that's that."

"Mom," Frank continued, undaunted, "lots of girls go to college."

"Yeah, and lots of girls end up old maids."

"Maybe some, but most of them get married."

Lilly on the defensive, "I already told her she can go to Wayne, but not Michigan! It's too expensive."

"It's not as expensive as medical school," he said in his deliberate voice. And after letting the words sink in for a minute, he delivered the order, "Mom, let her go."

And Lilly, looking at Edie peeping over her brother's shoulder, and remembering that she had not been there the day of the piano competition, decided maybe she should give in this time. "Okay," she said to her daughter, "so you can go to Michigan."

In August, Edie's parents moved out of their duplex on Pasadena Avenue, which they sold to a Negro family, and into their brand new two-story house on Freeland Avenue, near 7 Mile Road. The new house had not only a living room, dining room and kitchen, but three bedrooms, three bathrooms, and a den. Ironic, Edie thought, all those years of living with one bathroom, and sharing her bedroom-den, and now just when she was leaving home, she could have had her own bedroom and bathroom.

In September, 1954, Stanley and Frank started medical school at Wayne, and Edie entered the University of Michigan.

The Sunday before classes were to begin, Stanley drove her up to Ann Arbor and helped her move into the dorm. He carried her new portable typewriter, a graduation present from her parents, her suitcases and her cartons of books and clothes into the room she would share with Sandy Stahler. Edie was so excited she couldn't stand still, flitting back and forth from the window to the door. "Oh, it's so beautiful here. Stanley, come look out my window."

"It looks just like Detroit to me."

"Oh, Stanley, where is your romance? It looks nothing like Detroit. Detroit is a big ugly city, this is a beautiful little town. I know I'm going to love it here."

"I'm sure you will," he said, his left lid closing slightly. "But now, I've got to go."

She came to him, put her arms around him, a feeling of melancholy coming over her. "I feel like this is an ending," she said.

"It's not an ending. It's a beginning, for you." A moment of thought. "You know, you really should start dating other boys."

Although he'd said it before, this time sounded different, as if there were no choice. "I suppose I should."

"Don't look so sad," he said, "we'll still see each other."

"Will we?" she asked.

"Of course. Detroit's only an hour away."

"If you have a car. But on my bicycle it'll take a lot longer than that."

"Then Thanksgiving time. You'll be coming home for Thanksgiving."

"If I can get a ride."

"You'll get a ride. Or maybe I could come up sooner if I'm not too busy studying."

"You'll probably be too busy studying."

"Then Thanksgiving time."

She held him tightly, felt she could not let him go. "I'll miss you," she said.

"I'll miss you, too," he said, and then he was out the door.

She stood for a moment, knowing she would miss him terribly, but sure he was not out of her life, and then she knelt down and began unpacking her books. It was time for her new life, her new school, her new friends, and whatever adventures the University of Michigan had to offer.

Chapter Two
Florence, Italy, 1943

The thing that Gianna Camerini loved most was being in the kitchen with Anna, the cook. She liked school, and she liked ballet class, and all her pretty dolls, but she loved helping Anna make pasta and bread, and wonderful cakes and cookies. She loved everything about the kitchen. She loved the feel of the raw dough in her hands, she loved the taste of the fresh fruit and vegetables, and she loved the various smells: garlic, basil, oregano; onions and mushrooms frying in the pan; sauces cooking on the stove; and best of all, the smell of bread, cakes and cookies baking in the oven.

And then, suddenly, everything changed. First, Bianca, the maid was gone; then Anna left, hugging her to her big bosom, crying, "I'm so sorry, bambina mia, but I must leave."

Gianna missed Bianca and Anna terribly, especially Anna, and she asked her mother, "Why can't Bianca and Anna come to our house anymore?"

"It's the government," her mother told her. "They will not allow it."

"But why, mama?"

"Because we are Jewish."

Gianna knew now what she had always suspected. It was bad to be Jewish.

A few weeks after Bianca and Anna left, Gianna's father came home early from his jewelry store, looking haggard and upset, and took Gianna on his lap, "Camina, daddy can no longer go to work, and you, my child, can no longer go to school. But don't worry, my darling, I will teach you at home."

"But why, papa? What have I done?"

"You have done nothing, bellina, mia. It will all be better soon." Gianna knew it was because she was Jewish. And now she wished she wasn't Jewish. She didn't want to stop going to school. She didn't want to be an outcast.

On September 9, 1943, Gianna's papa walked into the apartment and said, "The Italians have signed a treaty with the allies. It's over." And he picked Gianna up and swung her in the air. "Now I can get my business back and you can go back to school."

Gianna was elated. "And will Anna come back and Bianca?"

"Yes," her father said. "Yes." And her mother and father hugged each other and then her, and her mother said, "Thank God, Thank God."

That night, all of Gianna's relatives came over, her aunts, uncles and cousins, and Gianna and her mother made a giant pot of pasta with oil and garlic, and cut up apples and oranges for dessert, and everyone was happy and joking, hugging and kissing, and Gianna was most happy because she had been allowed to help her mother cook the dinner. But in a few days, the city became strangely quiet, deserted, people spoke in whispers. Her father, and her two uncles, Alberto and Carlo, drove out to the countryside, and while they were gone, a man in a business suit came to their door and told her mother, "You must be ready to leave at a moment's notice."

When he had gone, Gianna asked, "Who was that man?"

"He is from the underground. We must leave Florence."

Gianna felt very frightened. Where would they go? What would they do? Where would they sleep tonight?

Her mother said, "I will get you a suitcase. Take some underwear, some socks, dresses, a sweater. Take your coat. Everything else must be left behind. Everything," she repeated as she waved her hand, and Gianna followed her eyes to the bulky dining room table, the 12 high back chairs, the lace tablecloth, the gold candelabra, the crystal chandelier, the china cabinet and all its shiny pieces of silver and crystal.

"And what about papa?"

"He will be back in time. Now go," her mother said. "Get ready."

Gianna left the room, thinking about the underground. What did it mean? Were she and her relatives going to crawl into big tunnels under the earth, like snakes on their bellies?

Later, her mother came to her room. "No, Gianna, you cannot take all the dolls. We don't have room. You must pick one. Just one." And Gianna chose the one with the white apron, to remind her of Anna.

It was the middle of the night and Gianna was awakened by her father carrying her out to a waiting car. The man from the underground was driving. They drove to her Uncle Alberto's apartment, and there Uncle Alberto, Aunt Sofia, cousins Pietro and Miriam, all carrying suitcases, squeezed into the car. Gianna could feel the heat of their bodies, the smell of their breath. Gianna was on her father's lap, Miriam and Pietro on their parents' laps, the suitcases on top of them.

"Move over," Pietro said, "I have no room."

Gianna was pushed so hard against the window, she thought it would break.

The seven of them drove past the apartment buildings, the churches, the piazzas to the countryside and then turned off on a narrow dirt road which wound up, up the mountain to an iron gate, and past the iron gate onto a bumpy road and there before them was a huge villa. Gianna couldn't tell if this was a dream or real, but the car stopped and everyone piled out, and her papa carried her up the stone walk, into the villa, up the stairs, down a hall, and into a room, where clinging together in a corner were her Uncle Carlo and Aunt Silvia clutching their three-year-old son, Stefano. "Ernesto," Aunt Silvia said, "Thank God, it is you. And the others?"

"They are coming."

And Gianna, feeling safe in her father's arms, finally fell asleep.

The next day Gianna and her cousins explored the villa. It was deserted except for the ten of them, and a layer of dust covered everything. The children ran from room to room, and then outside to the garden overgrown with weeds, to the gravel road that led to the front gate. They followed the iron fence that surrounded the villa, their fingers dragging along the cold metal, to the side of the house where they discovered a parapet, a landing enclosed by its own fence, where they could stand and look all the way down the mountain to the village below.

The children spent most of their time playing outdoors, but they knew that if they heard an airplane or saw a car approaching, they must run into the house at once. "At once!" they were instructed several times a day. They never saw a car, but the airplanes passed overhead at least once a day. And then they would run inside and the ten of them would huddle together at the front window, waiting for the sound of exploding bombs, the sight of smoke rising in the distance, and then the planes returning, before the children could go out and play again.

The children did have fun, jumping off the small brick wall, running about the grounds, climbing trees, playing hide and seek in the rooms of the villa, but there was never a moment when Gianna could relax. She always knew that danger was lurking just beyond the gate, that death was waiting in the trees.

Every afternoon Gianna's father, Ernesto, would sit in the garden with the children and give them lessons. Even Stefano, who was only three but already knew his alphabet and colors, had to participate.

The children were surprised that Ernesto had remembered to bring books and paper the night they escaped Florence.

"Sometimes your father thinks of too many things," Pietro, who was ten, complained.

But Gianna was happy with the lessons. She liked reading and listening to the others read, and having her papa instruct them in math and the laws of nature. "See how the sun moves from east to west every day? But it is not the sun that is moving. It is the earth. This is a law of nature."

"And is it also a law of nature that we must hide in this villa?" Pietro asked.

"No, Pietro, it is a law of man, for men are not so wise as nature."

"And how long must we be here?"

"Until man comes to his senses, or is taken over by men who have not lost theirs."

One afternoon as they were about to start their lessons, they saw dust rising in the horizon.

"Quick, children, into the house," Ernesto said.

Gianna's stomach was doing flip-flops as she ran into the villa. She crouched beside a cracked window with her cousins, and watched as a truck pulled up and two men dressed in overalls got out. They spoke a few minutes to Gianna's father, then got back in the truck and drove away.

Ernesto came into the villa where all the aunts and uncles and cousins were waiting to hear what the men had said. "The Germans have invaded Florence. It is no longer safe for us here. We are leaving tonight. Everyone get your things together."

And everyone ran off to their different rooms and Gianna began to shake. Her father scooped her up, "There is nothing to fear, bellina mia," he said. "We will be all right."

But still that night sitting on her mother's lap, waiting for the underground to pick them up, Gianna could not calm down. She kept imagining them, the Germans. She thought they must be ugly giant bugs with protruding eyeballs, black tentacles, claws on their arms and legs, and each time she closed her eyes, she saw them coming after her, chasing her, their giant claws about to grab her.

"Aaah," she woke with a scream.

"What is it, camina?"

And Gianna began to cry and clutched at her mother, wishing she was back home, safe in her own bedroom.

"It's all right," her mother said, smoothing her hair. "You just had a bad dream. Everything is all right."

But Gianna could not stop shaking. And then the truck was there, and they all climbed into the back and lay down, and one of the men who had been there this afternoon, covered them with straw so that Gianna could hardly breathe. "Are you all right in there? he asked.

"Yes," Gianna's father said.

But Gianna wanted to scream, "No, no, I can't breathe." And yet she knew she had to be brave like the others. Even little Stefano was not saying a word. Gianna had to be silent, too.

So they drove and drove, and Gianna thought her lungs would burst. Every time she tried to inhale, she inhaled dust. She cupped her hands over her nose and took a breath. But it was dust, nothing but dust. She was going to die. She was going to suffocate. And then just as she thought she could not last another minute, the truck stopped, the hay was pulled off them, and Gianna sat up and inhaled the cool night air. How wonderful it was to breathe.

Her father lifted her up and Gianna looked around. They were in a valley surrounded by hills, and in front of them was a stone farmhouse. A man and a woman stood at the door. "Come in, come in."

"How can we ever thank you?" Gianna's father asked.

"Our reward will be in heaven," the farmer answered.

The farmer and his wife, Salvatore and Teresa, led the ten of them down a rickety staircase to the cellar, and then brought them some thin blankets and two sheets. "I'm sorry," Teresa said, "it is all we have."

The adults spread the sheets and blankets on the stone floor, and everyone, clinging together, lay down to go to sleep. And then, Gianna lying beside her mother on the cold hard floor realized she did not have her doll. It must has dropped from her hand when she had her nightmare. "My dolly," she said to her mother. "I left my dolly."

"I'm sorry, child. We cannot go back for it."

Oh no, Gianna thought. How could she live without her dolly? How could she go to sleep? Who could she cuddle and hug and kiss? She began to cry; she felt now that she had lost everything.

Gianna hated the cellar. It was dark and damp, and Gianna's shoes were always wet, someone always had a runny nose, a cough they had to stifle, and it smelled horrible--they had to use the coal bin as their toilet.

The days passed slowly in that cellar, especially for the children. The children were not allowed to make any noise, not even when the planes passed overhead. Not even when the bombs exploded. They were not allowed to run or jump, they were not allowed to cry or laugh, and they were not allowed upstairs or outside. They were not even allowed near a window during the day because some passerby might see them, and then that person might report them to the Germans, and then some unspeakably horrible thing would happen to all of them, including, Teresa and Salvatore, the kind people who had hidden them.

Salvatore and Teresa brought food down to them twice a day. Even though it might only be a meager portion of white beans, everyone lived for these moments. It was the only thing they had to look forward to in their bleak day.

Still, Ernesto tried to keep the children occupied. There was no more paper left for lessons, and even if there were, it was too dark to see, so Ernesto had the children recite their multiplication tables, in a whisper, and then they would take turns telling stories, also in a whisper. Ernesto's stories were always the best because he left every story unfinished. The children were always left with something to look forward to the next day: finding out what happened. And then at night, after all the lights were out as far as the eye could see, Ernesto would take turns lifting the children on his shoulders and let them look out the cellar window at the animals in the barnyard.

Teresa and Salvador had two chickens, a gray-striped cat named Princessa who strutted about the barnyard as if she owned it, and two dogs. It was the dogs which captivated Gianna's heart. One was all black and named Nero; the other was white with black spots and named Pepe. She loved to watch them play, and often they would come over to the window and she felt if she reached out her hand she could touch them. How she longed to go out and play with them, just for a minute. Just to pet their soft fur, just to hold them.

And then one night, Nero was not there. Oh no. He couldn't have been killed. The Germans couldn't have gotten him. "Papa," she asked. "Is Nero dead?"

"I think," her papa answered, "maybe she is having her puppies. Haven't you noticed how her stomach has been growing?"

"Yes, but I thought she was eating too much."

"No, she is going to be a mother. We will wait. Perhaps one night she will bring her babies to visit you."

Shortly after Nero stopped coming, Gianna took to climbing the rickety ladder after the others were asleep, to see if Nero had returned. And finally, one night when Nero had been gone for 27 days--her father made a mark on the wall for every passing day--she was rewarded, for there was Nero and trailing behind her were two puppies, the most precious, fluffy little beings Gianna had ever seen. How she longed to go outside to hold them, to cuddle them. She knew her papa would never allow it. She knew it was dangerous, and yet it was so late, no one could possibly be awake at this hour. If she could only go out just this once, take one of those puppies in her lap, hug it, pet it, then she would be content to spend the rest of her life in this cellar. As if they heard her thoughts, the puppies settled right outside the window. Just out of her reach. It was dangerous. Yes, she knew it was dangerous, but if she was very quiet, no one would ever know. She looked around; all her relatives were sound asleep. It was completely quiet in the house, and outside. Slowly she crept up the cellar stairs, carefully unhitched the cellar door, pushed it open inch by inch so that it wouldn't creak, found herself in the kitchen, pushed open the kitchen door, and then was hit with the fresh air. How wonderful it was, how sweet. She inhaled deeply, knowing she had done the right thing. Just to smell the fresh air was worth everything. And then she closed the door behind her and went in search of the puppies. They had moved further into the yard. There was a full moon and she could see as well as if it were daylight. They were just up ahead and she followed them, happy to be outside, to be free, if only for a few minutes. And then Nero and the puppies stopped in a clump of bushes. She caught up to them and Nero barked at her, hovering protectively over her babies.

"I'm not going to hurt them," Gianna whispered. "I just want to hold them." And Gianna approached Nero and began to pet her, looking longingly at the puppies who came close to her and began sniffing at her. She was enjoying herself so much that she didn't pay attention when Nero barked again, and then she heard a crunch in the bushes, and she knew someone was standing in front of her. She saw the black boots first, and then the uniform, and then the gun pointing at her.

She panicked. Oh God, what had she done?

A voice was speaking to her in German, and she did not understand the words. Pretend you belong here. Pretend you did nothing wrong, she told herself.

"What are you doing here?" the voice then said in broken Italian.

"Playing with the dogs," she repeated.

"Where do you live, little girl?"

Ayyy. If she told him the truth, he might know the farmer and his wife had no little girl. If she told him she lived some other place, he would surely find out she was lying. "Over there," she pointed.

"Come I will take you home," the German said, putting his gun back in his holster.

He pulled her up and she saw a car with another soldier waiting by the road. They exchanged some words in German, and then the other soldier came over and the three of them walked toward the farmhouse. What should she do, run for the woods? What if they killed her? At least the others would be safe. But it was too late for that, she had already pointed out the place she lived and if she ran they would know something was wrong. No, she had to pretend everything was all right, that she belonged to Teresa and Salvatore. She watched the earth as the black boots crunched in front of her and then the soldiers banged on the farmhouse door. Immediately a light came on. By now, she knew all those below must be awake, must know she was missing, must know what danger they were in. Salvatore got to the door first, but behind him, Gianna could see Teresa in her blue chenille bathrobe.

"What is it?" Salvatore asked.

"We found your little girl outside playing with the dogs."

For a minute Salvatore didn't know what to do. Then he reached for Gianna. "Giannina, what are you doing out so late?"

"I went to play with the puppies," she said.

"Is she your child?" the first German asked.

"No," Teresa said coming to get her. "She is my sister's child, just visiting from Florence."

"Is anyone else in the house?" the second German asked.

"No," Salvatore said. "Just my wife and Gianna."

"I think we'll have a look," the first German said. The two of them walked down the hall to the rooms in back. Teresa, Salvatore and Gianna did not move, did not speak. When they returned to the kitchen, they walked over to the cellar door. "Where does this go?" the first German asked.

"To the cellar," Salvatore answered.

The German tried to push the cellar door open but it was locked. "Why is this locked?"

"We don't use the cellar in winter. It is too cold and damp."

"Do you have a key?"

"Yes, in my bedroom."

"Go get it."

Salvatore was walking to his bedroom when the soldiers began talking to each other and laughing, and then one kicked at the door, once, twice, again, and it broke from its lock and flew open. "Never mind the key," the other soldier said with a grin on his face. And then the two of them pulled their guns again, and one his flashlight, and they descended the stairs. Gianna could hear their footsteps on each stair, the first, the second, and she thought of her papa, her aunts, uncles and cousins, and all her fault, all her fault, and then the soldiers were back up the stairs and in the kitchen.

"You're right, it is too cold and damp down there," the first German said.

They put their guns back in their holsters and were turning to leave when they heard a noise behind them. And there sauntering across the floor was Princessa.

"So you have a cat," the first German said.

"Yes, to keep away the rats," Salvatore said.

"I hate cats," the second German said and pointed his gun at Princessa.

No, oh no, Gianna thought, and then an explosion shattered the silence.

Gianna screamed. She saw Princessa's body leap up, splatter against the wall, and then fall limply to the floor.

Teresa put her arms around Gianna who was now sobbing hysterically.

"Tell your niece she better stay indoors at night," the second German said, "or she might be mistaken for a cat."

Both of the Germans laughed, then put their guns back in their holsters and walked out the door.

Gianna was shaking so violently, she thought she would break. Salvatore took her in his arms and carried her down the cellar steps, where her ashen-faced family was waiting. "It's all right," Salvatore said, "you're safe. You're all safe. But we will no longer be able to keep you here. Tomorrow you will have to leave."

Gianna's papa took Gianna from Salvatore's arms and covered her face with kisses and tears. "Thank God," he said. "Thank God, you are safe."

"Oh, papa," Gianna said, "I'm so sorry. I'm so sorry. Can you ever forgive me?"

Her father held her tight and stroked her hair. "As long as we have you, bellina mia, everything is all right, everything is forgiven."

But Gianna would never forgive herself. She was a horrible, terrible person. She had endangered the lives of everyone she loved. And for what? To pet a puppy.

The next night, after it was dark, a truck pulled up at Teresa and Salvatore's house. It was larger than the first truck they had traveled in, and after kissing and hugging Teresa and Salvatore, the ten of them crept into the back of the truck and again, hay was heaped on them so they could hardly breathe and they were transported away from Teresa and Salvatore's. Aunt Silvia, Uncle Carlo and cousin Stefano were dropped off at one farmhouse and the remaining seven were driven to another farmhouse.

Again a man and woman were waiting at the door for them. They were named Luigi and Rosa, and they fed the seven fugitives hot coffee and hot water with sugar, before taking them upstairs to the bedroom the seven of them would share. There were two mattresses on the floor, and pillows and blankets. Each family would sleep on one mattress.

Living in this farmhouse was better and worse than living in the cellar. Better because it was dry and light, and it had a toilet, just a wooden bench with a hole that went to the ground below, but it had a door, and privacy, and the smell was minimal.

It was worse than the cellar because the Germans were scouting the area for men to work for them. Luigi would come into their room any hour of the night or day and hurry Gianna's papa and Uncle Alberto and Pietro outside where he would bury them until the patrols passed. Sometimes they might be gone for days. And the whole time, Gianna was in a panic that she would never see her papa, or uncle or cousin again, that they would be caught or suffocate to death under the earth. She thought it would be better to be back in the cellar. Safer. And she thought, it was all her fault that they had to leave the cellar, and if her father and uncle and cousin died, that would be her fault, too.

When the Germans came into the house, they were not surprised to see so many women and children living in one house. It was how things were now with all the men gone to war.

On the days the men were not in hiding, they stayed in their room with the green shutters closed. Their meals were brought up to them twice a day by Luigi or Rosa. And whenever possible, Gianna's papa continued with the children's lessons. He asked Luigi to bring him paper, pencils and books and Luigi brought him paper, pencils and the only four books he could find: two picture books, a history book and an accounting book.

"What do we need the accounting book for?" Pietro asked.

"It's good to know everything," Gianna's papa said.

But the children never did open that book.

When the children tired of their lessons, Gianna's papa would take them into the storeroom, and there they would sit on the stone floor watching the ants for hours. Gianna's papa pointed out how intelligent the ants were, how each one knew exactly where he was going and what he was supposed to do.

As the days progressed, the German patrols were coming less often, and if Luigi thought it was safe, he would bring the seven of them into the kitchen to eat supper with him and Rosa. Every day, Gianna prayed that tonight would be the night she would see Luigi's smiling face at the bedroom door, "Would you like to join us for supper?"

How Gianna loved being in Rosa's kitchen, all of them gathered around the walk-in brick fireplace, the big black kettle, the paiola, bubbling and steaming, sipping sugar water and dreaming of what delectable treat lay in store for her. It reminded her of the blissful hours she had spent with Anna.

Rosa baked bread fresh each day, and sometimes she would make Fetta Unta. She would cut enormous slices from a huge loaf of bread, toast it, cover it with oil and garlic, and ahh, what a treat. She served a lot of potatoes and beans. White beans. There were sacks of them in a corner of the kitchen. And sometimes she would make vegetables or pasta. But whatever she made, every bit of it was delicious, and every bit of it was eaten.

While the German patrols were coming less often, the airplanes were coming more often, several times a day, dropping bombs so close that the farmhouse barely stopped shaking from one attack when another started. Every time a bomb exploded, Gianna could not help thinking about Princessa and what it must feel like to have your body blown into a thousand pieces.

And then one day, there was silence. Rosa came running into their room all excited. "We heard on the radio. The war is over. The Americans are coming."

The seven of them looked at her in disbelief. Could it be true? Were they safe? Was Gianna's body going to remain whole and together? Gianna's father opened the green shutters and looked out. It was a beautiful bright day and there was no sound except the singing of the birds. One by one, the seven of them came to the window, Gianna coming last, for she was the most afraid, and they all stood looking out--at first blinded by the yellow sunlight, but then able to see the blue sky, the billowy white clouds, the colored patches of farmland, the hillsides covered with vineyards and olive trees, and in the distance, the tall cypresses and clusters of little houses with their red tile roofs.

There were all holding each other and waiting, waiting for some sign. And finally over the hill they came, a group of soldiers in Jeeps, silent at first, and then as they approached, the noise from their engines wafting through the open window getting louder and louder, so that finally Gianna had to cover her ears to block out the sound. Gianna's father, Ernesto, picked Gianna up so she could see better, and she watched the jeeps come closer, closer. "They're Americans," Ernesto said. And everyone began to laugh and cry and hug each other.

One of the Jeeps parked in front of the house, right outside their window and a young soldier jumped over the side of his vehicle, looked up at them, waved, and in a few minutes was in the kitchen door, up the stairs, and standing at their bedroom door. He was shorter than Gianna's father and he had red hair and freckles. "Hi," he said, with a big smile on his face, "I'm Jerry Freyer from St. Paul, Minnesota, and I've come to liberate you."

Ernesto translated his words, and they all surrounded him, hugging him, kissing him, and he picked Gianna up and pulled a bar of chocolate out of the pocket of his tan uniform and gave it to her. She wanted to eat it, but she also wanted to save it, to remember Jerry Freyer and this glorious moment for the rest of her life. When he set her down, Pietro was already at the stairs. "I'm going outside," he said, and Gianna ran after him, but at the kitchen door, she stopped. "C'mon," Pietro said, "don't be a fraidy cat. We're free." Cautiously she stepped outside, felt the sun on her face, breathed the fresh air, and then took off after Pietro. He was across the yard, across the garden, and down a hill, running until Gianna could run no more, and then both of them plopped down on the grass, spread their arms and legs as far as they would go, and gulped the sweet, fresh air.

"Gianna, Pietro," Gianna's mother called from above. "Come back." Gianna and Pietro squinted up at her. They didn't want to go back, they wanted to lie here forever. "You must come back at once," Gianna's mother called again. Reluctantly, they lifted themselves off the ground and began the long trek up the hill. What had seemed like such an easy run down, was now impossibly difficult. They were out of breath and their legs hurt. Finally, they made it to the top, where two American soldiers picked them up and carried them to their waiting Jeeps.

The seven of them were taken to a resettlement camp where, in a few days, they were reunited with Silvia, Carlo and Stefano. The Americans didn't know what to do with any of them. Their apartments in Florence had been taken over by other families, all of their possessions were gone, taken by the Germans probably, they had no papers, nothing to identify them, on purpose.

Ernesto wanted to go to the United States where he had cousins living in Detroit, Michigan. He would no longer feel safe in Italy or anywhere else in Europe. But a few weeks after he filled out the papers, he became gravely ill. The doctors put him in a hospital, and every day, Gianna and her mother would come and sit by his bedside, holding his clammy hands, wiping his feverish forehead. But every day he became weaker, his coughing spells lasted longer, and one evening he said to his wife, "Ida, you must promise me that no matter what happens to me, you will go to America."

And Ida, weeping and clasping his hands in hers, said, "I promise, Ernesto."

Gianna was looking at her father's face, the face she adored, now so thin and withered, and suddenly, her father became very quiet, as quiet as that moment before the Americans arrived. His eyes were open, but he was not breathing. And Gianna knew, her papa was dead. And then, her mother looking up, screamed "Ernesto," and threw herself on his body, sobbing uncontrollably.

Gianna crawled onto the bed, next to her sobbing mother, her dead father, and began to cry. What was she going to do without her beloved papa? Who would take care of her? Who would protect her? Who would love her? Who would teach her and forgive her for all the bad things she had done? She thought of the night of the puppies, the black boots, the gun, and Princessa, and put her hands to her temples. Without her papa there to comfort her, she must never think of that night again.

When Gianna and Ida returned to the camp, all the relatives gathered around them, trying to console them.

"My life is over," Ida told them. "I may as well have died with Ernesto."

"No, Ida," Uncle Alberto said, "you must go on living. You must go on living for Gianna. She needs you. You will come to America with us. It is what Ernesto wanted."

Ida put her arms around her daughter, "Yes, I will go to America. I will go on living. For you, Gianna. For you. You're all I have left."

And looking into her mother's eyes, red and swollen from crying, Gianna swore that she would never leave her mother. Never.

Chapter Three

Edie didn't miss Stanley as much as she thought she would. She was too enamored with Ann Arbor. While it was only an hour's drive from Detroit, it was a different world. The typical little college town. Edie loved the old wood houses with the big verandahs, the weeping willows, the huge oaks with their low hanging branches, their leaves already turning red and orange. The campus itself was small, one large square with a diagonal walk cutting across it, the place to meet. "Meet you at the diag," one student would say to another. Most of the buildings were either on this square, or on the streets surrounding it, and most of them were old, made of red or yellow brick, some covered with ivy. There were also a few modern concrete buildings in the square and bordering the square, and then the bookstores, restaurants, boarding houses and dorms branched out in all directions.

Edie loved being at Michigan. She loved living in the dorm and being surrounded by 200 people. She loved being out on her own, away from her mother, being responsible to no one but herself. She loved all of her classes, especially English, and couldn't wait to start writing her short stories. But once she began, once she had to go into her room every evening after dinner to write, while the other girls were playing bridge, or at the library studying, or off on campus at this meeting or that, she wasn't sure writing was what she really wanted to do. In a way it was just like practicing the piano all over again, only now she was spending two hours a day at the typewriter keys instead of the piano keys. She didn't want to be locked away alone in her room anymore. She wanted to be with people.

But if she wasn't going to be a writer, then what could she be? What would fill all her criteria: exciting, challenging and sociable. The girl down the hall was an actress and she convinced Edie to try acting. "It's so much fun."

So the next semester, Edie enrolled in two acting classes, and the following semester got the part of Mrs. Winemiller in *Summer and Smoke*. She had no trouble memorizing her lines, but when the time came for the rehearsals, she panicked. She loved everything about the theater, hanging out with the theater people, going to their parties, being involved with the backstage production, and the plays themselves. The only thing she didn't like about the theater was actually being out there, on the stage, performing. It was one thing to know your lines, it was another to deliver them to five hundred people. Every time she stepped out on the stage, she could not help remembering the day of the piano competition. No, being an actress was not for her. She would have to find her forte somewhere else.

In the second semester of her sophomore year, she took a class in archaeology and found it fascinating. She imagined herself dressed in a tan safari shirt and pants, a wide-brimmed safari hat, traveling all over the world, discovering fossils and precious objects d'art. It would be exciting, maybe even more exciting than living in a penthouse in New York City. So that was it. She would major in archaeology

At the start of her junior year, Edie and Sandy Stahler moved out of the dorm into a boarding house. It was six blocks from campus, not such a great idea in the winter when the streets were covered with snow and ice, but the girls were in search of more privacy and better food. They had had enough of the dorms.

The "league" house, as it was called, was privately owned by Mrs. Stevens, a large woman with hairs growing out of her cheeks. There were twenty girls living there: two from Chicago, six from New York, one from Atlanta, five from various cities in Michigan, and the remainder from Detroit. The first floor of the house had a sitting room (with a piano), a kitchen, a dining room where the girls ate, and Mrs. Steven's private quarters. The second and third floors housed the bedrooms and bathrooms for the girls. Edie and Sandy's bedroom was on the third floor. It was unique because it had a walk-in closet with a window at the far end that overlooked the street. Edie and Sandy put a chair next to the window so that they could sit in their closet and enjoy the sun, or read, or look out at the sunset, or watch the people walking by on the street or see the guys as they came to pick up their dates. Most of the bedrooms were doubles, but there were a couple of triples, and all twenty girls shared two bathrooms. Each bathroom had two showers, three sinks and three toilets, but only two toilets had doors on them. Anyone who was shy could not have survived in Mrs. Steven's league house. And one got to know the truth about all the girls. Like Marsha Kay, who had a boyfriend, and always looked neat and clean, but left hair and makeup in the bathroom sink.

The most popular girl in the house was Babs Gordon, the girl from Atlanta. Not only was she pretty, but she was the only girl on campus with a Southern accent. There was a buzzer at the bottom of the stairs and by the telephone, and each girl in the league house had been assigned a buzz. Unfortunately Bab's buzz was dot dot dash while Edie's was dot dot. So every time the buzzer went dot dot, Edie's spirits would rise only to be dashed by the dash.

Edie thought she might bring this up at a league house meeting. "Ah, could I change my buzz, because the dash is killing me," but of course, didn't.

Actually, Edie had taken Stanley's advice, and by now, had dated a few boys, most notably a boy named David Eisenberg, a brilliant but boring physicist who lasted almost a whole semester. She was not really attracted to him or anyone else she went out with. Probably because she was still in love with Stanley. He would come up to Michigan for a Saturday football game, or see her on the occasional weekends she went home for a holiday or a family party, and they would get together over the summers when Edie moved back home and worked in her father's insurance office. Stanley had continued to date other girls while Edie was at Michigan, but as before, he kept coming back to Edie, and each time he did, their passion seemed to intensify, as if being apart brought them even closer together. They would make love for hours, kissing and fondling each other until they came. Stanley was now eager to go all the way, but Edie was still sticking to her plan to be a virgin when she got married, or at least until she was 22.

So it was that one Saturday afternoon in May, when Edie was nearing the end of her junior year, she heard her dot dot and ran down the stairs of her league house to find Stanley waiting for her. But he was not alone. He was with a girl. "Edie, this is Yelena. She just arrived from Russia and she's living with us until her parents arrive."

"How nice," Edie said, extending her hand.

"Yes," Yelena said taking it, "is very good for me."

Yelena was tiny, maybe five-feet tall, with curly brown hair cut close to her head, and a dark complexion. She seemed young, and boyish.

"Is it okay," Stanley asked Edie, "if we go visit a friend of mine? Zola Bitterman. He transferred here last September from Wayne, and since he was born in Russia, too, and I thought he might like to meet Yelena."

"Sure," Edie said, thinking that Yelena could stay with Zola, while she and Stanley snuck off somewhere and made mad passionate love for an hour. So they got into Stanley's car--he was still driving the 1948 green Plymouth, Edie in front, Yelena in back, and headed off to meet Zola Bitterman.

They arrived at Zola's apartment a little before five, and Zola Bitterman, unshaven and wearing shabby clothing, met them at the door. He reminded Edie of Jack Shine, same straight black hair and dark brooding eyes, but Zola was tall, and wore his hair long. "He's a poet," Stanley had told Edie, and he certainly looked the part.

His apartment was the biggest mess Edie had ever seen. There were books and papers everywhere, dirty coffee cups on the tables and desk, the furniture was old, stained, and torn, with little wisps of cotton sticking out here and there, and the kitchen was piled high with dirty dishes.

"Where do you want to go?" Stanley asked Zola.

"We could stay here," Zola said.

"How about the *Old German*?" Stanley asked.

"It's kind of expensive," Zola said.

"My treat," Stanley said. Edie knew Stanley didn't have much money, but apparently Zola had less.

"No, I can't let you do that," Zola said.

"Why not we eat here?" Yelena piped up.

Yech, Edie thought, in that kitchen? With all that filth and dirty dishes. "What about the hamburger place on East University?" Edie suggested cheerily.

"I be happy cook for you," Yelena butted in again.

And both men looked at her with admiration in their eyes.

"Okay," Stanley said, "you talked us into it. The guys'll go shopping and buy the food and you girls can get the kitchen ready." And turning to Edie, "Is that okay with you?"

What choice did she have? "Sure," she said, glaring at Yelena. "That'd be great."

So while the boys went shopping, Edie and Yelena cleaned up the kitchen. What a disaster. There was even a raw egg lying hardened to the linoleum floor. Edie washed the dishes, while Yelena dried, and then Edie worked on getting the dry egg off the linoleum while Yelena scoured the counters and kitchen table. Yelena was just getting out the pail to wash the kitchen floor when the boys appeared with hamburger meat, buns, lettuce, tomatoes, cucumber, and a gallon of red wine.

"Now we cook," Yelena said, and set to work seasoning the hamburger meat while Edie cut up the lettuce, tomatoes, and cucumber. When the hamburgers were done and the buns were toasted, they all sat down to eat. The hamburgers were delicious and Edie wished she had watched what Yelena put in them.

After dinner, the four of them moved into the living room taking their half-finished bottle of red wine with them, and were listening to Zola read his poetry, when Zola's room-mate appeared.

He was short, smelled bad and was smoking a cigarette. Perhaps he was the messy one. Edie hoped so. Listening to his poetry, she was liking Zola more and more.

Zola's poems were angry poems, about the state of the world, about bigotry, about poor people, about man's inhumanity to man and his environment. Edie caught a concept here, a vision there, and she liked the sound of the words, the alliteration.

After Zola finished a particularly moving poem, the three of them sat in silence, not clapping, joined together in a common sadness. Finally, Zola spoke. "Well, I think that's enough of that."

"No, Stanley said, "I love hearing your poems."

"I'm sure the girls are bored," Zola said.

"No," Yelena said, "I love them. I like listen to you read for hours."

"Me, too," Edie said, hating being a "me-too".

"No," Zola said, "no more poetry. Let's talk about the rest of you. I'd especially like to hear about Russia."

Was that Edie and Stanley's cue to leave?

But Stanley turned to Yelena. "Tell them, Yelena." And Yelena began talking, about the communists, how difficult it was to live in Russia, how prejudiced the Russians were against the Jews, how her family had bought papers to get her out, and how scared she was sitting in the airport, every few minutes another soldier checking her passport, until finally, Thanks God, she was on the plane to Helsinki, and then to Detroit, to her parents' friends, Morris and Yetta Rader and their son, Stanley. And she smiled a special smile at Stanley.

Zola refilled all of their glasses, then turned to Edie. "And what about you, Edith Stern?"

The black eyes that knew all. Suddenly she was embarrassed. "I don't know what to say," she said.

"What are you majoring in?" he asked.

"Archaeology."

"Why?"

"Because I wasn't good enough to be a pianist, and it was too lonely being a writer, and I got stage-fright being an actress."

"That doesn't answer Zola's question," Stanley said.

"Yes, it does," Zola said. "It answers it perfectly." And their eyes met and held.

"How about if we go get some ice cream," Stanley said. "I've got to be getting back to study." Stanley, like Frank, was now in his third year of medical school.

So the four of them piled into Stanley's green Plymouth and drove out to Howard Johnson's for ice cream.

It was two weeks later, on a Saturday morning that Edie, again unexpectedly, heard her buzz. Dot, dot. No dash.

She primped her hair, put on lipstick and ran down the stairs to see who her surprise visitor might be. It was Stanley, and she was, as always thrilled to see him.

"Want to go for a ride?" he asked.

His famous rides. "Of course," she said.

They hopped into his car and drove out to the arboretum where they parked and began walking amidst the beautiful plants and flowers. It was spring and everything was turning green and pink and red and purple.

She couldn't imagine what he was going to say. Had the other night with Zola proved to him how much he loved her and couldn't live without her. Was this going to be the moment she had been waiting for since the night they met?

"Edie, I wanted you to be the first to know...."

Yes, Stanley. Yes.

"I'm in love with Yelena."

She felt like a pail of cold water had been dumped on her head. "You're in love with Yelena?"

"Yes, we're in love and we're going to get married."

But how could this be? How could he be marrying Yelena?

"She's really a wonderful girl," Stanley went on. "She's so different from anyone I've ever known."

Edie was feeling weak, her legs folding under her. She needed to sit down. She spotted a tree stump, and fell onto it.

"Do you know that she doesn't want to have kids?" Stanley continued, seemingly completely unaware of how all this was affecting Edie. "She wants to adopt them. She says having kids is selfish when there are so many kids already born who need a good home. Isn't that amazing?"

"Amazing," Edie said, a tinge of sarcasm in her voice.

"And she's so strong. You saw how she was the other night at Zola's. She's such a tiny thing, but when she sees something that needs to be done, she just goes ahead and does it."

"Yes, I noticed," Edie said, a bit more sarcastically.

"I guess you're pretty shocked," Stanley said.

"Shocked isn't the word for it," Edie said.

"I guess everyone's going to be. It is pretty sudden. We've only known each other for two months."

Two months, Edie thought. And she had been going out with him for five years! "That is a pretty short time," was all she said.

"I always thought that one day you and I would get married," Stanley said, looking down at her. "But then along came Yelena, and I can't help it. I'm crazy about her."

"I understand," Edie said, feeling the tears gathering behind her eyes.

And Stanley finally becoming aware of her, lifted her to her feet and put his arms around her. "You'll always be my best friend, you know."

It was too much to bear, being held by him for perhaps the last time, and the tears burst forth.

"Edie," he said, touching her cheek, "you're crying."

"I'm sorry," she said. "I don't want to cry."

"I know this must be a terrible shock to you."

"I'll get over it," she said.

He lifted her chin so he could look into her eyes, "Tell me we'll still be friends."

"We'll still be friends," she said.

Later, when he dropped her at the league house, she stood on the front porch watching his green Plymouth drive off, trying to steady herself. Two months. He knew Yelena two months and he was going to marry her. She felt so hurt, so betrayed. But she had no right to feel this way. He had never promised her anything. She always knew he was dating other girls. And besides, she had her own ambitions. She was going to be an archaeologist, travel the world, meet all kinds of interesting people, perhaps make an important discovery. But she knew, down deep, that if Stanley Rader had asked her, she would have done it--she would have given up all her dreams of fame and glory to be Mrs. Stanley Rader, to have his little green-eyed babies and live happily ever after in dull, boring Detroit.

"Goodbye, Stanley," she said aloud. "Goodbye to five years of waiting for you to love me as I loved you." Then she ran up the stairs, to her room, to her closet, and sat on the chair by the window, crying softly for what might have been, for what would never be.

Stanley's parents made the young couple a wedding, not a fancy wedding, but with a sit-down dinner, and a three piece band that played *April Love*, *True Love*, *Love is a Many Splendored Thing*, and every other song that had "love" in it. Edie was there, and so was Zola Bitterman, clean-shaven and wearing a suit.

It had been a difficult month for Edie. She hadn't been able to concentrate on her studies, she hadn't felt like being around people, she absolutely would not go out on a date, although both Beth Siegel and Greta Stein tried to fix her up, and she spent most of her spare time playing Mozart sonatas on the league house piano, or sitting in her closet, reading and gazing out the window.

But today, driving in from Ann Arbor with Sandy Stahler, she made up her mind. This had to end. She had to get on with her life. She had to get over Stanley Rader.

Zola Bitterman came up to her during the reception as she stood on the edge of the dance-floor with a drink in her hand. "This must have been a shock to you," he said.

"Yes, it was," she said.

"I've had a chance to talk to Yelena, and she's a pretty smart girl. Their kids will probably be geniuses."

"They're not going to have kids," Edie said, somewhat smugly, knowing she knew something he didn't.

"You mean because they're going to adopt?"

So they had told him, too. "I think it's pretty admirable," Edie said.

"It would be if it were true," Zola said.

"You don't believe it?"

"In case you haven't notice, people don't always do what they say they're going to do."

"I think you're pretty cynical."

"And I think you're pretty naive."

She didn't like being talked to this way. She wasn't sure she still liked Zola Bitterman. The band was playing, *Only You*. "Do you dance?" she asked.

"Yes, but only when the spirit moves me. I don't dance to order."

"Would you dance with me now?"

He looked at her, "No. But come visit me in my apartment some time. I'll dance with you then."

"I don't visit boys in their apartments."

He shrugged his shoulders. "Your choice."

Stanley's father, Morris, asked Edie to dance to *Smoke Gets in Your Eyes*, and by the time the dance was over, Zola had left.

Should she visit Zola in his apartment? She thought of it back in Ann Arbor, between her periods of depression. He was the only boy she'd met since Stanley who really interested her. She'd like to get to know him better.

Marilyn Friedman insisted Edie double date with her. Marilyn was going to a fraternity party and her date's friend needed a date. "Please, Edie, you've got to help me out."

"Okay," Edie told her, but as soon as she got to the party, she regretted her decision. She hated the party. Everyone was smoking cigarettes and drinking beer, and Edie hated both. She also hated her date. He was stupid, crass and insensitive. He got drunk and threw up, and Edie had to find someone else to take her home.

Back in her room, she went into her closet and sat by the window looking out at the sky. *Blue Moon, you saw me standing alone, without a dream in my heart, without a love of my own.* There had to be someone out there who was right for her. Someone who would love her and whom she could love. And then she thought of Zola. At least he had a soul. At least he was brilliant and idealistic. And his eyes. His dark brooding eyes. They were haunting her. Maybe she should go to his apartment. Maybe she should give him a chance.

The next week on a warm June evening, Edie decided she would stop by Zola's apartment.

She was as nervous as she had ever been as she knocked on his door. She knew if she told Frank what she was doing, he would be appalled. She could hear his voice now, "Nice girls don't go to boys' apartments." For a minute she thought of running away. What if he really wasn't interested in her, what if he already had a girlfriend, what if his girlfriend was with him now? What a fool she'd make of herself.

And then, there he was, opening the door, smiling, happy to see her.

"Edie," he said, "come in."

"Are you surprised to see me?"

"I'm glad to see you," he said.

She felt relieved and took a seat on the sofa between two puffs of white stuffing.

"Would you like some wine?" he asked.

"Sure," she said.

He poured from a half-empty gallon bottle.

"Is that the same bottle of wine?" she asked.

"It could be," he said, "I try to stay away from artificial stimulants."

"Not very typical for a poet."

"I try not to be typical." He handed her the glass of wine and then sat beside her right on a piece of stuffing. "So tell me, are you over Stanley yet?"

"I'm trying."

"Is that why you came over here? Did you think I would help?"

"I suppose that's one of the reasons," she said.

"And what's the other?"

"I like you."

"I like you, too," he said and leaned over and kissed her, his lips soft between the black stubble on his face. She was surprised by his kiss, but didn't pull away.

They finished their glass of wine, and he poured another, then got up and put a Dixieland jazz record on his record player. "Want to dance?" He held out his hand to her.

She set her glass down, and let him help her up. The wine was affecting her, she was feeling loose, uninhibited, and they danced to the music. He was handsome, she saw now, in spite of his long hair and unshaved face, and there was electricity between them, more than the wine and the music, something deep and touching. The record ended and they stood looking at one another.

"Maybe I better go," she said.

"Such a short visit," he said.

"Maybe it'll be longer next time."

"And when will that be?"

"When do you want it to be?" she asked.

"Tomorrow," he said. "What time are you finished with classes?"

"Three."

"Come over tomorrow at three. I'll make a picnic lunch. We'll go to the park."

"Sounds like fun," she said.

He walked her to the door. "It's hard to get over someone you love."

"Have you ever been in love?" she asked.

"No," he said, "not yet." And then he kissed her again. "See you at three."

All that evening and all the next day, Edie kept thinking about Zola. She had been touched by him in some way she had not been touched before. It couldn't be love, it was too soon, and yet, she felt this magical connection. She knew she was vulnerable; she knew she was on the rebound, and yet she could hardly wait for three o'clock.

When she arrived at his apartment, Zola was waiting for her with a picnic basket. He looked a bit rumpled and he hadn't shaved, but at least his clothes were clean, and his hair was still wet from the shower.

They walked several blocks to a park near a river, and after they had eaten tuna salad sandwiches on whole wheat bread and drank most of a bottle of Faygo orange pop, Zola stretched out on the grass, and Edie sat beside him.

"So tell me about you, Edith Stern," Zola said. He had his hands under his head and he squinted up at her through a bright yellow sun.

"I've already told you about me."

"Yes, superficial things. I mean real things. Things you never told anyone else."

"I don't have any deep dark secrets."

"Sure you do. Everyone does."

She tried to think of something to say. Something she'd never told anyone. "I guess here's something I haven't told anyone, except maybe Stanley. I've always wanted to do something," looking for the right word, "important with my life."

"Like being an archaeologist?"

"And a concert pianist, a writer, and an actress. My favorite book growing up was *The Fountainhead*. I always wanted to live a life like Dominique."

"That was my favorite book, too."

"Was it?"

"Yes, but for a different reason. I admired Howard Roark standing by his principles no matter what. But tell me, *why* do you do you want to do something important with your life?"

A flutter in her stomach. "Maybe to show everyone I'm as good as they are. Or better than they are."

"And who are these everyones?"

A chill down her spine. Did she really want to expose herself to this almost stranger? Did she really want him to know the worst about her? And then plunging forward with what she had never put in words before, "I guess the girls in elementary school who wouldn't play with me, the girls in junior high who didn't want me in their club, the boys who didn't ask me out on a date, I suppose my brother, Frank, and.." something she realized for the first time, "my mother."

"Your mother," he repeated. "Tell me about her."

"Well she must be the most popular woman in Detroit. She spends all her time at meetings, and luncheons, and playing Mah Jong and poker with her thousands of friends." And then feeling a bit of guilt, "But she's really a good person. She's raised a ton of money for charity." She pulled at a weed. "Unfortunately, she and I have never gotten along that well."

"And why is that?"

"Because we don't have the same values. All that's ever mattered to her is that I should be pretty and popular and marry a nice Jewish boy."

"And what matters to you?"

"I do want those things, too, but as I said, I don't want *just* to be someone's wife and someone's mother. I want to achieve something for myself."

He was silent for a moment and then he said, "I think you and I are very much alike."

"In what way?" she asked, again feeling a unique connection to him.

"I've always wanted to do something out of the ordinary with my life, too," he said. "I was never like the other kids. I never liked to play baseball or go bowling. I'd rather sit in the house with my books and read. My mother was always after me. We came to this country when I was five, and being a greenie from Russia, my mother wanted me to fit in. She was always telling me to go play with the other boys. But I wouldn't. I felt shut off from them, different. Probably some of it was my accent."

"And what was the rest of it?" she asked.

"I don't know. I just never felt that I was part of it--the whole Detroit scene. And the older I got the more I hated everything that Detroit symbolized."

"Like?"

"Like the fact that everyone is so goddamn materialistic. Money and possessions, that's all people care about. Instead of caring about each other. Instead of valuing the important things in life."

"Which are?"

"Beauty wherever you find it, nature, art, music, literature, and other people. Yes, other people for who they are, not how much money they have, or how many things they own. In Detroit, the total measure of a man is how much money he makes. If you've got money, then you're admired and respected, no matter how big a bastard you are. But if you don't have money, then no matter how good a person you are, or how good you are at what you do, you're a failure."

"Anything else?"

"I have lots more. Like regimentation. Everyone's got to look alike, everyone's got to dress alike, have the same haircut, wear the same shoes. They're like a goddamn army."

"Is that why you wear your hair long, and don't shave?"

"I do shave, occasionally, but I wouldn't shave at all, except it would break my mother's heart to see me in a beard."

"Tell me about your mother."

"She's the sweetest woman on earth. And she's not a typical Detroiter. She doesn't need much to make her happy, which is lucky because my dad, being a baker, doesn't make much. I'm probably the only thorn in her side."

"Then I guess we're both a disappointment to our mothers."

"Well in one way, your mother got her wish," he said. "You are pretty. You have the most exquisite blue eyes."

She lowered her head, "Thank you."

"I guess I've been monopolizing the conversation. Your turn," he said.

"Haven't you heard enough for one day?"

"No," he said. "I want to know everything about you." She felt a rush of heat. She looked into his eyes, and got lost in their blackness. "Kiss me," he said, and she leaned over and touched his moist lips with hers.

"I could make love to you right now," he said. "Right here on this lawn, under this tree, with only the birds to see."

"You could if I let you," she said teasingly.

"And would you let me?"

"No," she said. "Not until I'm 22."

He laughed. "Why 22?"

"It's a decision I made, that I would be a virgin until I got married, or until I was 22, whichever came first."

"And how old are you now?"

"21."

"Then I guess I'll have to wait a year," he said with a smile.

He sat up and began packing the used plates, the glasses, "Let's go back to my place."

All the way walking back to his apartment, they held hands, and chatted some more about his family, her family, the weather, Stanley; innocent enough, but inside, she felt the electricity passing between them.

Back at his apartment, he dropped the picnic basket in the kitchen, and then put on a record; it was songs by Chet Baker, *Oh, there will never, ever be another you.*

"Care to dance?"

He took her in his arms and they began to move to the music, but not like last night, this was more sensual, they were moving together, like one person, and she could feel the bulge in his pants. And then he kissed her, a sweet, gentle kiss. She put her arms around him, and he pressed into her. And then his tongue was in her mouth, and his hands were caressing her body, her arms, her back, her hair, and then he was unbuttoning her blouse and his mouth was kissing her breasts, the course stubble of his face scratching her skin. It was going too quickly, she hardly knew him, she was still in love with Stanley, but it was exciting, so very exciting. He took off his shirt and his chest was full of black hair; he was an ape-man. "You're an ape-man," she said.

He growled, "Do you like it?"

"Yes," she said, "but we've got to stop. I hardly know you."

"You know me," he said. "It's not a matter of time, but chemistry."

He lowered her to the floor, the music was soft and sad, and he was reaching in his back pocket for something, and then apparently giving up, and again she became lost in his caresses. His hand was under her skirt and his fingers were touching her in special places, and she was becoming so stimulated, so aroused that she knew if she didn't stop him now, it would be too late.

"Zola," she said, pushing him away, "I can't do this."

And leaning on his elbow, his black eyes looking down into hers, he said, "I love you, Edie. I've never said that to anyone else."

And in some strange way, she loved him, too. "Oh, what the hell," she thought, "I'm almost twenty-two."

It flashed through her mind that he should use something. She knew about getting pregnant and all that, but it couldn't happen the night you were deflowered, it was too remote to even consider. "Remember I'm a virgin," she said.

"I'll be gentle," he said.

He brought her to a climax with his fingers, so that her body shook violently from the orgasm, and then he brought her to another peak of stimulation and this time entered her with his penis. It hurt, and she felt blood escaping. Why hadn't he gotten a towel or a blanket? But that was Zola. When he let her go, she went into the bathroom, and sat on the cold porcelain toilet seat wondering how she felt. Was she happy or sad? Probably a little of both. Happy to have entered into the world of womanhood; sad to no longer be a virgin. The act itself was disappointing. There were no bells or whistles, and no real pleasure, except for holding Zola close and making him happy. She thought of Stanley. Wouldn't he be surprised? After all those years of necking and petting, she had lost her virginity on a one night stand to someone she hardly knew.

Zola knocked at the door. "Are you all right in there?"

"Yes," she said, "just daydreaming."

"Can I come in?"

"No!"

"I'm coming in," he said.

"No," she screamed again, but she hadn't locked the bathroom door, and he pushed it open and came and sat on the edge of the bathtub. He was still naked and she was too embarrassed to look at him.

He took her hand. "How are you feeling?"

"I'm not sure."

"Tell me."

"Embarrassed."

"What else?"

"Like I've suffered a great loss. But gained something too. I guess I'm a woman of the world now."

He smiled, "I guess so."

His smile encouraged her.

"I never thought when I came here this afternoon that this would happen."

"Didn't you?" he asked, looking at her with those black eyes that knew everything.

"Maybe I did," she said.

And Mr. Ape-man, naked on the edge of the bathtub, put his hands on the sides of her face and kissed her. "I meant what I said before," he said. "I do love you."

And sitting there amid the cold white porcelain, the harsh electric light, what could she do but believe him?

He walked her back to her league house and they stood kissing on the porch until the light flicked on and Mrs. Stevens opened the door. "Better hurry, Edith," she said, "it's almost eleven." And reluctantly, she and Zola let go of each other. Edie hurried up the stairs to her room, where Sandy Stahler was putting her red hair up in rollers.

"Where were you?" Sandy asked.

Edie didn't want to go into all of it, or any of it, she just wanted to crawl into bed with her memories of tonight, of Zola, and all that had taken place. "Just out studying," she said.

"Where are your books?"

"I guess I left them at the library."

"Uh huh," Sandy said.

And then the lights were out and Edie fell asleep dreaming of Zola Bitterman and hoping next time they did it, it wouldn't hurt.

She didn't hear from him the next day, or the next, and she began to wonder, had she misjudged him? Was he something other than what he seemed. Had he duped her, just to seduce her? Was she the biggest fool since the world began?

And then the next night it was raining, and her buzzer went off, dot, dot. No dash. She knew it was he. It had to be. She brushed her hair, put on lipstick and ran down the stairs to Zola. He was wearing a raincoat and carrying a dripping umbrella.

"Want to go for a walk?"

"In the rain?"

"It's only a drizzle," he said.

"Sure," she said.

She ran back upstairs, got her raincoat and a babushka, and within minutes, was back downstairs and out the door walking beside him, holding hands under his big black umbrella.

"I was so worried when I didn't hear from you," she said.

"You shouldn't have worried. You know I love you."

And the words were thrilling to hear.

They walked in silence for a while, the drops of rain hitting her face and hands in spite of the umbrella, and then he said, "Don't ever be ashamed of anything you've done. If it seems right at the time, then it is right."

"What a strange thing to say," she said.

He stopped walking and turned to face her. "There's something I have to tell you."

Her heart started pounding. It had to be something bad.

"I'm going away."

Oh no, the worst thing he could say. "But where? Why?"

"To find where I belong. Probably out west somewhere. As far as I can get from the big city. Somewhere where there's open space, room to breathe."

"But I don't want you to go. And this isn't a big city, it's a little town."

"Yes, and that's why I transferred here last September. I was going to leave Detroit last June, but my mother talked me into trying a year at Michigan. Well, now I've tried it, and I can see it's no different from Detroit. Same people just transplanted to a different environment. I have to leave, Edie."

"But what about me?"

"Come with me."

"But where?"

"Wherever the road takes us."

"You don't even have a car."

"No, but I have a thumb."

She thought of it for a moment, the two of them standing on a deserted highway, their thumbs out, a truck stopping, them jumping in and riding off into the sunset, like in some John Wayne western.

And then realizing how crazy she was for even thinking it, "I couldn't. My parents would kill me."

"Who are you living for? Your parents or yourself?"

"Myself. But I don't know if I have the courage to do what you're asking."

"You don't need courage, just desire."

"When are you leaving?"

"Tomorrow."

"Tomorrow! But that's before school ends."

"I know."

"But at least you should finish the semester."

"It won't have any bearing on my life whether I finish the semester or not. So why wait? I've made up my mind. I'm leaving tomorrow."

Had he known he was leaving when he seduced her? She took her hand from his. "And when did you decide all this?"

"Oddly enough, it was the other night. After we made love. It was you who made me decide."

"Me?"

"Yes. There's no bullshit about you and it made me realize how I've been bullshitting myself. I don't want to be here. I've never wanted to be here, so I'm getting out." He smiled. "Can I have your hand back now?"

She smiled, and gave it to him. "I'm going to miss you."

"Does that mean you're not coming with me?"

"How can I?" she said. "It's too crazy. I don't even know you. I don't even know if you really want me."

"I really want you," he said and kissed her, there, in the falling rain, which was coming faster and harder now.

"Can we go to your apartment?" she asked.

"My room-mate's there."

"But it can't end like this."

"Then come with me. This is your chance to live that exciting life you always dreamed of."

She thought of a T.S. Eliot poem, *Do I dare disturb the universe? Do I dare? Do I dare?* "I wish I were stronger. I wish I were more like Dominique, but I'm not," she said. "I'm so sorry, but I can't go with you."

He turned in the direction of her league house. The intensity of the rain had increased and it was now pouring. They began to run, and by the time they reached the porch of the league house, they were both soaked and out of breath.

"Would you like to come in and dry off?" she asked.

"No," he said. "I want to remember you like this."

"Soaked like a rat?" she asked, shivering a little.

"No, with the rain in your hair, in the soft light of the evening. You will always be a part of me, of everything I do."

"Will I ever see you again?"

"Yes," he said, "but I don't know when. Don't wait for me. Go on with your life."

"I hate that you're leaving."

"I love your honesty," Zola said. "You're not like anyone else."

They hugged each other, their wet raincoats entangling. And then he was down the stairs, down the block, turning to wave to her, and then around the corner and gone.

She stood for several minutes watching the empty street, watching the rain fall. *This is the way the world ends; not with a bang but a whimper.* "Go on with your life," he had said, but he was her life at this moment. She didn't know how she could go on without him. Maybe it wasn't love, but she felt more alone at this moment than that Saturday morning Stanley had driven off. She wiped the tears from her eyes and hurried up the stairs to the rest of her life without Zola Bitterman.

Chapter Four

Janet Camerini walked the three blocks from the campus of Wayne State University to the corner where her mother would pick her up. She did not want the other students to know that her mother still drove her to and from school, even though she was a junior in college.

It was November, 1957, and Janet was 20.

Although Janet had lived in the United States for 10 years, and attended Durfee Intermediate and Central High, the "Jewish" schools, she still felt like a foreigner. She knew that the other girls thought she was strange and she accepted the fact that she couldn't be one of them, that she couldn't belong to their clubs, go to their parties, or have a boyfriend. She knew the other girls couldn't understand her. They hadn't been through what she'd been through. They didn't understand what fear was and why her mother wouldn't let her take the bus, why her mother had to drive her to school each morning and pick her up each afternoon, and why her mother had to know where she was every minute of the day.

Janet and her mother, Ida, her cousins Pietro and Miriam, and Aunt Sophia and Uncle Alberto had all been brought to Detroit by her father's cousins, Ann and Rudy Gerwin, in 1947, and for the last ten years, Janet and Ida lived in the downstairs half of a duplex on Collingwood Avenue near 12th Street. Ann and Rudy had Americanized Janet's name from "Gianna" to Janet, and her mother had taken up sewing to make a living, enough to pay the rent, buy food, buy material to make their clothing, and keep their 1950 black Chevy running.

The day after Janet and Ida arrived in Detroit, Ann and Rudy had taken them to one of Detroit's best restaurants, Mario's, and from that moment on, Janet knew what she wanted to be when she grew up: a chef. For the past ten years, she had spent all her spare time shopping for food, cooking, baking, and studying recipes. She wanted to make everything in her mother's cookbook, and in the cookbooks at the library. She was hungry for new ideas, new combinations of the old ingredients, and new ingredients. She was intrigued by the little spice cans in the supermarket and wanted to own all of them. Each time her mother took her to the grocery store, she begged her mother to buy her one more little can to add to her collection.

"All you need is salt and pepper and garlic and olive oil," her mother would say, "and you can make anything delicious."

"I know," Janet would say, "but I want to try other things anyway."

"Then go ahead," her mother would say, parting with the twenty cents grudgingly, contemplating how quickly her fingers would have to sew to make that twenty cents. Eight minutes for basil, another eight for rosemary. Her mother visualized all money in terms of time.

When Janet was a senior in high school, she told her mother that she did not want to go to college, but that she wanted to get a job in a restaurant so that someday she could become a chef. Her mother's reaction was swift and left no room for argument, "Don't be silly. A chef is not a job for a woman. You'll be a school teacher. And that's that."

Janet knew that once her mother made up her mind, there was no changing it, so reluctantly, she enrolled at Wayne State University, majoring in elementary education.

She did well at Wayne, getting A's in almost every class, even physical education. She didn't want to take P.E., but it was a requirement, and shortly after the class began, Janet realized that she was a surprisingly good athlete, well-coordinated and strong like her father, and even though she weighed 160 pounds, she was a pretty fast runner. Her favorite sport was basketball. She wasn't good at making baskets, but she was very good on defense, getting back fast and covering the shooters on the opponent's team. But more than the game, she loved the teamwork, the camaraderie. When she was playing basketball, she didn't feel like an outsider, but one of the girls. All the girls wanted her on their team. All the girls were friendly. But no one was her friend. How she longed for a friend. Of course, she had her cousins, Miriam and Pietro (his name now Americanized to Peter), who lived just on the next block. And after their months spent hiding together, she had a special bond with them that no other friendship could approach. But she wanted one girlfriend her own age to giggle with, to spend time with, to tell her secrets to, especially the one secret she had told no one, that she had a crush on Greg Flusty. Greg Flusty had been in two of her classes before, and this semester was in her biology class. He was one of the most popular boys at Wayne, a sharp dresser wearing button-down shirts and V-necked sweaters, and always surrounded by a bunch of girls and boys. He wasn't handsome, but cute, with sleek blond hair and a dimple in the middle of his chin, like Kirk Douglas. She knew she was being childish, but still she could not help dreaming about him at night, thinking about him during the day, and writing his name in one of her notebooks in all kinds of handwriting, as the girls in high school had done, "Greg Flusty, Janet Flusty, Mrs. Greg Flusty, Mrs. Janet Flusty." She knew it was futile. Why would a popular boy like Greg Flusty look at her? Why would any boy look at her? She was ugly and fat. She hated her body, she hated being fat but the fatter she felt the more she ate. At least she could do that. She could eat whenever and whatever she wanted. She didn't have to wait for food to be brought down to her two times a day.

Now, as she approached her mother's black Chevy, her mother stuck her head out the window, "Gianna, over here."

As if Janet couldn't see her. "Call me Janet," Janet said with annoyance. It made her angry that her mother couldn't remember her name. But in the same instant she felt anger, she felt remorse. She shouldn't be mean to her mother, even verbally, after all her mother had gone through; was still going through.

Her mother had not aged well. She had lost stature and her back was beginning to hunch from leaning over a sewing machine for the past ten years. She seemed to be getting shorter and wider every year, and her smooth brown hair was now frizzy and gray. She did nothing to make herself attractive. She didn't even wear lipstick, and all the dresses she wore were black and looked as old as she did. It was as if she was still in mourning.

At least the dresses she made for Janet were colorful, even if they were nothing like the store-bought dresses the other girls wore.

"So, how was school today?" her mother asked as Janet got in the car and sat beside her.

"Fine," Janet said. It was always the same question, always the same answer. Janet knew her mother didn't want to hear any bad news. She only wanted to know that Janet was getting all "A's", that she was well behaved, that she was safe.

"Can we stop at Farmer John's on the way home?" Janet asked.

"We stopped there yesterday," her mother said.

"I know, but there are some things I want to buy."

"I have a customer coming at four."

"I'll only be a minute."

"It costs money to buy groceries."

"I just want some bay leaves and cinnamon."

"What are you cooking tonight?"

"Pot roast and apple pie."

Her mother sighed. Of course she would stop. Didn't she always give Janet whatever Janet wanted. Fortunately, Janet wanted very little. Food really--that was all she ever wanted. So if her mother let her buy a few little cans of spice, an extra green pepper or bunch of broccoli, what did it hurt? Her mother could never make up for all the horror Janet had suffered in Italy. If only they had left Italy sooner, if only they had seen what was coming. If only Ida had listened to Ernesto when he said they should get out.

Janet's mother waited in the car while Janet went to do her shopping.

Immediately as Janet walked through the door of the supermarket, she was transported into a magical world. A world that was infinitely fascinating, exciting, challenging. She walked through the produce section, eyeing the cauliflower, the broccoli, the carrots. The mushrooms were calling out to her, "Choose me." The eggplant was ripe and purple, the asparagus fat and green. "You can do something wonderful with me," the spinach said. But today, she would have to pass them by. She had loaded up on vegetables yesterday, and if she bought any more her mother would have a fit. "Why do we need all this? Two people."

Her mother probably didn't understand that Janet could never get enough. If she had one onion, she needed two. If she had three bell peppers, she needed four. She was always afraid she would run out of something she needed. And who knew what might happen tomorrow? Who knew if this food would always be there. No, she had to be prepared. She had to have a full store of food at home.

She reached for the bay leaves and cinnamon.

Soon after they arrived home, Ida's customer appeared, and Janet began preparing dinner. She rubbed the pot roast with fresh garlic, salt, paprika, the way Anna had done, coated it with flour and browned it in a frying pan with olive oil, all the while inhaling the wonderful aroma. When all sides were browned evenly, she transferred it into a heavy pot, added chunks of onion, carrot, potato, bay leaves and beef stock that she had made the night before, and put it in the oven to roast. Then she got out the flour and butter and made two pie crusts, handling the sticky dough delicately. She then peeled and pared a dozen apples, mixed them with sugar and cinnamon, filled the pie plates, and topped them with a mixture of brown sugar, flour and butter, and put them in the oven. She and her mother could never eat all the food she prepared so she would take some of the leftovers over to her Aunt Sofia or upstairs to their landlady, Mrs. Landau, and the rest she would keep in the refrigerator, just in case.

The odors from the oven permeated the house, and Ida's customer, Mrs. Levine, a heavy woman with large varicose veins, asked, "What is that wonderful aroma?"

"My daughter is making dinner," Ida answered getting down on her knees.

"How lucky you are to have such a *ballabusta* for a daughter."

"Yes," Ida said, marking Mrs. Levine's hemline with soap, "I'm very lucky." Ida was sure Mrs. Levine did not catch the underlying sarcasm in her words. Yes, she was lucky to have Janet; no, she was not lucky to have lost everything else she had in Italy so many years ago.

The next day was one that Janet would never forget. As she was leaving biology class, she heard some giggles behind her. She turned around to see what was going on and saw two skinny blonde girls standing next to her desk, rifling through her notebook. One of them called to Greg Flusty, "Greg, look at this."

Janet's heart dropped. Could she have left behind her notebook with the scribbles of, "Janet Flusty, Mrs. Janet Flusty"? Oh no, oh no. Panic gripped her stomach. Her face was on fire. Frantically, she searched her books. The notebook wasn't there! What should she do? Run away or go back and grab the notebook from Greg's hands. He was looking through it now, and laughing. It was like the night the Germans had found her outside Teresa and Salvatore's house, that same terror, that same fear. She had to retrieve it, she had to. She ran to Greg, grabbed the book out of his hands, and ran for the door, as Greg called after her, "I guess you must be Mrs. Greg Flusty. And I didn't even know you existed."

Janet ran as fast as she could, down the hall, out of the building, and the entire three blocks to the corner where her mother picked her up every day. Finally she stopped, panting for breath, so nauseous she thought she would vomit. All she could think of were the last words Greg had said, "I didn't even know you existed." That was the unkindest cut of all.

She could not go to her next class. She could never go back to her last class. She was too humiliated, too ashamed. And standing there, waiting the extra hour for her mother to arrive, the gray wool winter coat that had been remodeled again and again, wrapped around her, she made up her mind. This was it. She would quit Wayne and get a job in a restaurant no matter what her mother said. She couldn't continue at Wayne, she couldn't take the chance of seeing any of them ever again.

That night Janet made veal parmesan for dinner, but she couldn't eat. She was too sick over what had happened today and too scared to tell her mother what she wanted to do. She fiddled with the fork on her plate, and finally forced the words out, "Mama," she said, "there's something I have to talk to you about." And not giving her mother a chance to say anything, "You know I don't really want to be a school teacher. I want to quit school and get a job in a restaurant." And then she waited for the guillotine to drop.

"Janet," her mother said, too busy soaking her bread in the sauce to look up, "we already discussed this. A chef is not a job for a woman."

"But it's what I want to do," Janet pleaded.

Her mother lifted her head and pointed her chunk of bread at Janet, "Now listen, you have just one more semester to go after this one. You'll finish college, and then if you want to cook in the summers, you can do that." Then she went back to eating.

But I don't want to go back to Wayne, Janet wanted to cry out. I can't go back to Wayne. But if she said this to her mother, her mother would want to know why, and then Janet would have to tell her about Greg Flusty. She couldn't do that. She could never tell anyone about Greg Flusty.

Janet cleared the table and began washing the dishes. There seemed to be only one solution. She would drop out of biology class and take an extra class next semester. That way she could still graduate on time. And as for Greg Flusty, she would have to block him out of her mind, just as she had blocked out everything else she didn't want to think about. She raised her wet hands to her temples as she had done so many years ago--the day her papa had died. She would never think of this again. She could bury Greg Flusty along with all of the other memories that were too painful to remember.

When the dishes were dried and put back in the cupboard, Janet marinated the beef flank steak for tomorrow night's dinner, and then set to work baking a three layer raspberry torte. For a moment, she panicked. Were there enough eggs? She looked in the refrigerator. Two dozen. Enough for the torte, yes, but tomorrow she would buy two dozen more, she must never take the chance that she would run out of eggs. Or anything.

Chapter Five

Three weeks after Zola left Ann Arbor, the semester ended. Edie went home for summer vacation to work in her father's insurance office, as she did every summer, and sometime in July, woke up feeling queasy, and the next morning vomited up her breakfast, and then realized she hadn't had a period in a long time.

It wasn't possible, she told herself. She couldn't be pregnant. But her breasts were swollen and tender, and each morning when she awoke, she felt sicker than the day before. It had to be something else, she told herself, and ran to the bathroom every hour to see if there was blood on her panties, on the toilet paper, in the pot, but nothing. She tried to hide how badly she was feeling from her mother, but her mother knew something was wrong.

"What's the matter, Edie? You don't look so good."

"I think it's a flu bug."

And then her father, "How come you're coming so late to work?"

"I wasn't feeling well this morning."

She should go see a doctor. She should find out the truth. But she knew. She already knew. She was pregnant.

She had to find Zola, to tell him. He had to help her.

She took the phone book into her room and looked through the B's. There were two Bittermans: Mark and Yuri. She called Yuri first. A woman answered the phone.

"Hello," Edie asked, "is Zola there?"

"Who is this?" a sweet European voice replied.

"A friend of his. Edith Stern."

"No, Zola's away."

Yes, she knew that. "I wonder, Mrs. Bitterman, if you might know how I could get in touch with Zola?"

"Is it something important?"

"Yes. Somewhat."

"Well, darling, I really don't. He writes us every now and then, but I haven't heard from him in a couple of weeks."

"Where was he when you last heard from him?"

"South Dakota."

"Well, if you hear from him again, could you please tell him to call Edith Stern. It's important."

"Certainly, darling. Let me get a pencil and I'll take your number down."

So it was not going to be easy to locate Zola. Now what to do? Call Stanley? He was almost a doctor. Perhaps he could help her. Perhaps he knew someone who could give her an abortion. Such an ugly word, abortion. But there was no choice. No one must ever know. Not her friends, not her brother, and especially not her parents.

The next morning, the sickness lasted longer than before. She was afraid to leave the bathroom, and sat on the pink and gray speckled linoleum floor beside the cool white toilet, waiting for the next wave to strike.

Her mother knocked on the bathroom door. "Edie, are you all right?"

"Yes, mom." Slowly she got up, flushed the toilet, doused her face with water from the sink, rinsed her mouth, and hesitantly opened the door to her mother.

"Edith, I insist you tell me what's going on."

She could contain herself no longer; the burden was too heavy. "I'm pregnant," she said.

"Oh no," her mother said, horror on her face. "How could such a thing have happened?"

And Edie wished she could die, crumple up in a little ball at her mother's feet and disappear. "I'm sorry, mom. I'm so sorry."

"Who was it?" her mother demanded, furious, threatening.

"Someone you don't know. Someone I hardly know."

Her mother's face was crimson, "Oh, Edie, how could you have done such a thing?"

"I only did it once, mom. Only once."

"Aach, only in the movies it happens like that." Her mother began swaying from side to side, "I think I'm going to faint." She headed for Edie's room, and Edie followed behind her, feeling more ashamed than she had ever felt in her life.

Her mother sat on the chair at Edie's desk while Edie sat on the bed.

"It was that Michigan," her mother said. "I should never have let you go there." Her eyes were wild. Edie had never seen her like this.

"It wasn't Michigan," Edie said weakly.

"Oh no? If you didn't go to Michigan, none of this would have happened."

Edie couldn't argue with that.

Her mother continued to shake her head back and forth. "What did I do wrong?"

"You didn't do anything wrong," Edie said, and then remembering Zola's words, "and neither did I."

"How could what you did not be wrong?"

"Maybe I was in love."

Hope flashing in her mother's eyes. "You think this boy will marry you?"

"I don't even know where he is," Edie said.

"Oy vey, what a tragedy," her mother said. "I never in my wildest dreams imagined such a thing could happen to me."

"It didn't happen to you, mother," Edie said a little defiantly, "it happened to me."

"And now we're all going to have to pay for it."

And Edie, thinking of her dad and brother, "I don't want dad or Frank to know."

"Of course I wouldn't tell them. You think I'd tell them such a thing."

Edie lowered her eyes. Of course not.

"There's only one solution," her mother said, "You'll have an abortion. How far along are you?"

"I think two months."

"Then there's not a second to lose. I'll have to get the name of a doctor." Her mother stood up, ready to swing into action, and when she got to the bedroom door, she turned and looked at Edie one more time, "I always thought you were such a good girl."

And Edie, needing to fight back asked, "What did you think I was doing until one, two in the morning with Stanley Rader all those years?"

"I didn't think you were doing that!" her mother snapped back and left the room.

Edie showered and dressed. Her overwhelming emotion was relief. Someone finally knew. She didn't have to carry this secret alone anymore. But she also felt anger--against her mother. Her mother didn't care what Edie was going through. All she cared about was how this was going to affect *her* life. All she cared about was herself. But then wasn't that how it had always been.

When Edie arrived downstairs, her mother was hanging up the phone.

"Well, I called my doctor, and I have a number to call."

Things were moving too quickly. Edie needed time to think. She envisioned this tiny embryo inside of her. Did she really want to destroy it? "What if I want to keep the baby?"

"Keep the baby?!" Her mother was aghast. "You must be out of your mind. It's out of the question. You are going to have an abortion and that's final."

Edie was quiet for a moment thinking it wasn't her mother's decision. It was hers. Her mother couldn't make her do what she didn't want to do.

Lilly, mistaking Edie's quiet for fear of the surgical procedure said, "It's not so bad--having an abortion. I had one."

Edie was astounded. "You had one?"

"Yes, after you were born. Dad and I didn't think we could afford another child."

"And you don't have any remorse?"

"I didn't have any choice, and neither do you."

"I still want to think about it."

"There's nothing to think about. If you have this baby it'll ruin your life. Who'll marry you? How will you earn a living? How will you live?"

"I don't know," Edie said, "but I do know a live creature is growing inside of me, a person who is half me and half Zola and I don't know if I can kill it."

"Zola," her mother said. "So that's his name. What kind of name is that?"

"Russian," Edie said.

That afternoon Edie called the Bittermans and arranged to come over that evening. She wanted to meet them; she wasn't sure why.

Zola's mother, a short round woman, and Zola's father, a lean, tall man who lumbered when he walked, met her at the door and welcomed her in. Both Zola's parents still spoke with an accent. Their house was tiny, and the furniture old. There were little crocheted doilies on the arms of all the chairs and sofa, and old-fashioned lamps that hardly cast any light.

"Did you crochet these?" Edie asked Mrs. Bitterman, pointing to an intricate white doily.

"Yes, it is a hobby of mine," Mrs. Bitterman said. She had made tea and served it in glass cups with cubes of sugar. She was as sweet as Zola had said she was, and Edie already felt a great affection for her.

"Tell me, Edie said, "have you heard from Zola?"

"Yes," Mrs. Bitterman said, getting up and walking over to the mantelpiece. "A postcard. Would you like to read it?"

"If you wouldn't mind."

Edie took the card in her hand, carefully, as if it might break. There was a scenic picture on the front of mountains and pine trees. She turned it over and read, "Dear Mama and Papa. I am in Montana now. I like it here. It's wide open. I may stay awhile. Don't worry, I'm fine. Love, Zola."

"He's such a talented boy," his mother said, "but I worry about him. So discontent. Always, his whole life. Never like the other boys."

"Zola's okay," his father said. Then to Edie, "She worries too much about him.

Mrs. Bitterman continued, "I don't like it. A boy out there in the wilderness with who knows what kind of people."

"Zola will manage," his father said, kindly.

Should she tell them, she thought. They were so trusting, so enamored with their son. Should she blow up their world. But she needed their help. "Mr. and Mrs. Bitterman. There's something I have to tell you." The room became still. "I'm going to have a baby. Zola's baby."

For a moment, there was silence.

"Does Zola know?" Mr. Bitterman asked.

"No. He left before I could tell him."

"Oh, my poor darling," Mrs. Bitterman began to cry, and came to Edie and kissed the top of her head, then sat beside her and took Edie's hands in hers. "I knew Zola would get into trouble one day, all those girls he brought home, and now it has happened, the worst kind of trouble," she said almost to herself. And then to Edie, "Tell me darling, what are you going to do?"

"I don't know," Edie said feeling even more lost than when she arrived.

"I'm very ashamed of my son," Mr. Bitterman said. "He shouldn't have left you."

"He didn't know," Edie repeated.

"Is there anything we can do?" Mr. Bitterman asked.

"Just help me find him," Edie said.

"I wish we could," Mrs. Bitterman said. "If only he'd call; if only he'd send us an address."

"Maybe I should go to Montana and find him," Mr. Bitterman said.

Maybe I should, Edie thought. "I don't want you to do that, just if you do hear from him, please tell him what's happened." And then getting up, "I'm so sorry I brought you this bad news. It's just that I need to find Zola."

"We know," Mrs. Bitterman said. "And the minute we get a telephone number or an address we'll call you."

"Thank you," Edie said, hugging them, and then she was back on the street, alone again, wondering again, what to do about the baby. She touched her stomach and thought she felt something move. But it was too soon, it was impossible to feel life this early. Unless this baby was trying to tell her something. Unless this baby wanted to be born.

She needed to talk to someone. She called Stanley.

He stopped by on his way home from school the next afternoon, and sitting in the den, on her mother's new blue sofa, she told him.

"Why you little slut," he said, in his joking way. "I can't believe you went all the way with that bum."

"Why are you calling him a bum?" she asked. "I thought he was your friend."

"He is, but he's also a bum," he said, still joking. And then in a more serious tone, "How could you let yourself get involved with him?"

She thought of Zola, his black eyes, the things he said to her, his kisses. "We had something, Stanley. Something special."

"I'll say you did," he said, sarcastically, looking at her stomach. "So what're you going to do?"

"That, my dear, is the 64 dollar question," she said, trying to keep the conversation light.

"And if you answer it correctly, you get a box of Snickers."

"Or a seven pound bundle of joy."

"Well I, for one, think you're crazy to even consider having the baby. What's it going to get you?"

"That's the trouble with you, Stanley. You always think in terms of what it's going to get you."

His left eyelid began to droop. "Oh, the irony of it. Yelena's dying to have a baby and you get pregnant."

She was taken aback by his words. "But I thought you weren't going to have any babies. I thought you were going to adopt."

"We changed our minds."

She thought of that afternoon at Stanley's wedding. "Zola was right."

"About what?"

"He said you would change your mind." If only she knew where Zola was, she could call him right now and tell him he was right. If only she knew where he was.

"Well, if you're asking my advice," Stanley said, "I say, have the abortion. There'll be other babies."

But they won't be Zola's, she thought.

The days were passing and Lilly was getting desperate. Edie was avoiding her, refusing to talk about the abortion, refusing to set the date. Lilly needed help. She didn't want to tell her husband or Frank, but someone had to put pressure on Edie. Someone had to talk some sense into her.

She decided to tell Ben first. She told him on a Sunday night after the 10 o'clock news, when they were alone in the bedroom, and as she expected, he was devastated. "How could she have done such a thing?" he asked in an accusatory tone, as if it were Lilly's fault.

"I don't know," Lilly said defensively. "I feel just as bad about it as you do."

"No," he said, "no one could feel as bad as I do."

"You've got to talk to her, Ben. You've got to talk her into having the abortion."

"You talk to her," Ben said. "That's your job."

"But I have talked to her and she won't listen to me. Please, Ben."

He looked at her with glazed eyes. "How am I going to talk to her, I don't even know if I can look at her."

So Ben was not going to be any help. She should have known that. Ben had never wanted to be involved with any problems at home. That was Lilly's department. He ran the office; she ran the house. It had always been that way. And up to now, Lilly hadn't minded. She didn't want Ben interfering with her decisions. But now she needed help, and if she wasn't going to get it from her husband, then she would have to get it from her son.

Frank seemed more upset than Lilly felt, and wasted no time in confronting Edie. "How could you be so stupid? Don't you know about birth control?"

"Of course, I do. But I didn't think anything would happen."

"That's what they all say," he said. "Well now that you're in this pickle, there's nothing to think about. It's just a little blob of protoplasm. Get rid of it." Spoken with unquestionable authority.

Edie knew Frank was right. She knew her mother was right. She hated the fact that her father was avoiding her, that he couldn't look her in the eye. But still she delayed making a decision. She didn't think there was anything morally wrong with having an abortion, but when it came to this baby, her baby, she didn't know if she could take the steps to end its life.

It was the end of August, almost three months since she had conceived and school was starting in two weeks. She stood before the full length mirror on the back of her closet door and put her hands on her bulging stomach. It was simple really. She loved this baby. Had loved her or him from the first moment she realized a live human being was growing inside her--a person created from the magic that had existed between her and Zola. She could not kill it.

She went into the kitchen. A big pot of chicken soup was simmering on the stove and her mother was peeling carrots at the kitchen sink. "Mother," she said, "I've made up my mind, I'm going to have the baby."

Her mother grabbed the edge of the sink as if she had lost her balance, "Oh no, oh no."

"I'm sorry, mother. I know you're disappointed in me and dad and Frank will be disappointed in me, and maybe I am being stupid, ridiculous, insane, but this is my baby and I'm going to keep it."

Her mother was shaking. "You're right, you are insane."

"Please, mother, there's nothing you can say I haven't already said to myself."

And Lilly, still not wanting to give up, said, "How will you live? You can't even support yourself, let alone a baby?"

"I've already thought of that. I thought I could move back home, transfer to Wayne, and switch into teaching. That way it wouldn't cost you any money and I'd be able to earn a good living as soon as the baby comes."

Her mother searched her mind for some way to get out of this mess. If Edie had the baby, it would ruin Lilly's life. "What if you go live with your Auntie Bea in Cleveland or your Auntie Anne in Chicago until the baby comes? Then we could make up some story about you adopting it."

"I don't want to go live with Auntie Bea or Auntie Anne, and everyone's bound to see through any story you might invent."

Lilly wanted to scream. She wanted to grab her daughter and shake her until she came to her senses; she wanted to handcuff her and drag her off to the doctor's. But she knew there was nothing she could do. "Okay Edie, you win. You want to ruin your life, then go ahead."

"I'm really sorry, mom."

"Sure, you're sorry," she said. "What do you care what this is going to do to the rest of us? Selfish. That's what you are."

Guilty as she was feeling, Edie could not tolerate the word "selfish" from her mother. "Me, selfish? What about you? All you care about is what everyone's going to think about you. You don't care at all about me."

"And why should I? Did you care about me when you made this decision? Did you care that this is going to ruin my life? That's right, ruin my life."

And Edie felt like she was sinking into quicksand. Maybe it was too much. Too much to put her family through. But on the other hand, should she kill her baby just to avoid their discomfort? "Maybe I should quit school. Stay in Ann Arbor. Maybe that would be easier for you."

Her mother thought it over. Yes, it would be easier, but if Lilly turned her back on Edie, refused to help her in her time of need, wouldn't the world think even less of Lilly? "No," her mother said, "I don't want you to do either of those things. You'll live at home, you'll finish school, and that'll be the end of it." And her mother turned back to cutting her carrots.

Edie felt totally miserable. She wanted to comfort her mother. She wanted her mother to comfort her. But there was a chasm between them that could not be crossed. "Well," Edie said, "I guess I better call Wayne and start making arrangements."

That night, Lilly told Ben of Edie's decision.

They were lying in bed together propped up against pillows, Ben reading the Detroit Free Press, Lilly reading *Dr. Zhivago.* She tried for an hour to get the words out and finally said, "Edie's decided to keep the baby."

Aside from the slight ruffle of Ben's newspaper, Ben did not appear to hear her.

"I said," she repeated a little louder, "Edie's decided to keep the baby."

"I heard you the first time," Ben said.

"Then why didn't you answer me?"

"What should I say?"

"Say how you feel."

"I feel rotten, like somebody stabbed me in the heart. That's how I feel."

And Lilly crumbled, "Oh Ben, how are we going to get through the next few months."

"I don't know," he said.

When Edie came down to breakfast the next morning, Frank was at the sink rinsing out his cereal bowl. He turned to look at his sister, disgust in his eyes. "I can't believe you're doing this."

"Please, Frank, let me explain..."

"If you have this baby, Edie, I swear, I'll never forgive you."

She sank into a chair. "Please, Frank, I can't stand you being angry with me."

"Then have the abortion," he said.

"I can't.

"Then don't bother talking to me again because I won't answer." And he picked up his books and slammed out of the kitchen.

Edie sat trembling at the kitchen table. It's going to be too difficult, she thought. I can't go through with it. But then she felt a flutter in her stomach and moved her hand to try and catch the baby's movement. "You're there," she thought. "You're alive." And aloud, she said, "Don't worry baby, no one's going to hurt you."

Edie started Wayne the following week. The plan was that she would go to school for one semester, have the baby, and then go back to finish school the following September. She still had the $400.00 she had saved from the ballet school and giving piano lessons, and she would use that money to pay for a baby sitter. If she worked over the summer and lived at home, it would all work out.

Wayne was, as she expected more like high school than college. She met up with the same boys and girls she had gone to junior high with, and they hadn't changed. They were still, in her opinion, superficial, materialistic, cliquish. Unfortunately Edie wasn't in anyone's clique. They all said, "hi," and "how've you been?" but no one wanted to get together with her outside of school. Did they know?

Still, going to school was the good part of her day. Being at home was more difficult. Her father walked around as if someone had died, her brother Frank wasn't speaking to her, and her mother's eyes welled up with tears every time she looked at Edie.

Edie needed a friend, someone to talk to. But all her friends were at Michigan or Michigan State, except for Naomi Parker who was now married and living in Atlanta, Georgia, where her husband was stationed in the army.

There was Stanley, of course, but she didn't want to call him. He had a wife; it wasn't right of her to invade his happy home, unless she was desperate.

By her fourth month, Edie could no longer button her skirts and had to make the daunting journey to buy maternity clothes. It was a degrading experience. All the clerks wanted to know about her husband, how long she'd been married, and was this her first. Then, trying on the clothes in the dressing room, the reality hit her. She really was going to be a mother. She really was going to have a baby. Suddenly she couldn't breathe, and then she began to shake. What had she gotten herself into?

But the worst was yet to come. The day she appeared at Wayne in her maternity top and skirt, all eyes were upon her. Maybe they had suspected before, but now they knew. There were whispers and stares all about her and no one wanted to come near her, as if what she had was contagious. As the days progressed, all the "hi's" and "how are you's?" stopped. Everyone was avoiding her. But still Edie kept trying to find a friend. She tried chatting with the girls before class and after class, she tried joining a study group, she asked people to go to lunch. But they were all busy, or in a hurry, or weren't eating today.

She even tried calling Debbie Bernard, a girl she hadn't seen in years, but who'd been in her club in junior high. Maybe she wouldn't know about Edie. Maybe she would want to get together. "Debbie, hi, it's me, Edith Stern."

"Edie, hi. It's been years."

"Yes, too many. Say how would you like to go to a movie tonight? Talk about old times?"

"Oh, I'd love to, but I'm already going to the movies."

"Well then," Edie said, pushing herself, "maybe I could go, too."

A hesitation on Debbie's part. "Oh, I'm terribly sorry, but not tonight. Maybe some other time."

"Sure," Edie said, "some other time."

She put down the receiver. Did Debbie Bernard know? Did every single person in Detroit know?

She thought of calling Stanley but held back. She wasn't that desperate, yet.

Instead, she went to her room and again looked at herself in the full length mirror behind her door. What she saw was a fat, dowdy girl, burdened with responsibilities, rejected by her family, and without a friend. Where was that young, carefree, energetic girl she had been just four months ago? She lay down on her bed and began to cry. But softly, so no one would hear.

The day that Edie had gone to buy maternity clothes was one of the worst days of Lilly's life. It meant that she could no longer hide the truth. That she would have to tell her friends that her daughter was pregnant.

Lilly Stern had spent her entire life cultivating friends. From the time she was a little girl, it had been the most important thing in her life--to be popular. She had been the middle child of three girls. Bea was the oldest, Anne was the baby and Lilly was nothing--or at least that's how she felt. So she set out to make her place in the world. She started working on it in elementary school, inviting girls over, being extra nice to them, doing them favors, remembering their birthdays, and by the time she was in high school, Lilly Kaplan was the most popular girl at school. And after she was married, it continued. Even when Frank was little, she invited people to dinner, went out with "the girls" while Ben stayed home and babysat, joined a bowling league, a mahj group, started a husband and wife poker club. And when Frank was old enough to take care of Edie, she started in with her organizations, the Temple, volunteer work. By the time Edie started college, Lilly was busy every day of the week. She had a luncheon, meeting, or card game every afternoon or evening. She was invited to every Bar Mitzvah, wedding, anniversary party. She had three dates for every Saturday night, her calendar was booked four months in advance and her phone never stopped ringing. She was a success. And now, just as she was about to relax, just as she felt she had enough friends, her daughter was about to topple her world like a house of cards.

She decided to tell her mother, Edie's grandmother, first. Her mother, Rose Kaplan, had moved to Palm Beach, Florida, two years ago, with her new husband, Arthur Koenig. Lilly's father, Sidney Kaplan, had died of lung cancer ten years earlier, and her mother waited eight years before finding the right man to marry, a retired furrier, who, after they were married, took her off to Florida to escape the bad weather in Detroit.

Dialing the phone, Lilly thought, "Thank God, my mother isn't here to witness Edie's pregnancy."

After the "hellos" and "how are you's", Lilly told her mother about Edie.

There was a moment of silence. Lilly could see her mother's face turning purple over the telephone line. And then her mother snapped at her, "I blame you."

"Me?"

"Yes, you. You were always too busy gallivanting around with your friends to pay any attention to Edith."

"That's not true," Lilly said, indignant. Her mother was a fine one to talk after how little attention she had given Lilly. "I was always there for her when she needed me."

"That's not the way I saw it," her mother said.

Lilly wasn't going to argue with her mother, and after a few more minutes of talking and a polite "Goodbye", Lilly hung up. She was upset with her mother for accusing her instead of supporting her. But could her mother be right? Could it be her fault? Lilly thought back to all those afternoons when she got home just a little bit late, of all the times she couldn't attend a program at school, how busy she was on the telephone every time Edie wanted her attention. She thought of that morning of the piano competition. And as she made her way to the kitchen to cook dinner, she wondered if, in some way, she had failed her daughter.

After dinner, Lilly continued on with her ordeal. She called her sisters: Bea in Cleveland, and

Annie in Detroit, and heard it in both their voices, the pity.

Then she began calling her friends.

She called one the first day, two the second day, three the third day and by the fourth day, everyone knew. Every friend, neighbor, relative, everyone she'd ever met, everyone she'd never met. And it was hard, it was humiliating to go to a meeting, or a luncheon, to the supermarket, the bakery, Northland, to even walk out in front of her house. Everyone was talking about her, whispering about her, pointing a finger at her. Everyone was appalled, shocked, embarrassed. And a few friends didn't call her back, and a few friends stopped calling her, and she wasn't invited to Betty Levine's annual Halloween party, but for the most part, her friends stuck by her, and in some way it was gratifying, for it proved that some people really did like her, no matter what.

At the beginning of Edie's seventh month, Mrs. Bitterman called Edie. She had received a letter from Zola with a return address, and she had already written him that Edie was pregnant. Would Edie like his address? Yes, of course, and Edie copied it down, and then sat staring at it for several minutes. Should she write him?

She pondered for days, to write or not to write, and then before she could make a decision, there it was, in the mail, a letter from Zola. She took it into her room and shut the door. Her heart was racing as she sat on her bed and opened it. She was almost afraid to read the words. They could make her spirits soar, or crash them into the ground. They could take her out of Detroit, or leave her here to rot. Her fingers were trembling as she unfolded the sheet of paper torn from a spiral notebook, and read,

"Dear Edie,

I received my parents' letter telling me that you are pregnant. It was both terrible and wonderful news. I am not ready to be a father at this time, but paradoxically, am thrilled that I am going to be one. I'm sure these are the same kinds of feelings you must be having. It's hard to believe that our one night of love has had such a cataclysmic consequence. The more I learn, the more I believe in powers beyond us. I believe this baby wanted to be born. I know you're going through the hard part and I admire your courage. As for me, I will do whatever you want. I will come back; I will bring you here; I will marry you. Just tell me what you want. You have often been in my thoughts, but when I left Michigan, I wanted to sever all connections to my past life, even to my parents, although I write them periodically to let them know I am still alive. But I am not afraid of responsibility; only stagnation. Let me hear from you.

Lovingly, Zola."

She set the letter down, feeling there was more between the lines, then in them. He admired her courage. Did that mean he wanted her to be even more courageous and have this baby without him? He wanted to sever all connections to his past life. Wasn't she a part of that life?

She re-read the letter again and again, and in a few days was ready to write back to him.

"Dear Zola,

Thank you for your letter, but as I made clear to your parents, I don't really need any help with this baby. I am quite capable of managing on my own, and my mother is providing any help I need. I thank you for your offers, but I chose none of the above. You are welcome to see your child any time you happen to be in Detroit, but you don't need to come back or take me away, or marry me, or support me. I don't regret anything that's happened and I don't feel guilty. I hope that you find whatever it is you're looking for, and I hope I do, too.

Love, Edie."

She was happy with her letter. It said it all, in the lines and between the lines, and the only word, she pondered was "love" at the end. Was it "love" she wanted to send him, or hate, anger, resentment. If he really cared, he wouldn't have asked what he could have done, he would have done it. But then, if he really cared, he wouldn't have left in the first place.

She decided to leave the "love," sealed the envelope, and walked it over to the mailbox on the corner. As she dropped it in, she said out loud, "Goodbye, Zola."

Chapter Six

Edie's baby, a girl, was born on March 2, 1958. And looking at this tiny, helpless creature, holding her in her arms, breast feeding her, Edie thanked God that she had not had an abortion. She could not imagine loving anything or anyone as much as she loved this baby.

Edie's mother and father were as enthralled with the baby as Edie was. They could not get over how beautiful she was, how tiny, how much she looked like Edie. Edie didn't think the baby looked anything like herself, with her headful of black hair. If she looked like anyone, it was Zola.

After all the months of tension, both of Edie's parents had come through for her. From the moment she went into labor, they were both at her side, comforting her, encouraging her, fussing about her like two mother hens. And once the baby was born, her mother spent all day, every day at the hospital, and her father came every afternoon, not really to visit Edie, but to stand at the nursery window and look at his new granddaughter.

Edie wanted to name the baby, Wendy Stern. There was a fight about that.

"Her name should be Bitterman," her mother said.

"But I hardly remember Zola Bitterman and he's not going to enter into the fathering."

"Again, you're only thinking of yourself," Lilly said. "Think of Wendy. Everyone will know you weren't married. At least give the child a fighting chance." And then in a tone that sounded just like Frank, she said, "Name her Bitterman."

Bitterman. Such an ugly name for such a sweet little baby. But her mother was right. Wendy would have enough to contend with not having a father. Better Bitterman, than bastard.

The Bittermans came to the hospital the day after Wendy was born, bringing her a fancy pink dress and a soft brown teddy bear. They, too, were thrilled with the baby, and Mrs. Bitterman told Edie, "Now, you be sure to let us know if there's anything we can do, or if you need any help."

"I will," Edie said. Mrs. Bitterman was so sweet and loving that in a way Edie felt closer to her than she did to her own mother.

Stanley also came by to see the baby, but Frank did not. Edie was terribly disappointed in her brother. She had hoped that once the baby was born, Frank would forgive her, but it looked like he wasn't going to be won over so easily.

"Did Frank say anything to you about the baby?" Edie asked Stanley, trying to sound nonchalant.

And Stanley sensing the disappointment behind her words, said, "If I were you, I wouldn't expect too much from Frank."

The day Edie's parents brought Edie and Wendy home from the hospital, Frank stayed hidden in his room until right before dinner when Wendy woke up screaming. Then as Edie was changing her diaper on the bathinet which was now a permanent part of Edie's bedroom, along with an oak crib and high chest of drawers, Frank came walking in. "So this is the new baby."

"Yes," Edie said, glowing. "Isn't she beautiful?"

"Beautiful," he said, "and noisy. I guess I'll be spending a lot more time at the library now."

And he turned to leave.

Edie was fuming. "Is that it?" she asked. "You haven't even looked at her."

"I've seen all I want to see."

And now all the frustration and anger that had been building for the past months came rushing out, "She's just an innocent little baby. How can you be so mean?"

"I'm not mean," he said pushing his horn-rimmed glasses back up his nose, "I'm just in a hurry."

"Well, I'm sorry for taking up your valuable time," Edie said as sarcastically as possible.

"My time is valuable," he said, a look of contempt in his eyes, "and I don't have time to stand here and argue with you." And he was out the door.

Edie wanted to throw something at him, to cry, to scream, but Wendy was doing enough screaming for both of them. Edie took her baby in her arms, unbuttoned her blouse and sat at her desk chair to feed her. "What do I care," she said aloud, holding her baby close. "What do I care about old Uncle Frank? I have you."

Frank left Edie's room more upset than Edie was. He couldn't figure it out. All his life he had doted on his little sister, taken care of her, cared about her. He had taken her to Tiger baseball games, helped her with her schoolwork, taken her for chocolate sodas whenever she was upset, and gone to her piano competition, cutting an important class in quantitative analysis to do so. He had even talked their mother into letting her go to Michigan. He could kill himself for that. If she hadn't gone to Michigan, she would never have met Zola. Zola. He'd like to kill Zola. And now she had made him the laughing stock of Detroit. All his friends knew, everyone in his medical class knew. Had Stanley told them? No, Stanley was a good guy--he wouldn't have done that. He wouldn't intentionally hurt Frank. But someone had. Someone had spread the word. And now everyone who had always looked up to him, was making jokes about him. "You hard up?" he heard one of his classmates whisper to another, "maybe you should call Frank's sister." How humiliating! Frank couldn't understand why he was being punished this way. He had always been so sure of himself. Knew exactly what he was going to do. He was the elder, the big brother, the smart one. When he studied, his mother shushed everyone in the house; when he spoke everyone listened. He was going to be a doctor, what could be better than that? And now Edie, his little sister, in one stupid action, had fucked up his whole life. He would never forgive her.

When Wendy was three months old, Edie got a job as a checker at the A & P on Davison and Linwood. She wanted to help out with the expenses at home, and she needed some time away from her mother. Her mother was constantly telling her what to do, especially concerning Wendy, "She's too hot, she's too cold, you should do this, you shouldn't do that". Edie wanted to talk back, but as long as her mother was supporting her, she didn't feel she had the right to.

She had planned to hire a babysitter, but was surprised when her mother offered to babysit.

"But what about your meetings?" Edie asked. "What about your organizations?"

"I'm kind of tired of all that," her mother said. "I think I'd like to stay home for awhile and take care of Wendy."

Edie was amazed and moved, that her mother was willing to give up all the things that were most important in her life for Wendy. "Well that'd be great with me," Edie said.

Lilly was also amazed at her offer. It's true that things hadn't been the same with her friends since Edie became pregnant, but still to give up everything to stay home with Wendy was pretty drastic. But the words had come out so spontaneously that she knew it was what she really wanted. She just loved that little girl like nothing on earth, and couldn't think of being away from her for a whole day, let alone leaving her with a babysitter.

She spoke to Ben about it. "I can't believe how crazy I am about Wendy." They were lying in bed together, the lights out.

"I know what you mean," Ben said. "She's really something that little Wendy."

"When she smiles at me, my heart could break."

"I know what you mean."

"I mean I'm afraid I love her more than I ever loved our children."

"I'm sure not."

"And I worry about her," Lilly said. "I'm so afraid something will happen to her."

"You worried about our kids, too."

"No, Ben. I didn't have time to worry about our kids. I was too busy taking care of them, and the house, and all our social engagements. Maybe because I was younger, I didn't realize all the things that can go wrong. She's so precious to me."

"I know," Ben said. "I think about it, too." And he was silent for awhile.

What was he thinking, Lilly wondered. Ever since that night she told him Edie was pregnant, he had become so closed, so silent. She couldn't get anything out of him. "What are you thinking?" she asked.

"I'm thinking that it's time I forgave Edie."

"But you've been so nice to her and the baby."

"Nice on the outside, but still angry on the inside."

"Yes," Lilly said, "I know what you mean." And Lilly had to admit she felt the same way Ben did, that deep in her heart she had never forgiven Edie. "Maybe it's time we both forgave her."

Ben pulled her to him. "You're my sweetheart, Lilly."

"And you're mine, Ben," she said, tears coming to her eyes, and she was glad that she had chosen Ben over Hymie the doctor, and Sam the lawyer, and Abie the millionaire. He had what the others lacked, a heart.

The next evening after dinner, Ben asked Edie, "Is it okay if I take Wendy out for a walk?"

"Sure," Edie said.

Ben lifted his grandchild out of her infantseat. "Come on my little cookie pie, grandpa's going to take you for a walk." He paused for a moment and then came over and kissed the top of Edie's head. "You did the right thing," he said, "having Wendy," and walked out the kitchen door.

Edie's mother reached across the table and put her hand on Edie's hand, "Thank God," she said, "thank God you didn't listen to anybody, but yourself."

A week after Edie began working, on a Sunday afternoon, Frank was at a friend's studying, Wendy was taking a nap, and Edie and her dad were in the den watching a Tiger baseball game, when the doorbell rang. "I'll get it," Lilly called out.

In a few minutes, Lilly entered the room and after her, standing in the den doorway, was Zola. Edie felt her body go numb, as if she'd just been injected with Novocain. "Zola," she said.

"Hi, Edie," he said. And then seeing that no one was moving, he explained, "I came to see my daughter."

He looked awful. He had a gigantic beard that covered his entire face, with two little peepholes for his eyes. He was dressed in creased army fatigues, and carried a knapsack on his back.

Edie, feeling as if she were in a dream, got up, walked over to him, and kissed the black hair that covered his cheek. He smelled of sweat and tar. Then she turned to her parents who were both looking as stunned as she felt, and announced, "This is Zola Bitterman. Wendy's father."

Ben looked like he wanted to punch Zola in the face, but instead he walked over and shook his hand. "Glad to meet you," he said pleasantly, a salesman to the end.

Edie's mother only stood and stared. Edie knew what she must be thinking, "How could my daughter have had sex with this gorilla?"

"Would you like to clean up?" Edie asked Zola.

"I would," he said, dropping his knapsack on the rug. "I do have a clean shirt with me, but first I'd like to see my daughter."

"Of course," Edie said. "Come, I'll show her to you."

Edie's heart was racing as she led him down the hallway to the baby's room. Had he come just to see the baby, or did he have some other motives? And if he did, what might they be? They tiptoed over to the crib.

"She's gorgeous," Zola whispered.

"Yes," Edie said, proudly, "isn't she." Not a question.

And they both stood admiring the human being they had created.

What if Zola wanted to stay? Edie thought. What if he wanted to marry her? She pictured the two of them settled into a little bungalow in the suburbs of Detroit. Zola going off to work each day, clean shaven and well dressed, and Edie staying home and taking care of the children. She turned to look at Zola and wondered if he was thinking the same thing.

Later, after Zola had washed and changed into a clean blue shirt, and eaten a tuna salad sandwich, and after Wendy had awaken and been fed, Zola sat holding his daughter. "I've never been as enchanted by anything as I am with this baby," he said, shaking his head from side to side, as if filled with the wonder of her.

"She looks just like you," Edie said, finally relaxed and smiling.

"Well, she's got my hair and eyes, that's for sure." And then looking at Edie, "I don't suppose you'd consider coming back to Oregon with me?"

Immediately Lilly walked over to Zola and took Wendy from him, while Edie thought, is it me he wants or his baby?

Ben stepped forward, protectively. "You know we don't know anything about you."

"What do you want to know?" Zola asked.

"Well, for one thing, what do you do for a living?" Ben asked. That would be the most important thing to her parents.

"I'm a bartender."

And both parents grimaced. Of all the things he could have been, bartending wasn't even on the list.

"And where do you live in Oregon?" Lilly asked accusingly, holding Wendy over her shoulder and patting her on the back.

"At the top of a mountain with a bunch of other people."

Edie could see it was getting worse every minute.

"What kind of people?" Lilly asked.

"Actually, it's a commune," Zola said.

And both parents grimaced again.

"It's really a great place," Zola continued. "We share all the money and all the tasks, and it's fun." Then looking at Edie, "I think you'd like it, Edie."

"And where is this commune?" Ben asked, continuing the interrogation.

"Right outside of Medford. We don't have any electricity or plumbing, but we do have a lot of little kids." Again looking at Edie, "What do you say, Edie?"

Edie had kept quiet through all of this, watching her parents take command, letting them ask all the questions she should have asked. But for once, she didn't resent them for it; she appreciated the fact that they were looking out for her best interest. Or perhaps Wendy's. Now, all eyes were on her. The thought of going to Oregon was tempting in a way. It sounded different, exciting. But she had to consider what was best for Wendy. And what seemed best for Wendy at this moment was keeping her in this warm, safe, loving environment. Her parents were holding their breath and she knew they were thinking that it was better for Edie to be an unwed mother in Detroit, than to take their precious granddaughter off to a commune in Oregon with this ape-man. "I think for now you'd better go on with your life and I'll go on with mine," Edie said to Zola, and she could feel her parents' relief.

"Your choice," Zola said, and Edie felt a little disappointed that he had given in so easily. If he really wanted her and Wendy, he should have put up more of a fight. Jack Shine all over again.

"Well, I better be going," Zola said getting up wearily. "I'm bushed."

"Indeed you are," Lilly said under her breath.

"What's that?" Zola asked.

"Nothing," Lilly said.

Then, turning to Edie, Zola said, "I'd like to come by tomorrow and spend some more time with Wendy before I leave."

"When are you leaving?"

"I figure I'll hitch out of here sometime in the afternoon."

"You mean you hitched all the way to Detroit from Oregon?" Lilly asked, a mortified look on her face.

"Yes," Zola said.

"How awful," Lilly said.

"No, it wasn't," Zola said. "You meet interesting people on the road."

And you expected my daughter to hitch back with you? Lilly's expression said.

"I have to go to work in the morning," Edie said, "but my mom will be here."

"Then I'll be by in the morning."

Edie walked him to the door. "I'm glad you came," she said.

"I never thought it would be like this."

"How is it?"

"I came because I thought I should see my daughter. But now I feel the responsibility. I want to do something for her."

"What can you do?"

"Move back."

And Edie, touched by his offer, "No, Zola, you can't do that. You won't make her life better by ruining yours."

"I know you're a good mother, Edie, and I can see your parents really love Wendy. I feel good about that. But shouldn't I be doing something too?"

"Oh, Zola, Mr. Ape-man," and she wrapped her arms around him, and felt enveloped by his arms, his hair, his warmth.

"There's no one like you, Edie. I knew that the first night we met."

"Just go," she said. "Go back to your mountain. We'll do fine without you."

"I'm going to send you money," he said. "As much as I can."

"We don't need your money," she said, kindly.

"I'm her father," he said. "I want to help support her."

And Edie, now close to tears, "Of course. Send what you can."

"And I'll stay in touch," he said. "You'll always know where I am. If you ever need anything, let me know."

"I will," she said.

"Sure you won't change your mind and come with me?"

One final moment of temptation, and then staving it off. "No, Zola. I don't know where my life's going to lead me, but I don't think it'll be Oregon."

"Okay, then," he said, looking as if he wanted to stay, but didn't know how, "I guess this is goodbye for now."

"For now," she said.

And he hugged her one more time, then hoisted his knapsack onto his back, and was out the door.

She stood leaning her back against the closed door, tears running down her cheeks, so filled with emotion that she thought she would burst. Was it love for Zola? Or was it anger and frustration. Anger that circumstances had conspired against her so that she and Zola couldn't be together; frustration that Zola was who he was. If only he were a "normal" person, but if he had been "normal", she probably wouldn't have fallen in love with him, or let him make love to her on their second date--if you could call it a date--and then Wendy wouldn't be here today. She reached for the hanky in her blouse pocket. It was too painful to dwell on what might have been; she had to deal with what is. She wiped the tears from her eyes and went to check on Wendy.

Chapter Seven

In September, Edie quit her job at the A & P and started back to school. Zola was sending $25.00 a week, and Edie insisted that Lilly use the money for more help in the house. Mrs. Giles was still coming once a week, but it wasn't enough. Her mother was working too hard. "Okay," Lilly said, "I'll see if Mrs. Giles can come more often, but no one's going to take care of this baby but me."

Edie was glad to be back at school, although she hadn't minded working at the supermarket. It was fun in a way. She liked chatting with the customers, she liked her co-workers, and she liked seeing what people bought, what looked good to eat, what didn't, what was in season, what wasn't. But it had been tough, standing on her feet six hours a day and then going home to take care of Wendy. She was physically tired and she welcomed the chance to be a student again.

She was in teacher training and while she had always considered teaching a boring career (as Mr. Dow had said, those who can, do, those who can't, teach), she was really enjoying it. She loved the children, surprised that each one was a unique personality, and she decided that maybe helping 30 or 40 little kids learn was also "doing" something. For the first six weeks, her class observed master teachers, and then each student received an assignment for practice teaching. Edie was assigned to Winterhalter Elementary, as was Janet Camerini, a peculiar girl who was in most of Edie's classes. Janet was a most unattractive person. She never spoke unless spoken to, and she was heavy, with fuzzy brown hair, and dressed in odd, if perfectly-fitted clothing. Often Edie would look at her and wonder what was she thinking, what kind of person was she? She was not someone Edie would have picked for a friend, but since they would be teaching at the same school, Edie offered to drive her. Edie's dad had just bought himself a brand new yellow Buick, and given Edie his four-year-old white Pontiac.

"I don't know," Janet said. "My mother usually drives me."

"Well then, I'll save her the trouble," Edie said. "I promise I'm not a bad driver."

"It's not that," Janet said.

And Edie wondering, does she know about me too? Was this going to be another Debbie Bernard? Frank? "Well, it's up to you. Let me know."

It was a big step for Janet. One she wanted to take. She was twenty-one, now, almost twenty-two, but she still felt like a child. Her mother made all her decisions for her and was in total control of her life. She wouldn't even allow Janet to get a driver's license even though Uncle Alberto had taught Janet how to drive. The only freedom Janet had was when she was in the kitchen where she could cook whatever she wanted, as much as she wanted. Driving with Edie would be a chance for Janet to spend time with someone her own age, someone who might turn out to be a friend. Janet could not let this opportunity pass her by.

That night, her knees trembling, Janet approached her mother. "Mama, I'm going to be driving to student teaching with this girl in my class."

"You don't need a ride," her mother said, looking up from her sewing machine. "I drive you."

"But she's driving anyway and it'll save you the trouble."

"It's no trouble for me. I enjoy doing it."

"Mama, really, I can't have you waiting outside the elementary school for me. It's too embarrassing."

"Why should it be embarrassing to have your mother there for you?"

"You don't understand."

"No. I don't understand."

"Please, mama. She's a nice girl."

Her mother thought a moment and then asked, "Jewish?"

"I don't know. Her name is Edith Stern, so I assume she's Jewish."

The doorbell rang. Probably a customer.

"Well, I don't like it," her mother said.

As her mother made her way to the front door, Janet called after her, "Well I'm going to do it. I'm going to tell Edith tomorrow that I'm driving with her."

And before her mother could say another word, Janet escaped to the kitchen and began banging pots and pans so that she would not hear whatever else her mother might have to say.

Janet came to Edie the next morning, shyly, "If the offer's still open, I'd love to drive with you."

"Of course," Edie smiled, "it's no trouble at all."

The second morning of commuting together Edie told Janet about Wendy, and the third morning together, Janet told Edie that she was born in Italy, and the sixth afternoon together, over coffee at Darby's Restaurant, Janet told Edie about her year spent in hiding, and her life before and after that year, and finally, feeling like a teakettle that had been boiling for years and now finally had a spout, Janet told Edie about Greg Flusty. Janet was shaking when she finished the story and Edie got up and came over to her and hugged her. "My poor, Janet," she said. "You've been through so much. Nothing bad should ever happen to you again."

And Janet began to cry, not because of anything that had happened to her in the past, but because she finally had a friend.

From that moment on, the girls became inseparable, having dinner together and spending evenings and weekends together, preparing lesson plans, correcting papers, taking Wendy to the park, and cooking dinner together. And the more they talked, the more determined Edie was to make it all up to Janet, all those years of suffering, both in hiding, and since.

She took Janet shopping for clothes. "Your mother's a wonderful seamstress, but she doesn't understand fashion. You've got to dress like one of them to be one of them," Edie told her. "And your hair. You'll come to my beauty shop and we'll get you a good haircut." Of course, money was a problem, a big problem. Janet didn't have any and her mother wouldn't let her get a job. "No," Ida said. "Your studies are all that matter. There will be plenty of time to work after you become a teacher."

So Edie took some of the money she'd saved while working at the A & P and bought skirts, blouses and sweaters two sizes too large, took off the tags, washed them, and miraculously found them in her closet. "Oh here's something from my heavier days," she'd say and give it to Janet, amazed that it fit Janet perfectly.

"Are you sure you want to give this away? It looks brand new," Janet would say.

"I probably only wore it once or twice."

Did Janet suspect? Perhaps. Perhaps subliminally. But she never let on, just accepted graciously whatever Edie handed her.

Lilly saw what Edie was doing and didn't object. "I feel sorry for the poor girl, too. As long as you don't go overboard."

"Now," Edie said to Janet, "we have to go on diet. I know you're the greatest cook in the world, and your cakes are to die from, but we have to forego these little pleasures for the greater good."

And Janet, like the obedient child she was, listened and did whatever Edie told her.

By the time student teaching ended, Janet was feeling much better about herself. She had lost ten pounds, her hair was cut short, like Mary Martin's in South Pacific, she had a nice wardrobe, she had a driver's license (Edie had insisted on her taking the test), but most important, she had a friend, and a new family, and a sweet little adopted niece, Wendy. Janet could not understand what Edie saw in her--Edie was such a normal girl, and so pretty, but Janet never doubted Edie's love for her and Janet shared all her feelings, dreams and ideas with Edie, especially her dream about becoming a chef.

"If you want to be a chef," Edie said, "then that's what you should be."

It was a Saturday afternoon and they were driving Wendy to the park.

"But how does one become a chef? Just walk into a restaurant and say, I want to cook for you?"

"There must be schools," Edie said. "We can find one."

"Maybe in New York, maybe in Paris."

"Then that's where you should go."

"But how could I afford it?"

"I'll support you."

"Sure," Janet said, looking out the window.

"I'm serious," Edie said. "My life's kind of on hold right now with Wendy to take care of, but at least I could help you."

Janet was touched. She knew enough of Edie to know Edie meant what she said. But she also didn't think it could ever happen. She shrugged her shoulders. "It's a pipe dream," she said.

"No," Edie said. "It doesn't have to be. You can do it if you want to." Then remembering her piano competition, "But you have to really want to."

"I really want to, but..."

"But what?"

And Janet thought of the promise she had made so many years ago, that she would never leave her mother. "I don't know if I can leave my mother."

Edie pulled the white Pontiac into a parking spot near the swings and slides. "You're going to have to leave her sometime."

"Then sometime I'll worry about it, but not now."

"Well let me know when that is. I'll be ready."

And looking at her friend, her one, her only true friend, Janet said, "What would I do without you?"

And lifting Wendy out of her carseat, Edie replied, "What would I do without you?"

In February both girls graduated from Wayne and got a job teaching, a real job, making real money, $400 a month, and Edie decided it was time to move out of her parents' home.

"I don't understand," her mother said. "What's wrong with living here?"

"I just need some independence," Edie said.

"Why, do I bother you? Do I tell you anything? I make sure that I keep my lip buttoned."

Edie wanted to laugh at that, but she wouldn't hurt her mother's feelings after all her mother had done for her. "It's not you, mom, it's me."

"But it'll be so much more difficult on you."

"In some ways, I guess."

"And what about Wendy?" her mother asked. "Who's going to take care of Wendy?"

"You could still watch her if you want, or I could hire a babysitter."

"You know I wouldn't let you do that," her mother said. And then a look of resignation. "So go, move out. I'll still take care of Wendy."

Edie asked Janet to move in with her. "We could get a three bedroom and if I paid two-thirds the rent, it wouldn't be that expensive for you."

"I'd love to move in with you, Edie, but there's that same problem, my mother," Janet said.

"You're going to have to leave your mother someday."

"I know you're right, but it's just so difficult."

Janet couldn't sleep that night. She wanted to move in with Edie in the worst way but how could she? How could she desert her mother?

Edie knew it might be a long time before Janet would be ready to move, so she rented a two bedroom apartment, halfway between her school and her parents' home, and moved in the first of March.

Edie loved living in her new home, even if it was tiny, and even though it meant a lot more work for her. She felt finally that she was an adult, responsible for her own life. She could do what she pleased, when she pleased to do it, and did not have to answer to anyone.

A week after she moved in, Stanley showed up.

He had been dropping by her parents' home from time to time just to say "hello", just to see how she was doing. But she hadn't seen him in at least three months.

"Stanley," she said, opening the door to him. "What are you doing here?"

He was wearing his white lab coat. "Well there I was cutting up dead bodies and I thought, 'I'd like to see Edie's new apartment.' So here I am."

She smiled, "Come on in."

She showed him through the apartment, and after they tiptoed out of Wendy's room, where Wendy was asleep, Edie asked, "How do you like it?"

"Cozy," he said, and plopped down on her new peach sofa.

"Want a Vernor's?" she asked.

"Of course."

She fetched him one and sat down beside him. "So how's Yelena?"

"Still trying to get pregnant," he said, his left eyelid wavering. "Sometimes I feel that God is punishing me for marrying Yelena. You know, like Faust. Only instead of giving up my soul, I've given up my babies."

"That's ridiculous."

"Anyone in your life?" he asked.

"You must be kidding," she answered.

He took a sip from the bottle, "I still can't get over it."

"What?"

"You and Zola."

"You mean that I had sex with him?"

"No, not that you had sex with him, God knows, we had sex together and plenty of it, but that you went all the way."

"That's what I mean," she said

He guzzled what was left in the bottle and then looked at her. "I often think of you and me, rolling around naked in your bedroom-den."

"Yes," she said, "those were the days."

He moved closer to her, and she snuggled into his shoulder and put her feet up on her mother's hand-me-down formica coffee table. "We've known each other, how long now?" he mused.

"Let's see, it was Sandy Stahler's sweet sixteen party. I'm twenty-three now. Seven years."

"And I'm almost a doctor, and married, and you're a teacher and not married, but with a baby, and here we are together again."

"Yes," she said, "but only temporarily. Soon it's home to Yelena."

"Yes," he said, looking at his watch and standing up, "and late at that."

"Will she wonder where you've been?"

"Yes, she will."

"And will you tell her?"

"No, I won't." He kissed Edie on the cheek and was gone.

He showed up again a week later, and then twice the following week. Each time he came by, she was delighted to see him. He was her only connection to male companionship, and even though he was a married man, he made her feel like a woman again, pretty, young, attractive. Like she hadn't felt since becoming pregnant with Wendy. If there's no man who thinks you're attractive, then are you?

"What is this," she asked him, "your stopping off place?"

"I like it here," he said, sprawling on the sofa.

She brought him a Vernor's. "But you have a home."

"I like it better here."

"Does that mean that you and Yelena aren't getting along?"

"She's a bitch," he said, setting his bottle on her mother's hand-me-down formica end table. "She's so bossy, and she knows everything. She's like a little Napoleon. And as far as sex is concerned, we don't have sex anymore, all we do is try to make a baby."

"Poor Stanley," she teased.

"You're a bitch too," he said grabbing her and beginning to tickle her, and she was giggling and struggling to get away, and then he was kissing her on the lips, a warm, friendly kiss, and she realized she hadn't been kissed by a boy since the night she kissed Zola goodnight on the steps of Mrs. Steven's league house.

She pulled back. "You better go," she said.

"Yes," he said, "I better."

And then he kissed her again, but this wasn't a pleasant, friendly kiss, this had urgency and passion, and she was frightened. She tried pushing him away, "Stanley, stop."

"I'm crazy about you, Edie," he was saying, "you know that."

And now his hands were on her breasts and his mouth was smothering her. "Stanley, stop. Get off me." And she put her hands around his neck and squeezed as hard as she could, trying to strangle him, and finally, he let go. For a minute, he sat panting, his dark blond hair falling over his gray eyes, "Cockteaser," he said.

"I'm not a cockteaser," she said. "I never led you on."

"Oh no? What about all those years we spent necking and petting?"

"You knew I wanted to be a virgin when I got married."

"Oh yeah? Then what happened with Zola?"

She was furious. "Is that what this is all about? That I had sex with Zola and not you?"

"Maybe," he said.

"Get out," she said. "Get out and never come back."

"Admit it," he said, "you're still in love with me."

"I'm not admitting anything," she said.

He buttoned his white lab coat and walked to the door, "Okay, I'm going, but I will be back." And he closed the door behind him.

She sat shaking for several minutes. She was filled with anger at him and herself. Maybe she still had feelings for him, maybe she had led him on. It was so wonderful to be held by him, to be kissed by him. But she couldn't do this. She couldn't be Hester who earned her "A". She couldn't enter into an affair with a married man. Stanley had made his choice, and now he had to abide by it; there was no way she would hurt Yelena. She would have to make him understand that and if he didn't, she would have to stop seeing him.

In the summer, Edie went back to her job as checker at the A & P, and Janet got a job in a summer camp. Not with the children; she'd had enough of children, but in the kitchen. Cooking.

She had to beg her mother for weeks to let her go so far away from home, but finally her mother had given in.

The camp was in northern Michigan, amid a myriad of lakes and greenery. It was the most beautiful place Janet had ever been. She loved the fresh air, the lakes, the woods. She loved being away from her mother, but best of all, she loved spending all day in the kitchen.

She was one of three cooks who took turns preparing the various parts of the meal. One cook might do the main dishes one week, and the desserts the next. The cooks had help for the menial tasks, someone to peel the carrots, snip the beans, shell the peas. They had someone to wash the lettuce and slice the tomatoes and cucumbers. They had someone to spread the peanut butter and jelly or egg salad for sandwiches at lunch. But everything else was done by the three cooks. 200 meals for breakfast, lunch and dinner, including dessert.

By the third week, it was clear to all three, that desserts were Janet's forte, and the other two assigned her the task. she baked apple pies, cherry pies, blueberry pies, chocolate cake with fudge icing and white cake with chocolate icing, apple strudel, apple crisp, and apple brown Betty with caramel sauce, and her specialty, carrot cake with a cream cheese icing. And then there was chocolate pudding and butterscotch pudding and jello all served with Janet's hot fresh-baked cookies.

She still helped with other meals: spaghetti sauce for the spaghetti, chicken cacciatore without the wine (it wouldn't do to inebriate the little campers), and meatloaf with Janet's secret ingredient: Italian seasoned croutons. The other two cooks, in fact, were happy to delegate whatever they could to Janet: more time off for them, and as for Janet she was eager to do more, to do everything, to do it all. She was never happier than when her hands were covered in dough, the smell of fresh blueberries or apples baking in the oven, and all the pots bubbling and boiling, even if it was summer, and hot in the kitchen, even though some days the sweat poured down her forehead into her eyes, and down her arms and neck, leaving big wet spots under her armpits and down the middle of her back. Although she was on her feet all day, she was never tired. She felt a constant surge of energy, like she was an artist filling a blank canvas, and she couldn't stop until every inch of the canvas was covered with blazing color.

When the summer was over, the camp director called her to his office and thanked her for the best food he'd ever eaten. "If you'll come back next year, I promise you a raise. A big one."

Janet wanted nothing more than to come back next year, but she was afraid to make a commitment until she had gotten her mother's permission. "If I can," she said.

Sitting on the bus on her way back to Detroit, Janet became more agitated with each mile she got closer to home. It was going to be back to the same old routine, back to teaching and then home to mother. She was in a trap and there was no way out. She began to feel the muscles in her throat tightening, and then the exhaust fumes drifting in through the open windows became unbearable. They were filling her nose, clogging her throat until she felt she couldn't breathe. It was like being buried beneath a pile of hay. She stood up, trying to escape the feeling, and knew she couldn't go back to things as they had been. She had to do something about her life.

And holding onto the metal grips, swaying back and forth with the movement of the bus, she made up her mind. She would tell her mother tomorrow that she was moving in with Edie.

The next morning after she had eaten breakfast and cleaned up the kitchen, she forced herself into the living room where her mother was already bent over her sewing machine, sewing, sewing, always another skirt, another pair of pants, a blouse, a dress. "Mama," she said, "we have to talk."

Her mother looked up at her, her wire rimmed glasses far down her nose. "What is it, sweetheart?"

She had repeated the sentence over and over in her mind, but now her mouth felt sticky, as if she had swallowed a spoonful of peanut butter. She inhaled, trying to find the breath to speak. "I want to move out," she said.

"Oh, sweetheart, but why? Aren't you happy here?"

"Of course I am," she said, feeling more confident. "I just want to try living on my own."

"But there's no reason."

She remembered Edie's words, "Yes there is a reason. I need to grow up."

Her mother squinted at her. "It's that Edie, isn't it? She's the one poisoning your mind. I knew she was no good. Well, I don't want her in my house again. Is that clear? She's not to come here again."

"Mama, it's not Edie. It's me. It's my decision."

"Please Gianna. Please, don't do this to me." Her mother was up, moving from behind the sewing machine, taking Janet in her arms, crying, "You're all I have. There's just the two of us. How can I go on without you?"

Oh God, Janet thought, this is too terrible. She felt her confidence dissolve like sugar in a cup of tea. "All right, mama, I'll stay. All right, don't cry." And she patted her mother's head, until her mother finally let go.

So it was back to teaching, back to the children, back to living with her mother, and as the weeks progressed, Janet became more and more depressed, until finally, sitting in Edie's apartment one evening she began to cry.

"Oh, Edie, I'm so unhappy."

Edie was holding Wendy, who was about to doze off, her head resting on Edie's shoulder, "What is it?"

"I hate my life. I hate teaching. I hate living with my mother. I know what I want to do and I can't do it."

And Edie, feeling somehow that she had let Janet down, reached over and covered Janet's hand. "I know. I know how unhappy you've been."

"Oh, Edie, last summer was so wonderful, the most wonderful time of my life. I can't tell you how happy I was at camp, working in the kitchen. I want to be a chef."

"Then, that's what you're going to be. Tomorrow we're making a trip to the library."

"What's at the library?"

"Books about cooking schools," Edie said. "It's about time someone made a move around here. You're going to go to cooking school; you're going to get your wish." And to allow no further discussion, she picked up Wendy from the floor and went to change her diaper.

The next day, after school, the girls went to the library and found some articles in magazines on cooking schools. The best ones seemed to be in France. Edie copied down their addresses. "We'll write to them all," she said. "Apply to all of them."

"You expect me to go to France?" Janet said. "I can't even move out of my mother's house."

"If you get accepted, we'll find a way." Then perusing the pages in front of her, "This one looks the best, L'Ecole de Gastronomie de Jacques Patou. It's the only one that's bi-lingual." And then seeing Janet's downcast face, "Don't look so gloomy. It is possible. Everything is possible if you want it badly enough."

"It's a pipe dream," Janet said, feeling that nothing would come of this, but so touched by Edie's efforts that tears came to her eyes. "But thank you for looking. Thank you for trying. Thank you for everything."

Edie put her arm around Janet's shoulder, "What's a friend for?"

Back at the apartment, Edie composed a wonderful letter, about Janet's childhood, and how she had always dreamed of becoming a chef, and then sent it off to four cooking schools in France.

The day before Thanksgiving, Frank stopped by Edie's apartment.

"Well, this is a surprise," Edie said, feeling a touch of anxiety.

The only time she saw Frank was at family gatherings, or if she accidentally bumped into him when she was picking up or dropping off Wendy. The only time he'd been to her apartment was the day after she moved in, when he brought over some boxes she had left at her mother's. "I wanted to talk to you privately and in person," he said.

There was a tightening in her chest. Was he coming to apologize, to make peace, or to say something horrible to her. "This sounds serious," she said, trying to sound lighthearted, and resuming her place on the floor where she'd been playing with Wendy. Toys were scattered everywhere.

"It's not *that* serious," he said, sitting on her peach sofa. "It's just that I'm bringing a girl to Thanksgiving dinner."

She felt relieved and surprised. "A girl," she said with a smile. "Well, now we're back to serious."

"It's not that serious yet, but it might be." He seemed uncomfortable. "I was wondering if we could just not mention Wendy's parentage."

"Wendy's parentage?" What a peculiar way of putting it, Edie thought. And how insulting. "Did you expect that I would walk up to her and tell her my daughter's illegitimate?"

"No, no, of course not," More embarrassed. "It's just that I told her you're divorced and I'd like you to go along with it."

"You told her I'm divorced?" More an accusation than a question.

"Yes."

"I see," Edie said, trying to gather her thoughts. "In other words, you want me to lie. To make up a story."

"You don't have to lie, just don't say anything."

Edie thought it over. At this moment, she felt utter contempt for Frank, but what was the point of causing more friction between them. "Sure, Frank. Sure. No problem."

"I intend to tell her the truth later. It's just that she's a very fine girl from a very fine family."

What did that mean? That Edie wasn't a fine girl from a fine family. "Of course, Frank," Edie said. "I understand."

"Well then," standing up, "see you Thanksgiving."

"Yes," Edie said, "see you Thanksgiving."

Edie had tried to appear calm in front of Frank, but inside she was seething with anger, not just at his request, but because he hadn't said a word to Wendy. After he closed the door, she turned to her little daughter with the black hair and black eyes, who was now stacking her brightly-colored plastic donuts on their stand, and said, "Don't worry, sweetie pie, someday Uncle Frank will realize what he's missing by not having you in his life."

On Thanksgiving Day, Edie arrived at her mother's at ten in the morning to help with the cooking. Ben took care of Wendy while Edie and her mother made the turkey, stuffing, and side dishes and at four o'clock, Janet stopped by on her way to Thanksgiving dinner at her Aunt Sofia's, with three pies she had made for the Stern family: pumpkin, apple and cherry.

At five o'clock, Frank arrived with the girlfriend.

Edie had been curious about Frank's girlfriend ever since his visit, and she turned out to be the exact opposite of the girl Edie thought Frank would have chosen. Her name was Cookie, but she didn't look like a Cookie; she was thin and tall, almost as tall as Frank, and reserved, to the point of being cold. She was beautifully dressed (wearing an emerald green knit suit which matched the green of her eyes and her green eye shadow) and lots of makeup and jewelry. She was pretty, almost beautiful with her long blonde hair and a cute little nose, so that you might not think she was Jewish, but she was, which made Edie's mother happy. She had not gone to college but worked as secretary to the administrator of the hospital where Frank was doing his internship and that was where they met, getting into an elevator together.

Cookie hardly spoke to Edie, and stayed far away from Wendy, as if getting close to Wendy would soil her clothes.

After dinner, and after Janet's pies, which everyone agreed were "the best we've ever tasted," Edie and Ben lay on the floor groaning because they'd eaten too much and swearing they'd never eat again, and as Wendy crawled over them laughing hilariously because her mom and grandpa were acting so silly, Edie decided that in spite of Frank and Cookie, it had been a lovely day.

The day before Christmas, Janet came up with a plan. She'd move in with Edie gradually. She'd move a few things at a time, start spending some nights away from home, until one day she would be totally moved in.

The two girls went apartment hunting over the Christmas holiday, out on the icy streets, trudging through snow drifts, their noses and toes freezing, going from one place to another, until they found a passable three bedroom at a rent they could afford.

Ida didn't exactly realize what was happening, but maybe she did. Any maybe she knew the day Janet came back from summer camp was the beginning of the end.

Ida had said it all that day, and if Janet still chose to be the heartless, cruel girl she seemed to be becoming, there was nothing Ida could do about it. It was all Edie's fault, anyway. Anyone could see that. Edie had corrupted her baby. Who knew where it would end? Maybe with Janet pregnant, too. Bite your tongue, knock on wood, pooh, pooh, pooh, a million times. God forbid such a thing should ever happen.

Chapter Eight

Living with Janet, even part time, was wonderful for Edie. Not only did she have Janet's company, but the best damn food she'd ever eaten.

Stanley was still dropping by now and then, on Edie's terms: nothing sexual between them, except maybe a hug at the door. He was the only friend Edie spent time with except for Janet, and occasionally Sandy Stahler, who was still at Michigan getting her master's degree, and Naomi Cohen who was back from her husband's stint in the army and was now living in Oak Park, just five minutes from Edie's apartment. Naomi had a one-year-old baby boy, and yet Edie seldom saw her. Naomi was always too busy with her husband and her married friends to spend much time with Edie, and she never invited Edie to join them. But Edie understood. How could Naomi invite Edie, the single, unmarried mother to be part of her group? And even when they did get together, usually to take the children to the park, Edie would come home feeling more lonely than before she had gone, feeling that she didn't belong anywhere. Not in Naomi's world and not in any other world.

On the first Sunday in February, Edie's mother called to tell Edie that Frank and Cookie were getting married. "At the end of April. Isn't it wonderful?"

"Yes," Edie said "wonderful." She was trying to sound enthusiastic, but what she really felt was disappointment. All her life she had tried to be the kind of girl Frank would want to marry and now he was marrying an empty-headed materialistic snob.

"I don't know how I'm going to get everything done by April," her mother was continuing.

"What do you have to do?" Edie asked.

"I have to arrange for the liquor, and they want me to help pick the flowers and decide on the menu, and I have to make up my guest list, and buy a dress..." And then catching herself and her voice softening. "Oh Edie, I shouldn't be talking to you about all this."

Edie tried to sound bright, "Yes, you should. Of course, you should, mother."

"No, it's not fair."

"Of course it's fair. Why isn't it fair?"

"Because," her mother said, "because I'm never going to be doing all of this for you."

For a moment, Edie was paralyzed. She could carry her own pain, but not her mother's, too. "Mom, I'm sorry, but Wendy needs me. I'll call you later." She did not wait for her mother's reply. She could not have stayed on the phone another minute, or she would have burst into tears.

Edie was asked to be a bridesmaid at the wedding (she could hear her mother's words to Frank, "It would be a shame and a shanda if your sister wasn't a bridesmaid at your wedding") but Wendy, now two years old, was not asked to be the flower girl, was not even invited to the wedding.

"I'm really upset," Edie told her mother the afternoon after she got the invitation addressed just to: "Miss Edith Stern."

"You've got to understand," her mother tried to explain, "she's only two years old. What's the point of having a two-year-old at a wedding? She won't even remember it." The three of them were sitting in her mother's kitchen, Edie and Lilly at the kitchen table sipping coffee, Wendy in her high chair picking at Cheerios.

"I know," Edie said. "Still it hurts."

"Don't take it personally. Cookie wants a perfect wedding; she's not inviting any children."

"Yes," Edie said, putting another handful of Cheerios on Wendy's tray, "I understand perfectly."

And her mother looking pensively into her coffee cup, "If only you could find someone to come to the wedding with."

It was something her mother mentioned almost every day, but today it got to Edie. "Mother, why do you keep bringing that up? You know it's impossible."

"But you're not even trying."

"What do you want me to do, stand on a street corner?"

"You could join organizations, you could join the Jewish Center."

"Mother, you still don't understand, no boy will come near me, let alone ask me out."

"Well you don't have to shout at me."

And Edie, having heard enough for one day, lifted Wendy up and headed for the door. "I'll see you tomorrow."

All the way driving home, Edie was unsettled. She decided she better not have any more cups of coffee with her mother until after the wedding. She did not want to hear one more word about the dresses, the flowers, the band, and she certainly did not want to hear one more word about her getting a date for the wedding.

The Friday before Frank's wedding, Edie's grandmother, Rose, and her husband, Arthur, came in from Florida for the weekend, as did Edie's aunts, uncles and cousins from Cleveland and Chicago. Although Wendy could not go to the wedding, she still got to spend a lot of time with her great-grandmother, and all the other relatives who had never met her. Everyone seemed to adore Wendy, except of course, Frank and Cookie. The wedding itself was a lavish affair, with ice sculptures, hot and cold hors d'oeuvres, liquor, wine, a three course sit-down dinner, a five piece band that played too loud most of the evening, and for dessert, a sweet table loaded with all kinds of cakes, tarts, fruit, and a huge round of halvah. Edie felt beautiful in her pink gown, and danced almost every dance with her uncles, dad, step-grandpa, and cousins. All and all, it turned out to be great weekend.

Chapter Nine

The day after Frank's wedding, May 3, 1960, the letter from the L'Ecole de Gastronomie de Jacques Patou arrived. It was addressed to Janet Camerini, and Edie, who had gotten home first, didn't dare open it, but was standing at the door, Wendy in her arms, a big grin on her face, when Janet arrived.

"Oh, Janet, it's here!"

"What's here?"

"Your letter--from Paris."

Janet's hands shook as she opened it. And then her face showed concern, so that Edie thought she had been rejected. "I'm accepted," Janet said, in a daze. "They accepted me."

"Oh Janet, I knew it, I knew it," Edie said, jumping up and down. "You're going to get your dream come true. And Wendy and I are going to get to go to Paris." Edie began dancing around the room with Wendy. "Aunt Janet's going to be a chef. And you and I, pumpkin are going to get to go to Paris." Then seeing the forlorn look on Janet's face, "What's the matter?"

"Now what?"

"What do you mean now what? Now we're going to give notice at our schools, pack our bags, buy our airline tickets, and we're off to Paris."

"But how am I going to leave my mother?"

Edie put Wendy down, and took Janet's hands, "Oh Janet, Janet, don't you see, this is the chance you've been waiting for? The chance we've been waiting for. You've got to do it," Edie said, pleading as much for herself as for Janet.

"But don't I owe my mother something?"

"You owe her your own self-fulfillment. That's all you owe her." And looking into Janet's eyes, "Janet, do you want to be a chef?"

"It's all I want."

"Then it's settled. You're going to tell your mother and we're going to Paris. Now when do classes begin?"

Janet, consulting the letter, "September 5th."

"You've got four months. You managed to move out of your mother's house. You'll manage this."

"Oh Edie," Janet said, hugging her friend, "how can one person be so happy and miserable at the same time?"

"It's easy," Edie said. "It's how I feel most of the time."

Janet was afraid to wait. She took Edie's white Pontiac and drove immediately over to her mother's. When she walked in the door, her whole body was trembling, but she wouldn't allow herself to think. She walked directly into the living room, where her mother, as usual, was bent over her sewing machine. "Mother," she said, "a wonderful thing has happened to me."

Her mother looked up at her. Her eyes were clouded, expectant. "Yes, sweetheart?"

"I've been accepted to a cooking school."

"A cooking school?" her mother said as if she didn't understand the words.

"Yes. In Paris. I start in September."

"In Paris?" her mother repeated.

"Yes. It's the best there is."

"But I don't understand. You're going to a cooking school...in Paris?"

"Yes. I know it sounds crazy, but it's what I've always wanted to do."

"But Paris, it's so far away."

"I know it's far away, but I'll write you as often as I can, and I'll call you."

"I don't know, Janet...."

"It'll be all right, mama, you'll see. Edie's going to go with me. She's going to support me."

"Aach," her mother spit out, "I should have known. It's that Edie again. She's the one who got you into this."

"No, mama," Janet said, putting her hand on her mother's wrinkled arm, "I got myself into it. It's what I want to do. It's what I've always wanted to do. Be happy for me."

"How can I be happy for you when you're going to be thousands of miles away. You're all I have, Janet."

"No, mama, you have your sister, Sofia, and Uncle Alberto, and Peter and Miriam, and your cousins, Ann and Rudy, and Mrs. Landau. You should make friends, mama. You should have your own life."

"I'm too old for that, Janet. And too tired. I used myself up in Italy."

"Other people have gone on with their lives. Aunt Sofia has friends and goes out."

"And she also has a husband. A husband who didn't die in a resettlement camp."

And Janet got down on her hands and knees before her mother. "Mama, please. Please, let me go."

Ida pushed her glasses up her nose. "There are no cooking schools in Detroit?"

"No, mama. Not even in the United States. Not the kind of cook I want to be. I want to be the best."

It was a turning point for Ida Camerini. She looked at the anguish in her daughter's face and knew that if she didn't let her go, she would be losing her anyway. "All right," she said, "then go."

"Oh, mama," Janet said, putting her arms around her mother's waist, "Thank you. Thank you."

"Now, you better leave," her mother said, turning back to her sewing machine, "I have work to do."

Slowly, Janet got to her feet and walked to the front door. "Goodbye mama," she said, feeling like Hitler, the Nazis, Mussolini. She had just killed her mother again.

Edie was almost as worried about telling her mother as Janet was about telling hers. But it had to be done.

Lilly was appalled. "What do you mean you're going to Paris for a year?"

"Just as I said. I'm going to Paris so Janet can go to cooking school."

"But Paris is so far away. And what are you going to do with Wendy?"

"I'm taking her with me."

"But who will take care of her? How will you live?"

"I'm going to get a job and hire a babysitter."

"Sure someone who doesn't even speak English."

"I'm sure there are people in France who speak English."

Her mother shook her head back and forth in disbelief, "I can understand you wanting to help Janet, but how can you up and drag Wendy so far away?"

Of course it was Wendy her mother was thinking about, but Edie didn't resent her for that. "I know it seems kind of sudden, but I've been thinking about it for quite a while and I think it will be good for all of us."

"How can it be good for Wendy? To take her away from everything she knows, everyone who loves her?"

"Not everyone, mom. She'll be with Janet and me."

"Well I still think if you want to go with Janet, then fine, go. But you should leave Wendy here."

Now it was Edie's turn to be appalled, "Mother, I'm not going to leave Wendy here. She's my child, remember? Not yours."

Lilly was burning inside, but Edie was right. Wendy should be with her mother. Still maybe there was a way to hold onto Wendy for a little longer. "Well, if you insist on taking her with you, the least you can do is leave her here until you get settled."

"Mother, people move to other cities with their children all the time."

"But this isn't just another city. This is another country. You don't speak the language, you don't know anybody there, you don't have a place to live...what are you going to do, schlep a two-year-old all over Paris while you try to find an apartment?"

"I'm sorry, mom, but there's no way Wendy's going to be anywhere but with me."

But even as Edie spoke the words, she knew there was some validity in what her mother had said. Edie had no idea where they would be staying or who she could find to take care of Wendy. Maybe the wise thing to do would be to leave Wendy with her parents for a few weeks until she and Janet were settled, found a place to live, a babysitter. She would have to think about what was best for Wendy.

While Edie was making plans for her trip to Paris, Zola, on his mountaintop, was thinking about Wendy.

Since his visit to Detroit, he had been trying to think of some way to be with Wendy, and Edie, if possible. There was no way he would move back to Detroit. But maybe he could convince Edie to move to the commune.

He loved living here. He had enough private time to work on his poetry, and for the first time in his life, he felt like he belonged. Everyone on the commune shared his distaste for the materialism and self-centeredness of the outside world. They all valued the communal life style: everyone sharing, working together for the common good. Every task on the commune was done in teams: cooking, cleaning, washing clothes, even bathing. Every person was needed. Every person was important.

The commune was located just outside of Medford, Oregon, and everyone who lived there was under forty. There were lots of kids, a few married couples, a few unmarried, a few single people who interchanged partners, and there was Zola, who wasn't sleeping with anyone. It wasn't that his sexual desire had left him, it was that he was still tied to his middle class morality. You don't sleep with a girl unless you have special feelings for her; and you don't sleep with a girl if one of your buddies is sleeping with her. In a way, it made life easier--no romantic entanglements.

Some of the folk had jobs in town. They had to. The commune needed money to survive. Zola was one of them. He sent his $25.00 a week to Edie, and gave what was left to the commune. He was still working in the same bar in Grants Pass, and enjoyed the time he spent there. Most of his customers were men who came in wearing cowboy boots and western shirts with little string ties at their collar. Zola loved chatting with them, hearing about their farms and ranches, their houses, fences, crops, vineyards, horses, cows, dogs, chickens, wives and girlfriends. They did not talk about theater, art, music, books, movies or current events. Zola found it refreshing. Real.

Most nights after dinner, the folks of the commune would gather around an outdoor fire and two or three of them would play the guitar and the others would sing. A story or two would be told, or a joke, and then the children would be off to bed, and then some of them would roll their own marijuana cigarettes and start passing them around, and a few of them would snort cocaine, and a couple of them would drop some pills. At first, Zola had resisted. He was against all artificial stimulants. He had never smoked and seldom drank, but at some point refusing seemed silly. What was his problem, everyone wanted to know. The drugs they were using weren't like heroine. They were harmless enough. Non-addicting, pleasurable. "Go ahead, Zola, take a chance," Big Red said, a huge, robust man with red hair who had helped build the cistern. And so Zola had taken a puff or two, inhaled some little white dust, even tried the pills, because it was, after all, a part of experiencing life. And now it had become part of his daily routine, something he looked forward to, getting stoned every evening. And perhaps it was in this state that he thought the most about Wendy. He had dreams about her floating above his head, like a Chagall painting, calling out to him, "Daddy, Daddy, I miss you."

"I miss you, too" he said aloud, feeling his body drifting in space.

And as the weeks passed, and the months, he began thinking about her more and more. What would she look like? Was she walking, talking? What would it feel like to hold her in his arms. She became the subject of all his poems, and he could not look at any of the other little kids on the commune without feeling some remorse. He had a child, too. A daughter. He was a pop, a dad, the old man, yet his child didn't even know he existed. What profit a man if he have the whole world and lose his only begotten daughter? He wanted to see her. Had to see her. But not in Detroit. Not in the phony surroundings of all he had left. No, he wanted her here, in the wide open spaces of the commune. And Edie should come, too. They could be a family.

He told all this to Sheila, whose old man had skipped out on her a month before. Sheila listened to him patiently, took him into her bed, made love to him, comforted him. "Yes honey, it would be good for you. A father has rights. You should see your daughter."

"You're right," he said, "I'm going to call Edie. She can come, too. I always told her that."

"Sure," Sheila said, on top of him, moving slowly up and down on his penis, "she can come, too, as long as I come first," and she bent over and kissed him on the mouth.

The next day Zola went into town and called Edie.

It was August 15, a week before Edie was to leave for Paris. Edie had found a job the month before, through a friend of a client of her father's, at the American School in Paris. She would be teaching children ages five, six and seven, and making more money than she was making now. The added bonus of her job was that her school was located less than a mile from Janet's.

She had also decided a month ago, after debating back and forth with herself for three months, that she would leave Wendy with her parents, just until she got settled, just until she found a babysitter, and had immediately moved back into her parents' home so that Wendy could get re-acclimated to living there.

This afternoon as she was sorting through her clothing, trying to decide what to take and what not to take--how does one pack for a year?--the telephone rang. Edie answered it, wondering if she should take the black or beige cardigan, "Hello."

"Edie, is that you?"

Her heart stopped. It was Zola. "Zola, how are you?"

"I'm fine. And you?"

"I'm fine, too," trying to keep her voice steady.

"Listen, Edie, the reason I called, I've been thinking a lot lately about Wendy. About the fact that she doesn't even know who I am and I've decided I'd like her to come and stay with me."

Edie's face turned hot. "Zola, you must be crazy, calling up and proposing such a thing."

"You could come, too."

"No, I can't," she said, "I'm leaving for Paris on Sunday."

"Paris?!" Now it was his turn to be surprised.

"Yes. A friend of mine is going to cooking school there and I'm going with her."

"And what about Wendy?"

Hesitating, should she tell him? Would that make his request seem more reasonable? "I'm going to leave Wendy with my parents. Just until I get settled there, just until I find a babysitter for her."

"Well then that's great," Zola said. "Instead of leaving her with your parents, you could leave her with me."

"I couldn't do that, Zola. I don't know anything about you, where you live or how you live."

"I'm still on the commune, outside of Medford, Oregon. Why don't you come on out and visit? Then you'll see what a great place it is. The air is clean and fresh, the people are wonderful, and we have a lot of little kids. It would be great for Wendy."

"But Wendy doesn't even know who you are."

"That's my point," Zola said, "it's time she did. Look, Edie, you've had her two years. Maybe I should have her two years."

Two years! No way, she thought. But Zola did have some rights; he was Wendy's father. And it probably would be good for Wendy to meet Zola, to know she had a father.

"Well, let me think about it. Maybe I could let her come for a week or two."

"That'd be great," he said. "When can I call you back?"

"Tomorrow," she said. "I'll think about it tonight and you can call me tomorrow."

"Okay, tomorrow, same time," Zola said. And then after a pause, "As I said before, you could come, too."

"No, Zola," she said without a moment's hesitation, "I can't. I've made a commitment that I have to keep." And then more gently, "I'll talk to you tomorrow."

Edie set down the receiver in a complete state of confusion. She hadn't considered Zola in her plans. She felt he was out of her life forever--except for the $25.00 a week. And now he had just parachuted back in, and he wanted Edie's daughter. Maybe Edie, too.

Wendy and Lilly were sitting on the den floor building a huge tower out of blocks.

"That was Zola," Edie told her mother, sitting on the floor beside Wendy. "He wants Wendy to come stay with him in Oregon."

"That's ridiculous," her mother said with contempt. "Who does he think he is calling after two years and asking a thing like that?"

"Her father."

"Then where's he been the past two years?"

"He has been sending a check every week."

Lilly didn't want to give him any credit, but she couldn't condemn him falsely. "I have to admit he has done that."

Edie picked up a block, "I don't know what to do."

"You're not considering this, are you?"

"Maybe it would be good for her to know she has a father."

"No matter how weird he is," her mother said.

"Zola isn't weird," Edie rose to his defense. She could think him weird, but she didn't want anyone else thinking him weird. "He's just different from most people."

"Well I think you'd be crazy to leave Wendy with him."

Edie set her block on the top of the tower, and the tower began to sway until it all came tumbling down.

Edie couldn't sleep that night. What was the right thing to do? What was best for Wendy? The idea of Oregon appealed to Edie. According to Zola, it was clean, fresh, and the people were wonderful. It probably would be a good experience for Wendy. And there were lots of kids, he had said. Maybe that would be better than leaving her in Detroit with her mother. And Zola was a good person from a good family. Edie knew that for certain. Didn't Wendy deserve the chance to know her father?

By morning, Edie had made up her mind. She would fly with Wendy to Oregon, and if she liked it, she would let Wendy stay there for the two or three weeks it would take her to get settled in Paris. Her mother had already given her the air fare to fly back from Paris to pick up Wendy. It wouldn't cost much more to fly out to Oregon tomorrow and then again when she came to pick Wendy up. Yes, she would do it; she would let Zola have some time with Wendy, *if* she felt Wendy would be safe with him.

Zola was elated with the news, and that night, he made a decision. He was going to stop doing drugs. At this point, he didn't think there was anything wrong with it, but he was afraid Edie wouldn't approve, and he didn't want to do anything that would hurt his chances of keeping Wendy. He'd tell the others, too, that for the time Edie was there, no drugs. The commune did have rules about drugs: no drugs during the day, no drugs until all the children were asleep, but still Edie might not understand. Better to avoid the whole issue. He was happy that he had decided to stop doing drugs. And then, catching a glimpse of himself in the mirror, he thought it might also be a good idea to trim three inches off his beard. He didn't want his daughter to be afraid of him.

Edie finished packing on Friday night. On Saturday morning she would fly to Oregon, fly back Saturday night, and on Sunday morning leave for Paris.

The Bittermans, who were still seeing Wendy every week or two, came by that Friday night to say goodbye and to send their love and a million kisses to Zola. And Stanley came by.

"Watch out for those French guys," Stanley said. "I hear they're great lovers."

"Not as great as you," she said, kissing him on the cheek.

"Or as sterile," he said.

Naomi Cohen came over with her little boy, but not her husband, and Sandy Stahler called. Frank did not call or come over.

On Saturday morning, sitting on the plane to San Francisco, where she would change for a plane to Medford, Edie again explained to Wendy what was going to happen.

"You're going to go live with your daddy for just this many days," and Wendy held out her fingers and Edie counted up to fourteen.

Then Wendy, who was already speaking in sentences, said, "And you're going to Paris."

"Yes. But then in this many days," and Edie again counted to fourteen, you're coming to Paris to live with mommy and Aunt Janet."

"And my daddy has a beard--out to here," Wendy said, stretching her arms as far as they would go.

"Yes, but your daddy's a wonderful man and he loves you very, very much."

When she and Wendy emerged from the plane in Medford, Zola was waiting for them. It was a tiny airport and you could see from one end to the other. Zola walked up to them. He looked clean and his beard was neatly trimmed. "Wendy," Edie said, "this is your daddy." And Wendy held out her arms to Zola, as if she'd always known him.

"Oh my," Zola said, clasping her to him. "Oh my, she's so beautiful."

Edie had known that Wendy resembled Zola, but seeing them together was startling. Wendy had the same dark eyes, same dark hair, and same smile. Edie felt good about her decision. They belonged together: father and daughter.

Zola tossed Wendy's duffle bag into the trunk of the tiny gray Volkswagen he had brought to the airport, and the three of them squeezed into the front seat. Zola drove out of the city, and up a curvy road toward the top of a mountain. The little car shook every time they went over a bump.

"I guess I should'a brought the truck," Zola said.

"This is more fun," Edie said.

All the way up the mountain, Edie felt strange. She kept trying to look at Zola without him noticing that she was. Who was this ape-man? Who was this father of her child? Had she really been in love with him once?

And then they were there, a flat clearing, a parked truck, faded redwood picnic tables and chairs, an old wooden house off to one side of the clearing, and a few chickens. It reminded her of *God's Little Acre*, but still she liked it. She liked the open space, the fact that there were no cars, no traffic. And she liked the people, they all seemed so warm and friendly, if a bit unwashed. But when Zola explained how difficult it was to take a bath or a shower, to pump the water, to heat it on a wood stove, to pour it into the cistern or the big, round, metal washtub, she understood that everyone couldn't bathe every day. She didn't like that, and she didn't like the fact that there was no bathroom, that Wendy, who was now toilet trained, would have to use an outhouse. But on the other hand, it might be good for Wendy. Make her appreciate all the comforts she would have when she returned to civilization.

The kitchen squad cooked dinner, and the food was delicious, a ton of barbecued chicken, baked potatoes, and corn from the outdoor charcoal grill, and home-made bread and fresh-baked cookies from a bakery in town. They all ate together on the outdoor redwood tables and benches. Edie was becoming more and more enthralled with the place, happy about her decision. This would be a good place for Wendy. Wendy would grow here. Wendy already seemed at home, playing with the other children, and following one of the dogs wherever it went.

After dinner, Edie and Zola walked to the edge of the clearing and looked across the mountaintops at the setting sun.

"It is beautiful here," she said.

"But you don't think you could live here."

"I don't know," she said. "It's different."

"I'd really like you to stay," he said.

"I can't," she said. "I told you. I have a commitment."

He put his hands on her shoulders and turned her so that she was forced to look into his black eyes. "Can't you break it?" he asked.

She thought of it for a moment. It was tempting in a way. To have someone who would take care of her. To sit on this mountaintop with Zola, Wendy, and a bunch of hippies and let the rest of the world go by. But then she thought of Janet. There was no way she could disappoint Janet. "No," she said. "I'm sorry."

"I'm the one who's sorry," he said. "I'm going to miss you."

"But you have plenty of company," she said.

"But no one I care about as much as you."

His words filled her with joy. It was good to know he still cared for her. "If only...," she said.

"If only what?"

If only you had insisted that June night in the rain that I come with you, if only you had insisted that Sunday afternoon you came to see Wendy that I go back with you, if only you had insisted on moving back to Detroit. But there was no sense dwelling on what might have been. "Never mind," she said. "Let's join the others."

Everyone had gathered around the campfire, and they were singing songs and telling stories. Edie sat with Wendy on her lap, enjoying the spirit of togetherness, when she noticed Sheila, a young woman with long straggly hair, wearing a long black dress and leather sandals on her bare feet, hanging about Zola. Was she sleeping with him? Edie felt a gnawing in her stomach. Jealousy? But she had no right to be jealous of Zola. Did she think he would spend the rest of his life celibate? And even if he was sleeping with Sheila, Edie still believed everything he had just said to her.

When it was time for the children to be put to bed--all of the children slept in the same room-- Edie and Zola tucked Wendy into the little bed Zola had made for her.

"Now you know," Edie said, kneeling on the floor beside Wendy, "when you wake up tomorrow morning, mommy won't be here. You're going to stay with daddy for this many days," and Wendy, knowing the routine, held out her fingers so Edie could count them.

"And you're going to Paris," Wendy said.

"Yes," Edie said. "But if you want me for any reason, all you have to do is ask daddy and I'll come get you right away."

And Wendy, hugging the teddy bear the Bittermans had given her when she was a baby and that she slept with every night, said, "I like daddy, mommy."

And tears came to Edie's eyes, for now she knew she was doing the right thing.

"Maybe mommy will stay with you awhile, " Edie said and curled herself around her little girl. It all made sense logically, but still, it seemed impossible that she could leave Wendy.

Zola stood at the door, waiting for Edie, and when Wendy had fallen asleep, Zola, pointing to his watch, whispered, "Time to leave." Edie pulled herself away from her sleeping daughter, picked up her purse, took Zola's arm, and blinking back the tears, let him lead her out the front door. As soon as she was in the fresh air, the odor hit her. It was sweet and strange. All the happy folk of the commune, including Sheila, were still sitting around the campfire, passing cigarettes from one to the other, inhaling and blowing out the smoke.

She turned to Zola, "They're smoking marijuana, aren't they?"

Zola didn't know what to say. "It's not the way it looks. We have rules here. We only do it after the kids are asleep and anyway I've given it up."

"Well that's great," Edie said, disgust in her eyes. "That's just great!" And she turned and ran back to the dormitory, stuffed Wendy's clothes back into her duffle bag, lifted her sleeping daughter still hugging her teddy bear, and said to Zola who had followed her, "There's no way on earth, I'd leave my daughter with you now." Edie carried Wendy and her duffle bag out to where the two cars were parked, the Volkswagen and the truck.

"Edie, you're being unreasonable," Zola said.

"Are you going to drive me to the airport, or am I going to drive myself?"

Zola took the duffel bag from her, tossed it in the back of the truck, and opened the door to the front cab. He was devastated, furious with all of them and himself. He'd had her here, his Wendy, and now because they all fucked up, he was going to lose her. "Edie, please, try to understand."

"Don't say another word, Zola."

They drove in silence.

At the airport, the plane was already boarding. Edie carried Wendy; Zola carried the duffle bag and when they reached the gate, they stood staring at one another.

"So now what?" Zola asked.

"Now, I'm going to Paris as planned."

"And Wendy?"

"I'm leaving her with my parents as planned. And then in a couple of weeks when I get settled, she's coming to Paris with me."

"I'm sorry how things worked out," Zola said. "I guess I really screwed up."

"I blame myself. I guess I should have known there would be drugs on a commune, but I just never thought of it."

"It's really innocent enough," Zola said, "and I really have given them up."

"Maybe," Edie said, "but I can't take that chance with my daughter."

"This isn't the end," Zola said. "I'm not going to give up on being with my daughter."

"I've got to go," Edie said.

"Can I hold her one more time?" Zola asked.

Edie really didn't want to let go of Wendy, but she felt Zola had a right to one last hug. "Sure," Edie said.

Zola took Wendy in his arms, kissed her hair and whispered in her ear, "So long, little darling. Remember, that no matter what, your daddy loves you."

And then Edie took Wendy back, "Take care of yourself, Zola."

Zola watched as his little girl was carried aboard the plane, and then walked back to his truck and began the drive back to the commune. Now what to do? Follow Edie to Paris? Force himself into his daughter's life? But he wasn't worthy of her. She was so sweet and innocent and he was such a loser. They were all losers. All his supposed friends. They couldn't stay off the junk long enough to do him this one favor. Even Sheila, his beloved. She had stabbed him in the back, too. What was he doing with all these people anyway? Why did he need them so badly? To have a friend? To finally be accepted by some group? What an immature little child he was. Younger than his daughter, Wendy.

He drove past the outskirts of Medford, and then began the long climb up the mountain, until finally, he saw the light of the campfire ahead. They'd all be completely stoned by now and Sheila would be waiting for him with her magic little pills. He should get his things now, move out now, but he was too tired and depressed. Maybe he'd stay the night. But tomorrow he'd leave for sure.

Edie sat on the plane, clutching her daughter to her. Thank God, she thought, Thank God, I didn't leave Wendy with Zola.

The next morning, Edie woke up feeling as if she hadn't slept for days. She was groggy, nauseous, lightheaded. The events of yesterday had drained her physically and emotionally, and now she had to face the prospect of leaving Wendy. The more she thought about it, the more she thought it was impossible. Especially after all that had happened yesterday with Zola. "I can't do it," she decided.

She went into the kitchen to tell her mother, who was washing out the sink with Ajax. "I can't do it," she said.

"Can't do what?" her mother asked, turning off the faucet.

"I can't leave Wendy."

"Now stop it," her mother said, drying her hands on a yellow dish towel. "You're working yourself into a lather over nothing. You yourself said this was best for Wendy. Now calm down. Be sensible."

What her mother said was true. She had thought it all out calmly and objectively and she knew it was the right thing to do. She shouldn't let what happened yesterday with Zola affect her reasoning.

So she watched as her father loaded her suitcases into the car, and at eleven-thirty, Ben, Lilly, Edie and Wendy picked up Janet, and headed out to Willow Run airport where the two friends would catch a plane for New York, and then on to Paris.

All the way to the airport, Edie was filled with anxiety. She didn't know how she was going to part from Wendy.

And then they were at the gate, and everyone was hugging and kissing, and the loudspeaker announced their flight.

"We've got to go," Janet said.

And Edie, unable to look into Wendy's eyes, handed Wendy to her father, and then in the same instant, grabbed her back. "No," she said, clutching Wendy to her as she had done yesterday coming back from Oregon, "I can't do it. I can't leave her."

"But it's only for two weeks," her mother said. "You agreed to it."

"I don't care what I agreed to," Edie said, "I can't leave her." And she turned to Janet. "Go, move." And the three of them hustled past the stewardess taking the tickets.

"But she doesn't have any clothes," her mother called after Edie.

"I'll buy her clothes in Paris," Edie called back. "Goodbye, mom, goodbye, dad."

And once in her seat on the plane, the seat belt locked tightly around her daughter and herself, out of breath, and still trembling from what had just occurred, she turned to Janet, "I don't know what made me think I could leave her."

"I never thought you would," Janet said.

Chapter Ten

L'Ecole de Gastronomie de Jacques Patou was situated in the heart of the Latin Quarter. After spending a few nights in a pension, Edie and Janet found a furnished two bedroom apartment walking distance to both Edie's and Janet's schools. The apartment building was old. Not United States old. Hundreds of years old. Dull gray stone, zinc roof, peeling paint. But the apartment came with beds, a sofa, tables, lamps, a kitchen set, an assortment of chipped and unmatched dishes, a few pots, some odd pieces of silverware, and a bathroom with a bidet and bathtub.

Through their landlady, Mrs. Guineau, they found a babysitter on the next block, a young woman with a daughter Wendy's age whose husband was a student at the Sorbonne. Her name was Nicole Hubenette, and she was a delightful young woman, very animated, very talkative, and Edie and Janet joked that with Nicole around, the children wouldn't need a radio or a television.

The streets near their apartment were filled with cafes, bookstores, antique shops, art galleries, boutiques, jazz clubs, food shops, students, hippies, artists and musicians. The girls couldn't think of a more exciting place to live and for the few days before they moved into their apartment, they shopped the neighborhood for sheets, blankets, pillows, towels, a cheap set of stainless silverware, two good knives, a couple of proper pots for Janet, and four wine glasses--one could not live in Paris without wine glasses.

School did not start for either Janet or Edie for another ten days, so once they settled into their apartment, they had ample time to explore Paris.

Paris. So unlike Detroit. With its majestic buildings, beautiful gardens, flowers everywhere, outdoor cafes, markets, stores. One could buy anything on the street.

And there were people everywhere, walking, sitting at the outdoor cafes, sitting in the parks surrounding every beautiful building.

Edie and Janet walked whenever possible, taking turns pushing Wendy in her stroller. They walked to the Louvre, but after an hour were too tired to see anymore, so the next day they took the Metro and spent three more hours going from room to room, floor to floor. Then they walked through the Tuileries and sat on a park bench, watching the other people watching them. The next day they visited the Jeu de Paume, seeing every famous Impressionist painting they had ever seen in a book, and then on to the l'Orangerie where, in the basement, they saw the two oval rooms of Monet waterlillies. They walked to the Invalides and Napoleon's tomb, and on to the Eifel Tower, up to the 3rd etage, getting the most fantastic view of Paris they would ever see. They took a boatride on the Seine looking for lovers kissing on the banks, but saw only fishermen. They walked the Champs Elysee to the Place de l'Etoile and to the top of the Arc de Triomphe. They walked to the Ile de la Cite, toured Notre Dame, and explored Montmarte where they found everything they had already bought, cheaper. And they even took the Metro to the Cemetery Pere Lachaise, where they discovered the tombs of Balzac, Oscar Wilde, Chopin and Rossini. They spent a day at the zoo for Wendy, and another day at the puppet show at the Jardin du Luxembourg, but she was more interested in the children sailing their boats in the large pond, than in the puppets. And wherever they went, Janet would stop and read the menus posted outside the restaurants, and Edie would follow Janet into every charcuterie, boucherie, cremerie, boulangerie and patisserie, so that it might take an hour to walk a block. At every patisserie, they had to buy at least one irresistible pastry to share as they walked. They both wanted to try everything, taste everything, go everywhere, do everything, and when they got tired, they'd stop at an outdoor cafe for a cafe au lait or a Vittel and a lemonade or hot chocolate for Wendy, and spend an hour indulging in Paris' favorite pastime: watching the people go by. And then, they'd be off again.

Of all the sights, the most fascinating to Janet were the markets, indoor or outdoor. Janet could spend hours browsing among the fresh fruits and vegetables. And Edie liked it, too. She never tired of traipsing after Janet, looking, but not touching the mauve and yellow asparagus, the artichokes, the peaches, pears, strawberries, comparing them to all the fruits and vegetables that had passed through her hands when she was a checker at the A & P.

Janet loved all of the markets, but she especially loved the rue Mouffetard on Saturday and Sunday morning. The array was dazzling. Not only was there every variety of fresh fruit and vegetable, but there were the exotic ones: mangos, plaintains, papaya, white, red and green peppers, melons. And there were fishmongers, and butchers, charcuteries with their enormous selection of pates and sausages, and the cremeries with 200 varieties of cheeses. Janet thought that this is what heaven must be like: to be surrounded always by an inexhaustible amount of glorious food.

In the evenings, if it wasn't raining, the girls liked to sit at the outdoor cafes, drinking wine and watching the Parisians pass by. Usually they took Wendy with them, but occasionally, they would drop her at Nicole's, just to get her used to the lady she would be spending so much time with. They both loved Paris. How could anyone not love Paris?

And then it was the first Monday in September, and school started for both of them.

From the first minute Janet stepped inside of the 100 year old, three story building that was the L'Ecole de Gastronomie de Jacques Patou, she knew she had done the right thing, coming to Paris. It was her destiny to be a chef, and she could hardly wait to learn all she needed to know to cook all the wonderful dishes that were inside her waiting to be released.

She and the other eight students, one other woman, and seven men, were met by the chef's assistant, Henri, a tall, thin young man, who gave each of them a name tag, and a stiff white apron. He then showed them the freezers and refrigerators on the first floor before leading them up the stairs to the main kitchen, where the chef, Jacques Patou, a heavy-set middle aged man, wearing a white chef's coat, white apron, white scarf around his neck, white towel folded into his waist, and tall white chef's hat (gros bonnet) was setting out utensils on the table in front of him. There were nine chairs at the table with a towel on the back of each one. Janet was a little apprehensive as she took her chair. She hoped she wouldn't make a fool of herself--that she was good enough for this amazing opportunity.

At nine-thirty, the bell rang, and the chef looked up at them. "Bonjour, messieurs et mesdames," he said tipping his togue. He continued speaking in French, while Henri, standing beside him translated into English, "Welcome to L'Ecole de Gastronomie de Jacques Patou. You are all here because you want to learn classical French cooking. You will learn it, along with regional cooking. As you know this is a ten month course. The first three months I will teach you all I can about tools, techniques, ingredients, and recipes, for the next six months, each of you will be placed on the line in a fine restaurant, and that is where you will really learn to be a chef. Then you will return here for your final month, and if you are still with us, you will receive your certificate." He smiled. "I am sure you will all be with us." Then, "There will be two sessions each day, 9:30 to 12:30 and 1:30 to 4:30, and you will certainly have the best food in all of Paris, because you will get to eat your own creations." He took a breath, "Now for your attire."

He explained how to tie their aprons, crossed in back, then around to the front and tied on the side, so they made a convenient slot to hold their serviette (towel). He then explained how to fold their serviette, so that it would tuck into their apron, and yet be available to grab hot dishes, wipe drips, and dry their hands. "Cleanliness is the first rule of food," he said. "I change my serviette a dozen times a day and my apron when it gets dirty. A dirty apron is not the sign of a great cook, but a careless one."

He then spent the next hour explaining the importance of using the proper equipment, the knives, the heavy pots, the colander, the three sizes of sieves, the blenders, the cutting board, showing them each item as he discussed it. He talked about the art of slicing, dicing, carving. The vegetables must always be the same size or they will not cook evenly, as well as not look beautiful. He sliced an onion, a carrot, a potato. His hand moved so quickly, and cut so precisely that it was clear he'd been doing this since he was a child.

"Now," he said, "we will cook potage. We will start with potage, because potage is usually the first job a chef will have in a restaurant, and also because soup stock forms the basis of many other recipes. Also, because when I was child we had potage breakfast, lunch and dinner." He smiled and Janet was not sure if he was being serious or joking.

"Be sure to ask questions, if you do not understand."

He demonstrated making potato leek soup. When he was finished and the soup was simmering on the stove, Henri divided the students into three groups, and set them to work making the potato-leek potage. Janet was in a group with the other woman, Lucille Neumeier, and a man, Gordon Pratt, and the three of them worked together, cutting, dicing, mixing, smoothing, and constantly washing their cutting boards and utensils, while Chef Patou looked on and made comments, sometimes translated by Henri, sometimes not, until their soup, too, was simmering on the stove. The students cleaned up their work stations, put out place mats, napkins and spoons, and by 12 o'clock, they were all sitting down and eating the potage they had just prepared. "Ummm, delicious," they all agreed.

The next session began at 1:30. In this session, Chef Patou explained that good cooking depended on good ingredients and that they should always be sure to use only the freshest ingredients, that not only was it all right to vary a recipe to accommodate whatever was in season, but correct. French cooking was not heavy handed, but subtle, and French cooking was an art and like any true artist they must always strive for perfection.

He then demonstrated the making of three first courses: cheese soufflé, mushroom bouchees (incorporating the making of puff pastry), and leek torte (incorporating the making of a pie pastry). Then he broke the students into the same three groups and assigned the preparation of one of the appetizers to each group. Again the students set to work busily cutting, dicing, folding, mixing, blending until their dishes were in the oven and then again they cleaned their utensils and work places, set out their place mats, their napkins, spoons and forks, and at 4 o'clock, Chef Patou wished them a "Bon appetit" and they sat down to enjoy the product of their labor.

Janet was exhausted when she arrived back at the apartment. She wasn't sure if it was from the excitement of the first day, from the fear that she wouldn't be good enough, or from the hard work itself, but in any case, she was mentally and emotionally drained.

As Janet walked through the door, Edie was waiting for her as excited as a mother whose child has just come home from her first day in kindergarten. "So, how was it?"

"It was great," Janet said, picking up Wendy who ran to her, calling, "Aunt Janet, Aunt Janet."

"Everything you imagined?" Edie asked.

"Everything I imagined and more. I can't believe I learned so much in one day, potato-leek soup, cheese soufflé, and how to make puff pastry. Just being there, just wearing the apron, just learning to tuck a towel properly was worth everything. I can't wait for tomorrow. And how was your day?"

"The kids are adorable. The other teachers seem nice, and the walk is just right, as long as it doesn't rain."

"Then what will you do?"

"Wear my boots and carry an umbrella."

And Janet, tears coming to her eyes, "Edie, how can I ever thank you for all you've done, for all you're doing?"

"Don't say a word," Edie said. "Don't ever apologize, or feel guilty or thank me again. I'm having the greatest time of my life." Then taking her black-haired, black-eyed daughter who was reaching out to her, she said to Janet, "Now what's for dinner?"

"I'm too pooped to cook," Janet said. "Is it all right if we go out?"

Edie laughed. "So this is the great chef. One day of cooking school and she's too pooped to cook dinner."

"I'll do better tomorrow," Janet said.

The next day, Janet learned how to make the basic stocks and the five mother sauces. In the morning, they made the stocks: brown and white veal stock, brown beef stock, chicken stock, fish stock; and in the afternoon, they made the sauces: Hollandaise, Bechamel, Veloute, Brown sauce and Tomato sauce. Ms. Patou said it would be the only day they would have only bread and soup for lunch and dinner, and that tomorrow they would start preparing complete meals.

The next morning, when Janet entered the kitchen/classroom, Chef Patou was already busily cleaning out the innards of a duck. When the bell rang at 9:30, Chef Patou set his knife down and looked up at his nine students. "Bonjour messieurs et mesdames. This morning, we are going to make timbale de foies de volailla, canard a l'orange, and tarte aux pommes." Henri handed out the recipes, and as Chef Patou gave a detailed explanation of the dishes to be prepared, translated by Henri into English, the students made notes.

"C'est compris?" he asked every so often, not waiting for an answer.

The nine students again divided into what was now their set teams of three, and each team went to work to make one of the courses, while the chef and Henri bustled about answering the students' questions, helping them when they ran into problems. The students had now seen two demonstrations on how to make puff pastry, but incorporating the butter was still a difficult operation. By ll:30, the chicken livers, duck and tarte were all in the oven and by 12:30, each station was immaculate and set with its place mats and silverware, and after Chef Patou's, "Bon appetit," the students began sampling the dishes they had prepared. The timbale unmolded perfectly and was delicious, the duckling, prepared by Janet's group, decorated with skinless segments of orange was as beautiful to look at as to taste, but the apple tart was a failure, the apples were overcooked and the pastry was soggy. That threesome would have to do better this afternoon, but the other six had done marvelously well and Chef Patou was extremely pleased with them.

Each session from then on, went pretty much the same. Ms. Patou, or another chef would demonstrate three dishes, and then the class, divided into three teams, would make them. Occasionally, guest chefs would come and make a dish they or their restaurant was noted for. And whether Janet was watching or working, every day was exciting and exhausting.

Janet became very friendly with the other two members of her group, Lucille Neumeier and Gordon Pratt, but the other six members of her class seldom spoke to Janet or Lucille. Lucille Neumeier 32, big-boned, broadly built with short brown hair, looked more like a hiker than a cook, with her muscular legs and her brown boots that she wore to class each day. She was the assistant pastry chef at a fashionable restaurant in New York and thought if she took this class, she could "make" pastry chef. "It's not an easy world for a woman out there," Lucille told Janet.

"It's not such a great one in here, either," Janet said, thinking of the snubs they were receiving from the other students. Gordon Pratt, the other member of Janet's group, was 28, tall, slim, and quite handsome. He had straight brown hair, and brown eyes fronted by black-rimmed glasses, and he ate constantly without gaining a pound. "It's my metabolism," he said. "You've got to be born with it." He was from San Francisco, had been a short order cook for six years and now wanted to move up in the world.

Gordon and Lucille spent a lot of time at Janet and Edie's apartment. Both of them were staying in pensions, and they welcomed the chance to be in a "homey" environment. And Janet and Edie's apartment was "homey." Even though Janet and Edie knew living in Paris was temporary, they couldn't help buying little knick-knacks on their outings, a basket, a bowl, a silver box, an ashtray, candle holders, an exquisite quimper vase to hold the fresh flowers which Janet picked up almost every evening from a street vendor on her way home from L'Ecole, along with the fresh baguette from the boulangerie. And of course, with Wendy's toys always strewn about, it had to look like "home."

Because Lucille and Gordon spent so much time at the apartment, it wasn't long before Edie felt as close to them as Janet did. Especially Gordon. And Gordon seemed completely taken with Edie.

"I just love your room-mate," Gordon told Janet, "with her smooth creamy skin, her sparkling blue eyes and those luscious strawberry lips, voila, what a dish!"

Of course, Janet thought, it would be that way. Gordon would prefer Edie to herself. And Janet couldn't help feeling a little bit of resentment toward Edie for stealing Gordon away from her. Not that he ever belonged to Janet, but he was so kind to her in and out of class, so friendly, that she had begun to think that it was possible, that some man could love her. If it was going to happen, it would have to be a chef, someone who would appreciate her culinary skills. What else would any man see in her? She had begun to fantasize that she and Gordon would fall in love, that they would marry, have children. She imagined them opening their own restaurant, working side by side in the kitchen.

But that was before he met Edie.

"I think Gordon has a crush on you," she said to Edie one evening before Gordon and Lucille arrived, trying to find out how Edie felt about Gordon.

"Don't be silly," Edie told her. "Gordon's not interested in me in that way."

"How do you know?"

"Because he's queer."

Janet was shocked. It was something that had never entered her mind. "How do you know that?"

"Because my father had a client who was just like him."

"I can't believe it," Janet said.

"What, that Gordon is queer or that there are queers in Detroit?" Edie asked with a smile.

"Either one."

Janet needed to sit down. She felt utterly embarrassed, utterly stupid as she had that afternoon with Greg Flusty. How could she have gotten her hopes up over a man who was a total impossibility. She thought she would rather have lost him to Edie than because he was a homosexual. And then she had another thought. "No wonder Henri put Gordon with Lucille and me."

Edie's revelation did have an effect on Janet's attitude toward Gordon. The idea of two men having sex together, even though she wasn't sure what they did, seemed repulsive to her. But then she realized she was being as prejudiced toward homosexuals as the other members of the class were against women. She made up her mind to think of Gordon as she had always thought of him, a good friend, and the four of them continued to spend almost every evening together, either walking the streets of the Boulevard St. Michel (the Boul' Mich'), exploring the Rue de Seine or Rue Mazarine, or meeting for dinner at some restaurant they wanted to try.

If their landlady, Mrs. Guineau, could babysit, they would meet after dinner for a glass of wine at a favorite bar or bistro, or go to one of the popular jazz clubs, Jacob's Ladder, or Caveau de la Huchette in a cellar, or go to L'Abbaye and listen to folk singing. And always, always, the talk was of food. They talked about the recipes of that day, or another day, the restaurant where they had eaten dinner tonight, yesterday, last week, where they hoped to go tomorrow, and always there was criticism. "The potage was too creamy, the pastry was too moist, the pork was overcooked; the sauce on the fish needed more garlic, basil, lemon juice." Sometimes Edie wondered if these three knew there was a life outside of cooking.

Wine was almost as important to them as food, not just the wine, but knowing what wine went with what dish. They were learning regional cooking as well as classic, and if you prepared Grenadins de Porc Aux Pruneau, you had to have a Vouvray from the Louire Valley. Gordon and Lucille almost always brought a bottle of wine when they came over to the apartment, and opened it immediately, letting it breathe before they tasted it. Edie and Janet never had to worry about running out of wine; there were always several open bottles sitting on the kitchen counter.

Perhaps the most fun evenings were the ones when the three chefs cooked dinner. By this time,

Janet had accumulated quite a collection of cooking utensils, a cutting board, two sieves, a third knife for slicing meat and poultry, a casserole, skillet, wooden spoons, spatula, and wire whips, and the three students would stop at the markets after school, and bring home whatever was in season: meat, fish, fowl, fresh vegetables, fruits, and of course, the fresh baguette and flowers, and set to work. They'd butcher the meat, scale the fish, clean the fowl, then start on the sauces, the vegetables, and the desserts. It might take three hours to prepare one dinner, but when it was ready, what a treat!

As for Edie's job at the American school, she loved it. There were 22 children in her class, 12 boys and 10 girls, ranging in age from five to seven. Most of their parents were attached to the Armed Services in some way and the children were all well behaved, as if the discipline of the army had rubbed off on them. Within a week, Edie felt very close to each one of them. It was much different from teaching a class of 40 children in Detroit. It was quiet, relaxed and she could have a personal relationship with each child. For the most part, the children were bright and learned easily. Only two of them, six-year-old Timmy Lawsen and seven year-old Greg Wells needed extra attention, stumbling over their 1st and 2nd grade readers respectively. But she had time, all the time in the world, and patience, and would sit with them even after class, even after all the other children had been picked up or were playing out on the yard waiting for their parents to pick them up, and listen again to them read a story of a visit to the zoo, the bakery, the airport.

Sometimes she would join the children in the play-yard while they waited for their parents, and play tether ball with them, or handball. And she would always hug each child goodbye before he or she left. She loved each of the children by now: little Jeff Anderson who stuttered, and little Tracey Adams who still sucked her thumb, and Bobby Davis who liked to push the other boys around, but who always lingered longer than the others with his arms around her neck before his dad came to pick him up.

On a Tuesday night, eight weeks into the semester, the American school held an open house so that the parents could meet the teachers and see how the school was operated. The army dads in their uniforms, all assembled at one time in her room, were a forbidding bunch, but Edie kept a smile on her face and got through the evening with a minimum of discomfort, except when she met Josh Kelly's dad.

He was medium height, but powerfully built, with a square face, tanned skin and bristly blond hair.

He touched her arm, "I just wanted to thank you for being such a good teacher to my son. You're all he talks about."

And she could not help looking into the bluest eyes she'd ever seen and finding something unexpected there. "Why thank you," she said, trying to sound blasé.

"If I had known what a pretty teacher you were, I would have come by sooner."

Edie felt her cheeks flush. "Josh is a sweet little boy," she said. "You should be very proud of him."

"I am," he said, and finally moved away from her, letting Josh show him his desk and his picture on the bulletin board at the back of the room.

She continued greeting the other parents, but all the while she was conscious of Captain Kelly watching her.

And finally, when the open house was over and everyone had left, Captain Kelly, holding Josh's hand, came up to her again, "So what time does school let out?"

"Three," she said.

"I think it's time I assumed my fatherly duties and started picking up my son."

Again embarrassment. "I'm sure Josh will like that."

And Josh lifted up his arms to her and she bent down and hugged him.

All the way walking home, she felt totally unnerved. And yet there was no reason to be. Nothing had happened. Just a touch, a look, a remark that was not necessarily flirtatious. And even if something had clicked between them, nothing could come of this. He was a married man and if she had been able to stave off Stanley Rader, she could certainly stave off Captain Mike Kelly.

But later that night, lying awake on her bed, she could not stop thinking of him and his deep blue eyes--like Mellors, Lady Chatterly's lover, must have had.

While it was usually the mothers who came to pick up the children each day after school, in some cases, it was the father, if he was an officer and could arrange his hours, or was a student at the Sorbonne or Beaux Arts who was finished with classes by three.

Before open house, Mrs. Kelly, a pretty, blonde young woman, had always come to pick up Josh, but after open house, Captain Kelly began coming by every Monday, Wednesday and Friday. He always sent Josh out to play on the yard, and then stayed to chat with Edie. He was better looking than she first thought. He reminded her of Jack Armstrong, the All American boy. So unlike all the Jewish boys she had dated. With his blond bristly hair, his muscular body, his square jaw and deep blue eyes, he could have posed for a "Join the Marines" poster. And she liked his personality. He was not like Jack Shine or Zola, dark and brooding, but light and bubbly. Sunny, like Los Angeles. He was from Los Angeles and she enjoyed hearing about it. It had always sounded like such a beautiful place, but seemed so far away--farther from Detroit than Paris. He loved it there.

"It's got everything," he told her. "The ocean, the weather, excitement. I don't know why anyone would want to live anywhere else."

"Not even Paris."

"Well Paris is pretty great, too. But I wouldn't want to live here. You couldn't afford a house in Paris. You couldn't have a swimming pool. You couldn't have a backyard barbecue."

"A backyard barbecue," Edie laughed. "Yes, that's definitely more important than all the things Paris has to offer."

Captain Kelly, or Mike, as he asked her to call him, was an architect who had been in the R.O.T.C. in college, and was now in the Army for a three year hitch, stationed in Fountainebleau, and living in an apartment in Paris with his wife and child.

Edie looked forward to her talks with him. He was fun and he made her feel young and attractive, like she hadn't felt since becoming pregnant with Wendy, except for the night of Frank's wedding, and her rare visits from Stanley. But like Stanley, he was a married man and nothing could come of this.

And then on a Monday afternoon, three weeks after the open house, Mrs. Kelly came by to pick up Josh, and Edie was surprised at how disappointed she was. She hung around the classroom after the last child had been picked up, pinning pictures to a bulletin board and wondering why he hadn't come. Had he lost interest in her? And then, when she was about to leave, he appeared at the door.

"Hi," he said.

"Hi," she said. Then, trying to cover up how pleased she was to see him, she said, "You're too late. Your wife's already picked up Josh."

"I didn't come to pick up Josh," Mike said. "I thought we might have a coffee together."

It was a harmless request and yet it set her insides into turmoil. Chatting with him in the classroom was one thing; seeing him outside of the classroom put an entirely different perspective on their relationship. "No, I don't think so," she said. "I really have to get home to my little girl."

"No time even for a cup of coffee?" His voice was teasing and there was a twinkle in his eye. He was challenging her. Daring her.

She wasn't going to let him think she was afraid of him. He couldn't make her do anything she didn't want to do. And it was only a cup of coffee they were talking about. "All right," she said, "why not?"

They walked to a nearby outdoor cafe and he ordered espresso while she ordered cafe au lait, even if it was late afternoon and the waiter scowled at her. It was such a lovely day. She enjoyed sitting outdoors with him, sipping her coffee, talking about the States, Detroit, Los Angeles, her daughter, his son.

He put his army hat on the table exposing his bristly blond hair. "You know in all our talks, you've never said one word about your husband."

She thought of Zola with his black eyes, his great beard, still living on that commune in Oregon. "We're separated," she said, which technically wasn't a lie. "He's living in Oregon."

"Oregon! Do people really live in Oregon?"

"Wendy's father does."

He hesitated. "I notice you refer to him as Wendy's father, not your ex-husband."

"Well he is Wendy's father."

He studied her. Did he know more about her than she thought. He looked at his watch. "I've got to scoot," he said, "but will you have coffee with me again on Wednesday?"

"Yes, I will," she said and after he paid the bill and left her standing at the door of the cafe, she thought how quickly she had agreed to meet him, and how much she was looking forward to Wednesday afternoon.

On Wednesday afternoon they walked to the same cafe, and again sat outdoors, talking and drinking espresso for him, cafe au lait for her. "I can't tell you," he said, "how much I enjoy our talks together. You're the only person I can talk to. You know these army types."

"But you have your wife," she said, purposely injecting Cindy into the conversation, intentionally wanting to break the intimacy that was developing between them.

"Yes, my wife," he said. "She's very pretty, very attractive, but I'm afraid not very bright."

Edie winced. She didn't like him insulting his wife.

He seemed to catch her look. "Anyway, we don't have a real marriage. We're only staying together because of Josh. But I don't want to talk about my wife. I want to talk about you. What were you like when you were a little girl?"

And Edie trying to think of something to say, "Well, I loved to read, and I loved school, and I loved being with my big brother, Frank. He used to buy me chocolate sodas and take me to baseball games." Then somewhat wistfully, "I adored him."

"Is that past tense?" he asked.

She hesitated, how much to tell? "Let's just say, we're not as close as we used to be."

And Mike understanding she wasn't going to say any more on that subject, asked, "What else?"

She didn't have to think about her next answer. "Practicing the piano. I was always practicing the piano." And then she told him about the piano competition and how devastated she had been, but that it made her see that if you don't put your whole heart and soul into something you don't really deserve to get it.

"Yes," he said, "I believe that."

She drank the last drop of her cafe au lait, and said, "I think I'd better go."

After he paid the bill, they parted, he to the right, she to the left. "I hope we can do this again on Friday," he said.

"We'll see," she said. She didn't think she would go for coffee with him again. She was becoming too involved with him, liking him too much, feeling too good when she was with him. She'd better stay away from Mike Kelly.

But he didn't show up on Friday or the following Monday, and by Wednesday, she was beginning to feel depressed. Had she read the whole thing wrong? Was she the one pursuing him and he not interested in her at all? She felt ashamed and foolish and hoped he would never show up again. But then on Wednesday, there he was.

"Time for a cup of coffee?"

"No, I can't," she said, determined that she was finished with him.

"But I made a special trip down from Fountainebleau just to see you. You can't refuse," he said.

She looked into his deep blue eyes and felt her resolve melt like butter in a frying pan. "All right," she said, "but this is the last time."

He had a car waiting outside the school, a small gray Renault. "Come on, we're going for a ride."

"Where to?"

"You'll see."

She got into the car reluctantly, but once he began driving, she relaxed. It was fun being in a car. She hadn't been in one since coming to Paris, not even a cab; they were too expensive. As they reached the outskirts of the city, she asked, "Where are you taking me?"

"I told you, for a cup of coffee," he said.

"But where? Italy?"

"Not that far. I have a special little place that I stop for breakfast on my way to work. It's really charming." They were out of the city now and he pointed to a radar dish beside a shack on a hill. "That's a piece of my work," he said.

"The radar dish or the shack?"

"The shack."

"Pretty impressive," she said, jokingly.

"It's one of my better designs," he said, returning her jibe.

"Seriously...." she said.

"Seriously," he said, "you do what you can on the budget you're given."

"Well, it is kind of cute."

"I'd like to show it to you."

"Can you? I mean isn't it secret, or something."

"In a way, yes. But my best buddy works there. Tommy Cairns. He works 12 hours on, 36 hours off."

"I wouldn't mind those hours."

"Who would? Actually, he has an apartment right near you. 12 rue Bonaparte."

"Just a few blocks."

"Yeah. On the nights he works I go over to his place. He's got a set of weights and I work out."

"That's why you're so muscular."

"Yes, I like it. I like the body building and I like being alone. Gives me time to think."

"And what do you think about?"

He turned to look at her, "You."

And there it was, the very thing she had been dreading. She knew she should say something now. Put a stop to it now, before it went any further, but she sat mute, looking out the window at the passing scenery, the little houses on the hills, a red roofed church, the cows standing motionless, the flowers. How beautiful it all was and how happy she was feeling.

They were in a little town; he pulled over and parked in front of a hotel, Hotel Barbizon. It had a patio in front with tables with red umbrellas. He came around to her side of the car and helped her out.

"It's a lovely place," she said after they were seated at a table, "if a little far for a cup of coffee."

"Maybe you'll have a sweet," he said. "They have the best sweets here."

She was suddenly feeling very young, very carefree. "Yes, I'll have a tarte tatin."

He ordered while she telephoned Janet's school and left a message for Janet to pick up Wendy from the babysitter's. Then she returned to the table and sat looking at him. He was very handsome, she decided, seeing him sitting under the red umbrella. He had removed his hat, and the blond fuzz of his hair was glimmering in the sunlight. How would it feel to touch it? Would it be coarse or soft? She liked his build. He was square and solid. And she liked his smile, so bright and happy. He was smiling now and she thought how young he looked. Too young to have a five year-old child. "I never asked how old you are," she said.

He was sipping his espresso, she her cafe au lait, and both cutting into their apple pastries.

"Twenty-four," he said.

"The same age as I am," she said. And then, "You must have gotten married very young."

"I was eighteen," he said. "Cindy was only seventeen. The truth of the matter is, we had to get married. Cindy was pregnant." And looking directly into her eyes, "But I didn't love her. Don't love her now."

Edie took a bite of the luscious caramelized apples, the flaky crust. She wasn't impressed with the fact that he didn't love Cindy, but with the fact that he had stuck by Cindy. That he had married her.

"Don't get me wrong," he continued. "I liked Cindy. We had been dating all through high school and to tell you the absolute truth, I didn't mind marrying her. But my needs were different then. I just wanted someone pretty. Someone I could show off to the guys. And then after we were married, when I had to spend every day with her, when I had to talk to her, I finally realized the true meaning of "dumb blonde."

Edie looked down at her fork. Again she was annoyed that he was insulting his wife.

As if reading her mind, he said, "I'm sorry. I shouldn't be talking about my wife like that. I shouldn't be talking about my wife at all."

"It doesn't matter. We're just friends."

"But I don't want to be 'just friends.'" He put his hand on hers. "I'm crazy about you, Edie."

She looked into his deep blue eyes, "Don't," she said. "Please don't."

"I can't help it," he said. "I'm obsessed with you. I think about you all the time, and I make up all kinds of outrageous stories to get away from the base in the afternoon, just for the chance to see you."

"You're just unhappy in your marriage, that's all it is."

"No, dammit, it's more than that. And I know you feel it, too. Tell me you haven't thought about me."

"I have thought about you," she said, "but I've also thought that nothing can happen between us. You're married."

"But as I told you before, it's an empty marriage. If not for Josh, we would have been divorced years ago."

"But there is Josh. And you aren't divorced."

"Because I had no reason to be, until now."

They finished their coffees and pastries, and walked in the garden behind the hotel, holding hands amid the purple irises, the orange poppies, Edie feeling like Lara in *Dr. Zhivago*, and then beside an old oak tree, he kissed her, and she could not help responding. Her body did not know all the reasons she should not enjoy the kiss, or want it to go on. Her body did not understand that this was wrong, that he was married and had a child. Her body was selfish and stupid, and yearned for more.

"I'm going to get us a room," he whispered.

"No," she said, but he left her, and she started walking toward the car, her mind trying to take control, she had to get out of here, leave before it was too late, and then he reappeared, kissed her again, led her up the stairs to a small dark room, a bed with an iron headboard and brown chenille spread, and then it was too late. He was kissing her everywhere, caressing her, undressing her. "Do you have something?" she asked.

"We won't need it," he said.

"Yes," she said, "we do need it."

"Trust me," he said, "we won't need it."

And he was doing something to her no one had ever done, they were upside down, and his mouth was on her private parts, and God, it was so exciting, so unbelievably thrilling that she would do anything now, anything he asked, anything he wanted, anything to make it go on, please, please, don't stop, and then she reached a climax, and lay panting and soaked with perspiration on the bed.

"And now," he said, "you do me."

His penis was in front of her. She had never wanted to deal with a penis. She was afraid to look at it, afraid to touch it; she liked sex in the dark, but here it was, in her face, in her mouth, and it wasn't bad, it wasn't awful, and he was pumping, and her jaws were getting tired, and just when she thought she could not keep her mouth open another minute, he was at her again with his mouth, and she forgot everything, except the ecstasy she was experiencing, and when the white gooey substance was released in her mouth, she didn't care, because she was in heaven.

She spit it out in the sink and rinsed her mouth. He was lying on the bed, his knees up. She went to him, kissed him. He wrapped her head in his hands, "That was great," he said.

"Great," she said. "I've never experienced anything like it before."

"You've never gone around the world before?" he said.

"Is that what it's called?" she said.

"That, and 69."

"No," she said, "I've never experienced it before."

"You mean, I've had a virgin?"

"Almost," she said, a little embarrassed. "Actually I've only had sex once."

"Once!" He was astonished. "And you became pregnant? That only happens in the movies."

"That's what my mother said."

He looked at his watch. "It's late. We better get back."

On the way to her apartment, he passed 12 rue Bonaparte, a gray stone building, and stopped the car. "This is where Tommy Cairns lives," he said. "Second floor, first door on your left. He's going to be on duty tomorrow night and I'll be spending the evening at his place. Will you come visit me?"

"I don't know what to do," she said.

And stopping his car in front of her apartment house, he said, "I promise you an exciting time."

"I'll still have to think about it," she said.

And then he pulled her to him, and whispered in her ear, "While you're thinking about it, get a diaphragm, will you? I want to feel my cock inside you."

She shivered, feeling aroused just from his words.

"I don't know if I can do this," she said.

"You can," he said and let her go and she was out of the car, and up the stairs.

She wished he had said, I love you, but he had promised her something else, excitement. Sexual excitement. Something that had been missing from her life since that night in Zola's apartment.

Janet was waiting for her. "Where have you been? I was so worried about you."

"I'm sorry," she said, picking up Wendy who ran to meet her. "I just got tied up."

"Mommy, mommy," Wendy giggled.

The table was set, pots were bubbling on the stove. "What happened?" Janet asked.

"I've met someone, Janet."

"Oh, Edie. Tell me about him."

But she couldn't. She didn't want to tell Janet he was married and she didn't want to share any of what had just taken place. "Another time," she said. "Let's eat." But she just picked at her food. Although it was delicious, sautéed veal with mushrooms, braised carrots, and an apricot tart for dessert, she had no appetite. She had spent all of her appetite on Mike. Captain Mike Kelly.

After the dishes were done and the kitchen cleaned up, she sat on the floor playing with Wendy, putting pieces in a puzzle, then dumping them out and starting over, but she was exhausted, and as soon as Wendy was put to bed, she said goodnight to Janet and went to her bedroom and shut the door.

She undressed, but purposely did not bathe. She did not want to wash the feel of Mike Kelly off her. She lay on her bed in the dark remembering and reliving all that had happened at the Hotel Barbizon. It had been so thrilling, not just the lovemaking, but being held, being cuddled, being needed, being loved. She knew it was wrong, no matter what he said about his marriage, but still she didn't know how she could keep herself from going back to him at 5 rue Bonaparte tomorrow night.

The next afternoon, she went to a gynecologist and got a diaphragm and that night, after making sure Wendy was asleep, and telling Janet she might not be home until morning, she walked the few short blocks to 12 rue Bonaparte, where on the second floor, first door on the left, she found Captain Mike Kelly waiting for her.

From that night on, she began meeting Mike twice a week at Tommy Cairns apartment, living for the moments they would be together. He brought out feelings in her she didn't know existed, found places of pleasure in her body she didn't know she had, brought her to peaks of excitement she didn't think she was capable of. She was in a continual state of sexual arousal, and just thinking about him, she would feel a stirring between her legs.

She lost all her inhibitions. She didn't mind fondling his penis, taking it in her mouth. She didn't mind him seeing her body naked in the daylight. She bought black lace underwear, and began wearing high heeled shoes, black eye-liner, blue eye shadow, and red lipstick because he said those things excited him. Now, at twenty-four and already a mother, she finally understood what sex was all about, finally understood why people would kill to get it, or keep it, or not let it go.

It wasn't long before twice a week at Tommy Cairns wasn't enough for them. They needed to be together more often, so Mike began coming to Edie's apartment whenever he could get away. And if it was late, and Janet was asleep, they'd go into Edie's bedroom and make love, but quietly so Janet wouldn't hear them. And if Mike could come over in the daytime, when Janet was home, Janet would take Wendy to the park, so they could be alone for an hour; and if Janet wasn't home, and Wendy could be coaxed into taking a nap, they'd come together in a quick explosion of passion. At times Edie was ashamed of the way she was carrying on, like a common slut, but she could not control herself. The need for Mike was too great.

Edie wished that Janet was not a witness to all that was going on, not that they did anything sexual in front of Janet except an occasional kiss or hug, but even that seemed too much. Edie kept thinking about how Janet must feel. Janet didn't have a boyfriend, had never had a boyfriend. It must hurt Janet terribly to see Edie involved in such a passionate love affair while Janet had never even been kissed.

"I wish Janet would meet someone," she confided to Mike. "I feel bad that she's never had a boyfriend, never even been on a date. Maybe you know someone."

"I'm not in a position to double-date," he said, sarcastically.

"I didn't mean double-date. I just thought you could give her phone number to some nice young man. He wouldn't have to know about us."

"I'll think about it," he said.

"She's really a very sweet girl. A very wonderful girl."

"I didn't say she wasn't. I'm just in a very awkward position to fix someone up. Especially someone living with you."

And while Edie spoke of it now and then, Mike never could think of anyone to fix Janet up with, or if he did, probably didn't feel that it was worth the risk. Mike had agreed to let Janet know about their affair, how else could he go to Edie's apartment, but he didn't want anyone else to know about it. Gordon and Lucille knew Edie was seeing someone, but they never met him and they never knew his name.

In January, the three budding chefs left the school setting and started working on the line. Each of them was placed in a hotel restaurant, starting at the salad station, and when January turned to February, and Paris was covered with snow, they moved to the sauce station. In March, when the little chickens appeared at the markets, and the grass began to turn green again, they advanced to the meat and grill station.

Janet and Lucille had been assigned to Hotel Veronique, a small hotel on the West bank. It was American style which meant that all the meals came with the hotel room. It was a disappointment to Janet and Lucille. Since the hotel restaurant had a captive audience, and didn't have to depend on its reputation to draw patrons off the street, there was less need for creativity. Janet and Lucille both felt they had been placed at this restaurant because they were women. Even Gordon, who had been part of their threesome got a bustling restaurant near L'Opera. In a way, the Hotel Veronica reminded Janet of the summer camp she had worked at in upstate Michigan, and she viewed the hotel guests as the happy little campers. "Just give them something to fill their tummies" seemed to be the attitude of the chef. Still Janet was determined to do what she could with what she had, but every time she tried to add an ingredient, or change an ingredient, or make the presentation more appealing, she met with a scowl. Apparently the chef was just as unhappy to have been assigned two women as they were to be there. Still it was hard work and long hours. Some nights Janet would come home wondering if it had been worth deserting her mother in Detroit for this: to be a robot on the line in a third rate restaurant. She may as well have been on the assembly line in a Detroit auto manufacturing plant. At these moments of depression, she felt especially envious of Edie. Not because Edie had a man, but because she had Mike Kelly. Janet thought Mike Kelly was the most beautiful man she had ever met. Much better looking than Greg Flusty. Every time she looked at him, she thought of Jerry Freyer, the American soldier who had liberated her in Italy. Even though Mike had blonde hair instead of red, he had the same robust energy. She tried to avoid him, tried not to look into his blue eyes, tried not to see his smile that sent a chill through her body. She tried not to be around when he was there; she tried not to listen when he was in Edie's bedroom, tried not to picture what they must be doing, tried not to imagine what it would be like to be held by him, to be kissed by him. She kept telling herself that she was a stupid, foolish girl, that even thinking about him was absurd. No man would ever look at her, let alone a man like Mike Kelly, and even if he did, even if a miracle might happen, he belonged to Edie.

As much as Janet tried to avoid Mike Kelly, it turned out that they were often alone in the apartment, before Edie got home from school and before Janet had to leave for work. Janet usually stayed in her room until Edie got home, but one afternoon, when she was sitting at the kitchen table, drinking a glass of wine, and going over a recipe, Mike knocked on the front door.

"Come on in," she said, "the door's open." And then as he entered the kitchen, she looked up. "Edie's not home yet."

"Mind if I join you?" he asked, nodding to the glass of wine.

"Help yourself," she said.

He walked over to the sink where all the open and unopened bottles were lined up, chose a poully fuisse, poured it into a Montmarte glass, then walked over to the table, took off his hat, set it on the table, and sat next to her, so close that she could smell his after-shave lotion. It was spicy and sweet.

"So Edie tells me you were born in Italy," he said.

"Yes, I was."

"I knew there was something special about you. I couldn't quite nail it." He took a sip from his glass of wine and then said with a wink, "If you ever talked, I'd be able to tell if you had an accent."

She lowered her eyes, nervous to be talking to him, more nervous to be alone with him, "I'm sorry. I guess I'm not very good at small talk."

"Well I'm an expert at it. That's all I do. Between the army personnel and my wife." He put his fingers through his short blond hair. "I didn't know what the expression "dumb blonde" meant until I married my wife."

Janet knew she was blushing. It was bad enough that he was Edie's boyfriend, she didn't want to hear about his wife.

"I'm sorry," he said, "I shouldn't be talking about my wife like that. I shouldn't be talking about my wife at all. What I really want to talk about is you."

"Me?" What was there to say? She felt utterly tongue-tied. What could she talk about that would interest this handsome worldly man?

"Tell me, why do you want to be a chef?"

That was easy. "It's just something I've always wanted to do."

"Just like I've always wanted to be an architect." And then examining her face, he said, "I bet you were a cute kid."

"Why do you say that?"

"Because of your eyes. You have the most beautiful hazel eyes. Hasn't anyone ever told you that?"

"No," she said, almost too embarrassed to get the word out.

"Not even one of your boyfriends?"

She was ashamed to say the words, but still she said them, "I've never had a boyfriend."

"No one, sweet Janet? No one who saw behind the facade you present to the world. No one to see what a deep sensitive person you are? No one to kiss those sweet pink lips?"

She thought she could not take another minute of this, she was so filled with fear and embarrassment. "Please, Mike, don't talk like that."

"You know what I'd like to do right now?" he asked. "I'd like to kiss you."

Janet began to tremble. She had to get away from him, run to her room, run out the front door. But she couldn't move.

"Don't be afraid," he said. "It won't hurt, I promise." And he leaned over and touched her lips, oh so softly, and it was oh so lovely, unlike anything she had ever experienced. And then he pulled away. "Now that wasn't so bad, was it?"

"No," she said, still not able to look at him.

And then they heard the front door open and he stood up and perfectly at ease, his wine glass in his hand, walked over and embraced Edie.

It had only been a moment in time, only one or two seconds in Janet's life, and yet Janet could not forget that kiss, could not stop thinking about it, reliving it. She thought of telling Edie what had happened. But what would she say? That she liked being kissed by Mike Kelly. That she could not get him out of her mind. No, she was too ashamed to mention it to Edie. Better just keep busy. Better try to forget it. Better keep away from Mike Kelly. So she put all her energy into her job, trying to take joy in dicing the garlic perfectly, in making the smoothest sauce Hotel Veronique had ever seen, in stuffing her little chickens just right and then browning them to a perfect glossiness, in cooking the salmon to just the right tenderness, in arranging the grapes on the sole in a way that was pleasing to the eye--even this brought a look of displeasure from the grill cook--and in every way trying to be the best cook she could possibly be, given the parameters she had to work within.

It was April and in spite of the long hours Janet, Lucille and Gordon worked, sometimes not getting home until after midnight, they still managed to get together at least once a week. And if Edie wasn't spending the night with Mike, she would join them, and the four friends would meet at a cafe or bistro, and if it wasn't raining, sit outdoors, bundled up in their heavy sweaters, sipping an espresso, a glass of wine, or a hot chocolate. And while Edie listened, the three chefs would talk about veal and chicken, sweetbreads and rabbit, and what they would serve in their own restaurant if ever they were so lucky to own one.

In May, Janet would be returning to L'Ecole for her final month, and in June, she would be getting her certificate. She knew she should go home then, back to Detroit, back to her mother. She hadn't seen her mother in almost a year and was haunted by guilt every single day. But she didn't want to go back to Detroit. She wanted to go to Florence. She wanted to see her aunt, uncle and cousin with whom she had been in hiding, and she wanted to get a job cooking in an Italian restaurant. She felt if she didn't do it now, the chance might never come again.

But she didn't know if she could do it without Edie. And she didn't know if she had the right to ask Edie to go with her.

She broached the subject one evening after dinner. She and Edie were having a brandy, while Wendy was coloring at the kitchen table. No Mike tonight.

"Edie, I've been thinking about going to Florence when school is over."

Edie seemed surprised, but after a moment's thought, said, "Of course. You want to visit your relatives."

"I want to do more than that," Janet told her. "I want to get a job there. I want to work in an Italian restaurant. I want to learn all I can about Italian cooking."

"Sounds like a great idea," Edie said.

"Not that this wasn't the best year of my life," Janet continued. "I've learned so much and I'm so grateful to you for making it possible, but I'm Italian, or as Italian as a Jew can be, and I want to learn to cook Italian." And then, as if in an afterthought, "I don't suppose you'd want to go with me."

"I would," Edie said immediately. "Of course I would. I'd love to see Italy, live in Florence, but," a moment of hesitation, "I just don't know if I'm ready to leave Paris yet."

Janet got her meaning, and thought, of course Edie wouldn't want to leave Mike Kelly. What an idiot I was to think she would. "I understand," Janet said, "I didn't expect you'd want to go."

And Edie, worried that Janet might not go without her, and not wanting to disappoint her dearest friend, said, "Will you go even if I can't?"

"I suppose so," Janet said. "I've already checked with my aunt and she said I could stay with them. She said she has plenty of room." And not wanting to put any pressure on Edie, but wanting her to know it would be no problem if Edie decided to come, continued, "She said there would even be room for you and Wendy, if you decide to go."

And Edie, still concerned about Janet, said, "That was sweet of you to ask. Well maybe. Maybe in a month I'll know what I'm going to do. Maybe I will go with you to Florence."

And Janet, keeping her eyes on the brandy in her snifter, said, "It's selfish of me to ask. Do whatever's best for you."

"I will," Edie said. "I just don't know what that is at this moment."

It was 3 o'clock on the following Sunday afternoon. Edie had taken Wendy to a carnival at school, and Janet had just gotten home from work. On Sundays, after Janet prepared the large meal at lunchtime, she got the rest of the day off. She had just taken off her shoes and was preparing to lie down on the sofa to rest her feet, when there was a knock on the door.

Curious as to who it might be, she went to open it, and standing before her was Mike Kelly.

"Edie's not here," Janet said. "She's gone to a carnival at school."

"I know," he said, removing his army hat and exposing his bristly blond hair. "I didn't come to see Edie, I came to see you."

"Me?" she asked, her face turning hot.

"Yes," he said with his boyish smile. "Can I come in?"

"I don't know," Janet said, fear overtaking her. She didn't want to be alone with him. That was the last thing she wanted.

"There's nothing to be afraid of," he said, pushing past her and heading to the kitchen. She shut the door and followed him. He set his hat on the kitchen table. "Is it all right if I have a glass of wine?"

"Help yourself," she said, trying to sound calm.

He perused the wines and chose the Chateau Iguem, their most expensive bottle, then poured two glasses and handed her one.

She took it with shaking hands, hoping he didn't notice, hoping he didn't hear her heart which was beating so hard it must burst through her ribs.

"A votre sante," he said and clicked her glass.

He took a sip and she gulped down the entire glassful of sweet grapey liquid as if it were water.

She sat down at the kitchen table and he took the bottle of wine and sat across from her. "I've had the most God-awful day," he said. "I just had this terrible altercation with the Colonel. It's a heating problem. I told him we should put the ducts in the bottom of the wall, and he insists they should go at the top. Why? Because that's how it's always been. Of all the crap. No imagination." He picked up the bottle and poured them both another glass.

"I know," Janet said, feeling more relaxed, less tense, "it's like that for me, too. This chef I'm working with now, every time I present him with a new idea, he scowls at me. You would think a chef would want to try something different." And then she looked down, because she thought she had exposed too much of herself.

Mike smiled. "You know, you are deep. Deeper than most people suspect. And I understand you, Janet. I understand more about you than you think."

"How could you?" she asked.

"Because I do," he said. "I know how lonely and sad you've been all these years. I know how much you've wanted to be loved. How much you've wanted to be held by a man. And I know what a sweet, gentle person you are." He stood up. "Come over here."

She looked up at him. This couldn't be happening to her. This happened to other girls. Pretty, attractive, charming other girls. Girls like Edie. But not to fat, ugly Janet.

"Come here," he said again, commanding her as if she were a soldier in his army.

Slowly she stood, not feeling that she was part of her body, as if she was watching all this from across the room, and walked to him.

He touched her hair, he ran his finger along her ear, across her eyes. "Janet. My poor little ignored Janet. So no man has ever found you attractive. Well, I think you're beautiful." And then he kissed her, ever so gently, just like that first time. And she let herself go with it, enjoying it. And then he was kissing her eyes, her neck, her mouth again, and it was wonderful. More wonderful than anything she had ever experienced in her life.

Edie returned that evening, exhausted from her day in the sun, and from socializing with a hundred children and their parents at the game and food booths set up at the school, and found Janet already in her bedroom behind a shut door.

Edie knocked gently. "Janet, are you all right?"

"Fine," Janet called back. "I just have a little headache."

"Is there anything I can get for you?"

"No," Janet said.

"All right, then," Edie said. "Feel better. I'll see you in the morning."

Janet could not face Edie tonight, not after what she had done this afternoon. Perhaps she would never be able to face Edie again. What she had done was unforgivable, the worst thing she had ever done in her life, worse than exposing her family to death, because today's act had been intentional. She had stabbed her best friend in the back. It proved what she had always known about herself, that she was a horrible, terrible person, weak, selfish, and not to be trusted. But God forgive her, she was not sorry Mike Kelly had made love to her.

It was two weeks until the semester ended for Edie and Janet, and Edie was in a complete state of anxiety.

First, she didn't know if she should go to Florence with Janet or stay in Paris with Mike. Mike had been telling her for months that he was in love with her, that he was going to leave Cindy, that he wanted to marry her. He was going to tell Cindy tonight, tomorrow morning, next week for sure. But still, he hadn't told Cindy anything, and Edie was beginning to doubt that he ever would. And even if he did leave Cindy, did Edie want to marry him? He was handsome, he was charming, he was great in bed, but was he the kind of man she wanted to spend the rest of her life with? Would he be a good father to Wendy? And if he had done this to Cindy, mightn't he do the same to her?

But even more upsetting than the situation with Mike, was that something was the matter with Janet. Edie had never seen her like this. She was morose, brooding, monosyllabic. And she was avoiding Edie.

"Is something the matter?" Edie would ask.

"No, nothing," Janet would reply.

She was disappearing after dinner.

"Where are you going?"

"I have some things to do."

Edie tried to figure out what was wrong with her. It couldn't be her job--she had gotten over that months ago. Perhaps it was guilt over not going back to see her mother, or fear of going to Florence. But she had been happy about going to Florence. Excited. It had to be something else. Perhaps a man. Could there be a man in Janet's life? But if so, then why hadn't she told Edie? Why hadn't she confided in her best friend? And why so melancholic?

Edie's mind went rampant. Perhaps...it was a woman. Perhaps Janet was in love with a woman. Perhaps it was Lucille. If Gordon was homosexual, then why not Lucille? In a way it made sense. Maybe that's why Janet never had a boyfriend. But then, Janet had been so shocked about Gordon, and Edie didn't believe that Lucille was a homosexual. But what if it was some other woman. Someone she had met at the Hotel Veronique. Someone who seduced her as Mike had seduced Edie. Perhaps that was the real reason she wanted to leave Paris and go to Florence. Shame.

One evening, before she was to leave for 5 rue Bonaparte, Edie cornered Janet. "Janet, you've got to tell me what's going on with you."

"Nothing," Janet said, curt, as she had now become.

"Yes there is. It's all right. I can handle it. Whatever it is. Nothing is so bad that you can't tell me."

Janet could not stand it another moment, could not carry this burden another second. Her eyes filled with tears, and she collapsed sobbing on the sofa, "Oh, Edie, I'm so ashamed. I feel so guilty. You'll never forgive me. Never."

Edie came over and sat beside her, taking hold of Janet's hands, "What is it? You can tell me. You can tell me anything." It must be another woman. It must be.

"Oh Edie, It's Mike. We've been making love."

Edie dropped Janet's hands. For a moment, she couldn't catch her breath, and then there was a pounding in her head. Mike and Janet. It couldn't be. It couldn't be. She looked at Janet and her body filled with anger, disgust, hatred. Not for Janet, but for Mike. "How could he?" she said.

"Oh, Edie, I'm so sorry. I don't know how it happened. He kissed me one day while we were waiting for you to come home. And then, that day of the carnival, he came over and we were sitting in the kitchen drinking wine, and he kissed me again, and I was weak, Edie. I was too weak to stop him. I knew it was wrong, I knew I shouldn't be doing it, but I couldn't help myself." And then she was sobbing again.

Oh yes, Edie knew how that was. How charming Mike could be. How seductive. Had he gone down on Janet, too? The poor little thing, how could she have resisted that? Edie took Janet in her arms. "It's okay," she said, patting her back, "I understand. After all, the dirty rat seduced me, too."

"Oh Edie, I feel so awful," through her tears.

"How many times did you do it?"

Janet paused, as if she couldn't get the words out, "Every day."

Edie was aghast. "You mean every day since the carnival?"

Lowering her eyes, "Yes."

Unbelievable, Edie thought. Fucking her and fucking her best friend at the same time and probably fucking his wife as well. The man was insatiable. And then she wondered, were there others as well? All his talk of love, shmove, kabove, and all his talk of leaving Cindy and marrying her, what a bunch of bullshit. How stupid she had been. But she deserved it. She deserved every bit of misery she got for fooling around with a married man. And she vowed, sitting here, holding her dearest friend in her arms, that no matter what, she would never have sex with a married man again, no matter how long she lived, no matter how wonderful he was, no matter how much she loved him. Never, never, never again.

She let go of Janet and headed for the door.

"Where are you going?" Janet asked.

"I have a date with Mike," Edie said.

"Don't do anything crazy," Janet said.

"That's exactly what I intend to do," Edie said, "Something crazy."

Janet ran to the door. "I'm afraid for you, Edie. Don't do it, whatever you're thinking."

Edie looked back at her, "Nothing would be bad enough for him."

All the way walking to 12 rue Bonaparte, Edie was planning what to do, what to say. If only she could hurt him as much as he had hurt her and Janet.

Her fury propelled her the few blocks there, up the flight of stairs into the hall, to the first door on the left.

She pushed it open and saw him lying on Tommy Cairns' sofa. He did not turn to look at her, but unzipped his pants and allowed his erect penis to escape. He put his arms behind his head and closed his eyes. "I've been waiting for you, baby," he said. "C'mon and eat it."

"Eat it yourself," she said, "you fucking bastard," and she ran at him and began hitting him.

He jumped up and tried to grab her hands, but she was elusive. She wished she had the courage to grab his penis and yank it off, that would serve him right, but instead she just kept hitting at him.

"What the hell's the matter with you?" he said.

"You're a fucking bastard," she screamed through her tears.

And finally he had control of her, her arms pinned behind her back.

"What's going on?"

"Don't you know?"

Recognition shone in his eyes. "You found out about Janet," he said. "Look I was only trying to help the poor thing out. She doesn't mean a thing to me. I was just doing it for her. You were always saying how much she needed it, how much she needed a man. It's really your fault."

She wanted to throw up. She shook her head back and forth, "To think I really cared for you. What an idiot I was."

"You cared for me and you still do." He had forced her against the wall and was trying to kiss her.

Yes, it was just like him. He had no shame, no remorse, no conscience, and now she knew why she had never fallen in love with him. He had no soul.

"Well you're wrong, buddy," she pushed him away. "I hate your guts." And she was out the door and down the steps, while he stood in the doorway watching her, his limp penis still hanging out of his pants.

She ran down the street, past the people sitting at outdoor cafes, past the people looking in shop windows, past the people out for a stroll, tears streaming down her face, back to the two most precious things in her life, her daughter, Wendy, and her best friend, Janet.

The next afternoon at school, Mrs. Kelly came to pick up Josh, and Edie asked if she might have a word with her.

"Of course."

Edie was filled with apprehension as she sent the few remaining children out to the playground. She hated doing this, but felt she must. "Would you like to sit down?" she asked Mrs. Kelly, trying to delay the inevitable.

"No, it's all right, I'll stand," Mrs. Kelly answered, as if readying herself for bad news.

And for the first time, Edie looked at Mike Kelly's wife, really looked at her. She was a sweet young woman, she didn't deserve what she was going to hear. She didn't deserve Mike Kelly. And maybe it was wrong to tell her, to hurt her so badly. But maybe it was worse not to.

Mrs. Kelly was becoming impatient. "What is it you want to tell me? Is it about Josh?"

"No," Edie said, "it's about your husband."

Mrs. Kelly, Cindy, raised her hand as if to stop Edie. "I don't want to hear it," she said. "I really don't want to hear anything you have to say." And she turned to leave the room.

"I'm sorry, Mrs. Kelly. But there's something you have to know." Edie forced the words out, "I've been having an affair with your husband, and so has my room-mate."

Mrs. Kelly turned to look at her. Her eyes were glassy and there was a smirk on her face, "You're not the first, you know."

Her words would have cut like a knife just two days ago, but now all Edie felt was sadness. "I didn't know, but I should have." And then as Mrs. Kelly straightened herself up and headed for the door, Edie called after her, "Why don't you leave him?"

Cindy turned for one final look at her, "I don't think that's any of your goddamn business." And she was gone.

Edie collapsed onto one of the children's desks. It had been a horrible ordeal, one she never wanted to go through again. Why was life so unfair? She had wanted to hurt Mike, but instead had only hurt his wife. And now, the three of them, Cindy, herself, and Janet were all hurting, while Mike, the dirty bastard, was probably out fucking someone new, or old, or both, and not giving a damn about any of them. She should have killed him last night when she had the chance. Then he would never hurt anyone again.

It was clear that there was no longer any reason for Edie to stay in Paris, and a good reason to leave. She asked Janet if she was sure it would be all right with Janet's aunt and uncle if she and Wendy moved in with them.

"Oh Edie," Janet said, hugging her, "I'm so happy you're coming with me. I really was going to go without you, but it's so much better that you're coming with. I'm going to call my aunt right now and tell her the good news." And she ran to the phone, "I'm sure it won't be any problem."

And it wasn't.

School ended for both of them: Edie's 22 little children each receiving a report card with A's and B's in every subject, and Janet receiving a colored scroll, made for framing, dated the 8th day of June 1961, announcing that Janet Camerini was a graduate of L'Ecole de Gastronomie de Jacques Patou.

It was a night for celebrating, and the five of them, Lucille, Gordon, Wendy, Edie and Janet went to the one restaurant Lucille and Gordon had been dying to go to ever since they got to Paris, the frightfully expensive and very posh, La Tour D'Argent. They sat overlooking the Seine and the floodlit Notre Dame cathedral, and gushed through the entire meal over the Dresden china, the elegant service, and the marvelous food. "Oh, this potage Claudius Burdel is divine," and "the texture of this lobster Quenelle is extraordinary" and "this pressed duck is perfection."

The next morning, the girls began to pack. They had decided to drive to Florence. It was a chance to explore more of Europe, see the countryside, who knew when they would have another opportunity, and there was no urgency to get to Florence, except if their money ran out. So they put what they could in their valises, and put the rest in boxes, Janet's cookbooks, Wendy's toys, Janet's heavy metal pot, her skillet and knives, her sieves and casserole and cooking utensils, and Edie's quimper vase. Everything else would be left behind. They got their maps, planned their route, rented a Renault, had a farewell dinner with Gordon and Lucille at their favorite neighborhood bistro, and waited one extra day, hoping they could get a glimpse of Jacqueline Kennedy, who was visiting Paris with her husband. And sure enough, waiting on the packed street amid the cheering Parisians, Jacqueline Kennedy's entourage passed right in front of them and she waved to Janet, Edie and Wendy and they waved back to her.

And then the next day they were off to Italy.

They decided to drive through France to Nice, then along the Riviera, cutting inland to Pisa and then on to Florence. The drive through France was beautiful, the perfectly manicured countryside with the red-roofed little towns, steepled churches, cows on the hills, and flowers, purple, white, pink, orange, blooming everywhere. They stopped frequently for Wendy to go to the bathroom, or to read the menu of some quaint little cafe they passed, or to have a meal. They only ate at charming restaurants that had something interesting to eat. They didn't eat just because they were hungry, but for the ambiance, the adventure. And they were seldom disappointed. They stopped overnight in Lyon and spent the whole next day at an outdoor market and browsing the restaurants, patisseries, butcheries, charcuteries.

"If only the restaurants in the United States were half as good as they are here," Janet said.

"That's going to be your job," Edie said.

"Oh sure, I'm going to change all the restaurants in the United States, single handed."

"Why not?" Edie said. "May as well reach for the moon; the worst you'll do is end up with a few stars."

"You should be a poet," Janet said.

"One poet in the family is enough," Edie said, thinking of Zola and wondering how he was.

They spent another full day in Nice, sun bathing on the stony beach, and then drove through

Monaco, hoping that they might spot Princess Grace, which didn't happen, to San Remo and along the Italian Riviera. It was gorgeous, the blue Mediterranean on one side, the mountains on the other, the countryside, a patchwork quilt of different colors, and fruit trees, olive trees and vineyards. Then they were in Pisa and climbed to the top of the leaning tower and dropped two stones from the top and sure enough they both hit the ground at the same time. And then they drove on to Florence.

It had taken a week to get there, and by the time they found Janet's uncle's apartment, it was late, and the three travelers were exhausted.

Still when Janet saw her Aunt Silvia, her Uncle Carlo, her cousin Stefano, she felt a burst of energy and sadness, too. She had not seen them since the resettlement camp, fourteen years ago. And seeing their faces, her aunt and uncle a little older, Stefano, now all grown up, a young man of 19, she could not help but remember all the days they had spent together, in Florence before the war, and after, in the Villa and then in the cellar of that stone farmhouse where the worst night of Janet's life had taken place. There was much joy and so much pain...so much to reminisce.

Carlo and Stefano carried the girls' valises and boxes into the two bedrooms that had been set up for them, while Silvia sat the girls down in the kitchen and fed them tea and cookies and fruit and cheese. When Edie could no longer keep her eyes open, Silvia took her and Wendy to the bedroom they would share, turned down the cover, plumped the pillows, expressed concern that they would not be comfortable, promised they would get another bed tomorrow, apologized again that Wendy and Edie would have to sleep in the same bed, wished them a buena notte, and then closed the light and shut the door.

Edie wrapped her arms around Wendy. She was so happy to be in this warm and wonderful home, the whole world seemed bright to her, and she fell asleep instantly, with not one thought of Mike Kelly for the first time since that afternoon at the Hotel Barbizon.

In the kitchen, Janet and her relatives talked late into the night. They talked about Janet's mother, her life in Detroit, how she had come to go to cooking school in Paris, her plans for the future, and then they talked about the past, those days at the villa, the time they had spent in the cellar, and all the while they were hugging each other, crying a little, laughing a little. Finally Silvia insisted Janet go to sleep and took her off to her bedroom, tucked her in, kissed her good-night, and Janet fell asleep, thinking how thankful she was that she had decided to come to Florence. But her last vision before she fell asleep was of Mike Kelly.

Chapter Eleven

The Freni's apartment was on the first floor of a four-story building on Via Lamarmora, a narrow cobblestone street, in a lovely neighborhood of Florence. But wasn't every neighborhood in Florence lovely? The apartment was roomy, four bedrooms, fortunately for Edie and Janet, and furnished with heavy mahogany wood, dark brocaded fabrics, and little lace doilies like Zola's mother had crocheted.

Silvia, Carlo, and Stefano Freni were as sweet and loving as they had seemed that first night. Edie could not get over how they took the three of them in and accepted them as family, how they fussed over Wendy, brushing her long black hair, reading story books to her, and taking her for gelate every afternoon.

Edie and Janet wanted to see all there was to see in Florence, all the galleries, the churches, the piazzas, the parks, so between looking for jobs, they went exploring every day, sometimes with Silvia and/or Stefano, but usually just the two of them and Wendy. Edie and Janet took turns pushing Wendy's stroller, and went peeking in all the little shops, visiting the Piazza Mercato Centrale open air market, reading the menu posted outside of every restaurant, and Janet going inside the better ones to see if they needed a cook. They always knew exactly where they were by the Duomo, the great red dome that was the centerpiece of the city.

They left early in the morning, but they were always back in time for Silvia's lunch.

Silvia was amazing. Not only did she work in Carlo's leather goods shop, but she did all the cleaning in the apartment, and she cooked an enormous lunch each day. She made her own soups and pastas and while salads were not common at Italian meals, Silvia made a chopped antipasto salad, a recipe passed down to her from her mother, chopped lettuce, tomatoes, black olives, proscuitto, salami, provolone cheese, mortadella, to which she added garbanzo beans, pepperoncini, and tossed with salt and pepper, olive oil and balsamic vinegar. Edie could have made a meal of that salad alone, but it usually appeared after soup and pasta and veal or chicken. Still, she managed to eat enough of it to know it was the best salad she had ever eaten.

After a week in Florence, Edie was beginning to worry that they would never find jobs, when Janet went in to check on a job at the Ristorante Vittorio, just a few blocks from the Freni's apartment, and didn't come out for twenty minutes. Just as Edie was about to go in and see if Janet was all right, she came bursting out of the front door, beaming. "Guess what," she told Edie, "I got the job!"

Edie was more excited than Janet. "Oh, Janet," she said, hugging her, "I'm so happy for you."

"And more good news," Janet said, "they need a waitress."

Edie had been making calls trying to get a job teaching English somewhere, but being a waitress at the same restaurant where Janet worked was the best job she could think of. "Wait here," she told Janet, as she pushed open the door to Vittorio's Ristorante.

It was dark inside but beautiful. High ceilings, white-washed walls, dark-wood furnishings, white cloth tablecloths and napkins on every table, and at the far end, a bar, and the swinging doors into the kitchen. A tall man with an enormous mustache was seated at the bar.

He stood when she approached, and took her hand in his, "I am Vittorio," he said in English, "and you are Janet's friend?"

"Yes," she said, "I'm Edith Stern, your new waitress."

He smiled, exposing a full set of large white teeth, "You and your friend are very persuasive."

"You won't be disappointed," Edie said. "Janet's the greatest cook in the world."

"I am impressed with her Certificate from Jacques Patou," Vittorio said.

"If you're impressed with that," Edie said, "wait until you taste her food."

"Tell me," Vittorio said, "do you speak Italian?"

"I'm getting better at it every day," she said in English, and then added in Italian, "La mia famiglia mi insegnia."

He smiled, "Good. You're hired." He gave her two black dresses and two white aprons, one to wear while the other was being washed, a copy of the menu to study, and a schedule of the hours she was to work: lunch from 12:00 to 2:30, supper from 7:00 to 11. It was perfect. Not only would she get a rest between shifts, but she would get to spend all afternoon with her daughter. Outside in the sunlight, Janet and Edie hugged again. It was all too wonderful to be true.

Back at the Freni's, they shared their good news with Silvia.

"I'm going to have to find a babysitter today," Edie told Silvia.

Silvia thought a moment, "You know, we are not so busy at the shop now. Everyone is on holiday. I could take the summer off and take care of Wendy."

"I can't ask you to do that," Edie said, touched by her offer.

"But I want to do it. Carlo can manage a few months without me. Then in September, you can find a babysitter."

Edie was overcome with gratitude. How could she be so lucky, to have found this family, to be living in Florence, and to have someone as wonderful as Silvia taking care of Wendy. "I don't know how to thank you."

"Don't thank me. It is my pleasure."

The next day, Edie and Janet began their jobs at the Trattoria.

From the first moment Edie began working, she loved everything about her job. She loved interacting with the patrons--doing whatever she could to make their dining experience as enjoyable as possible; she loved the hustle bustle in the kitchen; she loved hurrying back and forth through the swinging doors carrying steaming plates of delicious food to her customers; and she loved watching Janet busy with what she loved most to do in the world, cooking.

A few days after Edie started waitressing, Vittorio set her to work helping out in the kitchen. "Would you mind washing the lettuce?" Vittorio asked one day. And then the next, "Would you mind slicing the tomatoes?" And then, "Would you mind coming in an hour earlier tomorrow morning, and I will teach you how to make the bread? It's easy," Vittorio said. And the next morning, he assembled the ingredients, the flour, the oil, the mayonnaise, and she put them all together, kneaded them to the right consistency, waited for the dough to rise, spread the dough on large flat pans and popped them into the oven. It was easy. It was fun. Edie felt she was the luckiest girl in the world: she had Wendy, she had Janet, she had the Freni's, and now she had this fantastic job.

It was two weeks later that Edie realized something was terribly wrong. Her breasts were swollen, her nipples were getting darker, and she woke up one morning and vomited. "Oh, God," she said to herself, "this can't be happening to me again."

When she felt well enough to leave the bathroom, she got out her diaphragm and held it up to the light, pulling it taut. And there it was, the tiniest of pinpricks. She thought she would faint. "Oh my God. Oh no." She kneeled beside her bed, "Please dear God, please don't let me be pregnant."

And just like three years ago, each time she went to the bathroom, she prayed she would see blood on her panties, in the toilet, but again, she knew, she already knew, just as she had known with Wendy, she was pregnant...with Mike Kelly's child. The thought of that alone was enough to make her ill. But there was a way out, and this time she was going to avail herself of it. She didn't want to tell Janet she was pregnant--it seemed in some perverse way that she was one-upping Janet, that she had gotten pregnant and Janet hadn't, and then an awful thought struck Edie, what if Janet was pregnant too, and too ashamed or scared to tell Edie.

Edie had to find out. She waited until everyone was asleep and then knocked on Janet's door. "Janet, can I come in?"

"Sure," Janet said. She was sitting on the edge of her four-poster bed unlacing her white leather shoes.

"Janet, is everything all right with you?" she asked.

"Yes, of course. Why do you ask?"

Edie's tension increasing, "I think I'm pregnant with Mike Kelly's baby."

Edie could not read the expression on Janet's face. Was it shock, horror, or something else.

Janet, herself, didn't know what she was feeling. She didn't want to be pregnant. She didn't want the shame, the embarrassment; she couldn't bear the thought of going home to her mother with a little bundle of joy and her mother saying, "Aaach that Edie...I knew she would get you into trouble." And she didn't want anything to interfere with her plans to become a great chef. And yet, wasn't there the slightest stinging in her gut, that this wondrous thing had happened to Edie and not to her? "What are you going to do?" she asked.

"Get an abortion, of course," Edie said without hesitation.

And Janet, trying to help, "Perhaps Silvia knows of someone."

And Edie remembering the awful scene with her mother three years ago, said, "I hate to ask her."

"But who else can you ask?"

"No one," Edie said. And then she burst into tears and clung to her friend, Janet. It all seemed too much to go through, again.

The next day Edie forced herself to go to Silvia. She hated asking Silvia such a thing; she dreaded seeing the disappointment, perhaps the disgust, in Silvia's eyes. But what choice did she have? Go back to Detroit, tell her mother, "Guess what, mom, I'm pregnant again, only this time I'm going to have the abortion." No, she had to try Silvia first. "Silvia," she said, "I need your help."

"What is it, carina mia?"

Could she say the words, brand herself a slut again. "Silvia, I'm pregnant and I need to get an abortion."

For a moment Silvia seemed stunned. "Mama, mia," she said lifting her hands to her cheeks. And then, her eyes softening, "I would help you, of course, I would help you, but it is not so easy to get an abortion in Italy."

And Edie feeling desperate, "Isn't there any way you can find someone?"

And Silvia, not seeing anything as evil compared to what the Fascists had done said, "I will see what I can do."

Within a few days, the nausea had subsided, and Edie was feeling good again, terrific, in fact--the sunshine before the storm. Now, she began thinking about the child she was carrying. It was Mike Kelly's baby, and she hated Mike Kelly, but it was also her baby. Another little Wendy. What a mistake that would have been, not having Wendy. It wasn't this baby's fault that its father was a bastard. No matter what kind of man Mike was, the baby was going to be a sweet innocent creature. The baby was going to be just like Wendy. She thought of her parents and what they would say, and Frank. Her parents, she was sure, would forgive her once they saw the baby. And Frank already hated her; what more could he do, hate her more? Then she thought about Janet. How would Janet feel about her having Mike Kelly's baby? But none of it mattered. As with Wendy, she had already made up her mind. She could not destroy this baby growing inside her.

"I may have found someone," Silvia said triumphantly one afternoon when Edie returned from work.

And Edie, whose legs were more tired than usual, immediately sat down and put her feet up on the brocaded crimson ottoman. "I'm sorry to have put you through so much trouble, but I think I've changed my mind."

"Mama mia," Silvia said. "But what will you do?"

"I'm going to have the baby."

"But the father...."

"I don't want the father to know. I hate him."

"Ah, it is often so, in such cases," she said, nodding her head.

"Maybe I should go home," Edie said.

"You mean, to America?"

"Yes."

"If you want, but there is no reason you cannot stay here."

"But I don't want to be a burden on you."

"You won't be. We love having you, and the little bambina. You can't take her from us."

"You are so kind," Edie said, tears coming to her eyes, again so grateful to have found this wonderful family, the Frenis.

When Edie told Janet that she was going to keep the baby, Janet felt again that twinge of jealousy. If only it had happened to her, if only she was pregnant with Mike Kelly's child. But then she realized the idiocy of her feelings. The reality was, she would probably never get married, never have a child. Better put all that aside and concentrate on her job. Better try to be the best chef that she could be.

Janet had been hired as souschef to the head chef, Renzo, which was quite a feat for a woman. She knew of no other woman in any restaurant in Florence with such a responsible position. She worked ten hours a day, six days a week, from nine in the morning until 2:30, and then from 6:30 to eleven. Fortunately, Vittorio supervised the break-down, so that at eleven o'clock, when the patrons were sipping their café latta or espresso, and finishing their cheese and fruit, Janet could go home, by then dead tired, craving only to take a hot bath and go to sleep, because the next morning she had to again be at the restaurant by nine a.m.

At first Janet's jobs were menial, cutting the vegetables, butchering the meat, cleaning the fowl and fish, but then she began making the pasta, fresh each day, and going to the open air markets to choose the vegetables, fruits, and spices, and then she began cooking the sauces, combining fresh tomatoes, fresh basil, rosemary, oregano, fresh garlic. She watched Renzo as he grilled the bistecca (t-bone steak) in olive oil and pepper, fried the fish, sautéed the veal, molded the spinach and simmered the risotto. Italian cooking did not use the five mother sauces that the French did, and olive oil was used instead of butter in many instances. Italian cooking concentrated on the flavor of the meat, fowl, fish, vegetables, more than on the sauce. But being a great cook still meant knowing how to blend the flavors just right, knowing what seasoning would best enhance the flavor of a particular item, and cooking it to the exact moment of doneness.

Until Vittorio hired Janet, he had been serving only fruit and cheese for dessert, but now he decided to turn Janet loose. "Buy whatever you need and let's see what you can do."

So she purchased her ingredients, fresh cream, sweet butter, fresh eggs, fresh apples and berries, and set to work. She made an apple tart; she made a babba au rhum, she made creme brule' and creme caramel, and gradually, the patrons began ordering these desserts in addition to their fruit and cheese. "Who is your new chef?" they wanted to know. And the restaurant began filling up earlier and earlier for dinner, as people who came late were turned away, and then earlier at lunch, and finally, Vittorio had to set some tables and chairs outside, because there was not enough room in the ristorante. Florence was a sophisticated city, but the people were excited about the new pastries at Vittorio's, and were startled to discover the "new chef" was a woman.

Janet was excited that people liked her pastries, but she was more excited about all she was learning from Renzo.

By the end of July, Janet was too tired from working, and Silvia was too tired from babysitting, to do any more sightseeing so it fell to Stefano to be Edie and Wendy's exclusive tour guide. If Wendy was going, they would take Silvia's Fiat, but if Wendy was napping, Edie and Stefano would zip about the city on Stefano's Vespa.

Stefano, on summer holiday from the University where he was studying to be a doctor, was only 19, but seemed older. He had wavy blond hair which he wore long, almost to his shoulders, blue-green eyes that changed color depending on the shirt he was wearing, and dimples in his cheeks when he smiled. He was quiet, gentle, intelligent. Much like Frank had been when he was a boy, Edie thought.

Edie knew she would never forget the first time Stefano took her and Wendy up to the Piazza Michelangelo for a view of "his" city, the city of flowers. She had been there before, but it had never looked so beautiful. With the sun casting a rosy glow on the red tile roofs, the towers and the spires, it was a dazzling sight. More enchanting, perhaps, then the view from the top of the Eifel Tower. "There are three Davids in Florence," Stefano told Edie pointing to the statue. "This one is a copy. Tomorrow I will show you the original."

The next afternoon, he drove Edie and Wendy to the Academy, and at the end of a long hall, enshrined in its own domed sunlit room, there it was, the original David. More moving than any statue Edie had seen at the Louvre. It looked to be about 15 feet high, and one could see every muscle, every tendon, the strength, the power, and yet the innocence of David.

"It's very beautiful, no?" Stefano asked. His English was excellent--he had studied it in school.

"Yes," she said, "only beautiful isn't an adequate word. It's overwhelming."

After, they walked in the park. "I've never been so taken by a sculpture before," Edie said.

"You must have seen a lot of them in Paris."

"Yes, Winged Victory, the Pieta, and lots that I didn't recognize or pay much attention to. I guess this is the first time I really stopped and looked, or else the statue itself is so compelling, that it makes you stop and look."

"I've grown up with it, and yet each time I see it, the effect is just as great. I feel not only David's power, but Michelangelo's."

She was impressed with his sensitivity. "I can't imagine any 19-year-old in the States saying that," she said.

"Perhaps I am old for my years," he said.

"You don't want to be old," she said. "Enjoy being young."

They bought gelates and headed home.

After seeing all of Stefano's favorite sights at least twice, Stefano and Edie settled on spending most afternoons taking Wendy to her favorite places: Boboli Park, rowboating on the Arno, and most often to the Giardino Dei Semplici. They would usually take a walk through the botanical gardens and then sit on a bench talking while Wendy played with the other children.

One of these afternoons, Edie asked Stefano about his childhood, the time he spent in hiding with Janet. "If you want to talk about it," she said.

"I don't mind," he said. "You know my recollections are hazy. I was just a child, Wendy's age. But I do remember being together with Janet's family at the villa. And I do remember her father giving us lessons. And I can't forget that horrible cellar and the night the German soldiers came. But Gianna must have told you about that."

"Some of it, yes. But go on."

"We were all hiding in the coal bin, the same place we went to the bathroom, and I was shaking so hard, I thought they would hear my bones rattling. They kicked in the cellar door, and then there was a shot, and I thought Gianna was dead. That we were all going to die."

He paused and Edie felt as she had when Janet told her this story, that she wanted to take him in her arms and protect him from anything bad that might happen to him in the future.

He seemed lost in reverie for a few minutes and then began talking again, "The next night, we had to leave. We were all stuffed into an old truck and covered with hay. I remember that I was choking to death from the dust, but we could not make a sound, and just when I thought I was going to expire, the truck stopped and they uncovered my parents and me and hurried us into an old stone farmhouse, where we stayed hidden until the end of the war. Gianna and the rest of the family were taken to another farmhouse."

"How terrible it must have been for you," Edie said.

"Yes, but I haven't told you the good part, the day the Americans arrived. My father took me into the kitchen, opened the door, and I ran across the field, waving my arms and screaming my lungs out, 'We're free, we're free' right into the arms of an American soldier." He smiled. "How we loved the American soldiers. They were so kind to us and gave us candy bars and gum." And then serious, again. "Of course, later when we were reunited with Janet's family in the resettlement camp, Janet's father became very ill. He must have contracted tuberculosis there. He was very thin and coughing up blood, but no one could do anything to help him. Finally he was taken to a hospital and it was there he died." He took a moment before he said, "The irony of it, the Germans couldn't kill him, but the resettlement camp did."

Edie pulled her knees up to her chest. "Maybe that's why you want to be a doctor, because of your uncle's death."

"Maybe."

Then, looking into Stefano's blue eyes, blue today because he was wearing a blue shirt, Edie said, "Well I'm glad you turned out to be such a positive person, in spite of all you suffered as a child."

"I am glad to hear you say that. Sometimes I worry that I am too.." he groped for a word, "melancholy."

"No, not at all. You're absolutely delightful." She smiled and watched for his dimples to appear as he smiled back.

Edie enjoyed spending time with Stefano. They never ran out of things to talk about. They talked about history, politics, the United States, art and music. He knew so much for someone so young.

In September, Silvia went back to work in Carlo's leather goods shop, Wendy started nursery school, and Stefano returned to the University.

Edie thought that once Stefano was back in school, she would see less of him, but there he was, almost every afternoon when Edie got off work, waiting for her on his Vespa, much as Stanley had waited for her in his green Plymouth at the ballet school. When she saw him, her heart would leap as it had when she had seen Stanley, but it had nothing to do with romance. She was just glad to see him. She'd hop on the Vespa behind him, and with her arms wrapped around his firm body, her hair blowing about her face, they'd scoot through the narrow streets, over the bridges, past the Piazzas, through the parks. She felt sixteen again. Until it was time to pick up Wendy from nursery school.

It didn't worry Edie that she looked forward to seeing Stefano's Vespa parked outside the ristorante, and it didn't worry her that she loved going riding with him, and talking with him, and going for walks with him, because it was all so innocent.

Until one afternoon, when Edie was in her fifth month, already wearing maternity clothes, and she and Stefano were sitting on a bench in the Giardino Dei Semplici and giggling about the fact that they were getting stares from all the passersby, as if they couldn't figure out if the two of them were married or not, when Stefano leaned over and kissed her on the mouth, and for an instant, Edie let herself go, felt a stirring in her body, and then, realizing what she was doing, pushed him away. "Stefano, stop. What do you think you're doing?"

"Kissing you," he said.

"Well, you shouldn't be kissing me."

"Why not?" he asked.

"Because you're 19 and I'm 25."

"What has age to do with it?"

"Everything!" she said. "You must never do that again, do you understand?" And without waiting for a reply, Edie stood up and marched back to the Vespa.

Without a word, Stefano put on his helmet and followed her.

If he was angry, then good, Edie thought, getting on the Vespa behind him. Anything to widen the distance between them.

That night, Edie lay in her bed, unable to fall asleep, looking at Wendy sleeping in the bed next to hers, and thinking about that kiss. Had she been kidding herself again? Pretending that she didn't have feelings for Stefano? Thinking that their relationship was nothing more than friendship? But after that kiss today, she could fool herself no longer. That kiss had awakened feelings she didn't know she had. They were nothing like the feelings she had for Mike Kelly. She could see now that Mike Kelly was pure sex. What she felt for Stefano was different, deeper. He was such a charming and sensitive young man, how could any woman *not* be attracted to him? But she was not any woman. She was six years older than he, with a child, and another on the way. She must not let her feelings get the better of her. Not just for Stefano's sake, but for Silvia and Carlo. She must never do anything to hurt Silvia and Carlo.

Two days later, she and Stefano walked to the Ponte Vecchio, where after browsing the jewelry shops, they walked to the edge of the bridge, and were leaning on the railing, looking down at the Arno, green and muddy today, when Stefano put his hand on hers. "Edie, I must tell you something. I am in love with you."

She turned to look at him. His face was red, from the sun, or embarrassment? "No, you're not," she said. "Don't ever say that again."

"But I am. I am in love with you and I want to marry you and take care of you and Wendy and the new baby."

She was so moved by his words that she could hardly speak, "Oh, Stefano, you're so sweet, and kind, but whatever you feel for me, it isn't love. I'm sorry if I led you on, but you must realize that if you married me it would ruin your life."

"I don't see how," he said.

"How would you go to college? Become a doctor?"

"I don't care about that now. I only want to take care of you."

"Stefano, please don't talk like that."

"I've already thought it out. I'm going to quit school and get a job working for my father."

"No, Stefano. You are not going to quit school. You are going to be a doctor. I don't want to discuss the matter ever again, and if you ever bring it up again, I'm going to leave Florence."

His eyes, green today, because he was wearing green, clouded over. Was it tears? "All right," he said, "I will do as you say. But will you do me one favor?"

"What is that?"

"Let me kiss you one last time?" He was like a little boy asking for one more piece of candy.

"No," she said, and then seeing the forlorn look on his face, she said, "Okay, once more, but never again."

He put his arms around her, and there on the Ponte Vecchio, in the bright sunlight, with the whole world to see, he kissed her again, gently, sorrowfully, until she had to push him away.

The people walking past were snickering, and smiling. And Edie wondered, what must they be thinking seeing this beautiful young man kissing this pregnant older woman?

As they began to walk back down the bridge, she said, "From now on we're just friends, okay?"

He smiled his dimpled smile, "Is it all right for friends to hold hands?"

"I don't think that's a good idea," she said.

"One last time?" he asked, in such a plaintive voice that she could not deny him.

"All right," she said, "one last time." And he took her hand and did not let go until they reached the apartment.

From that day on, he did not mention love or marriage again, and he did not try to kiss her, but she knew what his feelings were, in the touch of his hand, in the look in his eyes, a palpable energy connecting him to her. She hated herself for it, but she could not help thinking about him, wondering what it would be like to hold him in her arms, to feel his firm young body against hers. Sometimes she romanticized about marrying him. They could live with Silvia and Carlo until the baby was born, and then get their own apartment and hire a babysitter for Wendy and the baby. She would continue working at the restaurant while he went to medical school, and she would live in Florence happily ever after for the rest of her life. What was six years anyway? When they were old and gray it wouldn't matter. One night when she was dozing, half awake, half asleep, she even imagined their wedding. It would take place at the great synagogue. She would be wearing a white gown, her belly protruding in front of her, waddling down the aisle. Janet, her maid of honor, and Wendy her flower girl, both in pink, would be leading the way. Stefano and Carlo in black tuxedos, and Silvia in a long green satin gown would be standing under the Chupa waiting for them. And then as Edie got closer and closer to the chupa, she saw the look of horror in Silvia and Carlo's eyes. She jumped up, wide awake. No, no, such a thing must never happen. She had no right to all these fantasies, all these dreams. No matter what she felt about Stefano, or thought she felt, he was off-limits to her.

In November, when the weather turned cold and rainy, Renzo informed Vittorio that he was leaving, going to a restaurant in Milano. Janet held her breath. What would Vittorio do? Hire a new chef, or perhaps, perhaps...she didn't dare think it. That evening at 11 o'clock as Janet was leaving, Vittorio approached her and said, "You know, Janet, there are no women chefs in Firenze," Janet steadied herself for the bad news, "how would you like to be the first?" His face broke into a wide grin, his big white teeth flashing at her.

"Oh Vittorio," she said, hugging him. "Yes. Yes." She didn't want him to see her cry, but she couldn't hold back her tears of joy. It was really happening. She was really going to be the chef in a top restaurant in Florence!

Edie and the Freni's were overjoyed with Janet's news, and the following week Silvia and Carlo brought Stefano and Wendy to dinner at Vittorio's Trattoria to celebrate Janet's promotion. Little Wendy was all dressed up in a pink and white dress, black patent shoes, and a pink bow in her long black hair. Janet in her white pants and shirt and her white chef's hat cooked for them and Edie in her black dress and white apron waited on them.

Now Janet began working even longer hours, while Edie, who was finding it increasingly difficult to be on her feet, went to Vittorio and asked if she could work less. Vittorio understood. He told her to come in later, leave earlier. He hired another waitress and gave Edie more to do in the kitchen so that she wouldn't have to run back and forth taking orders and carrying food. But as November turned into December, she was feeling more and more guilty. She was already a burden on Vittorio, and the closer she got to her due date, the greater burden she was going to be on the Frenis. Soon she wouldn't be able to work, or pay Silvia and Carlo for her room or food, and after the baby was born, they would have to take on the full responsibility for her and Wendy and the new baby. And then there was the problem of Stefano. He was still picking her up from work most afternoons, and picking her and Janet up every night after work in Silvia's Fiat because he didn't want them to have to walk home in the cold. And while he hadn't said anything, she knew by his look, his occasional touch, that nothing had changed in his feelings toward her. She knew it couldn't go on forever like this; sooner or later, the dam was going to burst.

She dreaded going home to face her mother and father and Frank. She didn't want to leave Janet or the Frenis. She didn't want to leave this warm, safe place where she was loved, and she didn't know if she had the strength to make all the decisions and take all the actions necessary to leave Florence. But she knew she had to leave.

She told Janet the next evening. It was midnight and the two of them were in Janet's room, Janet lying on the bed, her feet up on a pillow, and Edie sitting at the foot of the bed; she was always looking to sit whenever possible.

"Janet," Edie said, "there's something I have to tell you. I've decided to go home."

Janet sat up on one elbow, "Oh, Edie, you're not going to leave me."

Edie averting Janet's eyes, "I don't want to leave, but I feel I must."

"But the Freni's don't mind about the baby. They want you to stay."

"I know they do," and then meeting the puzzled look on Janet's face, "but there are other considerations."

Janet lay back on her two puffed pillows. She had suspected something was going on between Stefano and Edie, and now she knew. "I understand," she said. And then after a moment of thought. "I should go with you."

"You mean, leave Vittorio?"

"No, I can't do that. Vittorio is depending on me. I meant go home for a visit. I should see my mother. It's been such a long time. I never dreamed when we left Detroit that we would stay away so long."

"That would be great," Edie said with enthusiasm. "You could fly home with me. I could use the help."

"Except that I can't go now. I can't leave Vittorio when we're so busy. Maybe in August when things are slower." Now Janet hesitated. "There is something else..."

And Edie concerned, "What is it?"

"Something I've wanted to do from the time we arrived in Florence."

"And what is that?"

"I want to go visit the farmhouse," her voice faltering. "You know, where I was in hiding."

And hearing the trepidation in Janet's voice, Edie asked, "Do you want me to go with you? Because if you do, I could stay an extra week or two."

"No," Janet said, "I've given it a lot of thought, and I think I need to go alone, if I can get up the courage to go."

"Are you sure you don't want me to go with you?"

"I'm sure, but thanks for offering." And then changing from one unhappy subject to another, "So, when are you leaving?"

"As soon as I can get a plane ticket."

"You know," Janet said, "this will be the first time we'll be apart since we met in teacher training."

"I know," Edie said.

"I don't know how I'm going to survive without you," Janet said.

"You will," Edie said. "We both will. We have to." Then lifting herself off the bed, "Would you like me to visit your mother?"

"I don't think that's a good idea," Janet answered. "She's not very happy with you."

"But maybe I could explain, make her see..."

"I don't think so. Anyway, I don't want to find out how much trouble I'm in with my mother."

And Edie, suddenly feeling very heavy with the baby, said, "I'm sure not as much trouble as I'm going to be in with mine."

The next night sitting around Silvia's lace covered dining room table, Edie told the Freni family that she was leaving, going back to Detroit, probably within the week. "I really want to be with my parents when the baby is born," she explained, hoping that Stefano would not think her decision had anything to do with him. Silvia and Carlo seemed disappointed that she was leaving. They said there was no reason for her to go, that they were more than willing to help her through the childbirth and with the infant after, but they understood her wanting to be with her family at a time like this, and Stefano, after waiting an acceptable amount of time, left the table without a word and went to his room.

Edie helped Silvia with the dishes, and then went to Stafano's room, and knocked on the door.

"Avanti," he said. She entered and closed the door behind her. He was sitting on the bed. "You could have told me," he said.

"I just did," she said.

"I mean, alone. Prepared me."

"I'm sorry, Stefano. But you knew nothing would ever happen between us."

"No," he said. "I thought it would. I thought...in time."

"Well, you thought wrong," she said.

Tears filled his eyes. "What am I going to do without you?"

She felt her insides crumble. She walked over to him and he put his arms around her waist and rested his head on her protruding belly. She stroked his wavy blond hair, "You will find some nice young girl to love."

"Never," he said. "I'll never love anyone but you."

"You will," she said. "You'll see." She wanted to tell him how much he meant to her, how much she would miss him, but she couldn't do that.

"Will you write to me?" he asked.

"I'm not very good at writing letters," she said. "But I will keep in touch with your family."

"When I'm graduated, and when I'm a successful doctor, I'm going to come to the United States. I'm going to find you."

She lifted his head, took out her hanky, wiped the tears from his cheeks, and looked into his blurred blue-green eyes. "Stefano, you must accept the fact that we are never going to be together. You must forget me."

"I'll never forget you," he said.

"Yes you will. In time you'll see that it was only your kindness that drew you to me. It isn't love, Stefano. You must believe me." She pulled herself away from him, made her way out his door to her room, where Wendy was sleeping peacefully. She leaned down and kissed her daughter's forehead, then walked to her bedroom window and looked out at the narrow cobblestone street. It was as dark and empty as she felt. And then she whispered the words she had never allowed herself to think, the words no one must ever hear her say. "I do love you, Stefano. More than anyone will ever know."

The next morning, she told Vittorio that she would probably be leaving within the week, and then spent the next few days making travel arrangements, packing, and finally, calling Detroit. She had rehearsed what she would say over and over again, but still her voice was trembling when she gave the operator her parents' phone number. She caught them just as they arrived home from a poker game, and when she had them both on the line, she told them that she and Wendy were coming home, gave them the airline, flight number and time, waited for their elation to subside, and then said, "There's something else I have to tell you. I'm pregnant and I'm not married and I have no contact with the baby's father nor do I ever wish to talk about him again." For a full minute there was absolute silence and Edie wasn't sure if they were still on the line. Finally her mother said, "Oh my God, this can't be happening again."

All of Edie's resolve to remain cool and objective, vanished. "Mom, dad, I'm so sorry to put you through all this again."

Another long pause, and then her father's voice.   "It's all right, Edie. We'll work it out. As long as you and Wendy are coming home."

Her dad's kind words made Edie feel even worse.

"Yes, of course, we'll work it out," her mother said in a scolding tone to Ben, and then to Edie, "Haven't we always stuck by you?"

Maybe not always, Edie thought, but this wasn't the time to bring that up. "Yes, you have," she said.

"What month are you in?" her mother asked.

"My seventh."

"God in heaven," her mother said. "And you never breathed a word."

"I didn't want to worry you."

Edie waited for a snide retort to that remark, but it didn't come.

Instead, Lilly ventured in a rather hopeless tone, "You wouldn't consider making up some story, would you?"

"Like?"

"Like you married an Italian and then got divorced."

And Edie still doubting that anyone would believe any story they made up, but wanting to do whatever she could to make this as easy as possible for her parents, said, "Yes, of course, I can go along with that."

"And what about the name?" her mother asked, sounding a bit more confident. "What are you going to name the baby? I mean the last name."

Edie remembered the fight about Wendy's last name. "The baby's last name will be" and in a moment of inspiration, "Freni," she said, very proud of herself for thinking of it. Now, every time she looked at the new baby she would think of Stefano, instead of the dirty bastard who had impregnated her.

"Good," Lilly said. "I like the name Freni."

And Edie was sure that she heard both her mother, and her father on the extension, give a sigh of relief.

"Now what time is the plane arriving?" her mother asked.

"Eight-o-seven," Edie answered.

"I can hardly wait to see Wendy," her mother said.

Meaning, Edie supposed, that she could very well wait to see her pregnant daughter. "See you tomorrow," Edie said.

"Yes," Lilly said. "Yes," Ben said, "see you tomorrow."

The next day, the scene at the airport in Florence was heart-wrenching for Edie. She didn't know how she could part from all these people who meant so much to her.

She hugged each one of them, Silvia, Carlo, Janet and then Stefano.

"I'll come for you one day," Stefano whispered. "You'll see."

"Don't," she said, touching his cheek. "I won't be waiting for you."

She took Wendy from Silvia's arms, and said to her daughter, "Say goodbye to everyone."

"Goodbye Nonna, goodbye Nonno, goodbye Stefano, goodbye Aunt Janet," Wendy said.

Edie hurried to the steps leading onto the plane, and then turned once more to wave goodbye to them. Goodbye Silvia and Carlo, how can I ever repay you for your kindness? Goodbye Janet, my soul-mate. Goodbye Stefano, how touched I was by your love.

And then they were up the stairs and on the plane, and Edie was tucking a blanket around her daughter, and trying to control the tears that were now gushing from her eyes.

"Why are you crying, mommy?"

"Because I'm so sad to be leaving so many people we love."

"Then why do we have to go?"

"Because Grandma Lilly and Grandpa Ben love you so much and miss you so much that I promised them we would come for a visit."

"And can we see my daddy, too?" Wendy asked.

And Edie looking into her daughter's black eyes, knowing that probably would not happen, but not wanting to disappoint her, said, "Maybe we can."

Chapter Twelve

Edie's parents met her at the airport.

When they first looked at her, they didn't seem to see her. It was as if they were in a trance, and then they both sprang into action, running toward her and Wendy, hugging and kissing them. "It's so good to see you, we can't believe you're really here," they both said. Then Ben scooped up Wendy and led the way to the baggage claim.

Edie walked beside her mother. She could feel the tension between them. "What's wrong, mother?" she asked.

"Nothing's wrong," Lilly answered, nervously. "What makes you think anything's wrong?"

"I can tell something's bothering you."

Lilly hesitated for a moment, and then she blurted out, "You're so big."

Edie was immediately plunged into the place she'd been four years ago with Wendy, an outcast, a misfit, singularly unattractive. "I'm in my seventh month, mother, almost eighth. What did you expect?"

Again Lilly paused. "I didn't expect you to be so....big."

On the drive home, Lilly and Edie sat in the back seat of her father's yellow Buick, Lilly insisting on holding Wendy who fell asleep as soon as the car reached the expressway.

"She's so adorable," Lilly said, kissing Wendy's forehead. "I've missed her so much." And then turning to Edie, "So how are you feeling?"

"Good."

Again an awkward silence between them, until finally Lilly said, "Your dad and I would like to know something about the baby's father."

Edie thought about her answer. She wanted to give them an answer that would preclude any further questions, "He was a dirty, rotten bastard and that's all I'm going to say about him."

For a moment there was only the sound of the car's radiator and engine, and then Lilly said, "Oh Edie, how could you have gotten mixed up with someone like that? How could you have gotten pregnant, again?"

And Edie thought, why did I come home? But she knew the answer to that. "I didn't try to get pregnant, mother. I was using protection."

"Yes, but you weren't married. Why didn't you wait until you were married?"

And Edie turned angrily to her mother, "Do you think every girl waits until she's married? I'm sure that most of the girls in Detroit who are my age are not waiting until they get married."

"I bet Cookie waited," her mother said, defiantly.

Edie knew it was useless talking to her mother. It didn't matter what Edie said, there was no way she was going to come out a winner in this battle. She was 25 years old, already a mother, about to be a mother again, but her mother still had the knack of making her feel like a naughty little girl. "Maybe I shouldn't have come home."

Now Ben, who had been silent since the drive began, spoke up, "Of course you should have come home. Where else should you be? You're our daughter and we love you no matter what."

Yes, dad, I'm sure you do, Edie said to herself, but I'm not so sure about mother.

The second day Edie was home, Stanley Rader came to see her. She hadn't seen Frank yet, but apparently he had told Stanley that she was back.

"So you've gone and done it again," Stanley said, following her into her mother's den.

"What's that?" she asked, feigning perfect innocence.

"Gotten yourself knocked up," in a teasing tone.

"It isn't called 'knocked up' if you're married," she teased back.

"You don't expect me to believe that story."

She turned to face him, looking on him as a bit of light in her dreary homecoming, "Frankly, my dear, I don't give a damn."

"I don't think there's a 'my dear' in that," he said.

"I only read the book three times," she said.

"That doesn't mean you know everything," he said, plopping onto her mother's new blue sofa. "So how was Europe, and tell me about your Italian husband."

"Europe was wonderful," she said, "and I don't wish to discuss my Italian husband. Why don't you tell me about you?"

"Everything's great," he said. "But of course, you don't know about Thomas Sterling Rader." He pulled out his wallet and showed her a picture of a chubby blond baby that looked very much like Stanley.

Immediately she remembered Zola's words at Stanley's wedding. "I don't suppose he's adopted," she said.

"Definitely not adopted. I worked long and hard for that baby."

"He's adorable," Edie said. "You should send Zola his picture."

"Why?"

"To show him that he was right." And seeing the confused look on Stanley's face. "About you not adopting a baby."

"Oh that," Stanley said. "Say, speaking of Zola, have you heard from him lately?"

"Just the $25.00 he sends every week."

"You mean all the way to Italy and France."

"No. Fortunately I was making enough so that I didn't need it. My mother's put it away in a bank account for Wendy."

"I wonder how the old boy is doing," he said.

Edie pictured Zola as he had looked the last time she saw him at the Medford airport, and felt a touch of sorrow. "So do I," she said.

"You know there's one thing I don't understand," Stanley said, half-joking, half serious, "how come you have sex with everyone but me?"

She smiled, "I guess you're just the wrong guy at the wrong time."

"And how do I get to be the right guy?"

"As long as you're married, you don't."

"Well than I guess there isn't any point in my trying to seduce you."

She laughed, "Stanley, you can't mean that. Would you really want to go to bed with me and my fat belly."

"Some men find pregnant women attractive. I happen to be one of them."

She wasn't sure if he meant it or not. Could he still have feelings for her? More probably it was just his ego that needed to be satisfied. "Well then, no," she said, "there's no point whatsoever in your trying to seduce me."

Later, when she stood at the door, watching him drive off in his new green Oldsmobile station wagon, she felt a sense of regret. How different her life would have been if she had married Stanley. How easy. How normal. But then again, she probably wouldn't have met Janet. She wouldn't have gone to Paris or Florence. She wouldn't have had the experiences she had with Zola, or that man in Paris, or Stefano. And she wouldn't have Wendy or this little unborn child she was carrying.

She shook the bad feeling from her and closed the door. Perhaps where she was now, was better.

Chapter Thirteen

Two weeks after Edie left Florence, Janet decided it was time to make the journey to her past. She asked Silvia if she could borrow the Fiat and if Silvia would show her where to go on the map.

"I know the way to the villa and the first farmhouse, but I don't know where your family was taken after we were dropped off."

"That's all I'll need," Janet said.

"Do you want me to come with you?"

Janet appreciated Silvia's offer, but knew this was a journey she must take alone. "No," Janet said, "but thank you for asking."

On the following Sunday morning, Janet equipped with Silvia's map and Fiat, set out for the countryside.

She drove slowly. It was a cold and windy day and looked like it would snow any minute. Janet had borrowed Silvia's heavy wool coat and wore a scarf, wool hat, and wool gloves from Carlo's shop. She drove to the outskirts of Florence, and several miles along the highway, made a turn, and another, drove up the hill on a narrow road only big enough for one car--had she really traveled this road before--made another turn, traveled a gravel road, and there in front of her was the rusted iron gate, and beyond it the stone villa. The villa was not as large as she remembered it, and the garden was all weeds. Janet sat in the car for several minutes staring at the villa, and then slowly got out, walked warily up to the front door, and knocked with the large brass knocker. No one came to the door, so cautiously, she pushed it open and stepped inside. She felt that she was in a dream, transported back to those days when she was a little girl, running up the stone steps to the rooms on the second floor, playing in the garden, standing on the parapet and looking down at the little villages below. She heard the echoes of those voices, her papa, her mama, Stefano, Miriam, Peter. And then she listened for the sound of the planes. But there was none. It was silent. She walked back outside to the parapet and stood for several minutes looking down below, trying to feel how Gianna had felt those many years ago, but she felt nothing.

She got back in the car and following her map, began her drive to the farmhouse. She saw it from a distance and her temples began to throb. The closer she came, the more terrified she became. She didn't want to do this. She didn't want to go there. She wanted to turn the car around and head back to Florence where she was safe, but some perverse force propelled her forward. And then she was there. It had begun to snow, and through the white flakes, she saw the barnyard where a few chickens were pecking at the ground. Beyond that was the clump of bushes where she had gone to pet the puppies, and directly in front of her, stood the old stone farmhouse. There was smoke coming out of its chimney. Someone still lived here. What if it was Teresa and Salvatore? Janet's heart began to race. She wanted to see them, but dreaded seeing them. She parked the car and willed herself across the gravel path, up to the front door, and knocked. A woman she did not know answered.

"Do Teresa and Salvatore still live here?" Janet asked in Italian.

"No," the woman replied. "Not for many years."

"I lived with them for a few months," Janet said, "during the war. Do you think I could come in and see the cellar?"

"The cellar?" the woman asked, dumbfounded.

Janet knew it was a strange request and debated if she should tell the woman that she had been a Jew in hiding. Would it elicit sympathy or scorn. She didn't want either. "Yes, the cellar," she repeated. "My name is Gianna Camerini and I live in Florence."

The woman looked behind Janet to see if anyone was with her or waiting in the car. "Avanti," the woman said.

Janet entered the kitchen, surprised at how small it was. A black kettle was hanging over the walk-in fireplace, and there was a loaf of bread on the table.

Janet looked to the spot where Princessa had been shot. She saw the German raise his gun, she heard the sound of the bullet, and she saw Princessa leap up in the air and then fall to the ground. And Janet knew. She knew that she had killed Princessa.

"The stairs are over there," the woman said, breaking into Janet's thoughts.

"Yes, I know," Janet said and walked to them.

She made her way down the narrow cellar steps into the dark and dreary cellar and then over to the window that looked out onto the barnyard. She didn't want to remember, but everything she had tried so hard to suppress all these years came filtering back to her in pieces. She remembered her papa holding her on his shoulders, so that she could look out at the two dogs she loved so much, Nero and Pepe. She remembered the night Nero was not there and her papa told her, "Maybe she is having her puppies."

She remembered looking for those puppies night after night, climbing that rickety ladder while everyone else was asleep, until one night there they were, just outside the window, just beyond her reach.

She remembered creeping up the cellar stairs, unhitching the cellar door, pushing it open inch by inch so that it wouldn't creak. She remembered being hit with the fresh air, and following the puppies to the clump of bushes. She remembered seeing the black boots of the soldier. And then, she panicked. Oh God, what had she done, what had she done. She squeezed her eyes tight, trying to blot out that feeling of terror, and when she opened them she saw a little girl sitting in the clump of bushes, reaching for a puppy. A little girl who was herself, but not herself. A little girl who did not understand the consequences of her actions, who did not realize she was endangering the lives of everyone she loved. A little girl who only wanted to pet the puppies, to breathe a bit of fresh air. And Janet began to cry for that little girl, that poor, stupid little girl who had suffered all the years of her life for that one selfish act. And soon, Janet was not only crying for that little girl, but for Princessa, and for all of her relatives, her mama, her dead papa, her aunts, uncles, and cousins, all of them who had suffered through that terrible time.

Finally, when she gained control of herself, Janet climbed the cellar stairs into the kitchen, thanked the woman who had let her in, and walked out the front door. She looked around the yard and wondered where were the puppies? Were they all grown old and died by now? And then, she looked up at the dark, gray sky, and with the snow falling in her eyes, her hands clasped in front of her, she prayed, "Please dear God, forgive me. And please let me forgive myself."

She was shaking all the way back to Florence, and felt that she had not put anything to rest, but had only brought to the surface all her feelings of anger, terror, and shame.

The next day, she went immediately to Vittorio. "Vittorio, I need to take two weeks off to see my mother."

"In August, yes."

"No," she said, "not in August, now."

"But you see how busy we are."

"I know and I'm sorry," she said, "but I must go home and see my mother. How about one week?"

"One week I can manage. But not a day more."

She called the airline, she called her mother and she called Edie. She would be arriving on flight 710. Could Edie pick her up?

It was freezing in Detroit the night Janet arrived. She made her way across the frozen slush to Edie's waiting car, her father's yellow Buick.

"Oh, Edie, I'm so glad to see you."

"Me, too," Edie said, hugging Janet, "but get in the car. It's freezing out here."

Since her visit to the farmhouse, Janet could think of nothing else, and as soon as she was in the car, before Edie could say anything, she said, "I did it."

"You did what?"

"I went back to the farmhouse."

"Oh, Janet. How was it?"

"I want to tell you about it, but not now. I want to talk to my mother first."

"All right," Edie said. "Whatever you say."

When they arrived at Ida Camerini's red brick duplex, Edie asked, "Will I see you tomorrow?"

"No, not tomorrow," Janet said. "Tomorrow, I want to spend with my mother. But the day after, for sure."

Janet got her suitcase and inched her way up the icy walk, feeling a mixture of fear and excitement. She hoped that her mother would be happy to see her, that she wouldn't be too angry with her for staying away so long.

She used her key to turn the lock, pushed open the door, and called, "Mama, I'm here."

There was no hesitation from Ida. She enveloped her daughter in her arms, covering her face with kisses. "Gianna, Gianna, you're here." And Janet let go of everything. She was a little girl again, safe in her mother's arms. And both women began to sob.

The next morning after breakfast, Ida and Janet sat in the den talking. "Mamma, there's something I want to ask you. When the war began, when you knew the Germans were coming, why didn't you leave Florence?"

"Your father wanted to," her mother answered without a pause, "but it didn't seem there was any need. There was an armistice. We thought the war was over. We had a big celebration. Don't you remember? You helped me cook dinner."

"Yes, mama, yes, I remember that. But earlier. When I wasn't allowed to go to school, when Bianca and Rosa had to leave us. Why not then?"

Her mother seemed a little agitated. "Florence was our home. We had our apartment there, our furniture, our relatives, your father's business. One does not just pick up and leave. And we didn't know. We didn't know how it was going to be."

"Yes, I can understand that," Janet said, but in truth, Janet did not understand. She continued, "Mama, last week I went back to the farmhouse, you know, Teresa and Salvatore's."

Now her mother seemed upset. "Why, Janet? Why did you do that?"

"I felt I had to."

"Oh, Janet, you shouldn't have done that. You shouldn't have put yourself through such torture."

"Mama, you know all these years, I tried to forget that night."

"What night is that, my darling?"

"The night I went outside to see the puppies."

"You were just a little girl, Gianna, just a little girl."

"But I did such a terrible thing, mama. I put the lives of all of you in jeopardy, just to touch those puppies, just to hold them."

"You didn't understand. How could you understand?"

"I knew, mama, I knew how dangerous it was."

"Janet, come here," her mother said, patting the place on the sofa next to her. And Janet walked across the room and sat beside her. "Janet, you must stop thinking about all this. What is past, is past. Nothing that happened was your fault. It was mine."

"Mama, what are you talking about."

"Oh, Janet, you're right." Her eyes became glassy. "Papa begged me to leave Florence. They all wanted to go, Silvia, Sofia, but it was I who wouldn't go. I couldn't bring myself to leave my home, my furniture, my belongings. I am the one who put everyone's life in jeopardy. Me. Not you."

Janet took her mother's frail hands in hers, "Oh, mama, please don't blame yourself." And Janet wished she could take back everything she had just said. The last thing she wanted to do was bring her mother more misery. "You didn't know what was going to happen. If you had, you certainly would have left. Promise me that you won't blame yourself."

"But I do blame myself," her mother said. "I always have."

And looking into her mother's eyes, now red and swollen as they had been the night her papa died, Janet realized something she had never realized before, that all these years, ever since her papa died, her mother had not only been carrying the burden of loss, but of guilt. "Oh, mama," Janet said, "I should never have brought all this up."

"No, Janet, it's better. Now it's out in the open, I don't have to carry it inside me anymore."

"Then maybe we'll both have some peace," Janet said.

And cradling her daughter's head in her hands, Ida said, "I pray you are right."

The following Saturday, Edie drove Janet back to the airport. In many ways, it had been a wonderful week for Janet. She had gotten to see Miriam and Peter, Aunt Sofia and Uncle Alberto, Ann and Rudy--the cousins who had brought them over from Italy, Mrs. Landau, the landlady, and of course, Edie and Wendy. But it had also been difficult. Talking about the past with her mother had been the most difficult. But perhaps in the long run it would be good for both of them. Now that they had faced it head-on, perhaps someday they would be able to forgive themselves.

Now it was time to leave. Time to return to her job in Florence, time to say goodbye to the people she loved most in the world.

"Don't forget to call me as soon as the baby's born," Janet said to Edie, when Edie dropped her off at the airport.

"The very minute," Edie said.

"I can't believe I'm doing this," Janet said, "going off to Florence all by myself."

"I guess you're all grown up now," Edie said, thinking of a line from Pinocchio.

"But inside, I still feel like a little girl."

"You'll do fine," Edie said. "Just be kind to yourself."

"How does one do that?" Janet asked.

"Think of all the goods things in your life, and never the bad."

"Is that what you do?"

"It's what I try to do."

"Then I'll try, too," Janet said. And then, "Did I ever tell you that you're the best friend a girl could have?"

"Funny, I feel exactly the same way about you," Edie said.

"I love you," Janet said.

"I love you, too," Edie said.

The two friends hugged, not wanting to let go. Then each wiped away her tears, and Janet headed for the plane, wondering when they would see each other again.

Chapter Fourteen

Brian Matthew Freni was born March 2, 1962, almost four years to the day of Wendy's birthday. He was a small baby and he had his father's blond hair and blue eyes, but in spite of that, within a minute of holding him, Edie knew she had made the right decision. It was worth any price she would have to pay to have this precious little boy in her life.

As soon as Ben and Lilly saw Brian, they were as enamored with him as they had been with Wendy, and Lilly, looking through the window of the nursery, decided that it had all been worth it, all the agony of the past few months. For it had been agony for Lilly. From the moment she heard that Edie was pregnant again, she had been hysterical. She didn't know how she could go through all that again. She didn't want to tell anybody anything. She didn't want their stares, their pity, their contempt. She wanted Edie to stay in Florence, at least until the baby was born, but Edie wanted to come home--how could she say, no. And then once she saw Edie at the airport, once she saw how large she was, she had been horrified. How was she going to face everyone again? If they had laughed the first time, how much harder were they going to laugh the second time. Lilly wished that she could hide Edie in the house, that she didn't have to be seen with her in public, that she didn't have to be seen with her at all.

And Ben's attitude toward the whole thing infuriated Lilly even more. She couldn't understand how he could be so calm through it all. "Doesn't it upset you at all that your daughter is pregnant with her second illegitimate child?" she asked him.

"Whatever's done is done," Ben said. "We lived through Wendy, we'll live through this."

And now the baby was here, and he was such a sweet, adorable little boy that nothing else mattered.

"Isn't he beautiful, mom?" Edie asked.

"Beautiful," Lilly agreed.

Edie decided to write to Janet, instead of call--she didn't want to take the chance that Stefano might answer the phone--and she mailed pictures of Brian, but didn't mention his last name. She didn't want Stefano to feel any attachment to her or her baby.

Frank and Cookie came to visit Edie after she got home from the hospital, bringing with them their one-year-old son, David, and a gift for the new baby. Frank still seemed distant, but at least he had come.

"Thanks so much," Edie said, opening the gift, a blue sweater, hat and booties. "We can certainly use something blue. Everything I have is pink."

"I'd offer to give you some of David's things," Cookie said with an enigmatic smile, "but we're expecting another baby."

"Oh how wonderful," Edie said. "When?"

"In seven months," Cookie said.

"Well that's great," Edie said, feeling some warmth for her sister-in-law for the first time since she'd met her. "Maybe one of these days, we could get together. You know let the kids play."

"Oh, sure," Cookie said, "that'd be nice."

But Cookie never did call Edie after that night, and they never did get together, except when Lilly invited Frank and Cookie to dinner.

By the time Brian was three months old, Edie was ready to go back to work. It was obvious she was going to have to stay in Detroit for some time to come. Where could she go with two little kids to support? But she wanted to move out of her mother's house and get her own place as soon as possible. She didn't like the feeling that she was her mother's little girl, again. She felt stifled, stunted, as if she'd taken a step backward.

She had a teaching job lined up for September, but she didn't want to wait until then. She wanted to do something now, and one afternoon in June, she noticed a "Waitress Wanted" sign in the window of a local Pizzeria. It was called Luigi's, and she went in to apply.

"You have to talk to Luigi," the cashier said, pointing to a man sitting at a back table going over some papers.

She walked up to him. "Hi," she said, "my name's Edith Stern, and I've come about the waitress job."

Luigi looked like he'd eaten too much of his own pizza. He was fat, balding, and chewing an unlit cigar. He looked up at her, "You had any experience?"

"Yes, I waited tables at Vittorio's Trattoria in Florence."

He squinted at her. "Florence, Italy?"

"Yes," she said.

"My family's from Napoli," he said. "Were you there?"

And they began talking about Italy, and his family and her family, and of course, it was a foregone conclusion that she got the job. He was paying $2.00 an hour plus tips.

"If you're fast and give good service," he said, "you could make three, four extra dollars an hour."

"More than I'd make teaching," she said. "By the way, I am a teacher and I plan to go back to teaching in September."

"That's okay," Luigi said. "I only expected to hire a college kid anyway who would tell me she was quitting school and planning to work for me forever."

He took her into his office, gave her three white dresses and two red and white checked aprons, showed her the kitchen, gave her a copy of the menu to study, and told her to be back at five.

Edie was excited. She liked Luigi and she liked the idea of working in a restaurant again.

In spite of the fact that Luigi's was not always full, Edie made good money, averaging $4.00 an hour, and as the summer progressed, she toyed with the idea of continuing to work for Luigi even after she went back to teaching. If she just worked weekends, she could make enough to have her own apartment, put Wendy in nursery school, and hire a babysitter for Brian.

Besides she didn't want to leave Luigi. He was becoming more and more dependent on her. He hated doing the books. "I can never get anything to balance. I know what number should be coming out, but it never does." So she took over his bookkeeping. And then if someone didn't show up, or someone couldn't work, it fell to her to make the phone calls, to get a fill-in, or fill-in herself. If the dishwasher broke, Edie would wash the dishes. If the cashier didn't show up, Edie would work the cash register. And even the ordering, "Edie, maybe you could figure out how much pepperoni we need. I always order too much or too little." Luigi didn't have a chef in the sense that Janet was a chef, just a cook who knew how to throw a pizza. And the menu was very limited, just pizza and green salad, so there was no need for a real chef. But Edie had ideas. "You know, this is a really good location, and you have plenty of room, I think we could fill this place up."

"How?"

"Let's offer something the other Pizzerias don't offer."

"Like what?"

"How about an antipasto salad, or some terrific desserts, or some homemade bread?"

"As long as it doesn't cost money."

"You've got to spend money to make money."

"I'm barely covering my expenses now."

"I know," she said, "so we'll start with something inexpensive. How about an antipasto salad? It's something I could make, it wouldn't cost a lot, and it might bring the customers in."

"I don't like the word 'start'," he said.

"What have you got to lose?" she asked.

"My shirt," he said.

"I'll buy you a new one," she said.

He studied her for a moment. Should he trust this young, inexperienced girl? What did she know about the restaurant business? Except she had worked in Firenze. And she was smart. "Okay," he said, "we'll try it."

The next day she ordered the ingredients and when they arrived, she chopped the Italian salami, prosciutto, provolone, black olives, lettuce and tomatoes into bite sized pieces as Silvia had done, then added garbanzo beans and pepperoncini, tossed it all with a dressing of olive oil, vinegar, and parmesan cheese and put it on the menu: "Antipasto salad." Within two weeks, everyone was ordering it.

"Now," Edie said, "we've got to do something about the bread."

"What?"

"We're going to bake it fresh. Focaccia bread, all they can eat."

"You're going to make me go broke."

"No, because we're going to increase the price of the antipasto."

"The customers won't stand for it."

"Yes they will, because they're going to get the best bread they ever ate, free."

"And who's going to make this bread?"

"I am."

"You know how to make focaccia?"

"I learned it from Vittorio."

Again, should he trust her? So far she'd been right. But now this bread business, it was another big step. "Okay," he said, "let's try it."

It was September, school was starting, but without Edie. She couldn't go back to teaching now, not when she had started on this adventure with Luigi and there was still so much to do. She was climbing a mountain and she wouldn't be happy until she reached the summit.

"Are you sure you're doing the right thing?" her mother asked.

"Absolutely."

"But all your training, all your education."

"I love what I'm doing, mom. What more could I ask for?"

Edie decided to call Janet, instead of write, for the exact recipe. She was more anxious to get the recipe than she was afraid that Stefano would answer the phone. Besides, it would be good to hear Janet's voice again.

Fortunately, Janet answered the phone and when she heard the reason for Edie's call, she laughed, "You must really be into this restaurant stuff. It sounds like you're taking over Luigi's."

"And loving it," Edie said.

"What did your parents say about you not going back to teaching?"

"My father doesn't care what I do, and my mother thinks I'm crazy. But what else is new?"

"Sounds like business as usual."

"How are things with you?"

"Great. I still love working at Vittorio's and I don't have time for much else." A pause. "By the way, Stefano started medical school in September. He always asks about you."

Sweet, sweet Stefano.

"But don't let me prattle on. This call is costing you a fortune. Get a pencil and paper and start writing."

It took Edie a few tries to get the bread exactly right, but once it was put on the menu, it was an immediate success. Now, not only was the restaurant filling up on the weekends, but during the week. A lot of people ordered just the Antipasto because they got the focaccia free, but still they ordered wine and drinks, and "Luigi's" was making more money than it ever had.

Luigi would watch over Edie's shoulder each week when she added up the books, waiting for the final number, and each week he was surprised and delighted. "I can't believe we're giving something away free and making even more money."

"Now it's time to raise the prices of our pizzas."

"I'm scared, Edie," Luigi said.

"Don't be. It'll be all right. No one's going to let a dollar stand in the way of getting a bargain."

And Luigi laughed.

So the new menus were printed, with the higher prices, and it didn't make any difference in the number of customers. If anything, they were even more crowded.

Lilly was upset with how much time Edie was spending at Luigi's. During the day, Edie was home with the children, but every evening she was at Luigi's.

"It's not healthy," her mother said. "You're a young girl, you should be going out with friends."

"I don't have any friends," Edie said, which wasn't exactly true. She was still in touch with Sandy Stahler and Naomi Cohen.

"Then you should make friends. You should join organizations."

"I don't have time."

"Then you should make time. Maybe you'd like to join the Jewish Center."

And Edie gritting her teeth. "I am not going to join the Jewish Center. Please, mother, stop nagging me."

"So this is going to be your life? No friends, no husband, just Luigi's restaurant?"

Edie braced herself against the kitchen sink. "Mother, I'm sorry. I'm sorry if I haven't turned out the way you wanted me to be. I'm sorry if my life isn't the way you thought it would be. But I'm doing the best I can."

"It isn't fair," her mother said, "it eats me alive. Here my daughter-in-law has everything, a big diamond ring, a beautiful home. And my daughter has nothing."

"But I do have something. I have Wendy and Brian. I have Luigi's. And I have you and dad."

Her mother sat on a kitchen chair, "I wanted so much for you. You were such a smart girl. Such a good girl. I never thought you would end up like this."

"My life isn't over yet, mom. Don't bury me, yet. Maybe one day you'll be proud of me. But I'll have to do it my way."

"When have you ever done anything any other way?"

The Friday morning after Thanksgiving, Gordon Pratt called from San Francisco. "How's my favorite school teacher?" he asked.

"I'm not a school teacher anymore," she told him, "I'm running a restaurant!"

"No kidding!" Gordon said. "I didn't know it was contagious."

"Well I guess it is."

"Listen, the reason I called is to tell you, guess who's gotten a job as chef at a fancy French restaurant in Los Angeles?"

"You?"

"Right on the button. I'm moving there next week."

"Oh, Gordon that's wonderful. I've always wanted to see Los Angeles," she said.

"Well, come on out."

"How can I?" she said.

"Get a job out here."

"Too chancy," she said.

"Well, let me know if you ever change your mind. I'll do whatever I can to help you."

"Thanks for the offer," she said and hung up the phone thinking, what a lovely idea, moving to Los Angeles. But it was impossible. There were the kids to think of, and Luigi. There was no way she could leave Detroit now.

In December, Edie told Luigi they should fix the place up. "Buy some tablecloths, get some plants, put some fresh flowers on the tables. Maybe add some other items to the menu."

"Why?" Luigi asked.

"To make more money," Edie said.

"I don't know," Luigi said.

"I think we should make this into a real Italian restaurant. You know, serve pastas and chicken and veal."

"I'm happy just as it is."

"But we're so limited. There isn't a really authentic Italian restaurant in any of the suburbs. You could be it."

"It's too big a chance," Luigi said.

"How could it be a chance? Everyone would still come in for pizza and if they don't want to order the new dishes, they don't have to."

"But I'd need a chef. A real chef."

And Edie thought of Janet. It was obvious that Janet was too high powered for Luigi's. Still Edie wrote to her.

"Dear Janet,

I know this is a ridiculous request, but my little restaurant in Oak Park needs a chef. It's not a very impressive place at the moment; we only sell pizza, and Silvia's antipasto, and Vittorio's bread, but I think we could make it into something. Especially with you as chef. You'd be totally in charge, and we'd only put on the menu what you wanted.

Please give the Frenis my love." And then she struck the word "love" and replaced it with "regards."

Two weeks later, she got a letter from Janet.

"Dear Edie,

Thanks for the offer, but actually I'm considering a job in New York. Lucille Neumeier's got two restaurants interested in me. I think if I'm going to be really good, I have to go to New York. Of course I will stop in Detroit to see you and my mother on the way. My love to all, especially yourself and Wendy.

Janet"

Edie felt embarrassed. How had she had the nerve to ask Janet to work at Luigi's? Because she wanted her here so much. Because she wanted Luigi's to be a success.

A week later, Edie received another phone call from Gordon Pratt. "Guess what, our manager's given notice."

"So?"

"So you'd be perfect for the job. What with your experience in France and Italy."

"But I was a teacher in France and a waitress in Italy."

"Well he doesn't have to know that!"

"Gordon, you're incorrigible. Anyway, I have a job. A job I love."

"But it's in dull, boring Detroit. Come on out here where the sun shines 365 days a year."

Edie looked out the window at the pouring rain. That would be nice. "Sorry, Gordon, I can't do it."

"Well let me know if you change your mind. I'll even find you a place to live and a babysitter."

"You must be desperate," she said.

"Not desperate. I just think it'd be fun, being together again, and in the restaurant business."

This time when Edie hung up the phone, she was more tempted than the last time she had spoken to Gordon. A job managing a "fancy" restaurant in Los Angeles, a chance to get out of Detroit. But again, there were the same considerations as there had always been. Luigi and the children.

Brian had just had his first birthday, Wendy her fifth. Brian was walking, babbling, a sweet, happy little boy with fine blond hair and deep blue eyes. Wendy was still in nursery school, but already reading simple story books. Her long black hair was down to her waist, but she wouldn't let her mother cut it. Considering who her father was, Edie wondered if the desire to grow hair could be hereditary.

And then one evening at dinner, Wendy asked her mother, "Mommy, what's a bastard?"

Everyone at the dinner table went silent--Edie, her mother, her father. Only Brian continued to babble.

"Why do you ask, honey?" Edie said.

"Because Janie down the street said I was a bastard."

The blood rushed to Edie's face and she began to tremble. She could handle any insult to herself, but she could not handle one to her child. "It means you don't have a daddy," Edie said, as calmly as she could. "Janie thinks because your daddy doesn't live with us, you don't have a daddy. But you do."

Wendy put a forkful of mashed potatoes in her mouth. "I know. Zola is my daddy."

"Right," Edie said, with a big smile.

"She said my brother was a bastard, too," Wendy said.

Edie thought about what she could do. She could go down the street and punch Janie's mother in the nose, or she could go down the street and tell Janie's mother what a cruel, heartless person she was, or she could move out of her mother's house to a different neighborhood where no one knew her. But that might be impossible in Detroit. Didn't every person in Detroit know who she was and what she'd done? And as the children got older, it could only get worse. The sins of the mother would be visited upon the children. She thought of Gordon's offer. It seemed the perfect solution, if not for Luigi. She hated leaving Luigi, but what choice did she have?

That night she made her decision and after the children were asleep, she went into the den and told her mother what she planned to do.

"But how can you drag two little kids across the country?"

"I dragged one little kid to Paris."

"But that was different. You had Janet."

"And now I have Gordon."

"Gordon," her mother said with distaste. "Who is this Gordon?"

"Someone I met in Paris. I told you about him."

"Yes, you told me he's queer."

"What does that have to do with anything?"

"Well, I don't like it. I don't like it one bit."

"Mother, I'm never going to allow what happened this afternoon to happen again."

For a moment, Lilly was silent. "Yes, I know, it was a terrible thing. But taking the children so far away from everyone who knows them, from everyone who loves them."

"I know, but anonymity has its advantages."

Lilly could not argue with that.

The next morning, Edie called Gordon.

"Gordon, I'm calling your bluff. Does your boss still want me?"

"He's desperate for you."

"Then tell him I'm coming. I just have to give my boss two weeks notice, maybe three. I think the beginning of May."

"Perfect," Gordon said. "And Edie, you won't be sorry. This is a fabulous restaurant. Especially the food."

"I hear they have a great chef."

"Wait 'til you taste my chantilly desserts."

Edie hung up the phone, feeling uneasy. She had taken the first step. Could she take the next thousand.

That afternoon she told Luigi that she was leaving; he didn't take the news well. "How can you desert me? What am I going to do without you?"

It was a terrible moment for Edie. She felt like a traitor, Lord Jim deserting his ship. "I'm sorry, Luigi, but I've got to get out of Detroit."

"But why?"

"Personal reasons."

"Personal reasons," he spat. "But what about my business?"

"It'll do fine. You'll do fine."

"And who's going to make the antipasto and the focaccia? Who's going to do my ordering and take care of the books?"

"You'll find someone."

"No, Edie. Maybe to do the books, maybe to make the antipasto, but not to do it all."

She looked at this fat, balding man with the cigar between his lips and felt her determination fading. And then she remembered why she had to go. "I'm sorry, Luigi, but I've made up my mind."

He looked at her for a long moment, then shrugged his shoulders, "Okay, if you gotta go, you gotta go."

She went to him and put her arms around him. "I love you, Luigi."

And with his cigar breath, he kissed her cheek. "You better find me someone good," he said.

"I'll do my best."

Edie immediately put an ad in the paper, called an employment agency, and told all the purveyors to spread the word, Luigi's needed a new manager.

It was a Sunday afternoon a week later, when Edie got home from the park with her children, that her mother met her at the door. "Call Janet. She's been trying to reach you."

Edie dialed the long distance operator who put her through immediately.

"Janet," Edie said, "what's wrong?"

"It's my mother. She's dying."

"Oh, Janet, I'm so sorry. What is it?" But even before Janet answered, Edie knew what it was going to be.

"Cancer," spoken in a hushed tone, as if, if you said the word out loud, it gathered more power.

"I'm so sorry."

"I just had a call from my Aunt Sofia. She doesn't think my mother will last the week."

"Where is it?"

"Her liver. She's been feeling very tired lately, and at first they thought it might be her heart, but they did a bunch of tests, and it's her liver. I'm flying home tomorrow and I was wondering if you could pick me up at the airport."

"Of course."

Janet gave her the time, the flight, the airline, and both women said, "I can't wait to see you," with Janet adding, "and I can't wait to see Wendy and the new baby."

Edie was at Detroit Metropolitan Airport an hour before Janet's flight was due, so filled with anticipation that she couldn't sit down and walked the terminal from one end to the other. Finally they called Janet's flight, and Edie ran to the gate, and when Janet emerged, the two friends flew into each other's arms and stood hugging for several minutes.

"Oh God, it's good to have you home," Edie said, "even if it is for such a terrible reason." Janet hadn't changed at all over the past year: she was still overweight; her hair was still in short tight curls, like Mary Martin; she still wasn't wearing any make-up; and she was dressed in the same white blouse and brown skirt Edie had given her when they first met.

"You're looking great," Janet said. Edie's hair was tied back in a pony tail (more convenient for work) with bangs that fell almost to her eyes, wearing white slacks and a pink blouse, and just a touch of pink blush and pink lipstick to pick up the pink of the blouse. She was thinner than she had been in Paris. "How do you do it?" Janet asked. "Stay so slim?"

"I never sit down," Edie said. "I'm either running after the children or Luigi."

"Then what's my excuse?" Janet asked.

"You like your own cooking too much," Edie teased.

The girls walked arm and arm to pick up Janet's luggage.

"I feel so guilty," Janet said. "How could I have let another year go by without seeing my mother."

"You didn't know your mother was going to die," Edie said.

"But I knew how much she missed me. I'll never forgive myself."

"Janet, you can't blame yourself for everything bad that happens in your life."

"I can't help it. That's how I feel."

Driving to Aunt Sofia's house where Janet's mother was staying since she became ill, Edie said to Janet, "I have some news for you. I'm moving to Los Angeles. I got an offer to manage Gordon's restaurant and I'm taking it."

"You mean, the Chez Helene?" Janet said.

"Yes."

"I can't believe it," Janet said. "You've become one of us."

Edie did not want to tell Janet at this moment the real reason she was leaving Detroit. Janet had enough on her mind. "So how about you?" she asked. "Anything happening with those two restaurants in New York?"

"As a matter of fact, I'm going to stop off there on my way back to Florence, and if one of them wants to hire me, then I'm going to take the job. I think I've learned all I'm going to learn from Vittorio. It's time to move on."

Edie pulled up in front of Sofia's house, and turned off the engine, but neither of them made a move to get out.

"You know," Janet said, "Stefano still hasn't gotten over you."

Edie was surprised; she didn't think Janet knew about her and Stefano. "Then you knew."

"We all knew."

"Silvia and Carlo?"

"Of course."

"But no one said anything. No one acknowledged it."

"I think Silvia and Carlo appreciated very much that you left when you did."

"But they asked me to stay. They almost insisted."

"Because they wanted to do what was best for you."

"Thank God I did what was best for them." Edie pictured Stefano's face as he had looked that afternoon he kissed her on the Ponte Vecchio. If only he had been older. If only she had been younger and single. She pulled her key out of the ignition and asked casually, "Tell me, is Stefano seeing anyone?"

"Yes, he is going out with a girl. Being in medical school, he doesn't have much time, but there is a girl. Luisa."

"Then what makes you think he hasn't gotten over me."

"When I left, he said to tell you, 'nothing's changed'."

"This is something that can never be," Edie said, as much to convince herself as Janet. "I'm glad he's seeing Luisa."

The two friends exited the car and went around the back to get the luggage.

"There's something I should tell you about Brian," Edie said. "His last name is Freni."

"I thought it was Stern."

"I didn't want Stefano to know. I still don't."

"Don't worry, I won't tell him." And then, lifting her suitcase, Janet said, "Well, it's time to think of other things."

"Shall I come in with you?"

"I think not. I better see her first. I don't know how she's going to feel about seeing you."

The two friends hugged.

"Call me as soon as you can," Edie said.

"I will."

Janet called Edie the next morning at nine and asked if Edie could come over.

"I'll leave right now," Edie said.

She was there within fifteen minutes and as soon as Janet saw her, she burst into tears and collapsed into Edie's arms.

"My poor Janet," Edie said, and stroked her hair. "It's all right, it's all right. Go ahead and cry. It's good for you."

Finally, after Janet's tears subsided, and she wiped her eyes and blew her nose, she asked if Edie would like a cup of coffee.

"No thanks, I've eaten. But I would like to see your mother--to say goodbye. Do you think she'd see me?"

"I don't know," Janet said. "I don't want to upset her."

"Whatever you think."

Janet thought a moment and then made up her mind. "All right, let's try."

Edie followed Janet into the bedroom. Ida Camerini was lying in bed, her head supported by several pillows. At her bedside was a pitcher of water and a glass. She seemed to be dozing. Janet bent over her. "Mom, look who came by to see you."

Ida's eyes opened and Edie went to her bedside. "Who is it?" Ida asked.

"It's Edie."

Ida's eyes tried to focus and Edie felt if she were going to say anything, she'd better say it now. "Mrs. Camerini, I just wanted to say how sorry I am if I've done anything to hurt you. I didn't mean to hurt you. I just wanted to do what was best for Janet."

And Ida, finally recognizing Edie, said, "You took my daughter away from me."

"I didn't mean to take your daughter away from you, Mrs. Camerini. I just wanted her to be able to do what she was meant to do: become a great chef. And she is a great chef."

Mrs. Camerini was silent for a few minutes, as if trying to comprehend what had been said. "Yes, she is," she said, finally, and closed her eyes. Janet embraced Edie, or Edie embraced Janet, it was hard to tell who was holding whom. "Do you think she forgave me?" Edie asked.

"Yes, yes, I do," Janet said, and then they both began to cry.

Ida Camerini died a week later. She went into a coma the day after Edie had seen her, but it took a whole week more until she died. Janet was with her day and night, sitting by her bedside, telling her about Florence, about Silvia and Carlo, about her job at Vittorio's, and begging her forgiveness. "I didn't mean to stay away so long, mama. I should have come home to visit you. Please forgive me, mama. Please open your eyes one more time and let me know that you forgive me."

But Ida Camerini's eyes would never open again.

She was buried on a Thursday morning. There were more people at the funeral than Janet expected. Edie and her parents were there, and Janet's cousins, Ann and Rudy, and of course Aunt Sofia, Uncle Alberto, Peter and his wife, and Miriam and her husband, but also several of her mother's customers, some with their husbands. And it was their presence that gave Janet the most comfort. To know that her mother had been appreciated, that she would be missed.

After an evening of "sitting shiva", an evening of mourning and remembrance, Janet began to sort through her mother's possessions, deciding what was to be retained, what was to be given away. Most of her mother's belongings were going to the Goodwill. Except for her clothing. That was to be thrown out. It was rags, all of it. The seamstress who dressed so many others had never taken the time to dress herself. Aunt Sofia would keep a table, a chest, a clock, and the sewing machine. Janet would take her mother's wedding ring, gold earrings, ivory brooch and ebony pin. Fifty-two years of life and these few pieces were all that remained of Ida Camarini. These and her daughter, Janet. And Janet felt this great sense of being alone in the world, of being unprotected from death, of being the last of her line. And this last was perhaps the saddest thought of all. Both her parents were dead and when she died, there would be no more Camerini family. Her mama, her papa and herself would pass on to oblivion as if they had never existed.

Finally, every paper had been thrown out or saved, every piece of clothing and furniture had been picked up or put away, all the bills had been paid, and it was time for Janet to leave for New York and the two interviews Lucille Neumeier had set up for her. Then it would either be back to Florence, or on to New York.

Edie drove Janet to the airport and once at the gate, Janet hugged Edie first, then Wendy, and finally Brian, and as she hugged Brian, tears came to her eyes. Even now, in her grief, she could not help thinking, but for a twist of timing, Brian might have been her child. "I'm going to miss you all so much," Janet said.

"We're going to miss you, too." Edie said.

"I hope everything works out for you in Los Angeles."

"I hope everything works out for you in New York."

"Aren't we something!" Janet said, amazed at their worldliness. "You going off to Los Angeles, me going off to New York. How did this happen to two little 'innocents' from Detroit?"

"I don't think I can be characterized as an 'innocent'," Edie said. "Unless, of course, you're referring to *The Turn of the Screw*."

"Yes," Janet said, "you have been 'screwed' many times."

"And what do I have to show for it?"

And Janet, with a trace of wistfulness, said, "Two great kids."

"I wouldn't have it any other way," Edie said.

After one more hug, Janet scampered aboard the plane, and Edie and her children stood by the window in the terminal, watching as Janet's plane took off. "Wave bye-bye to Aunt Janet," Edie said, and black-haired, black-eyed Wendy and blond-haired, blue-eyed Brian waved happily until Janet's plane was out of view.

Now, it was time for Edie to get on with her own plans. She hired a manager for Luigi's (a fifty-year-old man, who had recently sold his coffee shop in downtown Detroit "because the neighborhood had become too dangerous"), purchased two plane tickets (Brian would sit on her lap), and packed her and her children's belongings, sorting them into two piles: one which was to be shipped, one which was to be taken. Gordon called to say he had found her an apartment, and on the first Monday in May, a warm, sunny, spring day when all the grass and trees seemed to have turned green at the same moment, Lilly and Ben drove Edie and her children to the airport.

Sitting in the front seat beside Ben, Lilly could hardly speak. She was upset that Edie was leaving, but even more upset that Edie was taking Wendy and Brian away from her. She didn't know how she was going to get along without them. They had become the most important thing in her life. More important than all her organizations, clubs, friends. Of course she would still have Frank's two children, and of course she loved all her grandchildren the same--but still there was something about Wendy and Brian that made them somehow special. Perhaps because she saw them every day, perhaps because they didn't have a father. But what could she do? She knew that once Edie made up her mind there was no dissuading her, and Edie had made up her mind. She was leaving. And in truth, Lilly had known since the day Edie left for Paris that she would never be happy in Detroit again. "How you gonna keep 'em down on the farm, after they've seen Paree?"

Once in the terminal, Lilly's tears began to flow. "Now you take good care of them," she said to Edie.

"I will," Edie said. "Don't worry." And Edie felt her mother's heartbreak as if it were her own. "We've got to go," she said, pulling her children from her parents' grasp and hurrying to the ramp. She knew if she looked at her mother's face one more minute, she would begin to cry. She didn't know why she was so upset. It was more than that she would miss her parents. No matter how difficult her mother had been, Edie still loved her. Perhaps it was fear of what lay ahead. But it didn't matter the reason, all she knew was that her insides felt like they were breaking apart, and she couldn't let any of them know it, not her parents, and especially not her children.

"Come children, hurry," she said, with a smile on her face, "we don't want to be the last ones on the plane."

Chapter Fifteen

It was four in the afternoon when Edie, Wendy and Brian arrived in Los Angeles. It was a hot, bright, sunny day and Gordon was there to meet them. Edie had been feeling jittery all during the flight, but as soon as she saw the Los Angeles skyline, her spirits lifted. This was a chance for a new start. A time for her to think positive, to have faith in the future.

Gordon was taller and thinner than she remembered, now wearing gold-rimmed glasses and dressed in a navy blue leisure suit. How glad she was to see him. She put her arms around him and held on longer than she expected.

"You're looking great," he said, looking her over.

She was wearing beige slacks and a blue blouse which brought out the blue of her eyes, and her brown hair which was usually tied back in a pony tail was hanging loose, with her wispy bangs falling almost to her eyes.

"You're looking pretty great yourself," she said.

"Los Angeles agrees with me," he said. And then stooping to the children. "Hi, I'm Uncle Gordon. You, of course, are Wendy, and you must be the new baby, Brian."

"He's not so new anymore," Edie said. "He's 14 months old."

"Well, you take the little one and I'll take the big one," Gordon said, lifting Wendy in his arms and tickling her stomach until she began to giggle.

After all the bags were loaded into Gordon's gray Ford, he headed for the freeway.

Los Angeles was nothing like anywhere Edie had ever been. It was the opposite of Paris, Florence, even Detroit. All the buildings were new, low, spread out, the streets were wide, the houses were pink, yellow, green, and there were palm trees. She looked in wonderment at the tall, thin trees, with their clump of green at the top, swaying just slightly in the breeze.

"It's beautiful here," she said.

"When there isn't any smog."

From the back seat, Wendy asked, "What's smog?"

Gordon answered, "It's gooky yellow stuff in the air that makes your eyes water and chokes you."

"Yuck," Wendy said.

"Thanks, Gordon," Edie said. "I've been telling my kids what a great place Los Angeles is."

"Sorry, Edie, but one must be honest at all costs."

"Well I don't see any smog," Edie said.

"That's because it's May. Wait until July."

They were driving north on the San Diego freeway.

"Do you want to see the restaurant or your apartment first," Gordon asked. "Since it's Monday, the restaurant's closed, but I have a key."

"The restaurant," Edie said.

"I have to make tinkle," Wendy said.

"Is the restaurant far, or should we stop at a gas station?" Edie asked.

"We better stop at a gas station," Gordon said. And then, "Children! I'm glad I'll never have any."

And Edie, sensing his neediness, said, "I'll tell you what, you can have mine. They need a daddy anyway."

And Gordon, sensing her neediness, said, "It's a deal."

After the gas station stop, they drove down La Cienega, a beautiful wide street loaded with restaurants, "'restaurant row' we call it," Gordon told them, and turned on a smaller street, Beverly Boulevard, still charming but not as wide, where they parked, and all piled out of the car, and into Chez Helene.

Chez Helene probably resembled a thousand French cafes throughout the world, red and white checkered tablecloths, a bottle of wine sitting on each table and pictures of Parisienne landmarks, (the Eifel tower, Notre Dame, Sacre Coer) on the walls. "It's lovely," Edie said, having doubts that she was really capable of managing such a place. Luigi's had been a neighborhood pizza parlor--how much damage could she do? But this was a "real" restaurant, and Gordon had exaggerated her experience. "I just hope I'm up to it."

"Don't worry," he said putting his arm around her shoulders, "you'll do fine." And she felt comforted by his confidence.

"By the way," he said, "how soon can you start?"

"As soon as I get Wendy enrolled in school, and find two great babysitters," she said.

"Why two?"

"One for Brian during the day, he's too young for nursery school, and the other for the evenings."

"Well then," he said, "let's get started. Ready to see your new living quarters?"

"Can't wait," she said.

They drove another few blocks to Genesee, a narrow street intermixed with two-story apartment houses, and small private homes. Edie immediately loved the street because of the tall palm trees lining both sides of it. "Well, here we are," Gordon said, pulling up in front of a two story, light green stucco apartment house with a front courtyard, and outdoor steps leading up to the second story.

"The courtyard will be great for the children to play in," Edie said as Gordon unlocked the door to Edie's first floor apartment. Inside, Edie looked around. It was small, but cozy, with two bedrooms, a small living room and dining area, one bathroom, and a yellow and white tiled kitchen. The furnishings were sparse, a green plaid sofa and easy chair in the living room, a kitchen table with four chairs, and beds and dressers in the bedrooms.

"You like?" Gordon asked.

"It's fine," she said, looking through the cupboards and drawers in the kitchen, while the children chased each other from room to room. And then, standing in the middle of this tiny kitchen with its yellow and white tile, the feeling of depression that Edie had been trying to stave off since she left Detroit this morning, overtook her. What was she doing in this alien place, in this dumpy apartment, alone with this almost stranger, 2400 miles away from everyone and everything she'd known all her life?

"I've put some things in the frig for you," Gordon said.

She looked at him. He was such a kind and gentle person. Warm feelings flowed over her. He would help her through.

"You're a sweetheart," she said, coming to him and putting her arms around him. "I'm afraid I'm going to have to depend on you a lot these first few days."

"I got you out here and I'm going to do everything I can to make you happy. Now let's get these wild Indians together and go get something to eat."

It took several days until Edie found the right nursery school for Wendy, until she found two perfect babysitters, and until she got all her shopping done. Just like Paris, she had to buy dishes, silverware, pots, pans, bed linens, towels, soap and toilet paper. And by the time the three cardboard boxes arrived from Detroit with the rest of the clothes and toys, Edie was ready to begin work at Chez Helene.

Alain Schembri, the owner of Chez Helene, was a nice guy and reminded Edie of Luigi, except that he was from Dijon, not Napoli. He was also short, fat, and smoked a cigar, except never in the restaurant. He went out back into the parking lot if he wanted to smoke. He, too, hated paper work, and wanted her to do it all, as soon as possible. He also wanted her to take over all his other responsibilities. "It's the old ticker," he said, "I can't handle these problems anymore."

And she did take over. Her experience with Luigi paid off. It was as if it was Luigi's, except the menu was French instead of Italian. Even the clientele, same type of people as Detroit, except more casually dressed. "Does anyone ever wear a suit and tie in this city?" she asked Gordon.

"Only at the Escoffier room, as far as I know," Gordon said.

Gordon worked long hours in the kitchen. He started at nine a.m., even though the restaurant didn't open until ll:30, and some nights, he didn't get off until ten. He had a souschef and four cooks who helped with the preparation of the vegetables, fish, poultry and meat and then worked on the line preparing the salads and cold dishes and working the fish and meat stations, but Gordon and his souschef prepared all the soups and sauces, and Gordon had his hand in all of the entrees. Chez Helene did not make its own bread or desserts, although Gordon thought they should. And Edie agreed with him. Like Janet, Gordon had specialized in desserts: fruit tarts, mousses, soufflés, and he missed making them. The French bakery which did their baking was good, but not great, and while the restaurant was quite busy most nights, it was never full. "I'd like to try to fill you up," Edie told Alain. "I think we need to improve our desserts. And our bread. I'm a great believer in bread. I think Gordon should make them both."

"If Gordon makes the bread and desserts, we'll need to hire another cook," Alain said, hesitantly.

"Or, I could help out in the kitchen. I've done it before."

"Well, if you're willing to do that...."

"Yes," Edie said, eager to do anything to make the restaurant a success. It belonged to Alain monetarily, but emotionally, it belonged to her. It was an extension of herself, a test of her abilities, a measure of her self-worth. Perhaps she had messed up her personal life, but she would succeed in this.

So in addition to managing the restaurant, helping Gordon with the ordering of the food and wine, hiring and training the cooks, busboys, dishwashers, waitresses and waiters, attending to the uniforms, towels, dishes, and bookkeeping, Edie now began spending two or three hours each morning in the kitchen, assisting Gordon in the baking of the bread and pastries.

It was difficult putting so much energy into the restaurant and then coming home and trying to be a good mom. But she felt she was doing it. She felt she was giving as much to the children as she was to the restaurant. And as long as she kept moving, and didn't stop to take notice of how tired she was, she could get it all done.

Chapter Sixteen

Janet took one of the two jobs offered her in New York. It was at Lombardo's, an elegant Italian restaurant located on 57th between Fifth Avenue and Sixth. To start, she was to assist the souschef in making the desserts. It was not the job she wanted, but she took it because Mr. Lombardo, the owner, assured her that he had no prejudice against women, and that she could go as far up the ladder as her talent would take her.

"We're very impressed with your credentials and your experience," Mr. Lombardo told her at her interview. He was from Milano, and seemed like a very sharp, sophisticated man, wearing a silk suit, and a large diamond ring on the third finger of his right hand. It flashed through Janet's mind that he might be a member of the Mafia, but she had enough to worry about without worrying about that.

Mr. Lombardo's chef, Gerard, was also at the interview. Gerard had been trained in both French and Italian cooking. Currently the restaurant was doing only Italian, but both Mr. Lombardo and Gerard wanted to expand the menu to be more continental, and to include more interesting desserts. "It's a dog eat dog world out there, Janet," Mr. Lombardo told Janet, "and if your aren't leading the pack, then you're behind it. If you do well with the desserts, then we'll move you onto the line and from there, the sky's the limit." That was what Janet wanted, the chance to show what she could do.

Janet moved to New York two weeks after Edie moved to Los Angeles, and with Lucille's help, found an apartment on 79th and 8th. It was just a couple of blocks from Central Park. Janet would have loved to have an apartment facing the Park, but those apartments were exorbitantly expensive. At least this way she could walk by the park every day. She would never walk in the park. She knew about the muggings that took place there and she would never take that chance.

Her apartment was a one bedroom on the third floor of an old brick building. Not old like Paris, but old. Still she had a garbage disposal, and most importantly, the rooms were large and bright. She always kept her blinds up and her curtains open to let in the natural light, except in her bedroom when she went to sleep.

Janet's first day on the job was a disappointment. She had come to work that morning full of anticipation and excitement, but within ten minutes, she realized what she was up against. In spite of the fact that Mr. Lombardo had told her he had no prejudice against women, she was the only woman in the kitchen, and no one seemed happy to have her there, except Gerard. The souschef was a man named Arturo. He was from Bologna and finding out that for the last two years, she had been the chef of a first class restaurant in Florence made no difference to him. To him she was a woman and therefore inferior in every way.

The way he treated Janet was insulting. "Hand me the butter, hand me the baking powder, de-stem the strawberries." It was demeaning, but if she was going to get anywhere, she had better not antagonize anyone.

After two weeks of watching Arturo do everything while she did what any idiot off the street could do, he finally let her prepare two of their standard desserts by herself: tiramasu and cannoli.

They both turned out excellent. Gerard tasted and took note.

Within the month, Arturo was content to have her do all of the baking. Why not? She did the work; he got the credit. He was still nasty to her, never giving her a compliment, but turning over the baking was compliment enough.

Now, Gerard decided it was time to expand the dessert menu and went over some choices with Janet. They decided on tarte tatin, creme brule', and a chocolate soufflé, made to order: "please allow 20 minutes".

And Janet set to work.

Gerard was delighted with the results and so were the customers. Several of them complimented the matre'd on the addition of the new desserts, all the while complaining about how full they were.

Arturo did not like the new desserts. He went directly to Mr. Lombardo. "Italians do not like these rich desserts. We should keep it simple."

"That would be fine," Mr. Lombardo said, "if we were only going to be serving Italians."

Arturo turned away in a huff. He had not been consulted about the new desserts and he didn't like this woman taking over. It was too great an insult for him to live with, and within the week, he let it be known to the restaurant world that he was available. Two weeks later, an offer came and he quit.

Janet was not unhappy. She was sorry that she had been the cause of Arturo's leaving, but she was delighted not to have him peering over her shoulder, making comments and criticisms at everything she did. She was not learning anything from him. He was a total negative. Now she felt she could spread her wings. She talked to Gerard about trying some other desserts. Perhaps a special or two each night in addition to the regular desserts. A surprise for the customers--a reason for them to come back one more time that week. And Gerard liked the idea and let her go ahead. She pulled out all her recipes, studied each one, made changes here and there, a little less sugar, a little more fruit, a dash of cinnamon, a drop of vanilla. She prepared apple crepes, strawberry, blueberry and apple tarts, cherries jubilee, bananas flambé, and flaming soufflés with Grand Marnier. It was her time to be creative and she was going to take advantage of it.

Her desserts were a hit and Janet thought now the other cooks would be friendly to her, but they remained unapproachable. They had seen what had happened to Arturo and they didn't want anything to do with her. They especially did not want her invading their stations.

Occasionally she would ask Gerard about letting her cook something, but he always had the same reply. "You are doing so well with the desserts. The other can wait."

But Janet did not want to wait. She enjoyed the desserts, but she was not meant to make desserts all her life. She wanted to get into the heart of the food, the soups, the meat, the pastas, the vegetables. And so she continued to ask Gerard--not so often as to be a pest, but often enough so that he was aware she was anxious.

Janet's hours were from 9 a.m. until 2 p.m., and then from 4 p.m. to 9 p.m. After work, she'd take a cab home, take her shoes off, pour herself a small glass of red wine, and sit in her new brown leather recliner with her feet up watching whatever show was on television. At 11 o'clock she'd watch the news and then Johnny Carson until she got drowsy and went to sleep. Sitting there alone in her apartment, her eyes on the television screen, she'd often think of her year in Paris, her years in Florence. How happy she had been living with the Freni's, working at Vittorio's. How much she missed Edie, Wendy and Brian. Brian...she could not think of him without thinking of Mike Kelly, without remembering the thrill of being held by him, being kissed by him, being made love to by him. She'd try to shake them off, all her memories of him, but she could not get them to leave her mind, no matter how hard she tried. If only she had some company, some companionship, someone to talk to, someone who cared for her. She was 26, and yet she'd come such a short distance from her high school days. She was an outcast at work, her only true friend was 3000 miles away, and she was still without a man to love.

The only bright spot in Janet's life, outside of creating her desserts, were Monday nights--chef's night out. Almost every Monday night, she would get together with Lucille and Lucille's friends, all people in the restaurant business, and go somewhere for drinks, then out to dinner, then out for dessert, and finally end up at someone's apartment. One never knew who was going to show up, or how many--it was an ever-changing group. But always the conversation was the same, about food, wine, decor, other chefs, and how and when each of them could open their own restaurant. Janet enjoyed these outings immensely. For these few hours every week, she could feel that she really belonged, that she was part of a group, that people really liked her.

Three months after Janet began working at Lombardo's, the sauté cook left for a better position.

Gerard looked at her. "You think you can handle his job *and* do the baking?"

"I'll come at six in the morning, if I have to," Janet said, ecstatic that at last her chance had come.

The next day, in addition to making the desserts, Janet was put on the line, sautéing the chicken, veal, seafood and fish, and doing whatever else Gerard asked her to do.

The other cooks, remembering what had happened to Arturo, were even more hostile to her now that she was working beside them. Each morning when she greeted them, her stomach would twist in knots. But there was nothing she could do. She had to just hope that if she did her job well enough, in time, she would win them over.

Gerard was very impressed with her work and two months after she was put on the line, Gerard said to her, "Maybe it's time we got you an assistant for the desserts. I'd like you to be souschef."

Janet's eyes filled with tears. "Thank you, Gerard. I'll make you proud."

Mr. Lombardo hired an assistant pastry chef for Janet, and Janet began working alongside Gerard, assisting him in preparing the sauces and the soups, seasoning the meats, fish and fowl, and overseeing everything the other cooks did.

Lucille and her friends of Monday night, celebrated by buying Janet a bottle of champagne, and treating her to dinner. It was a gala evening and Janet felt like the queen of the ball.

Nine months after Janet began working at Lombardo's, Gerard got an offer to work for a Michelin 3 star restaurant in Lake Anecy, a little town in the south of France. It was too good an offer for him to pass up and he accepted it. Janet held her breath. It was just like at Vittorio's. Would Mr. Lombardo search for another chef, or would he give the job to Janet?

Two days after Gerard had given notice, Mr. Lombardo called her into his office. Janet was excited, but tried to appear calm. She knew it must be about the job. "You know," he said, pointing his cigarette at her, "I've been very impressed with your work, Janet, but this restaurant has never had a woman chef."

Almost the same words Vittorio had uttered, but in a more foreboding tone. The hot dog was before her nose and she wasn't going to let it get away. "But why, Mr. Lombardo? What's wrong with a woman chef?"

"It's common knowledge that the best chefs are men. Besides, women get married, they have babies. They're unreliable."

Janet wanted to say, "Look at me. Do you think anyone would want to marry me?" Instead she said, "I know it may sound as if I'm bragging, but I think I'm as good as any man. And I have no intentions of getting married."

Mr. Lombardo had a strange look in his eye. Janet couldn't tell what it meant. "The thing is," he said, "I've already hired another chef. Unfortunately, he has someone else in mind for souschef, but I do want you to stay on."

Janet felt her insides crumble. "But, Mr. Lombardo, how could you do such a thing?"

"I'm sorry, Janet."

Anger and disappointment surged through Janet's body, but when she spoke, it was almost to herself, "I thought you would give me a chance."

"I considered it," he said apologetically. "I seriously considered it. As I said you're a wonderful cook, but I just couldn't take a chance on a woman. I truly hope you'll stay on here."

"Where else would I go?" she asked.

She left his office feeling empty, hopeless, and stupid. She had done it again, made an utter fool of herself. How ridiculous she was to get her hopes up--to think he would choose her. She felt the tears bubbling up in her eyes, and ran into the ladies' room to hide. She didn't want any of them to see her cry. Then they would say, "What do you expect from a woman?" She wouldn't give any of them that pleasure.

She didn't know what to do, stay or leave. If she stayed, she would feel humiliated. But if she left, where would she go?

That Monday night, a new girl joined the group. Her name was Linda Sheridan and she was working in the salad station at Pierre's, an upscale French restaurant on Seventh Avenue. Linda Sheridan was petite and very pretty, with brown hair and brown eyes. Janet found herself sitting next to Linda all evening--during drinks, at dinner, and after dinner at a bar on Lexington Avenue, and after gulping down two Courvoisiers, Janet told her the whole story.

"Well, fuck Mr. Lombardo," Linda said. "Get a job somewhere else. He doesn't deserve you."

"I don't know," Janet said. "I don't think it's going to be better anywhere else. Look at Lucille. She also has a diploma from Jacques Patou and she hasn't done any better than I have."

"It's because we're women," Linda said. "They're afraid of us. And you know why? Because they know we're better chefs than they are."

"I don't know," Janet said. "I've met a lot of great male chefs."

"Whose side are you on?" Linda asked, with a sideways grin.

Janet drank one more Courvoisier at Linda's urging and then Linda said, "I think you're a little smashed. Maybe I better take you home."

"I'm really okay," Janet said, although she felt a little tipsy.

"It's no problem," Linda said.

They took a cab to Janet's building and Linda insisted on accompanying Janet up to her apartment. "It's really not necessary," Janet said.

"But I want to," Linda said.

Once upstairs with Janet's three locks bolted, Janet offered Linda a glass of wine.

"Sure," she said. "Will you join me?"

"No," Janet said, "I think I've had enough for one evening."

They sat together on the sofa and Linda said, "Nice place you got here."

"Thanks," Janet said, suddenly feeling very tired and a little awkward.

"The more I think about Mr. Lombardo the angrier I get," Linda said. "I think you should quit the dirty bastard."

"I don't know," Janet said.

"God, I'm smashed," Linda said. "Maybe I should spend the night."

"Sure, if you want," Janet said. "You could sleep on the sofa."

Linda, moving closer, "I was thinking more of your bed."

Janet panicked. It had never entered her mind that Linda was a homosexual. She was so feminine. "I'm not like that," she said.

"Have you ever tried it?" Linda asked. "You know once you've had a woman, you'll never go back to a man."

"I'm sorry, Linda. I just don't think I could do it."

Linda took her hand. "You could be making a big mistake. I could make you very happy."

Janet didn't know what to do. Take her hand back or leave it in Linda's. She didn't want to hurt Linda's feelings, but she didn't want to encourage her, either.

"How long's it been since someone's made love to you?" Linda asked.

"A long time," Janet said, a vision of Mike flashing into her mind.

"Then why don't we try it? What have you got to lose?"

Janet pulled her hand back. She was beginning to feel nauseous. "No, Linda. As I said, I'm not like that."

Then before Janet knew what was happening, Linda's arms were around her, and Linda's lips were on hers. It was awful, horrible, disgusting. Janet wanted to puke. She pushed Linda away. "Please," she said, "I want you to leave."

"Okay," Linda said, pulling back, "but I think you're making a big mistake." She stood up, a little wobbly, walked to the door, and turned to Janet with a smile, "Let me know if you ever change your mind." Then she unlocked the three locks, and was gone.

Janet sat motionless for several moments watching the door after Linda left. She felt the heat radiating from her body, as if she had a fever. She was embarrassed that Linda would think she would have sex with a woman. But more than that she was angry, not just at Linda, but at Mike Kelly, at Greg Flusty, at Mr. Lombardo, at all the people who had taken advantage of her all her life. She had had enough. She wasn't going to let them get away with it anymore. It was time to fight back.

The next morning, Janet called everyone she knew and told them she was looking for another job, and that day at work she told Mr. Lombardo she was quitting.

Chapter Seventeen

While Janet's career had taken a turn for the worse, Edie's couldn't have been going better.

Since Edie had come to work at Chez Helene, the restaurant had never been busier, nor made so much money. It was filled to capacity every day of the week, and people had to make a reservation a week ahead to be sure to get in. Edie wasn't certain if it was the food, the bread or the pastries. Each evening, she went around to the tables, asking, "How was your dinner?" trying to discern from her patron's answers where she was succeeding and where she was failing. It was important that each member of the team did his or her job perfectly from the chef to the busboys. And each time she got a, "You have the best bread in town," or "Your pastries are divine," she felt a special glow.

Alain was delighted, and decided to hire another cook and give Edie a break. She had been working too hard, and she had the petit enfants to take care of.

Edie's life had been hectic. Every morning she had to get Brian off to nursery school, and Wendy to public school. Then she rushed about the restaurant all day to get everything done, then picked up the children at three, just to feel guilty about leaving them again at seven. But now that Alain was giving her all day Saturday and Sunday off until four (in addition to all day Monday, the day the restaurant was closed), things became more manageable. On her days off, Edie would take the children to the park, to the beach, out to lunch, to the department stores, and of course, to the supermarket, as much to check what was bountiful and cheap as to do the week's grocery shopping.

Gordon usually came over one or two afternoons a week, between shifts, and always on Monday nights when the four of them would cook dinner together.

"We're just like a real family," Edie said to Gordon one Monday evening as she was at the oven broiling steaks, while he was at the stove sautéing champignons, and Wendy and Brian were fighting over whose turn it was to mix the brownie batter.

"Don't tell me you want to marry me," Gordon said.

"Oh, sure," Edie said, "exactly what I want."

Edie wondered if "gays" (a term she learned when she moved to L. A.) had a choice. If Gordon *could* be attracted to her, if he wanted to be. If he could fall in love with her.

"We sure would make a great team," Gordon said, "my looks and your brains."

"Yeah," she poked him in the stomach, "you got that right."

Wendy looked up from the brownie mixture, her face and hands covered with brownie dough, "Are you going to marry Gordon, mom?"

Edie's face colored, "No, darling, Gordon and I are just friends."

And later when the children were put to sleep and she and Gordon were watching television, their feet up on her coffee table, eating popcorn, Gordon said, "If only I were straight."

"That's a big if," she said.

Some evenings after work, or after the children were asleep, if Edie and Gordon had any strength left, Edie would get her babysitter to come over or stay later, and Edie and Gordon would go restaurant hopping with friends. As with all restaurateurs, the talk was exclusively of food and restaurants.

"This eggplant is divine."

"I heard that Pierre at Cafe de Paris is leaving for a restaurant in Chicago."

"The service at La Mere was dreadful. I sat for twenty minutes before they brought the water."

"The appetizers at Bellini's promised a great meal, but then the pasta came. Noodley and drenched with Del Monte tomato sauce."

"The Far East is going to be the next big influence on our food. You've got to go to Japan, Thailand, China if you want to keep up with things."

"What about Mexico?"

"If you're not already doing Mexican, then you're already too late."

"I hear that Bernard Postel has left Oceana and is opening his own restaurant. He's going to call it Atlantis."

A moment of silence. It was everyone's dream to someday open his or her own restaurant. And Edie felt it, too. What if Chez Helene was really hers? She couldn't work any harder, but the satisfaction would be so much greater.

No one talked about it more than Gordon. He was determined.

"I'm going to do it," he told her one Monday night after dinner, after the children were asleep and the two of them, too tired to go out, were sitting on the sofa watching T.V. and munching on popcorn.

"But where would you get the money?" Edie asked.

"I've got friends. People who've come into Chez Helene and admired my cooking."

Popping a handful of popcorn into her mouth, "You need a lot of money to open a restaurant."

"I know. But it's what I want to do. What I've got to do. Why should I spend my life working for Alain, or anyone else when I could be working for myself?"

"I know all that," Edie said, "but I don't think you realize how much is involved in opening a restaurant. It's a business and as a business it has to be financially sound."

"If Alain Schembri can do it, I can do it. I'm ten times smarter than that guy and 20 times a better chef."

"Exactly why he hired you."

"And with you as my manager, I couldn't miss."

A kernel was stuck in her throat. She gagged. "Me go with you?"

"Yes, Edie. You and me together. How could we miss?"

Edie felt the excitement rising in her chest. Her own restaurant, and with Gordon as her partner. She wanted to do it, but how could she? She was the sole support of her children except for Zola's $25.00 a week, and she couldn't do anything that would jeopardize her income. Besides it would be a rotten thing to do to Alain, both of them leaving at the same time. "I'm sorry, Gordon. I can't do it."

"Why not?"

"I'm not free like you. I have responsibilities."

"So do I and you're one of them. I wouldn't ask you to do this unless I thought it was a sure thing."

Edie turned off her desires. "I'm sorry, Gordon. I can't."

But Gordon would not let go of the idea, and on Mondays would drive around Los Angeles with Edie and the kids looking for locations. "Location is everything," he told her.

"Location is nothing without money."

"If we find the location, I'll get the money," he said. "By the way, your family's pretty well off, I understand."

"Forget it," she told him. "My parents don't have any spare money, and I wouldn't ask my brother for anything, especially money, and especially for anything as risky as a restaurant."

"With you and me, babe, how big a risk could it be?"

"I never said it was going to be 'you and me babe'."

"Where is your sense of adventure?" he asked in a teasing tone.

"I lost it when I had my second baby," she teased back.

"C'mon, Edie, you don't want to get old, fat and complacent do you?"

"Maybe not old and fat."

He looked at her. "I'm getting the feeling that you don't really want to go into this venture."

"What was your first clue?"

But Gordon continued to look, and talk about it and think about it, and then he met someone. An expensively dressed middle-aged man, who first came into the restaurant with his wife, and then began coming in alone, and waiting until Gordon was off duty, and then leaving with Gordon. Edie knew what was going on. The man, Lester Sterling, had become Gordon's lover.

Gordon now became "too busy" to come by Edie's apartment during the week, to spend Monday evenings with her, or to go out with the group, and Edie was feeling alone and rejected. She knew she had no right to be jealous of Lester. Gordon was just a friend. But she couldn't help herself. She felt deserted. She felt that Gordon was cheating on her.

It was a few weeks after the affair began, that Gordon came banging on Edie's door at 11 o'clock at night. She was already in bed, about to doze off. She pulled on her robe and hurried to the door, wondering who would be calling so late, but suspecting it would be Gordon. Who else would it be?

He bounced in the door. She had never seen him so elated. He wrapped her in his arms and lifted her off her feet. "We're going to do it," he said. "We're going to do it."

"Do what?" she asked.

"We're going to open *our* restaurant."

"*Your* restaurant," she said, sarcastically. "What happened?"

"Les," he said. "Les wants to support me."

"What about his wife?"

"I don't mean that way, silly," letting go of her. "I mean he wants to give me the money to open my restaurant."

Edie was disappointed in Gordon. She knew he was using Lester. She sat down on the sofa. "Gordon, do you love this man?"

"Love takes many forms," Gordon said sitting beside her.

"You mean, you're a whore."

"There are many types of whores," Gordon said.

"Yes," she said, "those who do it for money and those who do it for a restaurant."

He turned to her, suddenly angry. "Who are you to judge me? This is what I want and I'll do anything to get it."

She felt the sting of his words as if he had slapped her on her cheek. "You're right, Gordon," she said, "who am I to judge anyone."

"Just say you'll go with me."

All the same reasons to say "no" filtered through her mind, the children's security, Alain, the fact that Gordon was a scoundrel, but the bottom line was she wanted to do it. "I suppose if it doesn't work out," she said, "I could always get a job teaching."

"You mean you'll do it?"

A hesitation. "Yes," she said, still in doubt if she was doing the right thing.

Gordon pulled her to him and kissed her on the lips, "I knew you couldn't resist my charms." And then smugly, "No one can."

She wallowed in the warmth of his arms, and realized how much she had missed being with him. "Just one thing," she said, "we have to give Alain sufficient time to find people to take our places. We have to stay with him until he doesn't need us anymore."

"That wasn't my plan," Gordon said letting go of her. "What if he fires us as soon as we tell him we're going to be leaving? I need that job until my restaurant is ready to open."

She couldn't resist taking a jab at him, "Won't Les support you?"

"I think there's a limit to how much I can ask Les."

"Funny, I didn't think you had a limit."

"And I will abide no more sarcasm from you. Look Edie, we've got to do it my way."

"No, Gordon, I'll go with you, but only on condition that we're fair to Alain."

He looked at her, "You drive a tough bargain, lady."

"It's your choice."

"I accept," he said.

When she closed the door behind him, she looked at her watch. 3 a.m. in New York. She would have to wait until the morning to tell Janet the exciting news.

Gordon and Les scoured Los Angeles to find a choice location, and finally decided on a small store on Canon Drive in Beverly Hills. Then Edie and Gordon gave Alain their notice.

Alain seemed more upset over Edie leaving than Gordon leaving. "How will I find someone to replace you? You do everything. You know everything. Is it more money you want?"

It was Luigi's all over again. "It's not the money," she said, "and I love working for you. It's just that I want my own place. You understand."

"Everyone wants their own place. Wait until you see what a headache it is."

But it'll be my headache, Edie said to herself. Aloud she said, "I know you're worried, but I promise I'll find somebody good. Maybe someone better than me."

"There is no one better than you," he said.

She felt as bad as she had with Luigi, but there was nothing he could say that would make her change her mind. As soon as the store was turned into a restaurant, she was leaving with Gordon.

Edie found a new chef for Alain almost immediately, which was just as well because Gordon was busy meeting with accountants, attorneys, bankers, carpenters, electricians, plumbers, and once the work began on the new restaurant, he needed to be there every day to make sure things were being done right.

As Alain had predicted, it was more difficult to find a replacement for Edie, someone who could do all the jobs Edie had been doing. "Don't worry," Edie told Alain, "I won't leave until I find somebody."

But Gordon was after her, "I need you now. There are all these decisions to make now. I can't do it all by myself."

Edie didn't know where to run first: to the new site or to Chez Helene. And then there were the children. She would not give up her time with the children. She felt completely frazzled. There seemed to be only one way to satisfy everyone: give up sleeping.

On a Tuesday evening, just as she was leaving for Chez Helene, Gordon called. "You have to come over right this minute to see the wallpaper I've selected."

"Can't it wait until tomorrow?"

"No."

So she drove over to the worksite and Gordon showed her the paper. It had a cream background with tiny pink, blue and green flowers. "And here's the matching fabric for the chairs. Isn't it gorgeous?"

She picked up the sample and noticed the price. "Gordon, do you know how much this wallpaper costs?"

"Edie, if I'm going to do it, I'm going to do it right."

"But there are lots of pretty wallpapers that cost a lot less."

"This is going to be a quality restaurant, and I refuse to skimp on anything."

"You're very generous with Lester's money."

"He wants it that way."

Edie didn't feel it was her place to object. "Then go ahead," she said, and drove over to Chez Helene to supervise dinner.

At seven-thirty, the phone rang. It was Mrs. Mateus, her babysitter.

"Mrs. Stern, there's a man at the door who says he's Wendy's father. I don't know what to do?"

"What's his name?"

"Zola."

Edie felt a chill run through her. "Does he have a beard?"

"A very big beard," Mrs. Mateus said, a note of disapproval in her voice.

"Let him in," Edie said.

She told Alain she had to leave, drove like a maniac to her apartment, raced across the courtyard, opened the door, nervous as the first time she had knocked on his door in Ann Arbor, and there, sitting on her sofa, Wendy on his lap, was Zola.

"Zola," she said.

He looked up. "Edie."

His hair was longer and his beard more enormous than the last time she had seen him, so that you couldn't tell where his hair left off and his beard started. And it seemed to Edie he was wearing the same blue shirt he had been wearing four years ago.

Mrs. Mateus was at the kitchen door holding Brian, seeming a little upset. "I made him tell me Wendy's birthday and show me his driver's license before I let him in."

"It's okay," Edie said, "he *is* Wendy's dad." And Brian ran to Edie and she picked him up and kissed him.

"Are you going to be going out again, Mrs. Stern?" Mrs. Mateus asked.

"No," Edie said. "You can go home now. And thanks."

Mrs. Mateus, still seeming a little uncomfortable, left, and Edie carried Brian over to the easy chair opposite the sofa and sat down.

Wendy did not make a move to come to her mother, and Edie focused on Zola's eyes, Wendy's eyes. "Before I ask you what you've been doing for the past four years," Edie said, "I want to thank you for your checks, and your poems and your pictures." For the last year, Zola had been enclosing a poem or a picture for Wendy with his checks.

"It was the least I could do."

"Still, I, we, appreciated them." Then, "Now tell me what have you been doing for the past four years?"

"Well, the first three weren't very pretty. I stayed on at that commune, hating all the people, but so zonked most of the time, I couldn't make a move. Instead of *The Lost Weekend*, it was the lost three years."

"You had a girlfriend, didn't you?" Edie asked, hoping he would say "no."

"Sheila," he said. "She was a..." He stopped himself from using the word he was going to use and said instead, "slut."

Somehow Edie was relieved to hear that. "Then why did you stay with her?"

"Because I was out of my mind. Can you understand that? Me, who had avoided even alcohol before I moved out there. I was hooked and she was my supplier."

Edie became nervous seeing Wendy sitting on his lap. What if he was still on the stuff. "So what happened?"

"One of my buddies died. He was a guy I met at the bar. One day he wasn't there and I asked what happened. He had cancer of the pancreas. I went to see him in the hospital. He said, 'I'm dying, but you're dying, too, Zola. Promise me you'll get off the stuff.' At the funeral, standing there amid all the gravestones, and watching his box being lowered into the ground, I had an epiphany. It came to me that I wasn't dying, I was already dead. As lost to this world as my friend, and I made up my mind right then and there that things were going to change. That afternoon, I went back to the commune, packed my bag and left."

"Just like that."

"Just like that."

"You always were impulsive. What happened to Sheila?"

Zola glanced at Wendy before he answered, "She didn't miss me. She was involved with every guy on the commune, one way or another."

"And then?"

"And then I wandered a bit. I felt I had to be by myself, get back to my roots, and eventually I found this great place, also at the top of a mountain, a little shack, but I love it. It's in Idaho, about two hours from Boise."

"Yes," she said, "I noticed the new postmarks."

"Right," he said.

Wendy was climbing all over Zola, having a great time, and Brian, who couldn't stand all the fun Wendy was having, pulled away from his mother and ran over to Zola. Now both children were climbing all over Zola and he was tickling them both.

"Are you still writing poetry?"

"Of course. I have bushel baskets full of it."

"And have you sold any?" Edie asked.

"I haven't sent any out. It's not important that they get published; only that I write them."

Yes, that's what would be important to Zola. "Then, how do you earn a living?"

"In the winter, I fix Volkswagens," he said.

"And in the summer?"

"I work for the National Forest Service."

"You're a forest ranger?"

"No, a surveyor. I decide whose tree is whose, whose mine is whose."

"Sounds like fun."

"It is."

"So," she hesitated before asking her next question, "why are you here?"

"I wanted to see my daughter. I haven't stopped thinking about her all these years. Or you."

Their eyes met and Edie shivered. Was it still there? Her attraction to this man?

"I didn't come sooner," he was continuing, "because I didn't feel worthy of either of you. But now I've straightened myself out and I want you to come live with me."

Her first impulse was to laugh. "Zola, you can't be serious. Waltzing in here like this after all these years and expecting me to drop everything and run off with you?"

His eyes became more intense. "Nothing's changed for me since that night in Ann Arbor."

"Well they have for me," she said. "It's been six years, Zola. Things have happened to me. I have another child. I've built a life. Other people are dependent on me."

"So?"

She looked at him. It was a crazy idea, but still she felt unnerved. "It's impossible," she said.

"Will you at least come see where I live?"

"What's the point?"

"Maybe you'll like it."

Like I liked the commune, she thought, until I found out about the drugs. "Even if I wanted to, I couldn't possibly get away right now," she said. "I'm running one restaurant and about to open another."

"Well then, how about if I take Wendy for a couple of weeks and you could come whenever you have time."

The blood rushed to her temples. "You must be insane," she said. "I'm not going to let Wendy go off with you to God knows where."

"Then take off a couple of days, come with us and if you like it, she stays, if not, she comes back. I'll take Brian, too."

Again, she looked at him in amazement. What he was proposing was, of course, idiotic, and yet, she could not help picturing the mountain, the little shack, no worries, no cares, and Zola. "How do I know you're clean?" she asked.

"Because I'm telling you I am. I haven't touched anything in over a year."

"I don't know." Edie was tossing the idea back and forth. If she went with him or let her kids go, everyone would think she was as crazy as he was. She could hear her mother's voice now, "You must be crazy for even considering such a thing." But insane as it was, she trusted Zola. What was the harm in taking a look? What did she care what anyone thought of her anyway?

"Okay," she said, "maybe I am crazy, but I will come to your little house upon the hill. I just don't know when. I'll have to work it out."

He smiled, his pink lips parting beneath the bristle of his face, "You're going to love it there."

"Are we going to go live with my daddy?" Wendy asked.

"We're just going for a visit," Edie said.

"I want to go, too," Brian said.

"Of course you're going to go, Brian," Edie said. "We're all going."

"And we're all going to have so much fun," Zola said to Wendy and Brian who were pulling at his beard.

Edie looked at her watch. Eight o'clock. Time for bed for the children. "Have you eaten? Are you hungry?" she asked Zola.

"I wouldn't mind a cup of coffee."

"And do you have a place to stay?"

"No," he said.

"Well, you can sleep here. On the sofa."

"I'd appreciate that," he said.

"And now I think I better put the kids to bed."

"No, mommy," Wendy said. "I want to stay up. I want to be with my daddy."

"Me, too," Brian said.

Edie smiled. "Okay, I guess it is a special occasion. I'll make some coffee and put out some milk and cookies and we'll have a party."

"Goodie," Wendy and Brian said, jumping on and down on Zola.

In the kitchen, putting up the coffee, getting out the milk and cookies, Edie thought, what an absolutely amazing turn her life had taken. Zola Bitterman, the father of her child, was here. In the next room. And he wanted to take her and her children to the top of a mountain in Idaho.

After dessert, and after getting the children to bed, Edie and Zola sat sipping coffee in the kitchen and talking. "I guess I should have given you advance notice I was coming," Zola said.

"That would have been nice."

"Well I just woke up this morning and decided today was the day. And here I am."

"I guess that's what makes you Zola."

"Usually it's worked out."

She looked into his black eyes, trying to remember how he had looked the first time she saw him in Ann Arbor. "We're so civil," she said, "sitting here talking like this. Like you're not the father of my child, like we haven't not seen each other in four years."

"Edie," he covered her hand with his, "I'm so sorry for all the grief I've caused you."

"You haven't caused me any grief. Wendy and Brian are the best things in my life."

"But bringing up two kids alone. It can't have been easy."

"It was fine," she said.

"You know I still care for you," he said. "If you want, I'll move here to Los Angeles, get a job..."

"Shave your beard?" she interrupted, with a smile.

"If necessary."

She sighed. "Thank you, Zola. I thank you. It makes me feel good that you would do that. But I wouldn't ask it of you."

He looked down into his coffee cup, and then through the bush of hair that covered his face, she saw his eyes, glistening. "Do you have any feelings for me?" he asked.

"You're just a dream, Zola. I don't really know who you are. Sometimes I can't even believe that night happened. Sometimes I think about it, our picnic in the park, our walk in the rain. It was so romantic. But was it me? Was it you?"

"Maybe you should be the poet."

"I think I have enough jobs," she joked. She drained what was left in her cup. "Well, tomorrow's a busy day. I better get to sleep."

He leaned back on his chair. "I'm glad you're coming to Idaho. Maybe you'll like it there."

"I don't think I'll like it enough to stay."

"Who knows," he said. "Life is full of surprises."

"Yes," she said lightly, "I can vouch for that."

Zola helped her clean up the kitchen while she told him about Stanley. Stanley who wasn't going to have any children, now had three.

"And none of them are adopted?" Zola asked, sarcastically.

"Not a one," Edie answered.

And then as Zola helped her make up the sofa with sheets, a pillow, a blanket, he asked, "And what about Brian? You haven't told me about Brian's father."

She paused a moment. That was one subject she didn't want to talk about with anyone, including Zola. "It was a quick marriage in Florence."

"I see," he said. And then sympathetically, "You've had a lot of tough times."

"No," she said. "I've had a lot of wonderful times." And then turning toward her bedroom, "I'll see you in the morning."

It took Edie a long time to fall asleep. She could not get over the fact that Zola, Mr. Ape-man, the father of her child, was asleep in the next room. She could not stop thinking of all that had transpired tonight, that he still cared for her, that she had agreed to come visit him in Idaho, and that she was looking forward to it.

The next morning she canceled nursery school for Brian and summer camp for Wendy so the children could spend more time with Zola. At two in the afternoon she and the kids drove him to the airport. Wendy and Brian, who had been roughhousing with Zola all morning, didn't want him to go. Brian acted as if Zola were his father as much as Wendy's, and Wendy didn't seem to mind. "I don't have a telephone," Zola said at the airport, "but here's the number of the garage where I work, and I will call you every week to see when you're coming."

"All right," Edie said. "I don't know when it'll be, but I will be coming."

Zola hugged both children and Edie, and then moved off to board his plane. Edie watched him go, feeling a certain emptiness, like the day she parted from her parents to come to Los Angeles. He was a member of her family, her life--this bearded tramp who was Wendy's father.

That evening when Gordon called Edie at Chez Helene to see what time she would be stopping by to check the chairs he had ordered, she said, "You'll never guess who came to dinner last night."

"Sidney Poitier?"

"Not even close," she said. "Wendy's dad."

"No shit," he said.

"No shit," she said.

"And?"

"And I'll tell you all about it when I see you."

The next week, Edie hired a replacement for herself. He was a nice young man, whom Alain thought would be too inexperienced to steal, but what did he know about running a restaurant? He had a degree in business, had studied hotel management at a school in Arizona, and had worked in a restaurant for two years. "He'll do fine," Edie told Alain.

"We'll see. Meanwhile, stay on another couple weeks. Help the kid get his feet wet."

"Sure," Edie said, happy to get another two weeks salary.

Meanwhile, she and Gordon picked out the tablecloths and napkins, pink to go with the wallpaper and chair fabric, and continued to argue about the menu. Gordon wanted to serve everything in the world; Edie wanted to limit it. "If I have enough help," Gordon said, "I can make everything I want."

"Help costs money," Edie said.

"Money, money, money, that's all you think about."

"That's what you're paying me to think about."

"Eight appetizers is not too many."

She was tired of arguing with him. "Do whatever you want, Gordon."

"All right," he said, compliantly, "we'll make it six."

It was five weeks after Zola's visit. Edie had put in her last day at Chez Helene, Gordon's restaurant was set to open in four weeks. If Edie was ever going to go to Idaho, it had to be now. She made her plane reservation with some misgivings. Was she being a stupid romantic again? Or was she doing the right thing for Wendy and Brian? The next time Zola called, she gave him her flight information, and the second weekend in August, Edie and her two children were on a plane to Boise.

Zola met them at the airport, his black eyes showing through the hair on his face, his lips pink and smiling. He was so happy to see them. He hugged the children first, and then Edie, and then carrying Wendy on his shoulders and holding Brian's hand, he led the three of them out to his waiting pick-up truck, and the four of them squeezed into the cab.

"Not the most comfortable, I know," he said, in his deep voice.

They drove for two hours on a two lane highway, criss-crossing the Payette River, the mountains rising on both sides of them, sometimes through pine forests, other times along sheer granite cliffs. It was a beautiful ride. And then they passed the Cascade Reservoir, and the land was plush green, covered with flowers, and they rode up the mountain, beside another river, the Goose, and there in the clearing was Zola's wood cabin. He had built it himself, he told her. The four of them stepped out of the cab, stretched, inhaled the fresh, clean air. Ah, Zola was right. This was heaven.

The cabin had two rooms. One room was the makeshift kitchen with a table and four chairs, a sink nailed to the wall, a wood burning stove; the other room also had a wood burning stove with pipes to an iron bathtub, and two single beds.

"Well, it ain't much," Zola said, "but it's home."

"I've got to go potty," Brian said.

Zola looked at Edie, then at Brian. "I'm afraid the potty is out back."

Edie should have expected that. "Brian's never used an outhouse."

"It's not so bad," Zola said, "once you get used to it." And then he said to Brian, "Come on, big guy, I'll take you."

The four of them spent the next three days, hiking through the forest near Zola's cabin and up into the mountains, riding innertubes down the Goose River, and sunning and swimming at the beach of a nearby resort on the Payette Lake.

"It's even more fun in the winter," Zola said, "if you don't mind ten tons of snow and ice. But the skiing is great."

"I think I prefer the summer," Edie said.

Zola took them into town where they met his boss at the Volkswagen garage, and then the lady who would be baby-sitting with Wendy, or with Wendy and Brian, if Edie decided to leave them both. Mrs. Tucker was a warm, robust middle-aged woman who had raised seven children of her own. She fed them homemade oatmeal cookies and apple cider, and had a nice fenced-in yard with a swing set and sandbox, and two golden retrievers with whom the children fell instantly in love.

The night before Edie was to return to Los Angeles, she and Zola took a walk along the dirt path leading to the road. The sky was a canopy of stars and the crickets were rubbing their hind legs together in an hysterical rhythm.

In the three days that Edie had been staying with Zola, she had become used to the two-room cabin, the outhouse, waiting an hour for her water to heat so she could bathe, the endless black sky with its millions of stars. She had become used to the quiet, not the silence, for there were crickets and other animals about, but no people for five miles. And she had become used to Zola. His slow quiet ways, his patience with the children, his kindness and that bushy hair that covered his beautiful face. "It's been a wonderful three days," she said.

"It doesn't have to end," he said, taking her hand.

"Yes, it does," she said.

And Zola turning to her, pulling her close to him, "We belong together, Edie."

"Zola, please, don't."

"Say you'll stay."

And then he was kissing her, his lips so sweet between his bristly beard that for a moment, she considered it. How wonderful it would be to stay with Zola, to stay in this place of peace, to have someone who loved her, who would take care of her and her children. To be made love to. She was getting lost in his lips, his tongue. They could make love, right here under the stars. It had been so long since a man had made love to her. Since Mike. The memory of him made her shudder.

"What is it?" Zola asked.

"I can't, Zola."

"You can't what?"

"I can't make love with you; I can't stay with you."

He still held her, "Because?"

She was ashamed to say it, but nothing had changed since the first time he had asked her, since the second time he had asked her. "I just don't think I'd be happy here."

"Still trying to make your mark on the world?"

"Yes," she said. "I know it seems stupid to you, but I like being out in the world, and I like the restaurant business. I like the challenge, the struggle, and the success."

They turned back toward the cabin, walking in silence, still holding hands.

"And Wendy...have you decided about Wendy, yet?" Zola asked.

"Yes," she said, "I've decided to let her stay. But just for two weeks. And you'll call me every other day and let me talk to her. And if she wants to come home, you'll bring her immediately."

"Agreed. And as for Brian, can he stay, too?"

"I don't know what to do about Brian."

"I think you should leave him," Zola said. "It'd be good for him and it'd be good for Wendy to have her brother with her while I'm at work."

"But he's so young. I don't know if he could do without me. I guess it's a question of whether Wendy needs him more than he needs me."

"Well, think it over tonight."

"I will," she said.

They were at the cabin door.

"Then this is it," he said.

"Yes," she said, her stomach muscles tightening. "Zola, it isn't that I don't love you," she said. "Maybe I do, but I have to go back."

"I understand," he said.

"I'm sorry," she said.

"It's okay," he said. "We both have to live out our own master plan."

She put her arms around him and tears came to her eyes. Was leaving him one more mistake to add to the collection she had already accumulated? And then she pulled away and went inside to the bed she shared with Wendy.

She didn't sleep that night worrying about what to do about Brian. She knew it would be a good experience for him, but could she leave him? She debated back and forth all night, and the next morning, decided Brian could stay, but then all the way to the airport, the whole two hours in the truck, she was panicky, and finally when it was time to board the plane, she felt like she had at the airport with Wendy when she had left for Paris. She couldn't leave him. She picked him up. "I'm sorry," she said to Zola, "but I can't leave him."

"I understand," Zola said.

Brian put his thumb in his mouth and allowed himself to be taken. Perhaps he was afraid to stay, too. And Wendy, who hadn't let go of Zola the whole three days, now became quiet, not knowing where to go, to her mother, or to her father. Zola lifted her in his arms and brought her to Edie.

"Kiss your mother so long. You'll be seeing her soon. Just two weeks."

Wendy hugged her mother, "I love you, mommy."

"I love you, too, sweetheart."

And Edie turned to Zola, "Now, remember, you're to call every other day, and if she wants to come home, you're to bring her immediately."

"I promise," Zola said.

Then Edie kissed Wendy one more time and ran onto the plane, clutching her baby boy to her. Thank God she had decided not to leave Brian. She could never have left both of them.

Chapter Eighteen

Gordon's Restaurant, Chantilly, named for the whipped cream in his famous desserts, opened three weeks after Edie returned from Idaho.

Wendy was back, safely ensconced in the apartment, having had a wonderful two weeks with her daddy, and constantly asking Edie when she could go visit him again.

The restaurant had turned out to be exquisite. From the flowered wallpaper, the matching drapes and seat cushions, the pink tablecloths and napkins to the fine china and crystal wine goblets, everything exuded luxury. There was a basket of dried pink and blue flowers, and a white porcelain ashtray imported from France on each table.

Even the kitchen was outfitted with the most expensive pots, pans, utensils and appliances. Edie had fought Gordon on every purchase and lost every battle. Including the battle over the menu.

"We need at least four soups," Gordon said.

"Three is plenty," she argued.

"I gave in to you on the appetizers, I'm not budging on the soups."

"Okay then, four soups."

"And I want every kind of seafood--shrimp, scallops, lobster, crab, and of course, three or four fishes.

"Gordon, you have only so much time and energy. Why can't we keep the menu simple?"

"Because I don't want it to be another Chez Helene," he said.

Edie felt insulted. "What's wrong with Chez Helene?"

"It's boring," Gordon said. "Boring, boring, boring."

"But it's also profitable," Edie said.

"Look," Gordon said, "this is my chance to shine. I'm telling you, Edie, I can do it all."

She threw up her hands. "Okay, Gordon, have it your way."

So Gordon finalized the menu and had it printed on pink parchment paper.

He had the six appetizers, three soups and a soup du jour, four salads, and entrees of beef, pork, lamb, veal, duck, chicken, lobster, shrimp and fish. His specialties would be Beef Wellington, Tornadoes with champignons, Pork Chops Dijonnaise, veal chop Lyonnaise, and Duck a l/orange. His vegetables would include caramelized carrots and sautéed eggplant, as well as whatever was in season prepared in the classical French manner, boiled and tossed with butter, salt and pepper. Of course he would bake his own baguettes and his famous desserts: tart tatin, tarte aux fraises, chocolate fudge mousse, lemon mousse with caramel sauce, pecan pie, all topped with Chantilly, and creme caramel, creme brule', poached pears with raspberry sauce, and almond meringue cake with pralines. He would also prepare chocolate and Grand Marnier soufflés and Cherries Jubilee to order.

The prices were expensive. They had to be to cover their overhead. They were using the finest ingredients, buying fresh poultry, fresh fruits and fresh vegetables daily, importing cheeses from

France and they hired only male waiters, and outfitted them in top quality black uniforms. All of this was costly. But Gordon wanted to have a classy restaurant.

And it was.

Lester came by to see how the restaurant had turned out. Edie still had difficulty believing that Lester was "gay." He seemed so conservative in his expensive suits and ties, his simple gold wedding band. He was still married and Edie wondered if his wife knew the truth about him. How sad for the poor woman if she did. How even sadder if she didn't.

Edie was always very cordial to him, but he was never very friendly to her. Perhaps he was jealous of her relationship with Gordon, as she had been of his. "So how do you like it?" she asked him.

"Beautiful," he said. Nothing more. Not, "You did a great job, or Gordon did a great job," just "Beautiful."

"I think it turned out very well."

"Is Gordon here?"

"Yes, in back."

"Would you please tell him I'd like to get going."

What, to go screw? she thought. And then was immediately ashamed of herself for being so bigoted. If these two adult men wanted to screw, it was no one's business but their own.

"Gordon," she said, when she found him sitting at the desk in their office, "Lester's here."

He immediately got up. "Mustn't keep my angel waiting," he said, pinching Edie's cheek and heading for the door.

After several attempts, Edie finally got a restaurant reviewer from the L. A. Times out to review the restaurant, and except for the one negative comment that the warm goat cheese salad was made with indifferent cheese and tired greens, they received a rave review.

Still, business was slow.

"We've got to do something to get them in here," Edie said. "Your food is wonderful, Gordon, but the people won't know it unless they eat here."

"How about the ones who have eaten here? Aren't they telling their friends?"

"Maybe their friends can't afford it."

"Well, we could have a blue plate special," he said in his sarcastic way.

"Maybe that's not such a bad idea. An early bird, or a price fixe special dinner each evening."

"You want to try it, go ahead. I'm getting more depressed every day."

Edie knew just how he was feeling. All their effort, all the time and expense of creating this beautiful setting and wonderful food and still the threat of failure hung over their heads. They had to do something and fast. So they instituted an inexpensive dinner each night, complete with soup or salad and dessert, and business picked up, but was it enough?

At month's end, Edie went over the books while Gordon waited anxiously looking over her shoulder. When she punched out the last number, she looked up at him, "We're still losing money."

He sat on a chair and put his feet up on the desk, "Now what?"

"Maybe we should cut out a waiter. Maybe I should wait tables?"

"What and spoil our image?"

"I could wear black pants. Maybe no one will notice," Edie said half-serious, half-joking.

"They'll notice," Gordon said.

"We'll we've got to do something."

"How about advertising?"

"It's expensive. Just how much more money is Les willing to put into this?"

"I don't know. I think he's getting bored with me. You know all this work; I'm not as energetic as I used to be."

"Well, we've got to do something," Edie said.

Gordon sat upright and leaned toward her, his gold-rimmed glasses sliding down his nose, "Do whatever you have to. We can't lose this restaurant."

Edie felt horrible. She felt somehow it was her fault. That she wasn't doing enough. But she didn't know what else to do? She decided to let one of the waiters go and she began waiting tables. More time away from her children. But she had to do it. She had to do everything she could to save Chantilly.

The night after Edie started waiting tables, a male customer, who appeared to be in his early thirties, began coming into the restaurant. He reminded her of the boys she had gone to junior high with, the ones who always acted as if they were too good for her. And now here he was all grown-up, well-dressed, well groomed, medium height with curly brown hair. He always asked to be seated in Edie's station and chatted with her as much as her time would allow. He told her his name was Ken Rosenberg and wanted to know her name, what days she worked, what time she got off work, and finally, one evening, would she go out with him.

She was flattered. "Sure," she said, "I'll go out with you. I get off at eleven. Why don't we go for a drink?"

"I'll be back," he said.

At eleven, washing up in the bathroom, she regretted her decision. Why had she agreed to this? She was dead tired and she didn't feel like making small talk. Besides, nothing could come of this. Once he found out the gory details of her past, he wouldn't want anything to do with her--especially if he really was like the boys from her junior high. Maybe it would be better if he didn't show up.

But there he was at eleven waiting for her at the door. "Where to?" he asked.

"What's still open?" she asked.

"I know a place," he said.

She followed him outside and he opened the door of his Mercedes for her.

"Nice car," she said.

"I just got it," he said.

They drove to a restaurant on Wilshire Boulevard, and once inside sat in a red leather booth in the bar. It was dark and smoke filled. Edie ordered a vodka and tonic; Ken ordered a Scotch on the rocks.

"So tell me about you," he said.

"Well, I'm 28, I work at Chantilly, I'm from Detroit, Michigan, and I have two children." She watched to see how this last would affect him.

He carried it off quite well. "But you're not married." More of a statement than a question.

"No, I'm not married."

"Well," he sighed, "now that we have that out of the way."

"You don't mind that I have children?"

"I love children," he said. "I'd like to have a few myself."

The waitress set their drinks in front of them. "And you?" she asked. "Tell me about you."

He told her that he was 32, a CPA, that he'd never been married, that his father had died 5 years before, and that he still lived at home with his mother.

"How does that work out?" she asked.

"Great," he said. "She's my best friend, always has been. And after my father died, she really needed me. But now..."

"Now?"

"Life must go on," he said.

They talked some more about her past, his past, and then seeing her yawn, he said, "Maybe I better take you home."

"I left my car at the restaurant."

"Well then, how about if I take you home and pick you up tomorrow morning and take you back to work."

"I have to drop the kids off at school at 9."

"Then I'll be by at 8:30."

"Don't you have to be at work?"

"I have a good boss. Me."

She agreed to let him drive her home, and after he parked, he came around and opened the car door for her, and said, "May I?" meaning could he kiss her goodnight.

"Yes," she said. It was a gentle kiss and she was pleased with it.

"See you in the morning," he said, and drove off.

She stood watching his Mercedes turn the corner. Was it possible? Could something come of this? Could she fall in love with this man, be happy with him? Was he someone who would love her and her children? It was a lot to expect from one drink, one goodnight kiss. Besides, she had this terrible secret--two terrible secrets. She'd better tell him tomorrow morning. She didn't want to lead him on under false pretenses.

The next morning he appeared promptly at 8:30, kissed her good morning, drove the kids to school, and took her out for breakfast. She knew she should tell him over her English muffin and coffee, but it was such a beautiful morning, and she was feeling so happy that she didn't want to spoil it. If something came of this, there would be time to tell him later, and if nothing came of this, it would be just as well she hadn't told him.

He was waiting for her again that night at eleven, and kissed her goodnight again, and asked if he could see her the next night.

"I think you're rushing me," she said.

"I've waited 32 years for the right person," he said. "I don't want to wait any longer."

"I may not be what you think I am."

"Does that mean you have some deep dark past?"

"Maybe I do," she said.

"It won't matter," he said.

"Maybe it will," she said.

"Try me," he said.

"One day," she said.

As the days passed she began spending more and more time with Ken. He wanted to see her every night. He wanted to see her every morning. And he wanted to make love to her.

She put him off. She didn't want to take the chance of getting pregnant again, and she wasn't sure she was in love with him. Was it fair to go to bed with a man you don't love?

"I know you don't love me, now," Ken said, "but you'll learn to. I'm crazy about you."

She didn't know what to do. She liked him, she felt comfortable in his presence. He was a good man and kind to her children. But there was no magical connection with him, no electricity, no overwhelming passion as there had been with Stanley, Zola, the man in Paris, Stefano. Maybe at this stage of her life, it would be better to give up on the lightning flash at midnight and settle for someone who was nice. The kind of man her mother would choose for her: steady, reliable, successful. The kind of man who would be a good father to her children.

Was it fair not to go to bed with a man who loved you?

She decided it wasn't.

She knew she should tell him about Wendy and Brian before they got more deeply involved, but it never seemed like the right time. Besides, things were going so badly at Chantilly that she didn't think she could handle one more disappointment at this moment.

She outfitted herself with a diaphragm, and three times a week, Ken would rent a motel room, and they would make love. She concentrated on trying to satisfy him. She tried to be the wild woman she had been in Paris, imaginative, aggressive, and he was so grateful that she would take his penis in her mouth, that she would let him come in her mouth, that he took a long time fondling her, bringing her to a climax, so that sex was good with him. She enjoyed it. It was okay.

Chantilly, however, was not.

They had a lot of steady customers; they were almost full every Saturday night, but it wasn't enough. Between the food costs, the labor costs, and the rent, their expenses were too high. They needed to raise their prices, but were afraid if they raised them any higher, they would lose even more business.

It was a tightrope: to raise prices or lower them?

Lester was fed up. He had planned to finance this restaurant, but he hadn't planned on making it a lifelong commitment. It was draining him. There was a limit to what a good screw was worth, and now that Gordon was working so many hours, he wasn't even that good a screw.

"Maybe I should blackmail him," Gordon said.

"You wouldn't," Edie said.

"Of course not," Gordon said.

They were going to have to admit it; they were going to have to face the reality; they had failed. They would have to throw in the serviette; they would have to close their doors.

It was a nightmare. Their beautiful Chantilly was being torn apart. The creditors were there, taking things back, the tables and chairs, the kitchen equipment, the ovens and stoves, the shiny stainless steel counters, the bottles of liquor. Everything was being moved out the door and onto trucks, and all Edie and Gordon could do was stand and watch.

"I'll never do this again," Edie said. "It's too painful."

"We were good," Gordon said. "Weren't we good, Edie?"

"We were great, Gordon. The public just wasn't ready for us."

"Someday," Gordon said. "Someday we'll do it again. Someday when we have enough money to last."

But Edie didn't think that day would ever come. When would they ever have that much money?

"I feel worse for you than for myself," Gordon said. "You've got those bambinos to support and now you don't even have a job."

"It's okay, Gordon, I'll find something."

"I feel shitty. If I hadn't coerced you into coming with me, you'd still be working for Alain."

She put her arms around him, "I wanted to do it, Gordon. And it was exciting while it lasted."

His eyes were filled with tears, "Now what are we going to do?"

And seeing his tears, she began to cry, not for herself, not even for Gordon, but for Chantilly.

Finally they pulled apart, wiped their eyes, and walked across the almost empty restaurant that would soon be a ladies' boutique and turned off the lights.

"Take a basket of flowers," Gordon said. "You should get something out of this."

"You mean the flowers weren't repossessed?"

"No," Gordon said, "I paid cash for them."

"Okay," Edie said, "as a remembrance. I will treasure it always."

And they walked out the door together for the last time.

"Au revoir, Chantilly," Gordon said, and they hugged once again, and then headed off in their separate directions.

Chapter Nineteen

Edie could not go back into another restaurant. Not just yet. She felt decimated. She felt she had lost someone she loved. Chantilly was not just a collection of tables and chairs, it was a living, breathing entity; it was a presence. And it had its own unique personality, a composite of its beautiful furnishings, its waiters, busboys, its patrons, Gordon cooking in the kitchen, even Edie, scurrying back and forth, making sure everything and everyone was working. It had existed in this world and now it was gone. Torn apart piece by piece, and Edie needed time to mourn. She called Janet. "I can't believe how miserable I feel."

"Maybe you want to come for a visit."

"With what? Every penny I had went into that restaurant."

"I could send you some money."

"No. I can't ask that, but I'll tell you one thing. Never again. I couldn't live through this again."

"Hah!" Janet said. "You expect me to believe that. It's in your blood, Edie, and once it's in your blood, you'll never be free of it."

In spite of what Janet had said, Edie was determined to find a job in something other than the restaurant business. She searched through the want ads.

"It's ridiculous for you to have to get a job," Ken said. "Marry me. I'll take care of you. We'll buy a house with a nice back yard, with a swimming pool, and you can stay home and take care of the kids."

"Oh, Ken, I do love you, but..."

"I know, like a brother. Like you love Gordon."

"No, not like that," she said, "more than that."

"It's okay," he said. "I have enough love for both of us and in time I'm sure you'll come to love me as much as I love you."

"And if I don't?"

"I don't need you to love me; I only need to love you."

"I don't know, Ken. Let me think about it."

She went on two interviews, thought about teaching again, thought about another restaurant, and felt totally overwhelmed.

Ken came to dinner. She made him shrimp scampi, his favorite, spending too much money on the giant shrimps, but wanting to please him. After dinner, and after Edie had supervised the children's baths, read them a story, and tucked them into bed, Ken was waiting for her.

"Could we just this once make love in your bed?" he asked.

She was too weak to resist. "All right," she said. She checked to make sure the children were asleep, and then followed him into her room and locked the door.

Their love-making had settled into a routine. They fondled each other for awhile, he put his penis in her mouth until he could hold back no longer and then he came in her vagina. Sometimes if he was sure she had an orgasm, he would come in her mouth. Tonight she didn't have an orgasm, perhaps because she was worried about the children in the next room, but she was content just to feel close to him, just to feel loved, just to make him happy. When they had finished and she was lying cuddled in his arms, he again asked her to marry him.

She had been thinking about it. She felt she had no energy to go on with the fight. Marrying Ken would be an easy way out. It would mean accepting defeat; giving up on her dream of doing something special with her life. But he would be a good father to her children and maybe that was more important than any dream.

But she couldn't marry him without telling him her secrets, even though now was the worst possible time to tell him. With the loss of Chantilly, she didn't feel she could stand another loss. But she couldn't marry him without telling him. "I think it's time to tell you about my deep, dark past," she said.

"I don't really need to hear it," he said.

"Yes, you do. The only thing is you have to swear you'll never tell another living soul." She had to make sure no one in Los Angeles would ever know about her children.

"Now, you're scaring me," he said.

"I can't tell you unless you swear," she said.

"I swear," he answered.

"The thing is I wasn't married to either of my children's fathers."

She felt his body tense. "I thought you were married to Zola."

"I should have told you sooner, I should have told you before we got so involved. But I didn't want anyone to know."

"Then who is Zola?"

"He *is* Wendy's father, but I wasn't married to him."

"And Brian?"

"Brian's father was a man I knew in Paris. I wasn't married to him, either. I know it sounds like I led a pretty wild life, but it really wasn't. Zola and the man in Paris are the only two men I ever slept with...besides you."

"Is there anything else I should know?" he asked somewhat sarcastically.

She thought fleetingly of Stefano. "No," she said, "nothing else."

He got up and pulled on his pants. "It's late," he said, "I'd better go." They never spent the night together; Edie had to get home to her children, and Ken had to get home to his mother. He didn't want his mother to think Edie was the kind of girl who would sleep with him before they were married.

He bent over and kissed her. "I'll call you tomorrow," he said, and Edie listened as he walked to the front door and it opened and closed.

"Well that's the end of that," Edie thought, her eyes filling with tears. She shouldn't have told him. What a dumb, stupid thing to do. She could have just gone along and not married him, or she could have married him and not told him. At least she would have someone who loved her, someone to hold her, someone to take care of her. Obviously she cared for him more than she thought. Obviously she had screwed up her life again.

Ken did not drive immediately home; he drove around the streets of Beverly Hills, thinking.

It was quite a shock. Quite a shock. But then maybe that was part of why he loved her so much. She was different from all the other girls he'd known. She had a sparkle they didn't have. Perhaps she was a little too strong-willed and independent, but she was also fun, exciting, pretty, smart, Jewish, and great in bed. He loved that she took his penis in her mouth; that she let him come in her mouth. Neither of the other two girls he had slept with would let him do that. He was 32 already, still living in a bedroom in his mother's house. If he didn't make the move now, then when? Someone as good as Edie might never come along again. The important thing was that his mother never find out about her past, and if his mother never knew, then what difference did it make?

At the next corner, he made a right turn and headed back to Edie's.

When he got there, it was after midnight. He rang the bell and in a few minutes she came to the door, wearing her pink print robe. "Ken."

"I don't care," he said, "I don't care about any of it. I love you and I want to marry you."

And she opened her robe and enclosed him in her arms.

Edie's parents were thrilled that Edie was finally getting married, and to someone who sounded so perfect. "I want to make you a big wedding," Lilly said over the phone, "just like Frank had."

"No, mom, that would be silly. We'll just slip away to Vegas and do it quietly."

"Then you'll come back to Detroit for a reception. We've got to have some kind of celebration."

"All right, but keep it small, will you?" Edie knew it was a fruitless request. If her mother made a reception, it was going to be as extravagant as her brother's wedding, and there was nothing Edie could do about it. But maybe that was all right. Maybe her mother deserved some "nachos" after all the torture Edie had put her through.

As for Ken's mother, Liz, she would not hear of Las Vegas.

Liz was not thrilled about the forthcoming wedding. She did not like the fact that Edie was 29, that she was twice-divorced, that she had two children. Ken was only 32; he could have taken his time, looked around for someone better. It wasn't as if he was being forced out of her house. But if this was who Ken had chosen then Liz would make the best of it. But this was her only son, his only wedding, and she wanted it all: the band, the flowers, the bridesmaids and ushers, and the sit-down dinner.

"I waited all my life for Ken to get married," she told Edie. "You're not going to deprive me of a wedding, are you?"

"I don't know what to do," Edie said to Ken. It wasn't that she didn't want a wedding; it was that she didn't think she deserved one. Does a woman with two illegitimate children deserve a wedding?

"Let my mother have her wedding," Ken said. "She doesn't have much in her life, but me, and when I move out, she'll have even less."

"But I feel so embarrassed about it."

"Why should you feel embarrassed? You've never had a wedding, why shouldn't you have one now?"

"Because..." she hesitated, "I'm a mother with two children." She decided to leave out the word "illegitimate".

"So?"

"All right," Edie said, "but let's keep it simple."

Liz, however, had other ideas. She wanted the wedding at Temple Beth Hillel, she wanted 200 people, and she wanted Edie to wear a long white gown.

"I think that's going too far," Edie said to Ken.

"What's the big deal?" Ken said. "You think every girl who walks down the aisle is a virgin?"

"It's not that. It just seems so...silly."

"It'll make my mother happy."

And Edie remembering Cookie in her white gown, smiled, and said, "Yeah, what's the big deal? So all right, I'll wear a long white gown."

Now Liz wanted to know who their bridesmaids and ushers were going to be. "What kind of wedding is it without a bridal party?"

"But I don't have anyone to ask," Edie told Ken, "except of course, Janet."

"Well I have a ton of relatives and friends," Ken said.

"I suppose I could ask Gordon," Edie mused.

"With or without Lester?"

"Lester is long gone."

And Ken, not sure if she was serious or not about asking Gordon, said, "Could we just have him as a guest?"

Edie sensed an attitude in Ken she didn't like. "Why?"

"Because I just don't prefer him in the bridal party."

"Because he's gay?"

"Look," Ken said, "if you want him as a friend, fine. I just don't want him to be an usher at my wedding."

Edie thought for a long moment. She was disappointed in Ken, but she didn't want a disagreement over Gordon to spoil their wedding. "All right," she said, "you have your ton of relatives and friends and I'll ask Janet."

Six weeks before the wedding, Ken bought Edie a house in Encino, in the San Fernando Valley. It was a nice house, four bedrooms, one for each kid, and one for the kid they were going to have as soon as it was proper, and a large yard, plenty of room for a pool. "It's going to be your first order of business," Ken told Edie, "after getting pregnant, teaching the kids to swim."

Edie immediately set to work decorating their new home. She decided on country French, and purchased two sofas with a blue, yellow and red floral design, a side chair in a red-checked fabric, natural pine tables, and an armoire in a medium dark oak. The kitchen was also going to be blue and yellow with a touch of red, with a pine table, high back chairs with rush seats, and cushions with a small floral print. There were also baskets of dried flowers placed about the house, including the one from Chantilly, and the quimper vase she had brought with her from France sat upon her living-room coffee table.

A week before the wedding enough of the furniture had arrived so that Edie and her children could move into the house, and then two days before the wedding, Janet flew in from New York to be Edie's maid of honor.

Edie and the children met her at the airport, and after Janet had hugged Edie and Wendy, she bent down to Brian. He was holding a teddy bear and sucking his thumb. "Give Aunt Janet a kiss," she said. After a moment's hesitation he plopped a big wet kiss on Janet's cheek. She had not seen Brian since her mother died, and now she was struck by how much he looked like Mike. "You're such a beautiful little boy," she said, wrapping him in her arms and feeling a wave of love for him.

"You're the one who's beautiful," Edie said, as they began their walk to the baggage claim. Janet's hair was still short, but cut in a shag and smooth. She still wasn't wearing any make-up except lipstick, but she had lost fifteen pounds and the result was amazing. She was pretty--just like Edie had once predicted, and she looked stunning in her teal blue suit and black high heels.

"What did you do with your hair?" Edie asked.

"Do you like it?'

"I love it."

"It's something new I discovered--a beauty shop."

"And your suit. It's stunning."

Janet blushed, "I thought I'd get dressed up for the occasion."

"I don't think I ever saw you in high heels," Edie said.

"It's my only pair," Janet said apologetically.

"You don't have to apologize," Edie said. "It's okay to get dressed up."

"Yeah," Janet said, "I can see that from what you're wearing."

Edie was dressed in white shorts, a red t-shirt, and white tennis shoes. Her body was still slim and lithe, and her hair was pulled back in its customary pony tail and bangs. "I'm a housewife, now," Edie said. "No need to dress up."

They got the luggage and headed for Edie's blue Chevy Impala. "I can't get over the kids," Janet said, "how big they've gotten." Wendy, now seven, was tall and thin, her legs too long for her body. She had finally allowed her mother to cut her hair a few inches, but it still hung to the middle of her back. Brian, now three, was a chubby little boy with blue eyes and straight blond hair cut like the Beatles, long, almost to his shoulders.

"Can I sit in back with Aunt Janet?" Wendy asked.

"No, honey," Edie said. "Aunt Janet wants to sit up front with me."

"Please," Wendy said.

And then Brian, tugging at Edie's shorts and mimicking his sister, "Please, mommy, we want to sit with Aunt Janet."

So of course Edie gave in and Janet sat in the back seat on the drive to the San Fernando Valley, with Wendy sitting beside her and Brian sitting on her lap, even though Brian wasn't sure who Aunt Janet was.

That night, Edie got a babysitter so that the two friends could go out on the town. It was Edie's last night as a single person and she decided that they should both get dressed up and make it a real bachelorette party. They both wore black dresses and black high heels, and Edie made up Janet's face with blue eye shadow, black mascara, and blush, and again was astonished at how attractive Janet looked. Edie wore her hair hanging loose on her shoulders and brushed her wispy bangs off her forehead.

"You look beautiful, mommy," Wendy said.

"Yeah," Brian said, already in his pajamas and trailing his teddy bear, "and so does Aunt Janet."

Janet knelt beside him and took his hands in hers. "You're such a sweet little boy," she said, tears filling her eyes. And then, "You know I love you."

And Edie, standing and watching them was overcome with sorrow for Janet. Edie had Wendy and Brian, she was about to marry a wonderful man, and Janet had no one.

"Time to go," she said.

The two friends started by popping into a few restaurants on La Cienega where they tried a variety of appetizers. Then they drove downtown for duck at Paul's Duck Press, where Janet outlined her past year of jobs.

"Let's see, after Lombardo's, there was three months at Escargot, two months at The Three Horsemen, those miserable two weeks at Chatham's, and ever since, I've been at Tres Champignon."

"And you like it there."

"I like working for Jean Jacque, and being souschef."

"It must be difficult after running Vittorio's to have to be number two."

"Number two isn't bad, it's three, four and five that hurt."

When the friends had finished their dinner, they drove out to the Sea Lion on the beach, where they sat by a huge picture window drinking coffee and eating chocolate mousse pie, while the waves crashed against the shore and splashed onto the glass window.

"Ken seems like a nice guy," Janet said.

"He's a great guy," Edie said.

"But?"

"Why do you think there are any buts?"

"Because I knew you when," Janet said, with a knowing grin.

"Yes," Edie said, "in the heat of my greatest passion."

"Are we talking about the man in Paris, or Stefano?"

"Stefano was not passion. Something better. Something deeper."

"Is there something better than passion?"

"Yes," Edie said, without a moment's hesitation.

And Janet, still haunted by her memories of Mike said, "I'd settle for passion."

Edie, feeling again the sorrow she had felt earlier in the evening, asked, "You've never met anyone else?"

Janet thought of Linda Sheridan and began to blush. "There was one woman who tried to seduce me."

Edie was not as shocked as she thought she should be. "Oh Janet, tell me what happened."

And Janet told her about her encounter with Linda, and finished, "I don't know whether to laugh or cry."

"You know," Edie said, "back in Paris, when I couldn't figure out what was wrong with you, I thought it might be a woman."

"How wrong you were," Janet said, and the two friends felt a connection through their memories of Mike Kelly. "Well at least I won't die a virgin," Janet said.

"Then I guess we both owe him a debt," Edie said. "You won't die a virgin, and I have Brian."

On the drive back to the San Fernando Valley, Edie said, "I can't remember when I've had such a good time. I wish we could do this again before you leave."

"Me, too. I feel that Los Angeles has so much to teach me."

"It seems you'd know everything by now."

"'A chef is never done learning', to quote Jacque Patou. And he was right. There are always new techniques, new tools, even new ingredients. The Far East is having its influence, and Mexico. Especially in California. There must be all kinds of new spices and flavors that have become popular here that we in New York don't even know exist."

"Yes. Cilantro, black beans, blue corn tortillas. They're pretty popular."

"I want to learn all about them. I want to go to Mexico, and I want to go to the Far East--if I had the money or the time. I just wish I had enough time to try all of your fine restaurants, and some of the not so fine."

"We could go on a binge tomorrow before the wedding. But then I wouldn't fit into my gown."

"How about the day after the wedding? Do you think Ken would mind if we went restaurant hopping?"

"Not if he spends the day with his mother," Edie said with a bit of humor in her voice.

"Seriously?"

"Seriously."

"Are we having a mother-in-law problem here?"

"Not as long as I do everything she wants."

Janet, looking at her friend, "You're sure you want to go through with this?"

And Edie, "I'm sure."

And Janet sighing, "I hope you're not making a mistake, Edie."

"It won't be my first," Edie said.

The next day, Edie's parents, who would be staying at Edie's house for the next three nights, flew in from Detroit, and that evening, on August 21, 1965, after all the preparation, all the planning, all the shopping, Edie and Ken were married. Edie wore her beautiful white gown, Wendy was the flower girl, Brian was the ring bearer, and Janet was the maid of honor. There were five bridesmaids and five ushers, all relatives and friends of Ken, and after the ceremony, there were drinks, food and music. Edie did her best to play the blushing bride: she danced the first dance, posed for pictures, cut the cake and threw the bouquet to Janet, but all the while she was praying that she was not making a mistake, that Ken was the right man for her and that she would grow to love him.

That night after the wedding, Ken and Edie returned to their house in Encino, and for the first time since they'd met, they spent the night together. It was a treat for both of them not to have to get up in the middle of the night to "go home", but they made love quickly and quietly because Edie's parents were asleep in the next room and Janet was asleep on the sofa in the living room.

The next day, the first day of their marriage, Edie spent the day with Janet, and Ken spent the day with his mother. Edie felt a little guilty about going off with Janet, but she knew Ken loved being with his mother and Edie would be spending the rest of her life with him. Janet was only going to be in Los Angeles for one more day.

The two women started out by going to the markets in Chinatown, then Little Tokyo, and then walking the streets of Beverly Hills, looking in on all the restaurants that were open, reading menus, trying a dish a two, and then walking the streets of La Cienega, again going into restaurants and ordering things that looked interesting. It was like being in France again, on the hunt for new ideas, a well prepared dish, a different presentation.

They didn't arrive back at the house until eight.

Edie's mother was furious.

"I can't believe the first day of your marriage and you spent it with Janet."

"I asked Ken and he said it would be all right. We're going to spend the rest of our lives together and Janet's only here for four days."

"Still," her mother said, "it isn't right."

"If Ken didn't mind, why should you?"

"Because it isn't right."

There was no arguing with that.

Ken showed up five minutes later. He hadn't eaten yet; he and his mother had spent the day running errands, returning gifts, shopping, and he was starving. He wanted to take everyone out to dinner, but Lilly and Ben had already eaten with the kids, so he took Edie and Janet out, more restaurant hopping. What could be better?

That night, in bed, Edie asked Ken, "You're sure you don't mind that I spent the day with Janet?"

In a way, he did resent it, her shunting him aside as if he was a charm on her bracelet, throwing him a consolation prize--his mother. But he didn't want to be petty and he understood her reasoning, so he said, "Of course not."

"My mother was so concerned."

"It's okay," he said, "I understand."

And she put her hands on his naked buttocks, determined to be especially passionate tonight.

Janet left the next morning, and the following morning, Edie, Ken, Liz, the kids, and Edie's parents left for Detroit for the reception Edie's parents were giving the newlyweds.

Edie's parents had rented out the Rainbow Inn on Wyoming for the occasion and it looked as if everyone Edie had known her whole life was there. Edie's aunts, uncles and cousins had flown in from Chicago and Cleveland, and even her Grandmother Rose had come from Florida, without her husband, Arthur, who was too ill to travel. Sandy Stahler came in from Ann Arbor with her husband, Danny Lieberman, a research chemist at University of Michigan, and Naomi Parker Cohen attended, *with* her husband. All the guests were extremely warm and friendly to Edie, even those people who had once vilified her.

Zola's parents, Yuri and Olga Bitterman were among the first to greet Edie and wanted to know all about Edie's trip to see Zola and if they could spend some time with Wendy.

"I'm sure Wendy would love it," Edie told them.

Stanley and Yelena came over to say, "hi". Yelena was pregnant again with her fourth child, and she looked like a beach ball, round and colorful. In spite of the fact that she was dressed in an expensive sequin dress, that her hair was teased five inches above her head and that her round, pudgy face was covered with make-up, she was singularly unattractive. Stanley, by contrast, was still handsome, still a dashing figure.

"Can I have the next dance?" he asked.

"Of course you can," Edie answered, and he whisked her off, leaving Yelena standing there with a knish in one hand and an eggroll in the other.

"So," he said, "you finally found Prince Charming."

"Isn't he," Edie tossed back, feeling light-hearted, flirtatious.

"He seems like a nice guy. Maybe too nice for you."

"And what's that supposed to mean?"

"How much does he know about you?"

She felt the muscles in her chest tighten, "Everything."

"And he loves you anyway."

"Of course."

"You know I once loved you," he said. "Maybe I still do."

She felt a flutter in her stomach, "Stanley, what are you trying to say?"

His left eyelid began to droop. "Maybe things haven't worked out as I thought they would."

"Then I'm sorry for you," she said.

"Tell me you don't still have feelings for me."

"I don't still have feelings for you."

"I don't believe you," he said. "You don't love a person for five years and then stop loving them."

And suddenly all her tension vanished. Stanley was just being Stanley. He needed to feel that he still owned her. She looked into his gray eyes, "It's over, Stanley. It was over the day you married Yelena."

"What does marriage have to do with love?"

"Maybe nothing. But it is a commitment to another person. Whether you love them or not, there's no turning back."

"Sounds like a prison sentence."

"I didn't mean it that way."

"So if I asked you right now to run away with me, you wouldn't do it?"

"You wouldn't ask me, and I wouldn't do it. I belong to Ken, now."

"You belong to Ken. That's sounds so subservient."

"And he belongs to me, of course."

There were others about them now, waiting to talk to her, and Stanley leaned over and kissed her. "Don't forget, you once belonged to me."

Finally, the last guest had kissed Edie goodbye, all the presents were loaded into the family cars, and Frank and Cookie came over to Lilly's house, where Edie, her children, Ken and Liz were staying.

Edie went into the bedroom and changed from her white lace dress into blue jeans and was sitting on the floor looking under the bed for her slippers, when Frank entered the room.

"Here you are," he said.

"I had to get out of that dress," she said.

He seemed fidgety. "I just wanted to say what a good move it was on your part, marrying Ken."

Edie looked up at him, her big brother Frank, who hadn't spoken to her in any real sense since she refused to have an abortion with Wendy. "You mean you don't have to be ashamed of me anymore."

"I mean now that you're married, people will forgive and forget."

"Most people already have," she said.

Now Frank became annoyed, "You know, I came in here to try to make up with you, to try to have a decent relationship with my sister. Why are you trying to pick a fight with me?"

She tried to hold back, but she couldn't, and the words came tumbling out, "I guess because I resent you 'forgiving' me now. Where were you all those years when I needed you?"

"You're impossible," he said. "You've been impossible ever since you went away to Michigan. I'll never forgive myself for talking mother into letting you go." He turned to leave.

Immediately she was sorry. Why had she opened her big mouth. She wanted her brother back. She stood up. "Frank, I'm sorry. I don't know why I said all that. I don't want to fight. I want to be friends."

He turned to face her, his eyes were glassy. "I've missed you," he said.

"I've missed you, too," she said. And with one slipper on and one slipper off she walked over and embraced him.

By the time Edie and Frank entered the living room, the gifts were all assembled and ready to be opened. Edie sat beside Ken and together they untied all the ribbons, opened all the boxes, separating them into two piles, the take home and take back, while Liz commented on each item, "Give that electric frying pan back. You'll never use it," and "Another crystal bowl, just what you needed!" Cookie wrote up a list so Edie could send thank-yous, and they all drank champagne. It had been a wonderful evening and now Edie was ready to go back to Los Angeles and be Ken's wife.

Chapter Twenty

Janet arrived back in New York from Edie's wedding on a Tuesday evening. She had taken a bus to Grand Central Station and then a cab to her apartment on 79th and 8th. She never rode the subways at night.

Once inside her door, she hung up her black dress, her teal blue suit, and the pink taffeta dress she had worn to the wedding. She put her black high heels on a shelf in the bedroom closet, wondering when she would ever wear them again. Then, back in the living room, she poured herself a small glass of wine, turned on the T.V., and sat in her recliner with her legs up, thinking about her trip to Los Angeles. How lucky Edie was to have Ken. So he wasn't the great passion of Edie's life. He was still a nice man and he loved her. What Janet wouldn't give to have someone who loved her. It had never happened. Even the man in Paris who had aroused every emotion in her being had not loved her. He had only used her. She thought she would have a second glass of wine tonight, although it was against her rules. She didn't think she could face the long night ahead without it. She got up and walked to the kitchen. It had been a wonderful four days, but it had left her feeling more empty and alone than before she had gone to Los Angeles.

Janet stayed on working as souschef beside Jean Jacque at Tres Champignon for the next few months, and then on a Wednesday morning in September, 1964, just when she was about to leave for the restaurant, she received a phone call from Mr. Lombardo. It had been eighteen months since she had left him.

"Janet, can you stop by the restaurant on your way to work. I'd like to talk to you."

"Sure," she said. She took a cab over to Lombardo's and when she arrived, Marcel, the chef Mr. Lombardo had hired instead of Janet, came stomping out of Mr. Lombardo's office. Marcel took off his white apron, threw it on the floor, looked at Janet with venom in his eyes, and huffed out the door. Janet stood in amazement looking after him, and then Mr. Lombardo, dressed in a gray silk suit, came out of his office and said, "Janet, you're here. Please come in."

She took a seat in front of his desk where she had sat before--the day he had given her the devastating news--only this time she expected nothing. Her shell was up. There was no way he could hurt her as he had hurt her before.

He folded his hands in front of him, and said, "Janet, I can see now that I made a terrible mistake letting you go and hiring Marcel. Marcel has driven my business into the ground. I want you to come back."

Janet would not allow herself to think of what he might mean, but she could feel the blood pulsating through her veins. "In what capacity?"

"As chef."

The words reiterated in her brain. She wanted to jump up and run around the desk and fling her arms around Mr. Lombardo. But instead, she sat stoic, trying to control the tears forming at the edges of her eyes, and trying to keep her voice steady, casual. "When do you want me to start?"

"Today. This minute. Marcel's walked out and he's never coming back."

"I'll have to give my boss a week's notice."

"Then you'll do it?"

Her face broke into a wide grin, "I can't wait to start."

She floated out of his office. It had happened. It had finally happened. Chef at a first-rate New York restaurant. She thought of her mother, her papa, how proud they would be of her. And then she thought of Edie. She had to tell Edie. She went to the phone next to the ladies' room, and when Edie came on the line, she was so bursting with joy, she could barely get the words out, "Edie, you'll never guess what happened. Mr. Lombardo has just asked me to be chef at Lombardo's!"

Chapter Twenty-One

The year after Edie was married, she gave birth to a baby girl. She and Ken named the baby Melissa, after Ken's father, Marvin.

At first it was difficult managing with the new baby, being up all night with her feedings and diaper changes, and then trying to get everything done in the daytime that needed to be done: cleaning the house, cooking the meals, getting Wendy and Brian off to school, Wendy to ballet lessons, and both children to visit their friends. Fortunately, Ken hired a black lady named Ruth to help her out once a week, but still Edie was always tired.

And then, at 3 months, Melissa was sleeping through the night and life became easier.

Ken cut the cleaning lady down to once a month, and expected that Edie should have no problem managing everything.

And she tried. She wanted to be the perfect wife to Ken, to make up to him for not feeling the way she wanted to feel. She kept the house immaculately clean, cooked imaginative and delicious suppers, learned to play bridge, took tennis lessons, entertained his clients and friends with elaborate dinner parties every few months, spent every Friday night visiting his mother, and had sex with him whenever he wanted it, which turned out to be every Wednesday and Sunday night, except during tax season, when he might skip a week or two.

To the world, it looked as if they were a happy couple, but Edie knew she wasn't happy and suspected Ken wasn't either. When she tried talking to him about their relationship, he'd say, "Everything's fine. Stop trying to make trouble."

She didn't know what to do. Perhaps getting a job would help--maybe she was bored. But when she mentioned the idea to Ken, he was adamant. "If you wanted to go off and desert your children that was your business, but you're not going to desert mine."

And that was another problem. His attitude toward Wendy and Brian. Once Melissa was born, he separated the children into "his" and "hers." He was crazy about "his child". He couldn't wait to get home from work to be with her, to play with her, although he avoided most of the dirty work, ("Edie, I think Missy needs her diaper changed"). But the more involved he got with "his" child, the cooler he became to "her" children. He was too tired to read Brian a story; he didn't have time to pick Wendy up from ballet. He was annoyed when they giggled at the dinner table. Edie didn't know how to deal with it. Say to him, "You better be nice to my children, or else."

Edie was sure that Wendy and Brian sensed it, too, but she hesitated to mention it to them for fear she'd raise a problem where one didn't exist.

Then one Saturday afternoon when she picked Wendy and Brian up from friends they were visiting, in the new white Ford station wagon Ken had bought her, Wendy, her bright, brilliant eight-year-old said, "You know, mom, Ken's changed."

Edie tensed, "In what way?"

"Ever since Melissa was born. He doesn't like us anymore."

A sickening feeling came over Edie. "Don't be silly. Of course, he likes you. Who wouldn't like you?"

"He likes Melissa better."

Edie considered her answer. She didn't want to lie to her children, but she didn't want them to think their step-father didn't love them. "I guess it's only natural that Ken should be partial to his naturally born child. But that doesn't mean he doesn't love you."

Chubby little Brian with the long blond hair, now four, asked, "Are you partial to us, mom?"

Brian could break her heart. Brian who had no daddy, just her. "You're very special to me, but I love all of my children the same." Where had she heard that? From her mother. But when her mother had said it she knew it was a lie; she knew her mother loved Frank more.

That night she determined to talk to Ken about the situation. She waited until all the children were asleep, and when she and Ken were alone in the den watching television, she said, "Ken, there's something I want to talk to you about. I think Wendy and Brian are beginning to sense some partiality on your part towards Melissa."

"Why, what did they say?"

Immediately she was sorry she had brought Wendy and Brian into it. She didn't want him to feel any more animosity toward them. "It isn't what they said. It's what I see."

"Well, it's true," he said. "I do feel partial towards my daughter. Is there anything wrong with that?"

"Yes," she said, "if Wendy and Brian feel it."

"Look, Edie, I'm doing everything a father could be expected to do, under the circumstances. I pay for their food, their shelter, Wendy's ballet lessons, Brian's nursery school. What more do you want?"

"I want you to support them emotionally."

"Considering their history, I think I do a damn fine job."

Edie cringed. How could he have said such a thing? It was as much an insult to her, as to her children. "And does that mean, considering my history, you do a damn fine job, too."

He got up. "I don't want to argue with you. I just think you could be a little appreciative of me. Of my feelings, of what I do for you, not what I don't do." And he left the room.

She sat, shaking, for several minutes. What to do, now? Make a big fuss? Divorce him? Strike out in the world with *three* children to support? Take Melissa away from her adoring daddy. To what? What was there to run to? No, she would have to stay with him for now. Make the best of it. He wasn't, after all, an ogre. He was still a nice guy, a great father to his daughter. He just didn't love her children as much as he loved Melissa. She would just have to make it up to Wendy and Brian.

She looked at her watch. Ten o'clock. Too late to call Janet. She would call her in the morning. But she wouldn't tell Janet about any of this. There was nothing Janet could do to help and she didn't want to upset her friend. She just wanted to hear her voice.

Chapter Twenty-Two

Janet received Edie's call just as she was about to leave for Lombardo's. She could tell something was wrong, but Edie refused to tell her what it was--just hung up the phone with a promise to call again next week.

Janet was upset by her friend's call. She looked forward to hearing the brightness in Edie's voice and when it wasn't there, Janet felt scared. Was something terrible about to happen? And Janet incapable of preventing it?

Janet calmed herself. She must put this thought out of her mind. She must do what Edie was always telling her to do: think positive. She picked up her hairbrush, whisked it through her short brown hair, back to being fuzzy, and hurried out the door.

By the time Janet got to Lombardo's, Thomas, her souschef, was already there.

"How'd everything go last night?" she asked. She had taken the night off to go to Lucille Neumeier's fortieth birthday party.

"John didn't show up," Thomas said, "but what else is new?"

John was one of the dishwashers.

Janet went over to the crates of fruits and vegetables that had been delivered this morning, and began checking the sizes of the lemons, the oranges, the strawberries. They had paid for a certain size fruit, and each one had better be that size, not just the ones on top.

"We should fire him," Thomas said.

John was old, an alcoholic, and if Janet fired him what would he do? "He's here most of the time."

"How can you run a kitchen with someone so undependable?"

Janet had moved on to the green and red peppers. "If we fire him, who's to say we'll get anyone better."

"That's true," Thomas said.

Janet opened the refrigerator and stepped inside. Enough chicken, ducks, veal. "We're almost out of sausage," Janet said. Then stepping out of the refrigerator and closing the door behind her, "Let's get to work." Janet and her souschef, Thomas scrubbed their workboards, although they had been scrubbed yesterday at closing, and got out the pork, the spices, the grinders and began making the needed sausage.

The hours flew by; there was always so much to do. Lombardo's made its own pasta fresh each day and its own bread and desserts, and various people showed up during the day to do his or her job. But if someone didn't show up, then Janet and Thomas had to fill in. There wasn't a dull moment.

"The oven's acting up again," Alfredo, the pastry chef, growled.

"Look at these tarts!" Janet said, each one burned on the edges.

"It's not my fault," Alfredo said. "The oven's too hot."

"We can't serve these," and Janet took the whole batch and threw them into the garbage can.

"We might have scraped the edges," Thomas said.

"Not in my restaurant," Janet said. "Call the repair man, and Alfredo, start again."

"We don't have enough strawberries."

"Then make as many as you can, and get someone to start peeling apples."

If anyone should be fired, Janet thought, it was Alfredo. He was careless. But Mr. Lombardo loved Alfredo, and Janet had to put up with him.

Lunchtime was exciting, but dinner was the real show. It was as if everyone was in rehearsal all day, and at 6 o'clock, the curtain went up. By then, the kitchen was filled with cooks, dishwashers, busboys and waiters. All the pots were simmering with sauces or boiling with water, all the fry pans were shining clean and ready to go, all the ovens were baking or hot, and as the customers arrived, were seated, ordered, everyone in the kitchen swung into action. Thomas called the orders, and the cooks set to work, frying, tossing, combining the pre-set ingredients into the works of art Janet had conceived. There was constant activity, the doors to the kitchen swinging open and shut, the busboys and waiters hurrying in and out, getting the salads, the bread, then picking up the pastas, the veal, chicken, beef, and then the busboys getting the coffee cups, the espresso, more silverware and finally more tablecloths. It was a well oiled machine; everyone knew exactly what to do. And at the helm, Janet, the conductor of the orchestrated chaos, checked the soups, the sauces, the pasta, the meat, the fish; everything had to be perfect, and on time.

By 11 o'clock, things quieted down. The swinging doors stopped swinging so often, the waiters walked slower, the cooks were done. A few busboys and waiters carried coffee and dessert out to the few stragglers still finishing their dinners. And it was time for Janet to go home. She did not supervise the breakdown. Thomas did that. She did not have to count the silverware and the glasses, the pots and pans, Gloria, the manager, did that. Gloria even counted the tablecloths. "If I didn't count every single thing, within a week, we'd be robbed of everything," Gloria said.

Janet took a cab back to her apartment, feeling fulfilled, happy. Things had gone well tonight. She had done a good job.

Once inside the apartment, Janet took off her shoes, turned on the T.V., and was sitting in her brown leather lounger, sipping her glass of wine, when the telephone rang.

Her first thought was that it was Edie, but it was Gloria. "Janet, get here quick. We're on fire."

Janet called a cab, put on her shoes, and raced over to Lombardo's. The fire trucks were already there, spewing water on the black smoke emanating from her beautiful kitchen. "What happened?" she asked Gloria.

"A fire started in a stack of greasy frying pans waiting to be washed, and the next thing I knew the entire kitchen was in flames."

Thank God it hadn't started in the broken oven, Janet thought, then it would have been all her fault. And thank God, it had started after the restaurant was empty!

Mr. Lombardo showed up and began to cry. Janet was already crying.

"Don't worry, Janet," he told her. "I have insurance. We will rebuild. We'll make an even finer restaurant."

But Janet could not be comforted. It was her baby. And it was nothing but blackened rubble.

Janet hardly left her apartment for the next few days--she was too heartbroken over the destruction of Lombardo's. Yes, it was going to be rebuilt, but how long was that going to take? And what was she going to do in the meantime? In spite of her resolve to think positive, Janet could not help wondering why this had happened to her? Because things were going too well? Because she had finally let her guard down and was feeling secure? Was God trying to tell her something? Was he angry with her? Had he burned down Lombardo's just to teach her a lesson. That she had forgiven herself too soon; that she had not suffered enough.

And then the phone calls started coming in.

The managers of four Italian, two French and three hotel restaurants were after her. They wanted her to work for them. Her spirits lifted. Maybe God was not so angry after all. None of the job offers were exactly what she wanted: none of them were head chef. She wondered if it was because she was a woman, or that everyone expected she would go back to Lombardo's once it was rebuilt. But she had to do something, so she took the job of pastry chef at a French restaurant, Le Parc. The money would be almost as much as she had made at Lombardo's and it would be easy. Like a vacation. Just being responsible for desserts.

But working at Le Parc was not as she had envisioned. Perhaps because she didn't have enough to do. Perhaps because everyone acted as if they hated her. Especially the chef and the souschef. They never complimented her on anything she prepared. If she made the most beautiful and tastiest Bombe she had ever made, they wouldn't give it a nod. Although her tarte tatin was perfect, the apples not too soft, not too crunchy, the crust light and flaky, caramelized to perfection, they never said a word. And the other cooks weren't much better.

"What did you do at Lombardo's?" the grill chef asked her.

"I was the head chef."

"Oh," he said, and never spoke a word to her again.

She went home miserable each night. It was like her first year at Lombardo's. What had she done to make them hate her; what could she do to make them like her?

She didn't know what to say to them, so she just did her job each day, tried to make the best damn desserts New York had ever tasted, and prayed for the day when Lombardo's would re-open.

But Lombardo's was not going to re-open.

It took three months before Janet realized that Mr. Lombardo was stalling, that he really didn't want to open the restaurant again. And then the site was for sale.

By now, Janet was determined to leave Le Parc and she let it be known she was looking for a change. Back to an Italian restaurant preferably, back to being chef, if possible.

And again, miraculously, the calls came in.

She interviewed with a few places and decided to take the job as souschef at Umberto's. She didn't want to be second in command after being numero uno, but it was the best offer she got and anything was better than staying at Le Parc. Besides, if Umberto's didn't work out, she would get a job somewhere else.

Chapter Twenty-Three

It was March, 1969.

Melissa was three years old. She was a chubby little girl with brown curly hair like her father's, and she had his strong nose and brown eyes. Edie wondered if any of her children would ever look like her. Wendy, now eleven, was a beauty. She was tall and slender, her torso having finally caught up with her long legs, and she had Zola's dark eyes and dark hair. Brian, at seven, had lost his baby fat, and while he was short for his age, he was also slim, quiet and sensitive--like Stefano she often thought, and she made sure he wore his blond hair long, so that she would always think of Stefano when she looked at him.

Things were pleasant enough between Ken and herself. He was nice to her, she was nice to him. They were still making love, but only once a week now, every Sunday night, except during tax season when he was often too tired. Edie no longer looked forward to sex. It was something they were supposed to do--like brushing their teeth, instead of an expression of love between them.

Still, Edie would have been happy, if only Ken would let up on Wendy and Brian. He was constantly picking on them. They weren't helping out enough, they weren't doing their fair share, they were too demanding. "You have enough to do taking care of a Missy, you shouldn't have to wait on Wendy and Brian, too."

"I don't wait on them," she told him, "and I don't need their help. Anyway, they shouldn't be helping me; they're busy with their own lives."

"You can say that again. Does Wendy need piano *and* ballet lessons?"

"Yes, she does."

"And how many seven-year-olds get art lessons?"

"Brian is very talented. Did you see his beautiful watercolor on the dining room table? I want to encourage him with his drawing and painting."

"If you ask me he spends too much time with his drawing and painting. He should be out with the other boys playing baseball."

"I don't think he likes baseball."

"How can a seven-year-old know what he likes? You want me to take more of an interest in your children--okay, then, I've decided, I'm going to sign Brian up for Little League."

"You better ask him first."

"I'm going to sign him up, and he's going to go."

"Please, Ken, ask him first."

Ken turned to Edie with contempt in his eyes, and then he marched down the hall to Brian's room, while Edie stood and prayed that it would work out, that Brian would want to play baseball, that Brian and Ken could find some common ground on which to be friends.

"Brian," Edie heard Ken's voice filtering out into the hall, "I've decided to enroll you in Little League."

"But I don't want to play Little League."

"It doesn't matter what you want, you're going to do it."

"No, I'm not."

Edie moved closer to Brian's room, cringing with each word of this battle of wills.

"I'm your father and I say you're going to play."

"You're not my father. My father died in Italy."

There was a moment of silence and then Ken slammed out of Brian's room and as he passed Edie, he said, "It's all your fault."

"My fault?"

"Because you spoil them, you let them do anything they want."

"I treat them exactly the same way I treat Missy."

"Well I hope to God she doesn't turn out like Wendy and Brian," he said and stomped off.

Edie stood stunned for several moments. She could not understand his venom. Why was he so angry with her? She knocked on Brian's door. "Can I come in?"

"Sure, mom." He was sitting at his desk building a model car. It was another one of his hobbies, building model cars, boats and airplanes.

"I'm sorry if dad hurt you," Edie said.

"He's not my dad," Brian said. "My dad died in Italy."

And Edie bent over and hugged him. "He was trying to do something nice for you."

"No, he wasn't," Brian said. "He was doing it for himself."

And Edie thought, how could a seven-year-old know so much. "I love you, Brian," she said.

"I love you too, mom."

That night, when they were watching television, after the children were asleep, Edie said to Ken, "About what happened this afternoon...why were you so angry with me?"

"I think that should be obvious."

"It isn't obvious to me."

He reached for a handful of popcorn from the batch she had made. "I really don't want to discuss it," he said. "Let's just forget it, okay?"

She looked into his eyes. If she pursued it, she knew it would end as it always ended, with his leaving the room and then not talking to her for days. It was best to let some things go, she thought, and reached for the popcorn. "Sure," she said.

He looked relieved. "What do you want to watch?"

"Is there a movie on?" she asked.

In July, Wendy and Brian left to spend the summer with Zola. Wendy had spent at least a month with him every summer since that first one in Idaho, and Brian usually went with her for a week or two. Zola was no longer living in Idaho, but in Palo Alto, attending Stanford University and getting a degree in psychology. This summer, probably to get away from Ken who still hadn't forgiven him for not wanting to play Little League, Brian had begged his mother to let him go for the whole summer, too. "Please, mom, I promise I'll be good, and Zola really wants me."

"Okay," Edie said, "but if you get lonely, or want to come home for any reason, you'll let me know immediately. Ten weeks is a long time."

"I won't be lonely," Brian said, emphatically.

So Edie had taken them both to the airport and within a week of their departure, Edie was the one who was suffering from loneliness. She couldn't believe how much she missed them, how empty she felt. She tried to keep busy, taking Missy out every afternoon, to the park, to the zoo, to the supermarket and department stores, to visit friends, but still a depression hung over her.

Then, three weeks after Wendy and Brian had left, on a Wednesday afternoon, as Edie was taking Missy for a stroll in a mini-mall on Ventura Boulevard in Encino, she noticed a "help wanted" sign in the window of a little soup and sandwich restaurant.

Edie looked at the name, Quick Bite, and on a whim, decided to go inside.

It was a cute little place, 15 tables, but appealing.

"Hi," she said to the middle-aged woman behind the counter. "What kind of help are you looking for?"

"Just someone to help out lunchtimes."

"I see," Edie said, excitement building in her. And then, "Do you own this place?"

"Yes."

"Well how would I do?"

The woman looking from her to Missy, "Could you manage it? I mean with the baby?"

"Of course," Edie said with aplomb.

"Then you're hired," the woman said. "Can you start Monday morning?"

"No problem," Edie said, but when she was out the door, she said to herself, "What have I done?"

All the way home, she worried about what she was going to say to Ken. She didn't want to do anything that would drive them farther apart, but she wanted this job.

She told him as soon as they sat down to eat dinner.

"You took a job?" he said, anger blazing from his eyes.

"It's just part time," she said.

"I thought it was decided, that you were not going back to work. That you were going to stay home and take care of Missy."

"Yes, but for how long?"

"Until she doesn't need you anymore."

"Is that when she's five, ten, or twenty?"

"She's only three years old," he said.

"Old enough for nursery school, and it'd be better for her, anyway. She should spend more time with children her own age."

"Well I don't like it," Ken said.

"Please, Ken," Edie said, "I really want this job. And it's only three hours a day."

He was silent for a moment. "All right, but only three hours a day, and only while Missy's in nursery school."

"That's great," she said. "That's perfect."

By Friday, Edie had found a nursery school she liked, and on Monday morning she started work at the Quick Bite Soup and Sandwich Shop.

The owner of the Quick Bite was named Iris Mann. Iris was a no-nonsense kind of person, short, stout, with short brown hair streaked with gray. She had bought the shop with the money from her recent divorce settlement.

"I needed something to do to earn a living. I don't have an education, and fortunately, the kids are all grown up and out on their own so I don't have to worry about supporting them. I couldn't stand the thought of working in an office--isn't it terrible, I never learned to type, so I thought I'd try this."

"And how are you doing?" Edie asked.

"Just squeaking by."

"But well enough to hire some help."

"I had to," Iris said. "I can't handle it alone anymore. It's too exhausting."

"Well I hope I'll be able to help you."

"I pray you can," Iris said.

And Edie set to work. Iris made her own soups, two varieties a day, and fresh egg, tuna, chicken and turkey salad, served on a plate with lettuce, or in a sandwich. At least it was a simple menu and the food was fresh and delicious.

Edie came in early and helped prepare the salads and soups and then prepared the customers' orders at lunchtime. After a month, Iris confessed that the bookkeeping was overwhelming. Could Edie help her out? Edie knew Ken would be annoyed, but she couldn't see anything wrong with leaving Missy in nursery school an extra hour or two a day to help Iris. Besides it was something she wanted to do. So when Wendy and Brian returned from Palo Alto and went back to school, Edie extended the hours Missy was spending at nursery school and began adding the receipts each day, paying the bills, tracking the inventory, and soon she was dealing with the purveyors, doing the ordering, and trying to figure a way to perk-up the business.

Iris was "just squeaking by." There were just enough customers who came in to eat; and just enough "to go" orders to pay the rent and salaries.

It was a challenge for Edie. She wanted to help Iris as she had helped Luigi, Alain, Gordon--maybe not Gordon, although she didn't blame herself for Gordon's failure: Gordon had attempted too much with too little money.

"Maybe we should try some different breads," Edie suggested. "I'm a big believer in bread."

Iris was using the usual white, rye, and whole wheat. "Like?" Iris asked.

"Like some really grainy whole wheat, or Pita bread, or maybe some crusty French rolls."

"I'm afraid to take on any more expenses."

"I'll pay for it out of my salary."

"No, that isn't fair," Iris said. "Go ahead and order it. I'll pay for it."

So Edie found a good wheat, and changed the white to a good white, and ordered French rolls, and the take-out orders increased. Now Edie suggested adding sprouts to the sandwiches on request, and adding a few more vegetables to the salads.

"Like?"

"Like sprouts and broccoli and cauliflower."

"Raw?"

"Yes, raw."

"I don't know," Iris said. "I'm afraid to take on any more expenses."

"I'll pay for it out of my salary," Edie said.

"Here we go again," Iris said. "Okay, order it."

And the lunch trade increased. Now Edie suggested raising the price on the soup and serving it with French bread instead of crackers. And maybe Iris should start serving some desserts, and before Iris could say anything, Edie said, "I know, you're afraid to take on any more expenses."

Iris laughed. "Okay, go ahead and do it. Do anything you want."

So Edie found a French bakery that would deliver fresh baked desserts each morning, and people started stopping by mid-morning and mid-afternoon for coffee and a pastry.

As the Quick-Bite became busier, Edie felt energized. She had found something to give her the spark that had been missing ever since Chantilly had closed.

"Iris, I've been thinking," Edie said one afternoon before leaving to pick up Missy from nursery school, "what do you think about opening for breakfast? There are a lot of people working in this mall who need someplace to go for breakfast, to say nothing of all the office buildings around."

"I don't know," Iris said. "It means starting awfully early in the morning."

"But we could make so much more money. And it wouldn't be hard. Breakfast is easy. We've already got the bread for toast, you've got a grill for the potatoes, all we'd need are some frying pans for the eggs and omelets."

"It sounds like a big undertaking."

"Well I'm willing, if you are."

"What about your husband, what about your children?"

"If you're willing to do it, I'll work something out."

"I'll think about it," Iris said.

And while Iris was thinking about it, Edie was already planning the menu, what time they would open, what time she would have to get there, thinking about what kind of omelets they could make, thinking about muffins. And thinking about what she would tell Ken. That was going to be the difficult part.

Iris, of course, couldn't say "no." "What have I got to lose?" she said the following afternoon. "I can always take it out of your salary."

And they both laughed.

All the way driving home, Edie was in a panic. She wanted this so badly but was afraid Ken wasn't going to let her do it. Then what would she do? She couldn't explain to him why this was so important to her, except to say that she saw something that should be done and she wanted to do it. Even though the Quick Bite was only a little soup and sandwich place, she could make it a success. Maybe at this point in her life, she needed some success.

That evening when Ken arrived from work, she followed him into the bedroom and told him what she planned to do.

"Breakfast," he said, loosening his tie. "And how many more hours does that mean?"

And lowering her eyes, "A lot."

He sighed, "Edie, we made a bargain, 3 hours a day, remember? You're already up to 4 or 5, and now this."

She felt like she was a little girl being scolded by her daddy. "I know," she said, "but Ken, this is the way to make the business really go."

"Who cares about the business?"

"I do."

"You know this isn't your business. It belongs to Iris."

"I know that, but I still want it to be a success."

"Aren't you getting a little too emotionally involved? What if something goes wrong? Remember Chantilly."

"That was totally different. We were doomed from the start. But this business has very little overhead and no labor, except me. We can only go up."

"And what about us?"

"What about us?"

"I don't want this to cut into our life."

"It won't. I promise. I'll still be home every day at three, and I'll still do everything that needs doing." And then reluctantly. "There is one problem though. If I do this, someone's going to have to give Missy breakfast and drive her to nursery school."

And Ken hesitating.

"I could hire someone," she said.

"No," Ken said, "I suppose I could do it."

And hugging him, feeling that perhaps things could work out between them, "Oh Ken, thank you. You don't know how much this means to me."

"I'm afraid I do," he said, a touch of sarcasm in his voice.

So the Quick Bite expanded into the "quick breakfast." Edie had signs made and posted them on the window and the walls. "Now featuring--Quick Breakfast."

Edie tried different bacons, hams and sausages, and picked the three that were the leanest and tastiest, bought the frying pans and additional utensils they would need, sampled the cheeses and decided on the best Swiss and Cheddar for her omelets, and increased her vegetable order to include green onions, mushrooms, green peppers, red peppers, spinach, and avocados.

"I think we're taking on too much," Iris said.

"Don't worry," Edie said, confident that it would all work out.

And in spite of the ice-maker breaking, the dishwasher overflowing, a grease fire on the stove, and the refrigerator going on the blink one morning so that they had to throw everything out and close down for the entire day, within a couple of weeks, they were doing so well they needed to hire more help. Breakfast was a smash.

Iris was elated. "It's worth getting up early for this," she said. And then turning to Edie. "How can I thank you?"

"I'm the one who should be thanking you. I've never been so happy." And it was true. In spite of her problems with Ken, she had three adorable children, and this stimulating and fulfilling job. She felt she had found her niche in the world.

Ken pretended that the Quick Bite did not exist. He was serious when he said he didn't want it to cut into his life, so although Edie was up at 6 a.m., five days a week, she still had to do all she had done before and more. They still went to his mother's every Friday night, still saw friends every Saturday night, still had dinner parties for friends and clients, and now he wanted to play bridge every Tuesday night, he wanted her to learn to play golf and he wanted to go skiing. It was too much for her, but she couldn't tell that to Ken. It was part of the bargain. So she kept on: dozing on his mother's sofa while he and his mother talked, trying to keep count of the hearts, spades, clubs and diamonds at the bridge table, cooking an elaborate dinner for 10 or 12 people every two or three months, hitting golf balls at the range, and going up to Mammoth and practicing on the bunny hill because she was too frightened to get on the lift.

But she didn't complain and she wouldn't give up the Quick Bite.

Chapter Twenty-Four

Janet was careful. She was very careful.

She always took a cab home after work; she never rode the subway after dark, and she still never walked through the park, not even in the daytime.

But this Tuesday morning, she was feeling particularly happy. She had taken Monday off, slept late, gone shopping to Bloomingdale's, walked over to the Museum of Modern Art, spent several minutes gazing at her favorite Rousseau painting, and then gone to dinner and the theater with Lucille. They had seen *A Funny Thing Happened on the Way to the Forum*, and she had been chuckling all morning about Zero Mostel's antics.

She was back to feeling good about herself. It had taken a long time after Lombardo's burned down for her to stop looking over her shoulder, to stop expecting that something bad would happen if she relaxed her guard. It had taken all those jobs, all the restaurateurs after her, and now finally her promotion to chef at Umberto's to make her feel secure again. Oh yes, it was still there, lurking in the underbelly of her unconscious, fear, but this morning she was in too good a mood to notice it. She put on her yellow print dress, even some lipstick, and then smiled at herself in the mirror. She was a chef, a well known and respected chef of a world-renowned New York restaurant. How lucky she was!

She stepped out the front door of her apartment. What a beautiful day it was. The sun was shining brightly, there was a slight breeze, and the blue sky was filled with billowy white clouds. She decided to walk to work this morning. She wanted to enjoy this moment.

As she approached 57th Street, she spotted them, two young men with long straggly hair, wearing white undershirts, jeans, and leather boots. They were standing next to the alley of an old brick building. She thought of crossing the street to avoid them, why take chances, but she was feeling so strong and secure that she decided she would ignore them, just walk right on past as if they didn't exist. And then as she approached them, one moved toward her, flashed a knife, put his arm around her neck and pulled her into the alley.

"Keep your mouth shut," the other one said, "and you won't get hurt."

They pulled her to the ground and one was pulling her skirt up while the other had his hand over her mouth, the knife at her eyes. She heard a zipper, the rustle of clothing, and then she was overcome with terror, the terror of that night of the puppies when she had looked up and seen the Nazi soldier with the black boots and gun in his hand. Only now he did not have a gun, but a knife. She tried to scream, but no sounds came out. Her mind left her body and she floated above herself, watching the two Nazi soldiers, one standing guard, the other on top of her, ripping the insides out of that poor little girl she had once been.

Rage erupted in her. She would not let this happen again. She would not let that little girl go through that suffering again. She didn't care what happened, let them cut her to pieces, she would fight back. She assembled all her strength, swung her purse and hit the head of the one who was on top of her so that he reached for the back of his head, and dropped his knife. She grabbed the knife and plunged it into his shoulder, like he was a piece of meat on her cutting board. The blood spurted in all directions. He screamed. She jumped up, brandishing the knife at the one standing guard, and ran past him out to the street. "You bitch," he screamed. "We'll kill you for this."

She began to run, dropping the knife as she ran, and heard both voices from behind, yelling at her, "We'll find you, you bitch, and when we do, we'll kill you." She kept running, running down the street, until she could run no more, and then she flagged a cab and took it to the restaurant.

When she walked in the kitchen door, she was in shambles. She was sobbing, shaking. "Call the police," she told Charles, her souschef, and when the police arrived she told them what had happened. But they didn't comfort her, they accused her, as if it was her fault. They wanted to take her to the police station, to the hospital, but she wouldn't leave until she made a phone call. She had to talk to Edie, now, this minute. There was no one else in the world who could help her now, but Edie.

She looked at her watch. It would be 2 o'clock in Los Angeles. Edie would still be at the Quick Bite. She dialed the number there.

Edie was wrapping leftovers, when she got Janet's call, and after she heard what had happened, Edie said, "I'm coming to New York."

"But you can't," Janet said. "You have your family, your business."

"Don't argue. I'm coming. I'll be there just as soon as I can get a plane reservation."

"Thank you," Janet said, too needy to argue any further.

Edie immediately called the airline, told Diane, the new employee, "Here's the key. You can open tomorrow or not. I don't care," and left for home.

She had finished packing and was ready to leave for the airport when Ken got home.

"You're going to New York?" he said.

"Yes. Janet needs me."

"But the kids, the restaurant. How can you just pick up and go like this?"

"Because Janet needs me," she explained as if it should be self-evident.

"Yes, that's understandable," he said in a caustic tone, "if Janet needs you, you would drop everything."

She ignored his remark. "I've arranged for the babysitter to pick up the kids every day after school. All you have to do is what you normally do. I'll even drive myself to the airport."

"I see you've thought of everything."

"Janet was raped this morning," she said. "I have to go to her."

Ken's face showed concern. "I'm sorry," he said, "I didn't know."

"I'll be back as soon as I can," she said kindly, and gave him a quick kiss on the cheek, and was out the door.

She arrived at Kennedy the next morning at 5 a.m., took a cab to Janet's apartment, rang the bell, climbed the stairs, and found Janet waiting for her at the open door.

"Oh, Edie, I'm so glad you came," Janet said, and fell into Edie's arms, sobbing.

"It's all right," Edie said, caressing Janet's hair. "Everything's going to be all right."

Janet wouldn't go out of the house that day. "I'm so afraid," she said. "The police couldn't find them and I know they're going to be looking for me. They're going to try to kill me."

"They probably won't even remember what you look like."

"Yes they will. They were both watching me, and they must have seen me go by that corner before. No I won't go out."

So they stayed in the apartment all day and cooked lunch and dinner, and talked and reminisced and in the evening got into their robes and made popcorn and watched a Myrna Loy, William Powell movie on T.V. and when it was over, Janet said to Edie, "You know every time I begin to relax and start to think I'm just like everyone else, something terrible happens to me."

"Janet, you can't be blaming yourself for this."

But somewhere deep down at her core, Janet knew it was her fault. "Maybe somehow I led them on."

"That's ridiculous," Edie said. "Why would you even think such a thing?"

And Janet began to cry, "Because I want to be loved so badly."

And Edie held her close, "Oh, my poor Janet. Someday it'll happen to you. Someday someone will realize what a wonderful person you are. You have to believe that, Janet."

But Janet didn't believe it, even while she let Edie hold her and comfort her and pretended she believed it.

The next morning, Janet again refused to go to work or leave the apartment and Edie didn't know what to say to help her get over this. "Janet, you can't stay in the apartment forever. You're going to have to go out one of these days. Why not make it today?"

"They're going to be looking for me," Janet said.

"You don't want me to leave without seeing some of New York, do you?"

"I don't want you to leave at all."

"Listen, we'll take a cab, go somewhere. It'll be safe. I'll be with you. Is there some place special I should see?"

"I guess Greenwich Village," Janet said. "I suppose we could take a cab to Greenwich Village."

"Okay, then let's go. And maybe on the way we can stop at Umberto's. I'd love to see where you work. I've imagined it so many times in my mind."

"All right, but we'll take a cab."

They stopped at Umberto's first and Janet introduced Edie to everyone, and then they spent the afternoon walking the streets of Greenwich Village, in and out of art galleries, in and out of every restaurant they passed, and it would have been a wonderful afternoon if only Janet wasn't constantly on the watch for the two men who had attacked her.

On the third day, they went to the Museum of Modern Art and Janet showed Edie her favorite Rousseau, and then they walked 5th Avenue, and went to Bloomingdale's. "We won't have to worry about running into hoodlums at Bloomingdale's," Edie told Janet.

That night Edie reminded Janet that she was going home the next morning.

"I guess that means it's time for me to go back to work," Janet said.

"Can you manage it?"

"I guess I'll have to, it's got to happen sooner or later. But I'll tell you this, Edie, I don't think I'll ever be comfortable in New York again. Not with those two hoodlums out there, trying to find me."

"You'll be fine in a couple of days. You'll forget this ever happened."

"No I won't," Janet said. "I'll never forget. There are certain things you never forget."

"Then maybe you should move to Los Angeles," Edie said. "There are plenty of good restaurants there that would be thrilled to have you."

"It's a thought," Janet said.

"And then we could be together all the time and maybe one day we could open our own restaurant."

"Wouldn't that be something?" Janet said.

And on the fourth day after Edie arrived, she was on a plane back to Los Angeles, and Janet was alone again, wondering if she would ever feel safe again.

Chapter Twenty-Five

Janet tried her best. She went to work each day; she even went out with the group on Monday nights, but she could not shake the feeling that she was being watched, that she was being followed, that danger was waiting for her at every alley-way, around every corner. Even while she was working in the kitchen at the restaurant, she watched the back door, expecting her attackers to walk in, expecting them to find her.

She didn't know what to do: fight it through or take the easy way out -- escape to Los Angeles. She loved her job at Umberto's. She didn't want to leave it, but as the days passed, her fears got worse, not better. She could not sleep. Her dreams were filled with images of Nazis in black boots. She saw again and again the two young thugs, holding her down, the knife before her eyes, the blood spurting out of her assailant's shoulder. She felt dirty. She could not bathe enough. What had she done to incur this? Had she somehow sent vibes to them that she was lonely and wanted to be raped? Was it all her fault?

She called the police. Was there any news of her attackers?

Not yet, they told her.

"One of them had a stab wound," she said.

"Lady, we have a hundred stab wounds a day," they told her.

She hung up the phone more depressed than before she had called. There was no hope of catching them. The man she had stabbed was probably completely recovered by now anyway, and he probably had only one goal in life: to kill her.

Much as she hated to leave Umberto's, it was clear now. There was no way she could stay in New York. She called Gordon in Los Angeles. "Gordon, do you know of anyone who might be interested in a woman chef?"

"You thinking of moving to Los Angeles?"

"If I can find a job."

"Does Edie know?"

"I told her I was thinking of it, yes, but I thought you'd be in a better position to help me find a job. Edie doesn't really hang out with the restaurant people like you do."

"I'll see what I can do," he said.

Gordon spread the word. He told everyone he knew about Janet, her training, her experience, and within the week she received a call from Dominick's, one of the best Italian restaurants in Los Angeles. Could she come for an interview?

She made arrangements, and seated on the plane on her way to Los Angeles, for the first time since "it" happened, she relaxed.

The interview went well. They wanted her to start immediately.

"I'll need a week," she said.

"Take two weeks," Sergio, the owner told her. "You are worth waiting for."

She could not believe her good fortune. She was to start not as pastry chef, not as souschef, but as chef, and they were going to pay her a fifty dollars more a month than she had made in New York.

She went directly from the interview to Edie's house where she would be staying the night. Edie was waiting for her, and when Janet saw her, Janet began to cry.

"Oh, Janet," Edie said, "you didn't get the job."

"No, Edie, I got it. It's just that I'm so happy."

Edie took Janet's hands and began dancing around the room, like she had the day the letter came from L'Ecole de Jacque Patou. "Oh, Janet," Edie said, "it's too wonderful to believe. Now we can be together all the time."

Once Janet accepted the job, she couldn't wait to get out of New York, and a week after her interview, she had packed-up all her belongings and was back in Los Angeles, ready to begin work as chef at Dominick's. She stayed at Edie's until she could find an apartment and the two of them went apartment hunting together. Janet wanted to live near Edie, but realized it was more practical to live near her job, and her job was in Beverly Hills. They scoured the area and found the perfect place in a large apartment complex on the outskirts of Beverly Hills. It had a pool, jacuzzi, tennis courts, and Janet got three large rooms for half the price she had paid in Manhattan.

"I can't believe how much cheaper things are here," Janet said.

"Even Dominick's?"

"Much cheaper than Umberto's even though they're paying me more."

"Then we'll have to come to dinner one night."

"You've never eaten there?"

"No, too expensive for us. Ken doesn't like expensive restaurants."

"How about inexpensive restaurants?"

"He likes them all, except one."

And Janet looking serious, "How are things going between you?"

And Edie, not wanting to burden Janet, especially at this time, said, "Fine." Then taking Janet's hand, "Janet, I can't tell you how happy I am to have you here. Just think of all the fun we're going to have, restaurant hopping and market hopping and trying new dishes and new ingredients, just like I'm a real chef."

"There's nothing to be ashamed of in a good omelet."

"Maybe one day you could come by the Quick Bite and give me some pointers."

"Sure, I'll come by on my day off and do the cooking."

"Are you serious?"

"Why not? It'd be fun."

"No, I wouldn't let you to do that, but maybe you could make us some tarts."

"You mean every day or just on my day off?"

"Whenever."

"You little schemer," Janet said. "Now I know why you wanted me out here so badly." And both of them laughed.

It had been over ten years since they had lived together in Florence, but nothing had changed between them.

Ken was not happy about Janet's arrival. He liked Janet, but he didn't like all the time Edie was spending with her. It seemed they were either on the phone together, or out somewhere together, or Janet was at their house. They were like two teen-agers, except all their talk was about restaurants. Which restaurant was opening, which was closing, which chef was going where, about this fish dish, that veal dish, about rolls and bread and muffins. He was sick to death of hearing about restaurants.

He didn't know where to turn. He couldn't tell his mother how annoyed he was. He had stopped confiding in her the night he swore to Edie he wouldn't tell his mother the truth about her children--another way in which Edie had upset his life. Besides, he didn't want his mother to know that he was less than perfect, that he had made a mistake marrying Edie.

But he needed to talk to someone. First, he confided in his partner, Sherman Singer. And then, surprisingly, over lunch one day, he confided in the new girl in the office. She was a pretty young thing, sweet and innocent, passive and pliable. Nothing like Edie. How he had once admired Edie's strength and independence. Now how much he appreciated Maria Kent's weaknesses. She was so tentative, so afraid of making a mistake, so worried that she had done something wrong every time he called her into his office. But she wasn't stupid. She had graduated from Pierce Junior College with an AA in business. She did understand accounting procedures, and she did a good job. She wasn't a whiz, but she wasn't tough like those whizzes, either.

"You should feel better about yourself," he told her. "You're doing a terrific job."

"Thanks, Mr. Rosenberg. I really appreciate your telling me that. I don't have much confidence in myself. I guess because I don't have a bachelor's degree like the other girls. I did want to finish college, but my mother couldn't afford it. She's divorced, you know."

"And your father?"

She shrugged her shoulders, "Who knows where he is?"

Poor kid. She still lived at home with her mother. He thought he'd give her a raise, but it would have to be done surreptitiously. One couldn't give anyone a raise in the office without everyone else finding out about it. He thought he could at least take her to lunch a few times a week, at least save her lunch money.

It was obvious she idolized him, and she was so goddamn pretty.

He could not help fantasizing about her. What would she be like without clothes on? She had beautiful long legs, and she always wore hose and high heels, not like Edie who wore socks and tennis shoes. And her blouses, they were so clingy, so low cut, that one could see the split between her breasts. God, he was having terrible thoughts. He must cut them out. He must remember that he was 18 years older than she, that he was a married man, that he had a beautiful daughter who was a very talented tennis player, that his daughter needed all of his spare time to help her develop that talent. One doesn't treat things like that lightly. One doesn't throw away a whole family, a whole way of life, because of a cute twenty-year-old's tits.

Chapter Twenty-Six

It was four o'clock on Friday. Edie had stayed late to get the bank deposit ready and she was walking Iris to the bank at the other end of the mall, Iris holding the bag of cash, when Edie heard, "Don't move."

A young disheveled man was holding a gun at Iris' side.

Edie began to shake.

"Just give me the money," he said.

People were passing by but no one seemed to notice.

Iris handed him the bag. "Here."

He grabbed it and began to run, past the stores, to the street, around the corner, and all the while both women stood too panic-stricken to move or call for help.

When he was finally out of sight, both women clung together, still too afraid to move. Edie thought now she had some idea of what Janet had gone through. Only how much worse for Janet!

Edie and Iris reported the matter to the police who told them never to carry money unescorted again.

Edie didn't want to tell Ken about the incident for fear he would use it as an excuse to make her quit her job. She couldn't tell Janet about it for fear of recalling all the horror Janet had been through in New York. But she couldn't hold it in; she had to tell somebody. So she told Ken.

He was furious. "That's it," he said, "working is one thing, but taking a chance on getting yourself killed is another."

"But we weren't even in the restaurant," she said, sorry she had told him. "We were outside in the mall."

And Ken, trying to take full advantage of the situation, continued, "And what if someone comes into the restaurant and tries to rob you?"

"It could happen anywhere," she said, fighting back. "Look what happened to Janet."

"But it especially happens in retail stores."

"We've hired a guard."

"It's still not safe."

"Nothing is safe," she said. "Los Angeles isn't safe. As long as we don't carry money, we'll be okay."

And Ken, giving up, "Just do me a favor. Don't tell my mother about this. I'll never hear the end of it."

Edie had put up a brave front for Ken, but inside she was a wreck. She felt she had lost her innocence, that she could no longer take her safety for granted. She knew now that anyone anytime could attack her or her children, and there was nothing she could do about it. Every time she stepped out of her house, she was on alert. Was someone waiting to harm her? She was afraid to go to the mall, to the supermarket. She wanted to lock her children in the house and never let them out again.

Janet knew something was wrong. "Is anything the matter?" she asked Edie a week later when they were browsing through the newly remodeled Los Angeles County Museum of Art.

"No, nothing's the matter," Edie said, dying to tell her but controlling herself.

"You seem so fidgety," Janet said, stopping before a Van Gogh.

"It's nothing," moving on to a Cezanne.

"Is everything all right with Ken?"

"Yes, fine."

Edie seldom complained about Ken, but she had said enough so that Janet knew they had their problems. Maybe it was Ken, Janet thought, but she didn't ask Edie any more questions. When Edie was ready to tell her, Janet would be there to listen.

Iris not only hired a guard, she hired a service to pick up the cash and make deposits. Still it was obvious, she was not comfortable. Two months after the robbery, a year after Janet had moved to Los Angeles, she sat Edie down to talk.

"Edie, I've had it."

Edie got an uneasy feeling in her stomach. "What do you mean?"

"I mean I want out."

"Because of the robbery?"

"The robbery is part of it, but I've also decided it's too much for me. I can't take the work, I can't take the hours, my feet can't take the pain. I'm going to sell the place."

Edie went cold. Oh no. Then what would Edie do?

But before Edie could formulate the next thought, Iris said, "I thought maybe you'd like to buy it."

Edie felt a tingling throughout her body, and automatically responded, "Oh yes, of course I want to buy it." And then she thought of Ken. "The only trouble is, I think my husband would divorce me."

"No, he won't. Not if he loves you."

Ah, that was the question. "I suppose it wouldn't hurt to ask."

"We'll have to decide on a price."

"Ken could probably figure out what would be fair."

"Good," Iris said. Iris knew from Edie how honest and ethical Ken was.

"And what will you do?" Edie asked.

"Put my money in the bank and live on whatever interest I make. And if I don't make enough, I'll get a job typing."

"But you can't type."

"I'll learn how."

By the time Edie had taken off her apron, washed her face and hands, grabbed her purse, and was out the door, she was no longer thinking about Ken, but about Janet. This could be the opportunity they both had talked about, the chance to own their own restaurant. Of course, as it was, the Quick Bite was too unsophisticated for Janet, but it didn't have to stay that way. They could make it into whatever they wanted. Janet could cook anything she wanted. It wasn't just an opportunity for Edie, it was an opportunity for Janet!

As soon as Edie got home, she called Janet at Dominick's.

"Janet, we've got to talk. I have the most exciting news. I just got an offer to buy the Quick Bite."

"So?" Janet asked, sounding harried.

"Don't you see? This could be our chance."

"Our chance for what?"

"To own our own restaurant."

Janet laughed, "Edie, I'm not that kind of cook."

"But we can make it into anything we want."

"Look," Janet said, "can we talk later? I'm kind of busy."

"Of course," Edie said and hung up the phone, dejected. She had been so excited a minute ago, and now Janet had doused her enthusiasm like a fireman putting out a fire. It was just that Janet didn't understand. She would talk to her later. She would make her understand.

By the time Ken got home, Edie was more subdued herself. It was one thing to have your dream at hand, it was another to explain it to your husband. Edie dreaded the confrontation; how was she going to convince Ken to let her do it?

"Ken," she said over dinner, a tri-tip roast, baked potatoes, fresh broccoli, Missy sitting next to Ken, having just told him about her tennis lesson, Wendy and Brian on the other side of the table talking about school, "Iris wants to sell me the Quick Bite."

Ken turned from his daughter to his wife and immediately his expression soured. "And what'd you tell her?"

"I told her I'd have to talk to you about it."

He set down his fork, "I knew it would come to this."

"Ken, please try to understand. It's like a dream come true for me. I've already talked to Janet about it and..."

"You already talked to Janet?" he interrupted, disdain in his voice.

She lowered her eyes, feeling like a child caught in a lie. "Yes." And then looking back up at him, "I thought maybe she would go into it with me."

"Great," he said, sarcastically.

"Ken, if only you knew what this means to me."

"I'm afraid I do," he said, "and that's the trouble." He wiped his face with his napkin, and without finishing his dinner, got up and walked out of the kitchen.

Edie looked at Missy who seemed intent on her baked potato, and then at Wendy and Brian who had been listening to every word. "You children finish your dinner. I have to go talk to dad. I'll be back in a few minutes."

She went into the bedroom where he was standing by the sliding glass door looking out at their blue swimming pool, the flowers their gardener had planted, pink and fuchsia azaleas and golden-orange poppies.

"Ken," she said, "I'm really sorry if things haven't worked out the way you wanted."

"I thought I would take care of you, but it appears you're quite capable of taking care of yourself."

"It's not that, Ken, it's just that I need something in my life besides the house and kids."

"I think I've heard this story before."

And Edie, sitting on the bed, "What do you want me to do?"

"What I've always wanted you to do, stay home and take care of your family and give up all this restaurant stuff."

"I can't do that, Ken."

He glared at her, "Then do anything you damn please."

It was a moment of truth and she considered it. Giving it all up for Ken. Maybe that would make the difference in their marriage. Maybe then he would forgive her for not loving him. But she couldn't do it. She needed this restaurant in her life. "Ken, I hope you'll forgive me, but I've decided, I'm going to buy the restaurant."

"Then good luck," he said, brushing her off.

"But I can't do it alone," she said. "I need your help."

"If it's money you're worried about, half of everything I own is yours."

"I wasn't thinking about the money," she said.

"Then what?"

"Your moral support."

He sighed, exasperated, "Look, Edie, you can have the money, but don't ask for my moral support because you're not going to get it."

She felt miserable. She was hurting him and she didn't want to. But it was a question of his feelings or her survival. She had to hope that in time he would adjust.

Ken, standing at the sliding glass door was thinking, one more step into doom. He should be a good sport about it, he should be happy for her, but he wasn't. Still he could help her out with the financial end of it. He could do that much. He turned from the window, "You'll need to find out how much the Quick Bite is worth," he said.

"Yes. Iris is agreeable to you making that decision."

"She trusts me?"

"I've told her how honest you are."

Well, at least that was something, he thought. "I'll come by one day this week and go over the books. Anything else?"

"Not for now." She got off the bed and went to him, put her arms around him, kissed him. "Thank you," she said and waited for a hug from him, but did not get it. "Well, I guess I better go clean up the kitchen."

"Isn't that Wendy's job?" he asked, cool as he was before her kiss.

"She doesn't have time tonight."

"She never does," he said.

"I don't mind doing it," she said.

"You're on your feet all day, the least she can do is wash a few dishes after dinner."

"She's a young girl; she wants to have fun."

"You're spoiling her."

"I know, but what's a mother for?"

She left the room feeling relieved that her confrontation was over, guilty that she had upset Ken, grateful that Ken was going to let her do it, and annoyed that Ken was still picking on Wendy.

Edie waited until ll:30 that night, until Ken had gone off to bed leaving her alone in the den watching Johnny Carson, and then she called Janet.

"Janet, at last. I've been waiting all day to talk to you."

"You're nuts," Janet said.

"No, just excited. I keep picturing you in the kitchen at the Quick Bite."

"Edie, as I told you on the phone today, I'm not that kind of cook."

"But it doesn't have to be breakfast and lunch. We can turn it into lunch and dinner."

"I don't do tuna salad and omelets."

"Then I'll do those. You'll do the chicken and beef and veal and pastas."

"The place is too small."

"It's a beginning, and it is in a good location. Right on Ventura Boulevard."

"It is a good location," Janet agreed.

"We can dress it up. Put on tablecloths, candles, darken the lights, put some pretty pictures on the walls."

"I hate pretty pictures."

"Forget the pretty pictures."

"And the kitchen is too small."

"It's big enough."

"I don't know," Janet said.

And then Edie realizing what she was asking Janet to do, "I'm sorry, Janet. I have no right to ask you to give up Dominick's for a place like this."

"It's not that," Janet said, "I just don't want to get involved in anything that's doomed to failure."

"But why should we fail? The restaurant's been doing great so far."

"But change the character, change the menu, it could change everything."

"We won't fail. Trust me," Edie said.

It was a crazy idea, but the thought of having her own restaurant, of working side by side with Edie, was just too tempting. Janet suddenly felt lightheaded, as if she'd had too much wine. "All right," she said. "I must be crazy, but all right."

Now Edie hesitated. She had been so sure of herself all day. But now that she had convinced Janet to come with her, she began to worry that she wasn't doing what was best for Janet. The last thing she wanted to do was to take advantage of Janet's friendship. "Maybe you better think it over a few days," she said. "I'm taking the restaurant anyway. Maybe you want to wait to see how I do."

"No," Janet said, "I've made up my mind. I'm going with you. By the way, what are we going to do for money?"

"Ken says I have enough."

"And what about me?"

"I'll pay your half, and then when we're rich and famous you can pay me back."

"Sounds like too good a deal to pass up."

"I told you it would be."

"One last thing, Edie, no breakfasts."

"But breakfast is such a money maker."

"It's too long a day."

"I'll do the breakfasts, just until we get started."

"No, Edie. You have to make up your mind. Either it's going to be a fine restaurant or it's going to be a coffee shop. You can't have both."

"I don't see the harm in running it for breakfast, and then changing the menu for lunch and dinner."

"There may not be any harm, but I won't do it."

Edie was frustrated. She wanted Janet with her, but she also wanted to do it her way. "Janet, you're being so unreasonable. All those people are counting on my breakfasts."

"Sorry, Edie, but I won't budge on this issue."

"God, you were never such a hardnose when we were younger."

"Call it experience, call it confidence, call it stubborn, that's my deal."

Edie sighed. "All right, then stay where you are for a couple of months. It's going to take me that long to wean my customers away from breakfast and into dinner."

"Take all the time you want. I'm happy where I am. Just give me two weeks notice when you want me to join you."

"You're sure you want to do this?"

"I'm not sure. But I'm going to do it anyway."

Edie hesitated again, "Janet, there's one more thing I haven't told you. Two months ago, Iris and I were robbed."

"So that's it," Janet said. "That's what's been bothering you all these weeks."

"It didn't happen in the restaurant, it happened in the mall. Iris and I were pretty stupid. We were carrying a bag of money to the bank. But we've hired a security guard, and we have a service that makes the bank deposits for us. I didn't want to tell you about it, but if you're going to be working at the Quick Bite, you have to know."

Janet thought for a moment--to pass all this up for fear? No, she wouldn't succumb. "I suppose any restaurant can get robbed."

"If you don't want to do it, I'll understand."

"It happened to me walking down the street in New York. It could happen anytime, anywhere."

"That's exactly what I told Ken," Edie said.

"No, it's okay. Go ahead with the plans."

"I'll get started tomorrow," Edie said, and hung up the phone. She was exuberant. She wanted to dance, to sing, to wake up the kids and share this moment with them. The Quick Bite was going to be hers, and Janet was coming with her!

The next morning on her way to work, Edie stopped at a sign shop and had a sign made that said, "Edie's Quick Bite Cafe." When Iris saw it, she was a little surprised.

"I'm going to buy the restaurant," Edie told her. "I hope you don't mind if I put this up?"

"What if things don't work out?"

"They will," Edie told her, and hung the sign above the front door.

Ken came out during the week and went over the books. He was dressed in a suit and a tie and looked not only handsome, but formidable. Edie was in awe of him. Was this dignified professional really her husband? That evening when he came home from work, she followed him into the bedroom, came up behind him and put her arms around his waist. "I know it's not Sunday night, but...maybe we could go to bed early tonight."

"You don't have to pay me for checking the books," he said.

"It isn't that," she said, "it was just seeing you at the restaurant today. You looked so handsome."

He hung his jacket in the closet. "I've had a grueling day," he said, "maybe tomorrow."

Edie felt a coldness in the air, as if he had just turned on the air-conditioner. "Yes," she said, "tomorrow will be fine." And she left the room to go make dinner.

Ken took off his trousers, put on jeans. How ironic. His visit to the restaurant had turned her on. But it had had the opposite effect on him. He hated being in the place, everything about the place. And he especially didn't like seeing her there. She was so totally in charge, tough, confident, not the kind of woman he wanted to make love to. He pulled a sport shirt over his head and went looking for Melissa. Time to take her over to the high school and hit some tennis balls.

The next morning, Edie had another sign made and replaced "Edie's Quick Bite Cafe" with "Edie's Cafe".

Ken wrote up an offer and Iris took it to the attorney who had handled her divorce and after they negotiated a few changes, the attorney drew up an agreement, insisting that Ken co-sign on the promissory note.

On a Tuesday morning, two months after the offer was presented, when Edie walked through the door of Edie's Cafe, and turned the Closed sign to Open, tears came to her eyes. "It's mine," she said aloud. "Mine and Janet's." She wished Janet was with her to share this moment, but Janet would not be leaving Dominick's until Edie had phased out breakfast.

Now, there was no time to indulge her happiness, she had to get to work.

During the next few weeks, Edie applied for a wine and beer license, and continued serving breakfast and lunch, wearing herself out, because Iris walked out the door the day the papers were signed and never came back. Edie hired another cook and a waitress and Wendy came in to help before and after school, but still Edie always needed more help than she had.

Three months after the place was hers, Edie decided the time had come to make the transition to a "real" restaurant, and again she began to have second thoughts about Janet. Was it fair to take Janet away from a good-paying job to this untried venture. What if Edie's Cafe was only intended to be a breakfast and lunch place? What if it wouldn't make it as a fine restaurant? She thought back to her experience with Gordon and shuddered. She didn't want to live through that again, and she didn't want to drag Janet through it with her. Yet, she felt there would never be a better time than now. Better now.

She called Janet. "You want to help me pick out the tablecloths and napkins?"

"How about refurbishing the kitchen?"

"I don't think we'll need much."

"I'll come over Monday. We'll make a list."

"Okay. I'll do all the shopping. You continue on at Dominick's until the last possible minute."

"Sounds good."

On Monday, they met, walked through the place, decided on the placement of the tables, the decor, the color scheme. They went through the kitchen and made a list of containers, pots, pans, utensils. "The freezer and refrigerator are adequate," Janet said. "Thank God for that."

And then stopping in the middle of it all, Janet asked, "How's Ken taking all this?"

"As well as can be expected."

"I bet he wishes you'd never met me."

"This has nothing to do with you. I was in the restaurant business before he met me."

"Again because of me."

"Yes, but if it hadn't been this, it would have been something else. I would never have stayed home and been just a wife and mother." Then sitting down at one of the wood tables, "Tell me, Janet, what would you do? What if you met the man of your dreams and he wanted you to give up being a chef? Would you do it?"

Janet sat across from her. "I don't know. The whole thing seems so impossible--especially the part about me finding the man of my dreams."

"But what if it happened?"

"If I really had to give up being a chef forever? I don't know what I'd do." Then looking at Edie. "And you?"

"Maybe I could," Edie said, "*if* I was married to the man of my dreams."

They chose white linen tablecloths and napkins, and painted the walls white. It was a small place and they wanted to keep it looking neat. Edie had already purchased heavy stainless steel silverware, the kind Silvia and Carlo had, new pots, pans, utensils, and containers. They finalized the menu after a month of "making decisions and revisions that a moment would reverse." Edie had learned from her experience with Gordon not to attempt too many items and Janet agreed. "Let's keep the menu simple, but make every dish superb." The final version was printed on one page of heavy parchment like Gordon had used, but white instead of pink. Finally, Edie had the last sign made, "Edie's Cafe will be closing for breakfast, but opening for dinner, September 23." Janet gave her two weeks notice to Dominick's, and on September 23, 1973, Edie did not arrive at the restaurant until 9 o'clock, where she found Janet already busy, slicing and dicing the fresh vegetables she had picked up at the Central Market that morning.

They decided to serve lunch on the wooden tables, and then put the tablecloths on for dinner. It would save on the laundry bill, and they wanted it more casual at lunchtime. Brian was enrolled to come in every day after school to dress the tables, which pleased Janet as much as Edie. Janet still could not look at Brian, without feeling that in some way he belonged to her.

The place was filled that first afternoon. By now, Edie had a loyal following and all her customers showed up.

"We've just got to get them in the door," Edie told Janet, "your cooking will do the rest."

They kept the lunch menu simple: sandwiches, salads, omelets, and a special of the day, usually a fresh fish grilled and served with a light sauce, fries and salad for $4.95. They also served Edie's home-made focaccia bread and Janet's fresh pastries.

The menu at dinner expanded to include, chicken cacciatore, chicken Florentine, veal with roasted red and green peppers, veal parmigiana, veal with lemon and capers, Florentine beefsteak, the same fresh fish they served at lunch, several pastas, and a special of the day. The special might be duck, veal, lamb, or a shrimp or chicken dish, depending on what was in season, or inexpensive, or looked good to Janet.

Edie liked the idea of a daily special as a way to keep their customers tantalized and wanting to come back another night to try another special.

And it seemed to be working. The restaurant was full at lunch-time, mostly ladies out shopping, but also businessmen from the nearby offices, and at night, it was also usually full, even during the week. How many people did one need to fill 15 tables?

Edie kept the books and knew they were making a nice profit, and at the end of the month, Ken, their accountant, confirmed it. "You're doing all right," he told Edie.

"We're doing all right," Edie told Janet, and the two of them hugged.

The following March, when Wendy turned sixteen, she began waitressing dinners. As with Brian, it was a joy for both Edie and Janet to have Wendy with them. They were the original threesome, and Wendy felt closer to Janet than anyone in the world except her mother, father and Brian. Wendy was now in her first year of high school. She was as tall as Edie, 5'6", slender, with Edie's smooth clear complexion, but with long black lashes that shielded Zola's black eyes. She wore her black hair long, and parted in the middle. She was still getting mostly "A's" in school, and was as popular as she was bright. The phone never stopped ringing for her, and Ken was so annoyed by her constant phone calls, that Edie decided to get Wendy her own phone.

Another argument. "It's ridiculous," Ken said, "for a sixteen-year-old to have her own phone."

"It doesn't cost that much," Edie said.

"It isn't the money. It's the idea. Whatever Wendy wants, Wendy gets."

Edie's back arched. It was the same old tired line. "I'm not doing it for Wendy, I'm doing it for you. So you won't be bothered by her phone calls," she said and left the room.

Wendy was still spending at least a month every summer with Zola, but this summer, she told her mother she only wanted to go for two weeks. "I don't want to leave my job."

"It must be heredity," Janet said.

"Yes, but from you or me?" Edie asked.

When Wendy returned from her two week visit, this year without Brian who had opted to stay in Los Angeles to be with his friends, she told her mother that Zola had completed his PHD in psychology at Stanford, and was going to stay in Palo Alto and open his own private practice.

"You wouldn't recognize dad," Wendy said. "He's shaved his beard and he looks normal."

"But is he normal inside?" Edie asked, jokingly.

"He's still a little crazy, but no more than anyone else. And you'll never guess what else?"

"What else?"

"He's got a girlfriend and they're going to get married."

Edie felt a shock run through her. She hadn't seen Zola in ten years; she didn't expect him to be faithful to her, and yet the thought of him loving another woman stung a bit. "What's she like?"

"Just as ordinary as can be. About his age, 40, maybe, with three kids."

Another quiver. "He's really going all the way."

"He's absolutely crazy about her. They cuddle and coo all the time."

Edie tried to wipe it away. She didn't want to be jealous of Zola. He had a right to be happy. "Well, I'm happy for him," she said. "You know all the years we were apart, all the years you were growing up, he never had anything, and yet he sent me 25 dollars a week, every week, without fail. I'll always admire him for that."

"I know, mom. I really love him. He's a wonderful guy."

And Edie, looking at her daughter with love in her eyes, "You've got good genes, girl. Thank God for that."

"You did good, ma,"

"'Well,'" Edie, the teacher corrected.

"You did 'well'," Wendy repeated, and they got back to work.

Chapter Twenty-Seven

Edie's Cafe was doing "well."

So well in fact that they needed more space.

There were always people waiting at the door, Janet was always bumping into her assistants, and because they had crammed as many tables as possible into the space available, the waiters couldn't get by.

It was a year since Edie and Janet had gone into business together. Edie was still going home every afternoon from three to five to drive Brian and Missy wherever they needed to go. Wendy, now sixteen and driving, offered to take them, but Edie wanted to be with Brian and Missy as much as possible.

Brian was still working at the restaurant, coming in every afternoon after school to put the tablecloths on the wooden tables, and each time Edie and Janet saw him walk through the door, they'd both feel a lift. When Janet saw him, she thought of Mike Kelly. When Edie saw him, she thought of Stefano. He was such a sweet, sensitive, loving child. And with his long blond hair that Edie still wouldn't let him cut, and his blue eyes, he reminded her so much of Stefano that she could almost imagine he was Stefano's child.

Brian was in Bar Mitzvah training; his Bar Mitzvah was scheduled to take place in six months, on March 19, 1975, and Missy was also in Hebrew School.

Ken wanted her to have a Bat Mitzvah. He regarded her as his only child and it was important for her to carry on the tradition of his religion.

Melissa looked just like Ken. She had his curly brown hair, his brown eyes, and was built more like a boy than a girl: broad shoulders and hips, strong legs.

Ken wasn't happy about that. He would have preferred his daughter to be a petite, delicate thing, like Maria in his office, but it was not to be. Missy was never very interested in dolls or clothes. Maybe it was partially Ken's fault. Ever since she was a little girl, she had liked to play ball with him, and sit on his lap while he watched the Rams or Lakers on television. As soon as she was four he had started hitting tennis balls with her, and at five, started her on tennis lessons. She was amazingly gifted and Ken spent most weekends taking her to tennis tournaments, so that now, at eight years of age, she was ranked 19th in California in the 8 and 9-year-olds.

Ken had also taught her to ski, and she was just as talented on skis as she was on the tennis court. She loved skiing as much as he did and he took her for a weekend to Idyllwild or Big Bear every chance he got, and to Mammoth for a whole week every winter whether there was snow or not. He had given up on Edie ever becoming a skier and let her stay home. Anyway, he preferred being alone with his daughter.

Edie was relieved to be let out of the skiing excursions, but she tried to be at Missy's tennis tournaments whenever possible, even though Ken was never happy to see her there. It was as if this was his exclusive activity with Missy, and Edie's presence was an intrusion. Still, Edie went whenever she could, which wasn't too often since many of the tournaments were out of Los

Angeles, and the others were Saturday afternoon, the busiest day of the week at Edie's Cafe.

It was on a Saturday afternoon, as Edie was at home relaxing between lunch and dinner, that she received a collect call from Missy who was playing in a tournament at Cal State Fullerton. "Mom, I won my morning match. I'm in the finals. Maybe you want to come down and see me play."

"What time's your match?"

"4 o'clock."

"I'm supposed to be at the restaurant at 5."

"I know, but I thought you could come this one time."

"I don't know. I hate to leave Janet alone."

"Daddy works too, but he comes to all of my matches."

"But, honey, that's because daddy can go to work whenever he wants. I have to be there at lunch and dinner."

"Never mind," Missy said, and hung up the phone.

Edie sat staring at it for several minutes. She felt the muscles in her throat tighten. To let Missy down, or to let Janet down? It wasn't fair to make Janet carry the full load of a Saturday night dinner, but on the other hand, Missy really wanted her. That didn't happen very often. She called Janet at the restaurant. "Janet, would it be all right if I came a little late tonight?"

"How late?" Janet asked.

Edie calculated the time, two hours for the match, an hour to drive back. Tentatively, "Seven?"

"We have a full book tonight," Janet said, annoyance in her voice.

"I know, but I feel I have to go to Missy's game."

Janet hesitated another minute, but she knew there was no way she could deny Edie anything, "All right, but get here as soon as you can."

Ken was surprised to see Edie's car pull into the parking lot in Fullerton. He watched as she approached the courts and climbed up the bleachers to sit beside him.

"So you came," he said, not very happy.

"Yes, Missy wanted me here."

He looked at his watch, "You're never going to make it to the restaurant on time."

"I know," she said. She was determined not to let him upset her.

"By the way," he said, "Missy's the one standing to the right of the net."

She turned to him. "I think I can recognize my own daughter."

"Oh," he said. "I wasn't sure."

Edie decided not to answer him. If he needed these little digs, then let him have them.

Missy played beautifully. But in the third set, when Missy had the other girl down 4 to 2, she seemed to go to pieces. She lost the next four games and the match.

Edie was devastated and Ken looked as if he would cry. "She never falls apart like that," he said to Edie. "It's all your fault."

"My fault?" Edie asked, surprised.

"Yes, you made her nervous," and he scooted down the bleachers to where Missy was waiting for him, and enfolded her in his arms.

Edie refused to be intimidated by Ken and made her way down the wooden bleachers to where

Ken was still holding Missy.

"I'm so sorry," she said to Missy, "but you played a great game."

"It doesn't matter if I played a great game, mother, if I lost," Missy said.

And Edie felt chastised. Perhaps Missy also thought it was Edie's fault that she had gone to pieces. Perhaps Edie *had* made her nervous. "Well, I think it's important that you played well, and you did. I'm very proud of you." She leaned over and placed a kiss on Missy's cheek. "Now, I've got to run. See you tonight." The whole drive back to the San Fernando Valley, tears kept building behind Edie's eyes. She didn't know why she felt so sad. Because of her daughter's defeat, or because she felt so utterly rejected by Missy?

When she got to the restaurant, Janet's face was covered with perspiration and little wisps of hair were escaping her gros bonnet. "I'm sorry I'm late," Edie said, pulling the next order, and putting a dollop of butter in a frying pan.

"How'd the match go?" Janet asked.

"She lost," Edie said.

By eleven o'clock, the kitchen was spotless, Wendy had gone home, and Janet suggested they go for a drink to this new, trendy restaurant on Melrose.

It was always an internal struggle for Edie, to go out with Janet or to go home to Ken, but tonight it was an easier decision. By the time, they got to Francesca's, Janet had heard all about the match, and all of Ken's and Missy's remarks to Edie.

"What you need is a drink," Janet said.

"No," Edie said, "I'll just have my usual."

They ordered, a glass of red wine for Janet, an espresso for Edie, and a crepe with raspberry sauce to share.

"So," Janet said, "what are we going to do about Edie's Cafe?"

"If only we could break through the wall."

But they both knew that was impossible. The store on one side of them had three years to go on its lease, the other had two.

"There seems to be only one solution," Edie said, "We have to open a second restaurant."

"But there's the same problem there's always been," Janet said, "money."

"I know, but what if we could raise enough money."

"How?"

"Maybe we could find investors. Maybe my brother Frank would invest. He's got lots of money."

"Would you really ask a member of your family to invest in a restaurant?"

"If I thought it would be a success, and I know our restaurant would be a success. How could we fail with you as chef, and me as manager."

"Remember what happened to Gordon."

"Yes, but Gordon went into it in too big a way. We could have survived another year just on the money he spent on wallpaper! We could do it simply."

"Like Edie's Cafe?"

"Why not?" Edie said. And looking around the room, "Look at this place. It's not very fancy. Tile floors, white walls, plain wood tables and chairs."

"And lots of noise."

"We can do without the noise."

"I'd like it to be an authentic trattoria, like Vittorio's," Janet said.

"But we have to have your desserts."

"I guess if Vittorio could serve my desserts in his trattoria, I could serve them in mine."

"We can do anything you want. It'll be your restaurant."

"Could I really make every single thing I ever dreamed of?"

"Of course."

And after a pensive moment, Janet said, "Now, I'm worried. I'm afraid I've fallen behind. I should go to Mexico, China, Thailand."

"And I should go with you," Edie said.

"But when?"

"Once our new restaurant takes off."

They were both silent for awhile, each thinking her own thoughts about the new restaurant.

"What shall we name it?" Janet asked.

"How about Trattoria Nostra? Our trattoria."

"Sounds too much like the mafia," Janet said. "It would be good to keep the tie-in with Edie's Cafe. How about Edie's Trattoria?"

"No," Edie said, "I have one restaurant named for me, you should have one named for you. How about Janet's Trattoria?"

Janet, tentatively, "How about Trattoria Mia? My Trattoria."

"Yes," Edie said. "I like that. Trattoria Mia."

"Now," Janet said, "all we need is the money."

"You let me worry about the money; you worry about the menu."

Edie spent the next afternoon driving up and down Ventura Boulevard with a real estate agent looking at places that had been restaurants, places that could be restaurants. Janet refused to go. She didn't want the new restaurant to be in the San Fernando Valley. "If we're going to do it, let's do it right. It's got to be in town."

"I don't know why?" Edie said. "There's plenty of money in the Valley."

"Yes, but if people want a really good meal they come into town. We should open on Melrose. I tell you, Edie, it's going to be the next restaurant row, and we should get in early while the rents are still cheap."

"You call those rents cheap?"

"Cheaper than they're going to be in five years."

"But how are we going to switch our customers to the city. They won't follow us. We need to stay on Ventura Boulevard."

"Why don't you check with our accountant?"

"I suppose I'll have to sooner or later."

Edie had put off talking to Ken about a second restaurant, even though he knew they had outgrown their present location. But now, the time had come. She didn't look forward to the encounter, but it had to be done.

The next afternoon, she stopped by Ken's office.

"Well, this is a surprise," he said, standing up to greet her and then settling back into his black leather judge's chair. Edie sat on one of the two black leather pull-up chairs in front of his highly-polished ebony desk. Again, she was impressed with how formidable he was, here in his own surroundings. His desk, like his closet and drawers at home, was perfectly neat.

"I've come on business," Edie said.

"Nothing wrong at Edie's Cafe, is there?"

"No, quite the contrary. Janet and I have decided the time has come to open a second restaurant."

His face took on the look of someone who'd been told he had only two weeks to live. "I suppose I knew this was coming."

"Please, Ken, don't make it into a tragedy," she said. "It's a time to celebrate. We're a success. Doesn't that mean anything to you?"

"Yes, it means you'll be away from home even more."

"Oh, Ken, I wish you could be happy for me," she said.

"I didn't marry you to have a successful restaurant."

"But it's part of me. It's what I am."

"Love me, love my restaurant?"

"I don't object to you being a CPA."

"I spend less time working during tax season than you do any day of the week."

"That's not true."

He leaned back and folded his hands, resigned that it was a fait accompli. She didn't care what he thought. "So when are you planning to open?" he asked.

"As soon as we find the right location. That's one of the things I wanted to talk to you about: our location. I want to stay in the Valley, but Janet wants to move to Melrose."

"I'd stay in the Valley," Ken said.

"But Janet says Melrose is the place to be, and I trust her. She does spend all her free time restaurant hopping."

"And you don't?"

"That's not fair," she said. "I spend most of my free time at home."

"You couldn't prove it by me," he said. And then, "You'll need money. Plenty of money. A place, especially on Melrose, is going to be expensive, plus you'll need to furnish it."

"We want to do it simply except that Janet's got to have a proper kitchen. No telling what she can do with a proper kitchen."

"Know any millionaires?" Ken asked.

And then on an impulse, Edie asked, "Maybe you'd like to put some money in."

"Adding insult to injury."

"If it's a good investment, then why not?"

Ken hesitated. He hated helping her out, but on the other hand, it *might* be a good investment. "Even if I agreed," he said, "it won't be enough."

"I thought I'd ask Frank."

"It still won't be enough."

"Maybe he has some friends."

"Maybe."

And Edie tentatively, "Maybe you know someone?"

"I wouldn't put anyone I know into a restaurant. Too risky."

"Well," Edie said, "I'm going to keep looking and if I find the right place, I know we'll get the money."

"If you're going to get investors, you'll need something in writing. I better prepare a projection for a 120 seat restaurant based on your profit and loss at Edie's."

She felt a wave of warmth for him. Not only wasn't he going to fight her, he was going to help her. She wanted to touch his hand, embrace him, but he seemed so far away sitting behind his shiny black desk. "Thank you, Ken. I can't tell you how much I appreciate your help."

"What are husbands for?"

As soon as Ken's projection was ready, Edie mailed a copy, along with a Financial Statement from Edie's Cafe, to Frank. She hated asking her brother for money, or anyone else, but there was no alternative. She knew that Frank had made a lot of money in real estate investments, that he was a shrewd investor, and if Frank went for it, then she wouldn't feel guilty about asking anyone else.

When she called him a week later, she was filled with trepidation. After all they'd been through together, how could she ask him for money? But if she wanted the restaurant, she had no choice. His receptionist put her through. "Frank, how are you?"

"Fine. And you?"

"Fine."

"And the kids?"

"Great."

She forced herself to go forward, "Frank, I was wondering if you received my papers."

"Yes, I did," he said. "I even went over them with my accountant."

"And..."

"He says it looks good. The only problem is that it's the restaurant business."

"I wouldn't ask you to put money in unless I thought it was a sure thing."

"Would this be a loan, or would we own part of the restaurant?"

"Whatever you want."

"Well I do need a write-off desperately. Do you know what I paid in taxes last year?"

"No." Should she ask?

"Forty thousand dollars."

She gasped, thinking that if he gave her forty thousand dollars, she wouldn't need much more.

"Tell me," he asked, "is Ken going in on it?"

A little prick in her gut. "I'm not sure at this point. He's considering it."

"Well, let me think about it and I'll get back to you."

She couldn't let him hang up without making sure that he wasn't going into this for the wrong reasons. "One more thing, Frank, I don't want you to go into this because you feel obligated to me for anything that may have happened in the past. I only want you to go into it, if you think it's a good investment."

"I understand," he said.

She hung up the phone feeling drained. Could she go through this again and again? Yes, she told herself, because Trattoria Mia would never come into being unless she did.

After weeks of looking, Edie found the perfect place. It was on La Brea near Melrose. A little far from La Cienega, but cheaper because of it, and the building was for sale, not for lease. Ken liked that.

"If the restaurant fails," he whispered to her so the real estate agent wouldn't hear, "you'd still have the building. It's bound to go up in value."

"Can you get it for us, Ken?" Edie whispered back.

"Have you heard from Frank, yet?"

"No, but I'm sure any day now."

"What if he doesn't come across, what are you going to do?"

"I don't know," she said.

And she looked like such a needy little girl, so much like Melissa at this moment, that he said, "I'll come up with the down payment on the building."

Tears came to her eyes, and this time she did hug him, "Oh thank you, Ken. Thank you."

As Ken began negotiating for the building, Edie began making phone calls. She had already mailed a prospectus to everyone she knew and now it was time for the follow-up phone calls. Each time she dialed a number, she cringed inside.

After five straight rejections, she decided to call her childhood friend, Sandy Stahler Lieberman. Sandy was still living in Ann Arbor with her two daughters and husband, Danny, and still working part time as a pharmacist at the University of Michigan Hospital. Edie had kept in touch with Sandy over the years and felt close to her, but still dreaded calling her to ask for money.

"Sandy, hi, it's Edie," trying to keep it light.

"Oh, Edie, so good to hear your voice." Total warmth from Sandy. "Listen, I got your prospectus, and I would love to invest in your restaurant, it sounds so exciting, but I'm sorry to say, we don't have a spare dime."

"Why should you be different from the rest of the world?" Edie joked.

They chatted for a while longer and Edie hung up the phone feeling worse than she had with the other rejections. She hated asking people for money, especially friends. She didn't want to do it again. Ever. But there was no choice. Not if she wanted her and Janet's restaurant. She forced herself to call four more people, and got pretty much the same story, "We'd love to, but we just don't have the money."

She went to Ken. "Ken, maybe you'd reconsider and let me contact some of your clients."

"No way," Ken said. "I already told you I wouldn't put one of my clients into a restaurant."

"You don't have much faith in us."

"It isn't you, Edie, it's the business. The statistics aren't good."

"But we've done so well already. We're a proven commodity."

"Edie's Cafe is a little hole in the wall. This is a major investment."

"Still, we are a success. Doesn't that count for something?"

"Do you think I'd invest in it if it didn't?"

She called ten more people and got ten more, "I'm sorry" and then decided to send a copy of the prospectus to Stanley.

"I have no shame," she told him when she called a week later.

"You never did," he said.

"I wouldn't ask you, but I'm getting desperate," she said.

"What's a matter, your prince charming not supporting you in the style to which you wish to be accustomed?"

"This is a big undertaking, Stanley. Janet's putting everything she has into it, and I'm putting everything I have, and Ken's putting the down payment on the building, if we get it."

"Okay," he said, "I'll go $10,000.00."

"Just like that? You don't have to ask Yelena, you don't want to think it over?"

"No," he said, "what the hell. Call it for old time's sake."

"You don't owe me anything," she said.

"No," he said, "but maybe you owe me something. Anyway, I always wanted to own a restaurant, and besides, if it's good enough for Frank, it's good enough for me."

At the mention of Frank's name, she started to tremble. "Does that mean Frank is going in on it?"

"That's what he told me."

"Oh my God," she said, "that would be wonderful. Are you sure?"

"Of course, I'm sure. I guess the sister is always the last to know."

"If only it's true."

"You can count on it," he said. "Now, when do you need the money?"

"I'll let you know. And Stanley, thank you. I can't tell you how much this means to me."

"Just be a success."

"We will be."

Edie hung up the phone shaking. If only Stanley was right.

In the next three days, Edie called twenty more people and got three more pledges: the Wolfe's for $5000.00, the Fishers for $10,000, and Gordon for $2000.00.

Gordon was now the chef at Michele's, a French restaurant in Santa Monica. Very chic, very expensive.

"I'd give you more," Gordon said, "but I don't want to put a curse on you. You know what happened the last time we went into business together."

"But that wasn't your money; it was Lester's, remember?"

"How could I ever forget? I'm so shell-shocked from that experience I never want to open my own restaurant again." And before she could say anything, he added, "Only kidding."

On the weekend, she heard from Frank.

"Okay," he said, "I'll go the whole $40,000."

She felt herself lift off the ground and head for the sky. "Oh Frank, that's wonderful."

"But it'll be a loan. Three years to start. We can always extend it later."

"Three years is great," she said.

"You can have your attorney draw up the papers, or I'll have mine do it."

"Yours is fine," she said.

"When do you want the money?"

"I'll let you know," she said. "We're still negotiating on buying the building."

"You're buying the building?"

"Yes. Ken is putting in the down payment."

"Terrific," Frank said, "I like that."

"You're terrific," Edie said, tears coming to her eyes. "Thank you so much for believing in me."

"It isn't you I believe in, it's Janet," he said with a smile in his voice.

"Well then, you're smarter than I thought."

She hung up the phone thinking, $75,000--it was enough. She would have liked more, but they could do it on $75,000.

The next day, Edie's dad called. "Edie, we talked to Frank and we'd like to help you out."

"Dad, thanks so much, but I can't ask you." She felt uncomfortable taking her parents' money.

"You don't have to ask; we already decided. Besides it'll give us an excuse to come visit our grandchildren."

And then, it hit her. What if the unthinkable should happen? What if the restaurant should fail? Then all these people who had believed in her would lose their money. It was an enormous responsibility, and as much as she believed in herself and Janet, she vowed that if the unthinkable should happen, she would spend the rest of her life paying them back. Every one of them.

"I don't know, dad," she said.

"What's the matter, you don't need the money?"

"It isn't that."

"Then it's settled," her dad said. Put us down for $10,000."

"That's too much," Edie said.

"Just let us know when you need the money. And we all want to come to the opening. All of us. Frank, too."

"That would be wonderful," Edie said, tears escaping her eyes. "You're all so wonderful. I love you, dad."

"We love you, Edie."

The building was theirs. Ken called her at Edie's Cafe with the news. He and the owners had agreed on a price, and he was at the escrow office this very minute, opening escrow.

She set the receiver down and called across the kitchen, "Janet, we got it."

And Janet in the middle of an omelet, French fries, and 7-grain toast, ran to her, and put her arms around her. "Oh thank God. It's going to happen. It's really going to happen."

Now that the building was theirs, Edie and Janet's thoughts turned to fixing up the place: turning an empty stall into a fashionable restaurant. They would need an architect, they would need a designer, they would need a decorator.

Edie called Gordon. "Who did Michele's?" she asked.

"You like it?" he asked.

"Yes," she answered. "It's one of the nicer places. Simple and quiet."

"Guy by the name of Mike Kelly," Gordon said. "He's the best."

Chapter Twenty-Eight

When Edie heard the name Mike Kelly, she felt a jolt through her body. Could it be? The man from Paris, the father of her son. Of course she knew he lived in Los Angeles, that he was an architect, she shouldn't be shocked if it was he. But she prayed it wasn't.

She got his number from Gordon and called his office. It was located in Century City.

"Tell me," she asked his secretary, "did Mr. Kelly ever live in Paris?"

"I really don't know."

"Well does he have a son named Josh?"

"He has two daughters. Two little girls."

Then maybe it wasn't him. She hung up the phone relieved. It was a common name. It could be someone else.

She went to see his work.

Marvin at Marvin's showed her around.

"How do you like it?" he asked.

"It's beautiful," she answered. And then, "Tell me what does Mike Kelly look like?"

"Medium height, blond."

She went to see Le Grange. It was different from Marvin's but equally well laid-out. She was impressed. "Do whatever he tells you," Pierre, the chef, said. "I love my kitchen."

"Do you know if he was ever in Paris?"

"I think he was. In the army."

Now she was back to thinking it had to be him. But she didn't have to call him.

She went to Janet. "Janet, there's an architect I think we should interview. His name is Mike Kelly."

For a moment, Janet didn't comprehend what Edie had said, then her body began to shiver as if she were in the middle of a snowstorm, "You mean, our Mike Kelly?"

"I think so."

"Oh, Edie, what are we going to do?"

"I don't know."

Janet was completely unnerved. She didn't know if she could continue working. She didn't know if she could go back into the kitchen. But what else could she do? She had to keep her mind occupied. She had to keep her mind off Mike Kelly.

Edie pondered for days....should she call him? She didn't care about having him work on the restaurant. If he really was the best, she could handle that. It was Brian she was worried about. What should she do about Brian?

Finally, she decided to call him. If he really was Brian's father, there was no point in hiding her head in the sand. She had to know.

She called his secretary and arranged for an appointment. He would meet her at the site on Monday morning at l0.

Edie didn't want Ken to be there, but she desperately wanted Janet to be there. "What if it really is him? I can't face him alone."

"How do you think I feel?" Janet asked, already feeling totally distraught.

"Please, Janet, come with."

"Of all the architects in Los Angeles, why did you have to pick him?"

"Because he's the best."

Janet absolutely didn't want to go, but again, she couldn't refuse Edie anything. "Okay, I'll go. But you owe me one."

Ken wanted to be at the meeting. "It's going to be our biggest money expenditure of all. I think I should be there."

"But I'm just going to get his ideas," Edie told him, her voice a few pitches higher than usual. "I'm not going to sign anything. If I decide to go with him, then you can meet with him."

Ken gave her his disgruntled, "Okay, you win again," look and turned the channel on the T.V.

Both women were standing in front of the restaurant site at 10 in the morning, huddled together, nervous as schoolgirls on their first date, when he drove up.

He was driving a new Jaguar, and the minute he emerged from his car, both girls cringed. It was Mike Kelly all right. His army uniform was replaced by a suit and tie, his blond hair was styled to cover a receding hairline, but he was still broad and muscular, and his eyes were the same blue as Brian's.

"Good morning, ladies," he said.

"Good morning," they said.

And then he looked at them. It had been 13 years. "Don't I know you?"

"Paris," Edie said.

And he looked closer from one to the other. "I knew you in Paris?" he asked.

And it was clear to Edie that he didn't remember her. That long passionate affair, the father of her child, and he didn't remember her.

He looked down at his appointment book. "Mrs. Rosenberg," he said trying to place her.

"Yes," Edie said, "Edie Rosenberg."

"Edie," he said, recognition at last lighting his face, "of course." And turning to Janet, "and you're....."

"Janet Camerini."

Now he was embarrassed. "Edie and Janet. Of course, now I recognize you." And trying to re-coup, "You both look wonderful."

"Thanks," Edie said. Janet said nothing, but took a step backward trying to hide behind Edie.

"Tell me, what have you been doing all these years?" he asked.

"Working in restaurants," Edie said.

"And now, you're going to open your own place."

"Yes," Edie said, turning to the door, her hands unsteady as she tried to get the key into the lock. "Why don't we take a look."

The two women walked through the empty store with Mike Kelly, discussing where the reception area should be, how the kitchen should be laid out, but under all of the words, Edie was appraising him. He was still a very attractive man, still utterly charming in his conversation, still exuding the sinewy power of a lion. She could understand how she had been captivated.

Janet, walking on the other side of Edie, away from Mike Kelly, could not bring herself to look at him. He was the only man who had ever kissed her; the only man who had ever made love to her; the only man she had ever loved. And here they were, the three of them, standing around so civilized, speaking so pleasantly to one another. But all his attention was focused on Edie. So again, Janet was left out. Again, it was Edie getting the man. And as soon as she had this thought, she said to herself, "What am I crazy? Thinking this way about Mike Kelly. I hate him."

When they had finished discussing the design of the restaurant, the three of them walked outside.

The sun was directly in Edie's eyes and all she could see was Mike's glistening blond hair. "What happens now?"

"You decide if you want to use me or not," he said, a light emphasis on the word "use".

Edie shifted her position so she could see his face. He was smiling. She asked, "Don't we get to see any plans?"

"No. I don't work that way. I won't draw up any plans unless you're going to use me." Again that emphasis on the word "use".

"But how can we decide without looking at plans?"

"You can look at my other work. I can give you references. But if I give you the plans, who's to say you won't use them with another architect. I'm sorry but that's the way I work."

"I've seen your work," Edie said, conscious that her words could be taken another way, "and I like what you've done, but we'd also like something in black and white."

"Well, you heard my ideas. You know I know restaurants. And I'll work with you." A hesitation, and then with a twinkle in his eye, "I'll give you exactly what you want."

Janet did not miss any of the messages that he was sending, but it seemed to her that Edie was flirting back. Inconceivable!

Edie was also aware of his double entendres, and not only wasn't she flirting back, she was incensed. Thirteen years and he hadn't changed a bit.

"It's largely a matter of trust," he was continuing.

Edie wanted to laugh. She looked at Janet, who was looking very upset.

"Well, we'll have to think about it," Edie said.

"I'd like to buy you girls a cup of coffee. Talk about old times."

"We don't really have time," Edie said. And then, curious about why his secretary did not know about Josh, she asked, "Tell me, are you still married to Cindy?"

"No," he said, "we've been divorced for years. I have a new wife now, and two more kids." He opened his wallet, obviously proud. "Here they are, that's the little one, Karen, and that's the older one, Susan."

Edie found herself staring at two darling little girls, about 5 and 7, who looked like they could be Brian's sisters.

"They're very cute."

"And here's my wife, Peggy," he said, showing her a lovely blonde woman who looked remarkably like Cindy.

"And what about Josh?" Edie asked.

"Josh is doing fine. He's in college now."

"I can't believe it."

"Neither can I. University of Pennsylvania. He moved back to Philadelphia with his mother after the divorce. But he does come out for Easter, or Christmas, or a couple of weeks in the summer."

"How old is he?"

"Twenty." Then packing his briefcase, "And how about you? I assume there's a Mr. Rosenberg."

"A good assumption."

"And have you had any more kids?"

Her face turned hot. She could barely say the words, "Yes, two more." And her mind screamed out, *and one of them is yours.*

"Well, let me know what you decide. I think I can do a good job for you." And as he got into his Jaguar, he said to Janet, "Nice seeing you, too, Janet, after all these years."

Neither woman moved for several minutes. Edie was completely overcome by the thought that Mike had a son he didn't know he had, and Brian had a father he didn't know he had. And Janet was savoring Mike's last words, "Nice to see you, too, Janet, after all these years." Did he even remember that he had slept with her? Was she a real person to him, or just a shadow of Edie? She felt that she had gained nothing in the past 13 years. Although she was a well respected chef, known in Europe and in the United States, when it came to Mike Kelly, she was still the helpless little innocent she had been in Paris.

It was Edie who broke the spell, "C'mon," she said, "let's go." She pulled out her car keys and said to Janet, "Do you mind driving? I'm too shaken to concentrate on the road."

Janet wanted to say, "How do you think I feel?" But she didn't think she had the right to be as upset as Edie was. After all, Mike Kelly was really Edie's boyfriend. "Sure, I'll drive," she said.

As they crossed Mulholland drive at the top of Laurel Canyon, Edie said to Janet, "What am I going to do?"

"We'll interview a few other architects," Janet said. "See what they have to say."

"Not about that. About Brian."

Janet shook her head. "I don't know. It's a tough one."

"I never questioned it before. I was always so sure I had done the right thing. But now seeing him, even if he is a cad, doesn't he have a right to know?"

"The better question is, 'Doesn't Brian have a right to know?'"

"That's a whole other problem. He'll probably hate me when he finds out. What made me think I had the right to do this?"

"It seemed right at the time."

"No one knows," Edie said. "No one in the whole world but you."

"I can't help you on this one, Edie. You'll have to make this decision yourself."

"There's only one thing to decide. What's best for Brian."

But what was best for Brian? Edie slept fitfully that night, waking up several times in a cold sweat, visualizing the scene with Brian, telling him his father was not dead, but alive and well and living in Los Angeles. It would be awful. Brian would never forgive her. How could she have cheated him out of 13 years of having a real father? But Mike was such a bastard. Married, with two little girls and still flirting with her. How could she bring him into Brian's life?

Edie and Janet interviewed two other architects, and much as they didn't want to go with Mike, there was no comparison. The restaurant had to come first; too many people were depending on them. They asked for another meeting, this time with Ken. Ken listened to Mike's ideas and then said, "Before we sign with you, we'll need to see something on paper."

"Sorry," Mike said, "not possible. I walked through the place with you, I told you what I plan to do, what more do you need?"

"The three of them looked at each other. They had already decided they would go with him.

"All right," Ken said. "You start working on the plans, I'll draw up a contract."

"I've got one right here," Mike said, opening his briefcase and pulling out a two page document.

"I see you've thought of everything," Ken said.

"I've got to, in my business," he said. "But don't worry about a thing, you've made the right choice." And he shook each of their hands.

Although the next few weeks were busier than ever for Edie, continuing to run Edie's Cafe, and going back and forth to the new site to go over the plans, and then monitoring the construction once it began, Edie could not stop thinking about Mike and Brian. She took to spending more time with Brian, trying to find out who he really was, how this would affect him. She drove him to Hebrew School each day, and tried to be subtle, how had it been for him all these years without a dad?

"But I've had a dad. I've had Zola and Ken."

"But still without a real father of your own."

"My father's dead, mom."

"I know, but..."

"What's your problem, mom?"

He thought she was stupid. He didn't understand what she was getting at. He was well adjusted; he had accepted it all these years; she didn't need to bring Mike into the picture. She could let things go as they were.

But it kept nagging at her. And every time she saw Mike, it became harder to keep the truth from him. He was a philanderer, but that didn't make him evil. Plenty of men had extra-marital affairs, and he did seem to be a good father. If he had known she was pregnant, if he had known she had a baby, probably he would have tried to help; he would have sent money. He had cheated on his wife, perhaps was cheating on his new wife, but did that give her the right to keep his son from him?

Five weeks after the construction had begun, on a Friday afternoon, amid the sawdust, the carpenters, the bathroom walls going up, Mike walked over to her, "You know, Edie, I've been wanting to say something to you, ever since that first afternoon we met to discuss the restaurant. I want to apologize."

She looked at him, "For what?"

"For Janet. It was a rotten thing to do."

"And what you did to me wasn't rotten?"

"Not in the same way. We were two consenting adults." A pause. "We still are."

"And what does that mean?" she asked.

"Take it any way you want," he said. Then with a wink, "But it would be so easy to slip away for an hour or two. No one would even know we were gone."

"I see you haven't changed," she said.

"And neither have you. You're just as attractive now as you were 13 years ago. Perhaps more so."

"No, Mike," she said, "I have changed. I can see you now for exactly what you are."

"Oh, please," he said, "no lessons in morality. I'm a married man now, I was a married man then. You knew exactly what you were getting into."

"Yes," she said, "you're right. I was no better than you, but I hope I've learned something since then."

"Well, if you have, keep it to yourself. I'm not interested." He started to walk away, and then as if remembering something, he turned to her again, "If you ever change your mind, let me know."

She headed for the door. It was as if God were telling her something. This man is no good. Don't tell your son about him.

But in the end, she knew it was inevitable. The voice inside her would give her no rest until she told them. And of course she would have to tell Ken. But later. After she saw how things turned out.

Now she had to decide how? And when?

Should she tell Brian first, or tell Mike first? What if Mike didn't want to know, didn't want to have anything to do with Brian or his past? She better tell Mike first.

She made an appointment to see him at his office at 3 o'clock on a Thursday afternoon. She went directly from Edie's Cafe, arranging to have Wendy drive Brian and Missy to Hebrew school that afternoon. She was nervous waiting in the small antechamber and by the time his secretary said, "You can go in, now," she was completely unstrung.

She summoned her courage, walked into his office pretending she was completely at ease, sat before him, returned his smile, listened as he chatted about the progress of the restaurant. Did he think she had changed her mind about his offer? Did he think she was coming to start up an affair with him? "Mike," she said, "there's something I have to tell you."

His office was on the tenth floor. She could see out the window behind him, a few buildings, and then the brown-green mountains, splashed with colored houses and tall green palm trees, like a Cezanne painting.

He smiled, "You've run out of money."

"No," she said, "nothing as unimportant as that."

He leaned back in his chair, smug, expectant. "What is it?" he asked.

"You know, back in Paris, our affair, well, I became pregnant."

His look changed to shock.

She continued, "You have a son, Mike."

"I don't believe it."

"It's true."

"But you never told me, you never let me know."

"No, I didn't want to. I didn't want you ever to know and I wouldn't ever have told you, if I hadn't met you again."

He leaned forward, anger in his eyes. "But how could you keep such a thing from a father?"

"I thought at the time it was the right thing to do."

"How could it ever be the right thing to do?"

Shame crept up her neck. "I hated you. Don't you understand? I thought you were the rottenest scum on earth. Why would I want to share my son with you?"

"Then why are you telling me now?"

"Because I want to do what's best for him."

He stood up and walked to the window, his back to her. "I can't believe it," he said, as if digesting the news. "I have a son." And then turning to face her. "What's his name?"

"Brian," she said. "Brian Matthew Freni."

"Where did you come up with Freni?"

"An Italian family we stayed with in Florence."

"What have you told him about me?"

"I told him that you were dead."

"I mean now."

"I haven't told him anything."

He came and sat on the edge of his desk. She held her breath, waiting for the words that would determine Brian's fate. "I want to see him," he said.

She felt relieved. "It's going to be a shock to him."

"No more than it was to me."

"But he's young. Only twelve."

"Twelve. My God," he said.

"Almost thirteen," she said. "He's a wonderful boy."

"When can I see him?"

"I'll have to break the news to him."

"And I'll have to tell Peggy."

"How will she take it?"

He shrugged. "She knows I sowed my wild oats."

"And that you're still sowing them?" she asked pointedly.

He stood up, "Forget what happened in the restaurant the other day. I know I was out of line."

"I just don't want Brian to be disappointed."

"Don't worry, I won't disappoint him."

She left the office feeling heavy-hearted. She was glad that she had told Mike about Brian, and she felt sure that he would be a good father to Brian, but now she was faced with the forbidding task of telling Brian. She was not looking forward to it.

She came home early from the restaurant that night, at 8 o'clock, and found Brian in his room.

"Gee you're home early," he said.

She could hear her heart beating. "Brian, there's something I want to talk to you about."

"Oh oh, what'd I do now?"

How to say it? How to get the words out? "It's nothing you did. It's something I did."

He looked at her, more interested now, and sat on the bed. "What'd you do?"

She was trembling, trying to keep her voice steady. "I lied to you."

"You lied to me about what?"

He was so innocent, her beautiful, blond, blue-eyed son. She came and sat beside him and took his hands in hers. "Brian, I lied to you about your dad."

He pulled away. "I knew it. I knew it," he said, excitement in his voice. "He's alive, isn't he?"

"Yes, he's alive."

And then a moment's hesitation, "Is he insane?"

"No," she said, "he's not insane."

"Is he in prison?"

She laughed, in spite of her nervousness, or maybe because of it. "What makes you think that?"

"I tried to figure it out. Why you would never talk about him and the only thing I could figure out was that my father was either insane or a murderer."

"Oh, no, Brian, it's nothing like that. He's an architect. As a matter of fact, he's *my* architect, Mike Kelly."

"An architect! Then why didn't you tell me?" Confusion in Brian's blue eyes.

"Because I only just met up with him again. I haven't seen him since before you were born. I didn't even know where he was."

"But why did you tell me he was dead?" an edge to his voice. "Why didn't you try to find him?"

"I know this is going to be hard for you to understand. But at the time I became pregnant with you, I was very angry with him. So angry that I never wanted to see him again, I never wanted you to see him, I never wanted you to know he existed."

"But how could you do that, mom?" He jumped off the bed, away from her.

"I'm sorry, Brian. I know now I shouldn't have done it." And she got up and went to him, took him in her arms, smoothed his long blond hair. Mike's hair. "Please forgive me."

He put his slender arms around her, and after a moment he said, "I want to meet him."

"Yes," Edie said, "you will. Tomorrow if you want. He's very anxious to meet you."

"Yes, tomorrow. First thing in the morning. I want to skip school."

"All right, tomorrow at 9 o'clock. I'll call him and arrange it. He's waiting to hear from me."

"God, mom, how am I going to sleep tonight?"

"I don't think I'll be able to, either."

"Will you be there with me?"

"Of course I will."

"What's he like?"

She pondered for a moment, trying to think of a word that would sum him up without lying. "He's nice," she said. "I think you're going to like him." And then kissing the top of Brian's head, "I know he's going to love you."

Later, after all the children were asleep, and she and Ken were in bed together, she told Ken all that had happened that day.

"Jeez," he said. "Mike Kelly."

"Amazing, but there it is."

"I can't believe that in all these years you never told me the truth."

"I tried to, before we were married, but you didn't want to hear it."

"But you let me believe all these years that Brian's father was dead."

"I know, and I'm sorry. I can see now it was a mistake. I should have found Mike years ago. I should have given them to each other. It was selfish and stupid of me to keep them apart."

"I guess you were trying to do what was best."

"For myself," she said, and with that they both lay in the dark, not touching, not talking, thinking their own thoughts about the past and the present.

Chapter Twenty-Nine

That morning driving over to Mike Kelly's office, Edie didn't know who was more nervous, she or Brian.

Neither of them had gotten much sleep, and Brian was up at 6 a.m., showering and blowing his hair dry.

Now, Edie looked over at her son, dressed in a brown and white striped t-shirt and tan pants, and thought what a sweet, darling boy he was. She was proud of him, proud to be introducing him to Mike Kelly. She had done a good job with him. Mike would have to love him. And if he didn't, if he hurt her son in any way, she would kill him. She had wanted to kill him once before, but this time she would do it.

"Do I look all right?" Brian asked for the tenth time.

"You look gorgeous," she told him. And putting her hand on his, "I know this must be very difficult for you."

"I just hope he likes me."

"I know he's going to love you."

"But what if he doesn't?"

"Then we'll just go on with our life the way it was before."

"I still can't get over that you kept this a secret from me all these years. What could he have done that was so bad?"

Edie didn't know what to say. How could she explain it to a twelve-year-old? How could she tell him that his father had screwed Janet and her at the same time. She wanted him to think well of his father, but she didn't want to lie. "It's very complicated," she said, "but basically, I thought your father loved me, and I found out he didn't."

"Were you married to him?"

Painfully, "No."

Brian was quiet for several minutes. "I don't want you ever to lie to me again."

"I promise I won't."

"Are we almost there?"

"It's the tall building up ahead."

Edie pulled into the parking structure, and she and Brian held hands all the way up the elevator and into Mike Kelly's office. She could feel his hand quivering in hers. What a terrible thing she was putting him through. She should have told Mike Kelly as soon as she knew she was pregnant. How could she have done this to Brian?

As soon as they walked into the reception area, Mike's secretary buzzed him. In a moment, his door opened, and there he was. He was wearing a suit and tie, his hair perfectly styled, his blue eyes sparkling. He paused for one second, looked at his son, then came to Brian and put his arms around him, and Brian put his arms around Mike, and tears came to both their eyes.

After several moments, Mike held Brian away from him and looked him over, "God, you're a handsome boy."

"And you're a handsome dad," Brian said.

Mike put his arm around Brian's shoulder, "Come into my office," and Edie followed after the two of them.

Once in his office, Mike sat on the edge of his cherrywood desk and Edie and Brian sat in the two maroon chairs in front of the desk. "I still can't believe it," Mike said, "I have another son."

"And I have a real father," Brian said.

"It must be as big a shock to you as it was to me," Mike said.

"Bigger," Brian said.

Edie sat watching them, thinking that nothing Mike had done was as wrong as what she had done.

"There's so much I want to know about you," Mike said.

"And so much I want to know about you," Brian said.

"Have you had breakfast?" Mike asked.

"Yes, but I was too nervous to eat."

"Well then, why don't we go someplace and get acquainted?"

"That'd be great."

Mike looked at Edie. "Care to come?"

Edie stood up, "No. No, I think you two will do fine without me."

Brian stood up and came to hug her. "Thanks, mom. Thanks for letting me meet my dad."

And Edie could stand it no longer. She burst into tears. "I'm so sorry," she said, hugging Brian to her. And then looking up at Mike, "I'm so sorry to both of you. I should never have done what I did."

And Mike came and stood behind Brian and put his hand on Brian's shoulder. "It's okay. We're together now, and that's what counts."

And Edie, rocking back and forth with Brian, "Brian, can you ever forgive me?"

"Of course, mom. I forgive you right now."

"Thank you, sweetheart." And she kissed his cheek.

Mike took Brian's hand and asked Edie once more, "Sure you don't want to come with us?"

"No. I'll be fine. You two go along."

"I'll drop him at your house later," Mike said.

"Yes," Edie said, "that will be fine."

"Bye, mom," and Brian waved.

"Have a good morning," she said, and watched as the two of them, Brian, blond-haired, blue-eyed wiry, and Mike, the same, walked out the door.

Chapter Thirty

Everything was coming together at once.

The new restaurant was about to open, they were "breaking-in" a new chef for Edie's Cafe, and Brian was going to be Bar Mitzvahed.

Everyone was coming to town for the opening of the new restaurant and for Brian's Bar Mitzvah.

"If I'm ever going to have a nervous breakdown," Edie said, "it'll be now."

"I'll handle Edie's and the Trattoria, you handle the Bar Mitzvah," Janet told her.

There were going to be 110 guests at Brian's Bar Mitzvah. Edie hadn't intended on having that many people. She didn't want to flaunt that fact that Mike was Brian's dad. But at the same time she wanted Brian to have the party he deserved. So she invited everyone: Zola, his new wife and her three children, the Bittermans, Edie's mom and dad, Frank, Cookie and their four children, her aunts, uncles and cousins from Cleveland and Chicago, her grandma Rose and her husband Arthur from Florida, Ken's relatives, Mike's relatives, Ken and Edie's friends, and Brian's friends.

Edie asked Brian how he felt about having so many people at his Bar Mitzvah.

"Well, if it makes everyone happy," he said, "I guess it's okay."

"It's just that so many people love you," she told him.

Wendy asked if she could bring a date.

"Someone special?" Edie asked.

"Yes. Tom O'Neil."

"Another Irishman," Edie said.

"Why, who else is Irish?"

"Brian's dad."

"Right," Wendy said. "I forgot about him."

"So did I," Edie said, "for 13 years."

"I don't understand why," Wendy said, hoping for an explanation.

But as with Brian, Edie could not bring herself to tell Wendy the truth about Mike, especially since it involved Janet. "It's none of your business," Edie said, trying to keep it light and pinching her daughter's cheek.

"Well, all I can say is I hope my life's half as interesting as yours was."

"It better not be," Edie said.

Wendy was in her last year of high school, planning to start U.C.L.A. in the fall. She was now two inches taller than Edie, 5'8", still slim, beautiful, and still getting mostly A's, in spite of waitressing weekends at Edie's Cafe. When Trattoria Mia opened, she was going to become a waitress there. She was still undecided as to what to do with her life: become a college professor in English, or open her own restaurant someday.

"Become a college professor," Edie told her. "Owning a restaurant is just too damn much work."

"If it's so damn much work, then why do you do it?"

"Because I can't help myself. I guess it's in my blood."

"Well, maybe it's in my blood, too."

The opening of the new restaurant was set to take place three days after Brian's Bar Mitzvah. It was rushing things, but Edie's parents and Frank wanted so much to be there.

"What you're doing is crazy," Ken told her. "How can you do it all?"

"I don't know if I can. But I'm going to try my damndest."

"I think you're the most stubborn woman I ever met."

"I seem to remember my mother telling me the same thing."

"Well, she was right."

The morning of the Bar Mitzvah, Brian was called to the Torah. Edie's father, Ben, took the Torah from the Rabbi, passed it to Mike Kelly, who then passed it to Brian. Edie was very moved by the ceremony--the passing of the Jewish law from father to son to son. Thank God Mike had turned out to be a real father to Brian.

And later, over the challah and wine at the Oneg Shabbat, Edie's mother came up to her, "Well, it looks like everything's turned out fine."

"Yes, mother, of course it has. Did you ever have any doubts?"

"Believe you me, I had plenty of doubts. But I guess I was wrong. Every time I think that I didn't want you to have Wendy and Brian, I get shivers down my spine."

"And every time I think that I might not have had them, I get the same shivers."

That night there was a banquet: appetizers, salad, soup, chicken, kishka, ice cream sundaes for dessert, and a cake that Janet had baked. It had to be the most extravagant and most delicious Bar Mitzvah cake ever made. There was a live band that played the latest pop tunes, and "Balling the Jack", the "Hokie Pokie" and the "Bunny Hop" for the kids. Edie danced with her father, Frank, and then Ken, Zola, and Mike Kelly, all the fathers of her children.

Mike and Peggy Kelly were among the last to leave, and when Mike went to get Peggy's coat, Peggy came over to Edie, "You know, there's something I must say."

Something in her tone put Edie on the alert. "And what's that?"

"I just don't understand how you could have done it."

"Done what?"

"Not told Mike all these years."

Edie thought for a moment, what was her obligation to this second Cindy? Speaking up and telling Mike's first wife the truth, had only caused her anguish. Maybe it was better to say nothing. "It's a long story," she said.

"I'd like to hear it. Could we meet for lunch?"

"No," Edie said, "I think not."

"Please," Peggy said, "it's very important to me. Sometimes I feel that I don't know Mike at all."

"No, I'm sorry," Edie said, "it's really not my place to explain your husband to you."

"But I need to talk to someone," Peggy said.

Edie tried to read her eyes. Was Mike having an affair, now, while all this re-uniting with his son was taking place? And then seeing Mike within hearing range, Edie said, "I hope you're planning on coming to the opening of the restaurant."

"I wouldn't miss it," Peggy said.

Chapter Thirty-One

The next afternoon, Edie was sitting at a table at Trattoria Mia counting the tablecloths, the napkins, the towels, the aprons, when the door opened and Peggy Kelly walked in.

Edie was surprised and annoyed. She did not want to deal with Peggy Kelly at all, let alone two days before her new restaurant was going to open.

Peggy looked very pretty in black pants, a white blouse, a red jacket, her soft blonde hair turned under in a perfect page-boy, the way Edie had once wanted her hair to look. "I know this is a bad time for you, but I couldn't sleep last night," Peggy began.

"Neither could I," Edie said, "too much to do." She was still hoping to ward off whatever Peggy had to say.

Peggy sat on a chair next to Edie. "I'm just so desperate about Mike, I don't know what to do."

There were tears in Peggy's eyes, and Edie's heart melted. Nothing was more important than Peggy's misery at this moment. "What's the problem?" she asked.

Peggy began to cry. "I think he's seeing another woman."

But of course, Edie thought, how could it be any other way with Mike? "What makes you think so?" Edie asked.

"He's not interested in me anymore. He used to come home in the afternoons to make love, and now days can pass without him touching me." She wiped at her eyes. "The thing is, it's just what I deserve. You see, when I met him, he was dating my best friend."

Of course, Edie thought, it was his modus operandi--screwing two best friends at the same time.

Peggy was continuing, "I knew it was wrong to get involved with him, but I couldn't help it. He was so..." and she groped for the right word, "persuasive." Peggy looked into Edie's eyes. "He made me feel like no other man ever had."

Edie felt embarrassed. This woman, this almost stranger knew more about the most intimate moments of Edie's life than anyone else on earth, except Mike and Janet. "I know what you mean," Edie said.

"And now God is punishing me. And I deserve it. I deserve every bit of it."

That's exactly how I felt, Edie thought, but did not say out loud. "So what are you going to do?" Edie asked.

"I don't know. I have two daughters. Two daughters who are crazy about their daddy. How can I divorce him?"

"Yes, it's difficult."

"That's why I wanted to talk to you. You had a child with him, and yet you walked away from him. Why? How?"

Edie considered again, what did she owe this woman? And what did she owe Brian's father? Finally she made her decision, "Peggy, whatever happened between Mike and me was a long time ago. It doesn't really matter. Only you can decide what you want to do. I can only say that I don't think Mike will ever be faithful to any woman. If you can live with that, then stay with him; if you can't, then leave."

"Yes, yes, I know. It's just that I don't know if I *can* live with it."

"Even for your daughters?"

"Even for my daughters."

Both women sat quietly for a moment. And then Peggy said, "I guess I've taken enough of your time." And standing up, "I'm sorry to have bothered you on such a busy day, but I just had to talk to someone, and I didn't know who else to turn to."

"I don't think I've been much help."

"Yes, you have," Peggy said. "You said out loud what I knew was the truth anyway."

Edie watched Peggy out the door, and felt all her feelings of disgust for Mike stirred up again. He was a fucking bastard, but as long as he was a good father to Brian, she could put up with anything.

Chapter Thirty-Two

Would they make it in time?

The doors were scheduled to open at 6, but the day had started badly. The tomatoes didn't arrive. "How can I cook without tomatoes," Janet had asked, and Edie sent Wendy to the supermarket to buy a bushel of them. Then the eyes of the sole weren't clear and Janet said, "Scratch the sole Florentine from the menu." They couldn't find the corkscrews. "I know they were here," Edie said. "I remember seeing them." And she hunted everywhere and at 3 o'clock sent Wendy out to buy 10 more.

Now it was 5 o'clock and while the three assistant cooks were still slicing the vegetables, trimming the veal, deboning the chicken breasts, one of the waiters called to say he had the flu and wouldn't be in. Edie made frantic calls to everyone she knew, "Do you know a waiter who can be here in an hour and who wears a size 40 jacket and 34 pants?"

Janet, Edie, Wendy, and the waiters, busboys, and dishwashers, were all scurrying about, trying to get everything done: setting out fresh flowers, cleaning the bathrooms, sweeping the sawdust from the corners, adjusting the pictures on the wall--they had settled for a few reproductions of Cezanne still-lifes for now, to be replaced by original works of art when they had the time and money--folding the napkins, checking the silverware, the glasses, the utensils, the frying pans. Was everything there? Was everything handy?

They had sent out invitations to everyone they knew, and their reservation book was filled. They were giving free wine tonight, but everyone was going to have to pay for his or her dinner, even the investors. "I wouldn't have it any other way," Frank said.

Mike was very proud of the way the restaurant had turned out. "Everything in its proper place," he had said.

Janet was in the kitchen feeling like a debutante at a coming-out party. She had cooked thousands of meals before, but none as thrilling as this one.

Edie stood at the front door surveying the place, and bursting with pride. Trattoria Mia had turned out exactly as she and Janet had envisioned it.

The women had stuck to their white. White walls, white tablecloths, white napkins. They had purchased large, heavy, silverware, and two sizes of water glasses; the larger to be used for water; the smaller for wine. They wanted it to look as much like an authentic trattoria as possible. Each table had a miniature pepper mill and salt shaker, and a small vase of fresh flowers. The sugar and saccharine would be brought later with the coffee. A wine rack was placed near the bus station so the waiters could get to it easily. The kitchen was open to the restaurant, and if anyone wanted, they could look over the counter separating the kitchen from the eating area, and watch Janet and the other cooks at work.

The kitchen, in addition to the conventional stoves and ovens had an open grill, all the better to make fish, veal, chicken, and other grilled meats. And in the rear, not in view of the eating area, was the wine cellar, the restrooms and the office.

At five-thirty, Edie found a waiter who promised to be there by seven, and at six o'clock, Edie unlocked the door, and the guests began arriving. By seven-thirty, every table was filled.

It was a gala evening. Edie acted as hostess and cashier, Wendy waited on tables, and Janet cooked. Oh, how she cooked. Everything that came out of the kitchen not only tasted superb, but looked beautiful.

Janet and Edie had decided on a changing menu. They would have several standard dishes, but they would also have several specials each night, including appetizers, soups and desserts. Fish was put on the menu only as "Pesce del Giorno" and would change each evening, as would the desserts. In this way, the two restaurateurs felt they could utilize the freshest ingredients and keep their patrons tantalized.

For opening night, Janet decided to cook only from their permanent menu. She didn't want to attempt too much on this very important night.

As soon as each table was full, the waiter served a basket of assorted breads, including focaccia, and glasses of ice water. Then the patrons could order their wine and dinner. Appetizers, soup and salad were a la carte, but the main dishes came with vegetables (usually spinach, green beans, peas, zucchini, or whatever was in season) and a starch, which might be pasta, rice, cannellini (white beans), or potatoes, depending on what best accompanied the main course. Pastas were also available as a main course.

The menu read:

TRATTORIA MIA

Antipasti

Caprese (slices of tomato and mozzarella with parsley, basil, olive oil and vinegar)
Prosciutto with melon
Salmon carpaccio (thin slices of salmon with olive oil and lemon)
Sautéed scallops with garlic and parsley
Bruschetta (toasted bread with garlic and checca)
Polenta con funghi & Gorgonzola (crispy grilled polenta with mushrooms and gorgonzola)
Antipasto -- an assortment of meat, cheeses and vegetables

Le Insalate

Silvia's chopped salad
Insalate Mia (belgian endive and arugala with capers, olives and gorgonzola)
Insalate Mista (mixed greens with tomato and pine nuts)

Zuppa

Tuscan vegetable soup (Ribollita) with black cabbage, beans, garlic and rosemary
Minestrone (vegetable soup with tomato and pasta)
Zuppa de ceci (chick pea soup with fried bread squares)

Pasta

Spaghetti with meat sauce
Fettuccini with pesto
Pappardelle with eggplant and red peppers in a tomato-basil sauce
Spinach fettuccine with porcini mushrooms and green peas
Penne Puttanesca (tomato sauce with capers, olives, white wine and garlic)
Farfalle with shrimp, asparagus and mushrooms

Linguini with clams
Lasagna with spinach and a tomato meat sauce
Ricotta and spinach ravioli with saffron cream sauce
Gnocchi with a gorgonzola sauce.

Risotto

Risotto with wild mushrooms.
Risotto with seasonal vegetables, white wine and parmesan

Pesce

Pesce del Giorno (fresh fish of the day)
Shrimp sautéed with garlic, basil, lemon and white wine

Pollo

Pollo al matoni (half a chicken, flattened, seasoned with rosemary and olive oil and grilled)
Pollo mozzarella (chicken breast stuffed with tomato, mozzarella, parsley,
        thyme and marjoram and baked)
Pollo cacciatori (boneless chicken with fresh mushrooms, olives, peppers in a
        tomato sauce with dry vermouth)
Pollo Florentine (chicken with spinach and mozzarella)
Pollo Marsala (chicken with Marsala wine and mushrooms)
Pollo piccata (chicken with white wine, lemon and capers)

Vitello

Grilled veal steak with rosemary and olive oil
Roasted breast of veal with roasted potatoes
Veal scaloppine (with white wine and sage)
Veal Milanese, (breaded and sautéed in olive oil)
Veal Marsala (with Marsala wine and mushrooms)
Veal piccata (with white wine, lemon and capers)
Osso Bucco (braised veal shank over risotto)

Carne

Bistecca Fiorentina (grilled t-bone steak with olive oil and pepper in a wood burning oven)
Roast filet of beef with a Barolo wine sauce
Rack of lamb grilled with rosemary, olive oil and garlic

Desserts, including Italian and French, would be printed on a separate menu, and would change each day. Tonight's desserts were: Italian ricotta rum cake, zuccotto (a creamy ice-box cake with almonds, hazelnuts and chocolate bits), pistachio torte, Tarte tatin, fresh strawberry and kiwi tart, and apple crepes with chantilly.

The dessert menu would also include a tray of assorted cheeses and fruit, tonight served complimentary to every table.

Edie had put together a fine wine list; her years of experience with wine, and tasting the samples from the wine purveyors had paid off. They had good and great wines from California and some of the best wines of Italy: Asti Spumante from Piedmont; three medium reds from Lombardy; Pino Grigio, Merlot, Cabernet, Pinot Bianco; and Riesling from Trentino, white Soave and red

Amarone and Recioto from Veneto; Lambrusco from Emilia-Romagna; Orvieto from Umbria; Verdicchio from Marches; Frascati from Rome; pale red Montepulciano d'Abruzzo and the white Trebbiano d'Abruzzo from Abbruzzo; three Ischias, from Campania; the famous Vernaccia from Sardinia, and of course Chianti, Chianti Classico along with Brolia Riserva, Brunello di Montalcino, Montecarlo white and red, and Vernaccia di San Gamignano from their beloved Tuscany.

It was a marvelous evening for Janet and Edie. Edie felt it was the moment of her greatest achievement, and everyone she loved most, was here to share it.

Gordon showed up with a good-looking young man, "Can you believe I took the night off to go to someone else's restaurant?" he asked.

"I can believe anything about you," Edie answered.

Mike arrived but without Peggy. "Is Peggy all right?" Edie asked.

"Yes, she's fine," Mike said. "Just a little headache." Edie didn't press him further. Probably nothing had happened because Mike seemed perfectly at ease, very up-beat. But then again, he would. The man had no conscience. He sat at a table for two with Brian.

Ken sat at a table for three with his mother and Missy. Missy looked like a young lady in a pink dress and black patent pumps. Ken had insisted that Edie take Missy out and buy her something "pretty" for the opening; he couldn't remember the last time he'd seen her in a dress. It was another thing that upset Ken about Edie. She didn't seem to notice that Melissa was always in pants. You'd think with Gordon as a friend, Edie would be more conscious of these things. But she was so god-damn oblivious to everything but her restaurants. Ken felt the anger rising. And then he caught himself. Not tonight. Tonight was Edie's moment of glory. He'd give her tonight. But he couldn't help thinking what a great influence Maria would be on Missy.

The evening flew by with a bustle of activity, waiters scurrying back and forth to the kitchen, people oohing and ahhing at each new taste delight, and at ten o'clock, when Janet came out of the kitchen, everyone applauded. Janet doffed her Gros Bonnet, then stopped at various tables to chat, receiving handshakes, hugs and kisses before returning to oversee her kitchen.

By midnight, all of the diners, waiters, busboys, and the two dishwashers had left, and Edie and Janet sat drinking a glass of Chianti Classico at a plain wood table now stripped of its starched white tablecloth, heavy silver and glass tumblers. Both of them were utterly exhausted, but exhilarated, too.

"We did it," Janet said.

"Better than anything we could have imagined," Edie said, and they clicked glasses and drank.

"Yes, but what happens when our friends and relatives stop showing up," Janet asked.

"We'll be just as busy as tonight," Edie answered. "Why shouldn't we be? We've got the best chef in town."

"And the best manager," Janet said, and thought, maybe now, maybe that empty feeling inside of her would leave forever.

Later, when Edie got home, Ken was already in bed. Edie lay down beside him, feeling especially warm and cuddly, hoping he would take her in his arms, make love to her. "Wasn't it a wonderful night?" she whispered in his ear.

But he did not answer; he was already asleep.

Chapter Thirty-Three

Ken pulled into his parking spot in the subterranean garage of the apartment he had rented for Maria Kent, and looked around before getting out of the car. After all this time, nearly three years, he still checked to make sure no one saw him. Habit, or the conservatism of an accountant.

He walked up the stairs to the second floor and opened the door to the apartment.

Maria wasn't here yet. Probably got tied up at the office. That was a joke: the boss was here waiting while the secretary was still at work.

He walked over to the bar he and Maria had set up, and poured himself a glass of white wine, then took off his jacket, tie, shoes, and sat on the sofa, putting his feet up on the coffee table.

He hoped Maria would get here soon; he had a 2 o'clock appointment, and he did want to grab a bite to eat before he got back. Besides her, he smiled. He leaned his head back and closed his eyes and thought of her, her voluptuous breasts in those black lace bras she wore, her long legs in those impossibly high heels. Just thinking about her, his erection began to grow. But what he felt for her was more than sex, he told himself.

But was it love?

He loved being with her. He loved seeing her at the office, or here in their apartment. She was always smiling, always ready to do whatever he wanted, always trying to please him, existing for him alone. She had no ambition, no overpowering desire to achieve, no drive for success. She was just his.

Boring, one might think, but he loved it, ate it up, wallowed in it.

And she wasn't stupid. She knew what was going on in the world; she liked the same movies he did. She knew who Beethoven was and Rembrandt, and she could name at least three supreme court justices. She read *Time* magazine every week, as well as *Cosmopolitan*, and she had interests, besides "whatever he wanted to do." She liked to knit, and made beautiful sweaters, and she loved the sun. She sat out by the pool whenever possible, and loved to go to the beach. He had even gone with her a few times, but was too nervous to enjoy it. He was afraid someone would come by and recognize him, even though he wore sunglasses and a hat pulled low over his face.

And she had other qualities he liked. She was a devoted worker, and she was a devoted daughter. She stopped by to see her mother almost every day, even though her mother was giving her a hard time about their relationship.

The great thing about Maria was that she told him this, not as an ultimatum, and not as her sentiments, but only reporting how her mother felt about the situation. Now and then, he did think about it. Marrying her. There was a lot to be said for it. She would be a great wife, a great mother, and she was the greatest fuck he could ever imagine.

He heard her key in the lock and the excitement that had been building in him gathered momentum. She entered the room, threw her purse on the chair, and with deliberate motion took off her jacket, unbuttoned and took off her blouse, unhooked her bra, freeing her large firm tits, and then came to him, naked from the waist up, still in her skirt, those hose, and her incredibly high heels. It was enough to drive him crazy.

He cupped her breasts in his hands, then bent over and sucked her nipples. He ran his hands along her hose and under her skirt. She was wearing a garter belt, but no underpants. He didn't know if he could wait. He could just come now and make love to her after. He brought her to the floor, kissing her soft red lips, and then lying on the hard brown carpet, he ducked his head between her legs, and while she groaned, he thought, "Yes, I can wait. I want to savor every moment of this."

Chapter Thirty-Four

It was quite by accident they met.

Janet was having lunch at a newly opened restaurant on Wilshire Boulevard when he passed her table on his way out. "Are you expecting anyone?" he asked.

"No," she said, feeling uneasy. She always felt uneasy when he was around.

"Mind if I join you?" he asked.

"Not at all," she said, trying to keep her emotions under control. She mustn't let him know how much he meant to her.

She had ordered fresh water scallops on linguine and the waitress set the steaming plate before her.

"I'll have a glass of white wine," he told the waitress. Then to Janet, "I admire people who can eat in a restaurant alone. I never could."

"It's part of my occupation," she said, hoping she could hold her fork without shaking. "Trying new places, trying new dishes."

"You probably don't know it, but I'm quite a fan of yours. I come by your restaurant all the time. You wouldn't know, of course, you're always in the back cooking."

"Exactly," she said, concentrating on the food in her mouth, trying to identify all the flavors: shallots, basil, coriander, salt.

The waitress set his glass of wine before him. "So," he said, "you've never married."

"No," she said, seeing that her hand was steady and gaining courage from that fact.

"Why not?" he asked.

"No one's asked me," she said, trying to sound blasé, trying to sound like Edie.

He sipped his wine. "Does that mean I've been the only man in your life?"

She was afraid to look in his eyes. "Yes," she said.

"You know, Janet, I apologized to Edie, but I guess I never apologized to you for what I did. It was rotten."

Now she lifted her eyes and looked into the deep blue of his. "Do you really believe that or are you just saying it?"

"Half and half," he said and smiled.

She shook her head. "You haven't changed at all."

"Change is a relative thing," he said. "I have changed in a lot of ways."

"Name one."

"I'm getting tired of the chase."

"I guess you never heard, married men aren't supposed to chase."

"But I'm not married."

"I don't understand," Janet said.

"Peggy and I have split."

Janet was surprised. She wanted to ask, "What happened?" but didn't know if she had the right.

"Don't you want to know why?" he asked.

"If you want to tell me."

"I was having an affair. With a cute little blonde airhead." He sighed. "God how I hate those cute little blonde air-heads."

"Then why do you do it?"

"I can't help myself. Never can. Never could."

"But Edie has brown hair." She wanted to add, and so do I, but didn't have the nerve to say it.

"Yes, but I would never have married Edie, or you. I would never have married anyone who could hurt me."

Janet was confused by his words. "How could we hurt you?"

"Because you might have touched that part of me that I keep carefully hidden."

"So it's been the other way around."

"I'm sorry to admit it, but, yes."

"Still, you've only been married twice."

"Yes, but I've had many, many love affairs, sweet Janet. So many that I don't think I ever want another one."

"I guess we're in opposite places then," Janet said with a smile. "You're finished and I haven't even begun."

He smiled at her remark, then looked at his watch and drained what was left in his glass. "I have to get going, I have an appointment at two, but could we continue this talk tonight?"

The trembling began again. "I'm busy tonight," she said.

He seemed disappointed. "What are you doing?"

"What I do every Monday night, going restaurant-hopping with friends."

"Exactly what I planned to do. There's this great little restaurant at the beach I'd like to take you to. Can you cancel out of your other date?"

Of course she could cancel out. But what for? To have her heart broken again? "What do you want from me, Mike?"

"I want to get to know you better. You fascinate me."

"Me? What could be fascinating about me?"

"You're a genius with food. Geniuses have always fascinated me."

"I don't want to get hurt," she said.

"I would never intentionally hurt you."

"You did once."

"It wasn't intentional."

"Then what was it?"

"As I said before, I couldn't help myself. I needed the conquest. Every conquest. Everyone was a challenge to me. Even you, sweet Janet."

"Then what's different now?"

"As I told you, I've changed."

Could she believe him?

He put his hand on hers, "Just tell me you don't have any feelings for me and I'll leave you alone."

How could she tell him that? Not when she'd been in love with him all these years. She set her fork down. She had lost her sense of taste. She had lost her self control. All she could think of now was that Mike was sitting beside her, touching her hand. "I don't know what to say," she said.

"Say yes," he said.

"All right," she said, her heart pounding so hard she thought he must hear it. "All right, I'll have dinner with you tonight."

He told her he'd pick her up at eight that night. Janet began getting ready at six. She showered, put on her black hose, her black dress, her black high heels, blow-dried her short, fuzzy hair so that it was smooth and fluffy, and then thought about wearing blush and eye make-up. She looked in the mirror. Her face was so plain. But she decided against the blush and eye make-up. She didn't want to pretend she was something she was not. And then she realized that this was her first date. She was 39 years old and she had never been on a date before. But she didn't feel like 39, she felt like 2l, eighteen, younger than that. She felt like the teen-ager she had never been: carefree, innocent, excited. Oh God, I hope he likes me.

Mike arrived promptly at eight, driving his black Jaguar, and drove her to Julio's, a new restaurant at the beach. They sat by a picture window, dining on thick char-broiled swordfish, and after, they took off their shoes and walked along the beach. It was an unusually warm evening for January. The temperature had hit 80 during the day, and tonight was still balmy and so clear they could see a thousand stars in the sky. A warm breeze was blowing Janet's skirt around her legs.

Mike took her hand. "So," he said, "now that I know all about Jacque Patou and Vittorio and Umberto and Edie's Cafe and the Trattoria, maybe you'd like to tell me something about you."

"I've been talking about me all evening."

"Only the superficial stuff."

"Well," she smiled a devilish smile, "I could tell you about my love affair in Paris."

"Oh God no, please not that."

They walked a little farther, and Janet was finally feeling comfortable and at ease with him. "Why don't you tell me about you?" she asked.

"You don't want to hear all the gruesome details of my life."

"Yes, I do. Start when you were born."

"I was a great baby," he said.

"I bet you were," she said.

"But then when I turned twelve, I became a real terror. I was always getting into trouble. Cutting class, stealing things, smoking in the bathroom at school."

"I don't believe it."

"It's true."

"But you've done so well for yourself, becoming an architect."

"I was always talented in art. I was good with my hands. I used to make those boats from kits--you know the ones with all the little strings. And model airplanes. My room was filled with them."

"I'm not sure we had those in Italy," Janet said, thinking how wonderful this was. They were walking on the sand and talking just like any normal couple on a date. "But tell me, what happened when you were twelve?"

"My mother ran off with another man."

"How terrible."

"Yes, it was. I was very close to my mother. We had this really special relationship. I told her everything, she told me everything...I thought. And then one day, poof, she was gone."

"Did you ever see her again?"

"Oh yes. I went to live with her eventually. Her and her new husband, but it was never the same. She had another baby, a girl, and I was shunted aside like I didn't exist."

Janet wanted to put her arms around him, to comfort him, but she didn't know how, so instead she said, "It must have been very painful for you."

"Very," he said, seeming more ill at ease than she had ever seen him.

They walked in silence for a few moments, and then Janet asked, "What happened to your father?"

"My father went on with his life. I visited him some weekends. As few as possible. I hated him."

"But why? It was your mother who ran off."

"Yes, but it was my father who drove her to it. He was such a wimp. I guess I've spent my whole life trying not to be like him."

"And have you succeeded?"

"You bet I have. I've made sure that I'm the one doing the hurting, not the one getting hurt."

Janet felt a chill, as if a cold wind had just blown over her.

"I shouldn't have told you that," he said.

"Yes, you should have. I want to know everything about you."

"Even the bad stuff?"

"Especially the bad stuff."

He stopped walking and turned to face her, "Something's happening here, Janet. Do you feel it?"

She was looking into his blue eyes, remembering the warmth of his kisses, the strength of his arms. "Yes," she said.

And then he leaned over and kissed her. A very, sweet, loving kiss. "I want to make love to you, Janet, and if you were any other girl, I'd take you back to my apartment right now. But I'm not going to do that."

She was hurt, confused.

"I want to go slow with you, Janet. I don't want you to be another notch on my belt."

Janet looked down at the sand and barely whispered, "I don't care if I'm another notch on your belt."

He pulled her face up so he could look into her eyes. "I want 'us' to be different."

"We will be," she said.

He hesitated another moment. "All right," he said, "let's go back to my place."

They drove from the beach to Beverly Hills and all the way in the car, Janet was thinking what a fool she was. She was going against all her principles--he was a scoundrel, she could only be hurt by this, she should do what he said, go slowly, but she didn't care, she wanted him now, tonight. Who knew what tomorrow would bring?

Inside his apartment, he did not turn on the light, but took her in his arms the moment the door was closed behind them. "I never knew I could feel about anyone as I feel about you at this moment," he said.

She knew it was a lie, part of his line. He had probably said these same words to a hundred girls, but she didn't care, for now his lips were on hers, those soft moist lips from her dreams, and his hands were caressing her, undressing her, and the excitement was so intense within her, that she wanted to scream.

He picked her up after work on Wednesday night and Saturday night, and then they spent the whole day Monday together. It was that Monday, in the afternoon, lying naked on his king-size bed, the shades drawn, her head on his chest, that she told him about her childhood in Florence and the year in hiding. She could feel the muscles in his chest contract, and then he lifted her head so that he could see into her eyes and there were tears in his. "Janet, can you ever forgive me?"

For a moment she didn't know what he was talking about, "Forgive you for what?"

"For hurting you."

"Yes, Mike. You've given me so much happiness in the last few days, the past is forgotten."

He sighed a heavy sigh. "Janet, I have to tell you something. Last night I was with another woman."

She felt her body go cold. Oh no, no, no. She pulled away from him, hate in her eyes. It was easy to say you didn't care if you were hurt again, but the pain was more excruciating than anything she could have imagined. Betrayed again. She tried to run to the bathroom, to get away from him, but he was grabbing at her. "Janet, it's not what you think. I did it, yes, but not because I wanted to, but because I thought I should." And cradling her head in his hands, he said, "I'm afraid. Don't you understand? I'm afraid."

She saw the glaze in his blue eyes. "I won't hurt you, Mike."

"I cannot make a commitment. I can't."

"I know," she said.

"I want to go on seeing you."

"Just tell me something, Mike. How many women have you made that last speech to?"

"No one," he said. "You have to believe me."

"I do," she said. "I believe you."

He held her tight, and she could tell, it wasn't sex, it wasn't love, it was fear he was feeling.

He began picking her up every night after work, and now she was feeling better and better about herself. She lost her obsession with food; she no longer needed it, except for nourishment. The pounds were dropping off and her clothes were beginning to hang on her. Mike took her clothes shopping as Edie had done so many years ago, and she came out of the dressing room, modeling each item he had chosen, and buying whatever he liked.

"Am I too plain for you?" she asked. "Should I be wearing eye make-up?"

"You're beautiful just as you are," he said.

She told him about the rape in New York. He rubbed her shoulders and kissed her neck. "Life has not been fair to you," he said.

"Yes, it has," she said. "I have you. For now."

She was not deluding herself. She knew it was temporary. But she didn't care. For however long it lasted, she was going to treasure it.

And then, three months after their chance meeting, they were again walking on the beach after dinner at Julio's, when he turned to her and said, "Janet, I know you're going to think me absolutely nuts, but I want to marry you."

She dropped her shoes. Her heart was thumping. It was not happening to her. It was a dream. "You don't have to."

"But I want to. I want to spend the rest of my life with you."

"And the other women?"

"I can't promise I'll never stray again, but I don't feel I need to prove anything any more. And I promise you this, if it should happen, I will come to you and tell you."

"Then, yes," she said. "Yes, yes, yes." She grabbed his hands and began dancing in the sand. She was bursting with joy, and wanted to shout from every rooftop, "Fat, dumpy, Janet Camerini is going to get married. And to the man of her dreams!"

Edie knew something was up.

It was over a year since Edie and Janet had opened Trattoria Mia, and both their restaurants were thriving.

Edie spent her time shuttling back and forth between the two locations, running things at both places, while Janet spent all of her time at the Trattoria. But Janet still baked the bread and pastries for Edie's Cafe, and until four months ago, had been popping in every Monday to see how things were going.

But now Janet was "too busy" to pop in. And she was leaving Trattoria Mia early, while dessert was still being served, and she never went restaurant-hopping with "the group" anymore, and she had lost so much weight that she was almost as thin as Edie. When Edie asked her what was going on, Janet replied, "Nothing."

But Edie knew what it was. It had to be a man. Or a woman. Back to shades of Paris. Why would Janet confide in her about everything, but not about this?

So Edie kept her distance and waited. Eventually Janet would tell her; she knew that. It was only a matter of time.

The time came on a Monday afternoon in May. Janet showed up at Edie's Cafe a little after two. The lunch crowd had dispersed and Brian hadn't yet arrived to "dress" the tables for dinner.

Janet looked flushed, as if she had just finished making love? Edie hoped that was it. But if Janet was in love, why hadn't she shared her happiness with Edie?

"Edie, do you have time to take a walk?" Janet asked.

"Where to?"

"It's such a beautiful day. I thought we'd walk over to Balboa Park."

"Sure," Edie said, taking off her apron. She could hardly wait to hear what Janet was going to tell her.

They set out on foot up Ventura Boulevard, past the office buildings, the restaurants, the boutiques, and finally as they turned up Balboa Boulevard, Janet said, "Edie, I'm in love."

"Aha," Edie said, "I knew it."

"I was afraid you did."

"Afraid. Why afraid? I'm your best friend. Why haven't you shared this with me?"

"Because you're not going to like what you're going to hear." The park was ahead of them.

Just one more block. "Edie, I'm in love with Mike."

"Mike?" Edie asked, trying to think of some Mike Janet might be in love with.

"Mike Kelly."

At the mention of his name, Edie's head began to spin. Not Mike Kelly. Not him. She reached for Janet's arm to steady herself, "Oh Janet, no. Anyone but him."

"I'm sorry, Edie. I didn't mean it to happen. I hated him as much as you did, but there it is."

Edie couldn't believe what she had just heard. She felt angry. She felt hurt and betrayed. More by Janet than by Mike. Janet was her best friend. How could she have kept this secret from Edie? "But how could this have happened?"

"I bumped into him quite by accident one Monday at lunch. He sat down at my table and we started talking, and then it just happened. Something clicked."

"But Janet," Edie pleaded, "don't you see, he's just using you. He doesn't love you. You're just one more conquest to add to his list."

"No, Edie, you're wrong. This time it's for real."

Edie's anger went up a notch. "Like it was for real with Cindy and Peggy, and me?" She focused on Janet's hazel eyes. "Janet, I love you dearly, but you're making a big mistake. He doesn't love you. He doesn't love anyone but himself."

"I'm going to marry him, Edie."

Edie put both hands on Janet's arms. "Janet, don't do this. You'll be making the biggest mistake of your life."

And tears came to Janet's eyes. "Edie, you've always had a man. Why do you begrudge me this one chance for happiness?"

"Because I don't think you'll be happy. You're just letting yourself in for a lifetime of tragedy. He'll never be faithful to you. Never."

And walking onto the soft grass of Balboa Park, Janet said, "Maybe you still love him yourself."

Edie's body shook with anger. "I don't love him, Janet. I could never love him after all I know about him." And willing to say anything to stop this marriage, she asked, "Do you know why Peggy divorced him?"

"Yes, he told me. Because he was having an affair."

"And did he also tell you that while we were constructing Trattoria Mia, he propositioned me?"

Janet sighed, "Yes, he told me that, too."

"Then doesn't that indicate what kind of man he is? He'll never change."

And Janet stopping at a park bench, "I don't care, Edie. All I know is these last four months have been the happiest of my life. I love him, Edie. I've always loved him. And if he cheats on me-- then that's the chance I'll have to take."

The two women sat on the park bench, Edie thinking that this day that should have been pure joy, was pure hell. "Why did it have to be him?" she asked, almost to herself. "Of all the people in the world, why did it have to be him?"

Janet took her hand. "Please, Edie, be happy for me."

Edie turned to look at Janet, and thought about all Janet had endured, those years in hiding, that night of the puppies, the loss of her parents, the rape in New York, and a lifetime filled with rejection and loneliness. "All right," she said, "I'll try."

Janet took a breath. "We're going to be married next month. I was hoping you'd be my matron of honor. Will you be?"

What else could Edie say? "Of course."

The next evening at Trattoria Mia, Mike showed up at 10 o'clock. He came right into the kitchen, kissed Janet, and then came over to Edie who was wrapping the leftover tiramasu.

"Edie, I just wanted to say..." and he hesitated.

What, Edie thought. That he was sorry for the past, that he would be different in the future, that he had been a good father to Brian and that meant he would be a good husband to Janet. She didn't believe any of it.

"I just wanted to say, I love Janet very much, and I will make her happy."

But will you be faithful, Edie wanted to say. Instead she said, "I hope so."

"I'm glad you're going to be our matron of honor," and he squeezed her hand.

She pulled away from him, sickened by his touch. "That has nothing to do with you. I'm doing it for Janet."

"Will you never forgive me?" he asked.

"I gave you your son, didn't I?"

"But that was for his sake, not mine."

"I love Janet," she said. "As long as she's happy, I'll be happy."

He shrugged, "Well, a guy can't ask for more than that." He turned away from her and called to Janet, "You just about done?"

And Janet looking at Mike, radiant, as Edie had never seen her, "Just a couple more minutes."

Janet's wedding was to be outdoors, a candlelight ceremony at the Calabasas Inn. Janet wanted a rabbi, and Mike who couldn't get married again in the Catholic Church, agreed. They planned to have just their immediate family and best friends, but the list kept growing. "I feel really bad about this, Edie," Janet said.

"What's that?"

"All these people coming to the wedding."

"Why should you feel bad about it?"

"Because of your past relationship with Mike. Because Mike is Brian's dad. I just don't want you to feel embarrassed."

Annoyance in Edie's voice, "Janet, it's your wedding, do what you want." Edie was, in fact, embarrassed that her son's father was marrying her best friend. As with Brian's Bar Mitzvah, she did not want to put the spotlight on Brian's birth. But it was Janet's wedding. Edie had no right to put any limitations on Janet's celebration because of her sins.

Janet asked Wendy to be her maid of honor and Mike asked Brian to be his best man.

"Pretty weird," Brian said to Edie, "being best man at my own dad's wedding."

"But just think, now Aunt Janet's going to be your step-mother."

"That's pretty weird, too," he said. And then, "I still don't understand why you didn't marry my father."

He had brought it up every now and then since the night she had told him he had a father, and each time, she had told him the same thing she told him now. "I told you, Brian, I wasn't in love with him."

And Brian hesitating, "Then why did you have sex with him?"

And the blood rushing to Edie's face, "I loved him at the time."

"And then you stopped loving him?"

She didn't know what to answer. She didn't want to say anything negative about Mike and she didn't want Brian to think that she would ever stop loving Brian. "Sometimes with adults it happens that way. But I'll never stop loving you."

"I know, mom." She went to him, put her arms around him, rested her face on his fine blond hair. "Brian, I'm sorry if I've done anything to hurt you. It's just that at the time all I cared about was having you. I didn't think of any of the consequences."

"It's okay, mom," he said. "The way I see it, I had you for the first 12 years of my life, and now I have you and my dad for the rest of my life."

"That's a good way to look at it," she said, tears filling her eyes.

Edie didn't want to hear about the wedding, but Janet kept asking for advice. "Should I call it for 5:30 or 6? Should I get the pink tablecloths or burgundy? Should I wear a hat or a veil?"

And then one afternoon, she asked Edie, "Do you think Ken would give me away?"

Edie was surprised, "Why Ken?'

"Because he's your husband."

"I think he'd be delighted," Edie said. "He's been trying to give you away for years."

Janet laughed, so happy that Edie was joking again. "And I thought he liked me."

"He does like you. It's just that you've been a bad influence on me."

"I guess he's forgotten that Trattoria Mia was your idea."

"And that I started working at Edie's Cafe while you were still in New York."

"You mean the Quick Bite."

"Oh, yes. It's been mine for so long I forget that it once belonged to Iris."

And Janet hesitating, "There's something else I have to tell you."

And Edie braced for more bad news.

"Stefano's coming to the wedding."

Chapter Thirty-Five

The evening of the wedding as Edie dressed in her gauzy pink gown, pulling one side of her fluffy brown hair slightly off her face and fastening it with a rhinestone comb, she was filled with a myriad of emotions. She felt terrible that Janet was marrying Mike Kelly and that as Janet's matron of honor, she was part of the conspiracy leading the lamb to the slaughter. She felt terrible that Brian was going to be the butt of jokes, and prayed that he wouldn't hear them. And she felt excited about seeing Stefano again. She knew he was a doctor, had married Luisa, had two sons, and was coming to the wedding alone. Perhaps he'd be fat, dumpy, bald, smoking a cigar, the typical complacent doctor. But still her hand shook as she applied her mascara.

The ceremony was held outdoors in the garden of the Calabasas Inn, next to a waterfall, amid mountains and flowers, under a white lace chupa adorned with pink and purple flowers. It was a windy evening and all the women in their strapless gowns and filmy dresses were clinging close to their companions trying to keep warm. The candles in giant candelabras kept blowing out, while Edie standing next to Janet, and Brian standing next to Mike, kept trying to relight them. And there, before the 120 guests assembled, on July 3, 1976, the day after the Israeli's had rescued the people hijacked to Entebbe, and the day before the whole nation was going to celebrate its 200th anniversary, Gianna Camerini became Mrs. Mike Kelly.

After the ceremony, Edie kissed Janet, allowed Mike Kelly to kiss her cheek, took Brian's arm and headed for the dining room. There was nothing more she could do for Janet. From now on, Janet would have to manage on her own. Now, all of Edie's thoughts turned to Stefano.

She spotted him as soon as she entered the room. He was sitting at a table next to the dance floor, and he looked up just as she saw him. Their eyes met and held. He was not fat, balding and dumpy; he was still the sweet young boy she remembered. But he was also a man.

She started to walk over to him, but before she got there, the bandleader was calling up the bride and groom to dance, and then Edie and Ken, Aunt Sofia and Uncle Alberto, Miriam and her husband, Peter and his wife, Lilly and Ben, Ann and Rudy, and Frank and Cookie, and as Edie danced by, she saw Stefano watching her.

As soon as the dance was over, she walked directly to his table. "Stefano."

He stood up. He was only a little taller than she in her high heels, but more handsome than he had been as a boy. "Edie." A moment's hesitation. What were they? Past friends or past lovers. Then he put his arms around her and held her close.

"It's so good to see you," he said. "You haven't changed at all."

She was overcome with emotion, feeling that she would break down, begin to cry. But she held it in and smiled at him, "I'm a bit thinner than the last time you saw me."

"Yes, you were quite pregnant then."

He looked so wonderful. More wonderful than in her memories. Then standing back and observing him, "And you're a little gray," she said.

"We all get older."

"Well," she said, not knowing what to say.

"Can I buy you a drink?" he asked, knowing the drinks were free.

"Sure," she said.

They walked over to the bar.

"So tell me, what have you been doing all these years?" he asked.

"I'm sure Janet must have kept you informed...about the restaurants."

"Yes, I know all about those. I want to hear about you."

"Well, I've got three great children."

She ordered a vodka and tonic, he, a Scotch and water, no ice, and then she said, "I'd like you to meet them." He followed her to where Wendy was sitting. "You remember Wendy."

"Wendy. I can't believe it," he said.

Wendy, in her second year at U.C.L.A., stood up and shook Stefano's hand. She looked like a model, tall, slim, her black hair cut in layers cascading down her shoulders and back.

"I don't suppose you remember Stefano from Florence," Edie said to Wendy.

"Kind of," Wendy said. "Did you have a motorcycle?"

"That was Stefano," Edie said.

"Well, it's nice to meet you again," Wendy said and sat back down beside her blond-haired, green-eyed Irishman.

"Now," Edie said, "I want you to meet Brian." She wondered if Stefano knew that Brian's last name was Freni--she wondered if he knew that Brian was Mike's son. Of course, Janet must have told him. "Oh there he is," she said, spotting him. She took Stefano's hand and led him to Brian, her darling son. "Brian," she said, "I want you to meet an old friend of mine, Stefano, from Florence, Italy. I knew him when I was pregnant with you."

Brian, sipping a Shirley Temple, held out his hand, "I'm sorry but I don't remember you."

"Well I remember you," Stefano said. "I used to feel you kicking in your mother's womb."

Brian, with a smile, "I'm sorry, but I don't remember anyone I met before I was born."

And Edie and Stefano, laughing, and holding hands. "Such memories." And then after introducing Stefano to Melissa and to Ken, the two of them, deciding it was too noisy to talk inside, ended up walking in the garden, where Janet and Mike had just been married.

"It was wonderful meeting your family," Stefano said. "Especially Wendy. I have such fond memories of her. And you." He took her hand. "So it seems that life has been good to you, Edie."

"For the most part, yes." She did not think about her hand in his; it seemed so natural.

"Your husband seems like a nice man."

"Yes. He's very nice."

"But..."

"Why do you think there are any 'buts'?"

"My wife is very nice, too, but..."

"But?"

He turned to face her. "I think I've always loved you."

"It wasn't love," she said. "You were so young, so romantic. You were in love with love, not me."

"How do you know what I felt? What I've felt all these years?"

"Stefano, you were 19 years old."

"Yes," he said, "and nothing's changed."

They walked on, hand in hand, in silence, until they found a bench and sat down together, and then they talked some more about the time they spent in Italy, about Stefano's practice, his sons, and then he said, "You seem different, Edie."

"In what way?"

"Troubled," he said. "Not carefree like when I knew you in Italy. Although you had every reason to be troubled then, you were not so."

And Edie said, "It's just tonight."

"What is it? Tell me."

"It's just this whole thing, Janet marrying Mike Kelly." And she took a breath, "Didn't Janet tell you?"

"Tell me what?"

"Mike Kelly is Brian's father."

"You mean the man from Paris?"

"Yes," Edie said.

Stefano put his arms around her. "My poor girl," he said. Edie began to cry, and it was natural that Stefano should wipe away her tears, and it was natural that he should kiss her cheeks, her eyes, her lips. And it was natural that she should want the kiss to go on and never end. It was Florence again, and she was 25 again, and she was feeling all the feelings she had tried not to feel then. There was magic in the air, and she clung to him, shivering a bit from the cool wind and from the emotions surging through her.

The music from the reception hall was drifting out to them, "I feel the earth move under my feet...."

And it was what they were both feeling.

Edie pulled away. "We'd better go back," she said. "Everyone will be wondering where we are."

As they began walking back, he took her hand. "Will I see you tomorrow?" he asked.

"I don't know how that's possible," she answered.

"Come to my hotel room," he said.

"No," she said, "I can't. I have my family here. My mother, father, brother. I'll be busy with them."

"Can't you leave them for a few hours?"

"No, Stefano, it would be wrong."

"No," he said, "it would be right."

"How can it be right?" she said.

"Because we belong together."

"No, you belong to Luisa; I belong to Ken."

"If you will look me in the eye and tell me that you love your husband, then I will leave you alone forever."

"I can't tell you that," she said.

"Then come to my hotel tomorrow," he said. "I'm staying at the Hilton, room 420."

"I've been faithful to my husband ever since we met, 12 years ago," she said.

"And I've been waiting to make love to you for 15."

They had reached the double glass doors that led inside.

"I don't know what to do," she said.

"I told Janet I'd meet them for lunch. Come in the morning. Early," he said. "I won't sleep tonight."

"I don't know," she said. "I'll see."

Then they were back in the banquet hall, surrounded by people, music, talking, laughter, but Edie could not escape his blue-green eyes. They were watching her, and it didn't matter that Ken was there, that Mike Kelly had just married Janet, she saw only him. Stefano.

When she got home, and she and Ken were lying side by side under the covers, Ken said to her, "Who is Stefano?"

Her body tensed. "Janet's cousin. I stayed with his family in Italy."

"And his last name is Freni?" Ken asked, his tone more of an accusation than a question.

"Yes. I named Brian for his family: Janet's aunt and uncle." She felt uncomfortable and wanted to end the conversation. "Well, goodnight," she said.

"Goodnight," he said, turning away from her.

She was relieved he didn't want to make love to her tonight. She couldn't have done it. She was too filled with Stefano. She lay in the dark, thinking about him, remembering all he had said. And now, thinking about his kisses in the garden, her body came alive with sexual desire. How long had it been since she had made love? She and Ken hadn't made love for years; they had sex. And she couldn't remember the last time they had done that. Two weeks ago? Three weeks? Had Ken lost interest in sex? She knew that happened to older men, but Ken was only 44. He was too young to have lost his sexual desire. What could it be? Another woman? No. Not Ken. He was too conservative, too steady, too loyal. He would never cheat on her.

She got up and went into the bathroom, turned on the light and looked at herself in the mirror. But would she cheat on Ken? Was she an immoral person, after all? Had Frank and all the other people who had condemned her all these years, been right about her? She had made a commitment to Ken; she had sworn she would never enter into an affair with a married man again. But Stefano was different. With Stefano, there would be no risk to Luisa or Ken. Stefano would be leaving in three days and if no one ever knew, who would be hurt?

She turned out the light and crept back to bed. She wanted her night of love with Stefano. Her morning of love. She wanted him no matter what.

At eight the next morning, she was showered and dressed and found her parents already up and drinking coffee in the kitchen. "We're still on Detroit time," they told her.

"Well, I have to go check on a few things at the restaurant," she told them.

"On July 4th?" Ben asked.

"That's the restaurant business. But I'll be back for lunch."

"Take your time," Lilly said. "We'll be happy to spend the morning with the children."

"You can sit out in the yard today," Edie said. "It's going to be a beautiful day."

The sun was already shining, and the temperature was perfect, in the seventies.

Edie got into her car and drove to the Hilton. Frank, Cookie and the two children they had brought with them to the wedding were also staying at the Hilton. Edie prayed she wouldn't run into any of them. How could she explain her presence to them?

She took the elevator up to the 4th floor, dying each time the elevator door opened, and then hurried to room 420 and knocked on the door.

Stefano, wearing a robe answered it. "Edie."

He pulled her inside, locked the door, and drew her to him. He was naked under his robe, and she clung to his naked body, caressing his warm skin. He kissed her as if he could not get enough of her, as if he would never let go of her. "I have dreamed of this moment for so long," he said. "I can't believe you're really here."

"I shouldn't have come," she said.

"Yes, you should have," he said. "It is our destiny." And then, he undressed her slowly, making love to every part of her body and it was not the wild heat of passion as it had been with Mike, or the cold mechanics of sex with Ken, but the slow, loving caresses of a man who truly loved her.

Later, lying across his disheveled bed, she said, "The maid's going to wonder what's been going on in here."

"I'm sure it won't be the first time she's seen a bed in this condition."

She outlined his lips with her fingers. "That was wonderful, Stefano."

He leaned over, playing with a few strands of her hair. "But was it worth waiting 15 years for?" he asked.

"Was it?" she smiled.

"You should never have left me, Edie."

"I would have ruined your life, Stefano."

"You would have made my life."

"You wouldn't have been able to go to school. You would have had to support me and my babies. It would have killed your parents. I couldn't handle that."

"So instead we have both been miserable all our lives."

"I haven't been miserable. Have you?"

"No," he said, leaning back, "Not miserable."

"Even if I had stayed," Edie said, "even if we had gotten married, who knows how we'd feel about each other now."

"You are cynical, aren't you," he teased.

"I don't consider it cynical. Just realistic."

"But that's because you didn't marry the right man."

"I wonder how that happened," she said. "I was in love enough times."

"With Wendy's father? With Brian's?"

"Yes," she said. "With both of them, and with a childhood sweetheart. And..."

He leaned over her, "And?"

"And you," she said.

He kissed her, and she kissed him, and then they became lost again, lost in all the things they were doing to each other.

Time passed and they were lying in sweat, the room was still dark from the lightproof drapes.
"I wonder what time it is," she said.

He leaned over the nightstand and picked up his watch. "l2:30."

"Oh my God," she jumped up. "I said I'd be home for lunch."

"And I'm supposed to meet Janet and Mike at the Swiss Inn at one."

"We'd better hurry."

"No," he said grabbing her hand. "Let's cancel them all. Let's spend the day together."

"But how can we?"

"We'll call them on the telephone."

"But what will we say?"

"We'll tell them we're in love, that we want to be together."

"No, Stefano, not that. But I suppose we could tell them something."

Stefano dialed first, wanting to catch Janet before she and Mike left their hotel room. That was going to be their honeymoon, 3 days in a bungalow at the Beverly Hills Hotel, because Janet had to be back at work on Tuesday.

Janet answered the phone.

"Well, how was your night?" Stefano asked. And then laughing, "Yes, of course I know that, but still it was your wedding night." Then, "The reason I called is, something's come up, and I'm not going to be able to make lunch today. Dinner? Yes. What time? 8 o'clock? Fine. I'll meet you in the lobby. Good. See you then."

He hung up the phone and handed it to her. "Your turn."

Her mother answered after two rings and Edie told her she had run into some problems, nothing serious, but it would take some attending to. She'd be home in time to take them all to dinner. Could they manage without her? Frank and Cookie and the kids were there. Well, they could all go to Universal Studios. That would be a fun way to spend the day. Or watch the July 4th festivities on T.V.

"We'll be okay," her mother said. "Not to worry. We'll be fine. Business comes first."

Edie hung up the phone. "Well now what do you want to do?"

"It's your city," he said. "I'd like to see the ocean. We should have lunch, but I don't know. Why don't we take a shower and see what develops."

"You can't be serious," she said.

"I have to make up for all the years we missed," he said.

"Yes," she said, "but not in one afternoon."

He pulled her to him. "Why don't we try and see what happens."

It turned out that they did not go out. They did not leave the room, they did not even open the curtains until three o'clock when Stefano called room service and a waiter brought lunch to their room. Edie was starving by then, and they sat at the table, he in his robe, she with a sheet wrapped around her, drinking champagne and eating cheeseburgers. "I've always wanted an American cheeseburger," he said, "and today is my day to have everything I ever wanted."

Then they went back to bed, and lay talking and touching until Edie felt she had to leave.

It was almost 5:30 by the time she was dressed and ready to go.

"Do I look all right?" she asked.

"Perfect," he said.

"No one will be able to tell what I've been through today?"

"You look perfectly rested, perfectly content."

"And that's how I feel."

He kissed her before she opened the door. "Will I see you tomorrow?"

"What will I tell my family?"

"Think of something."

"All right, I will."

And she was gone.

When she unlocked her front door, they were all waiting for her.

"Where have you been?" Ken asked.

And she panicked. Did it show? Was her hair mussed, her makeup? Was there lipstick on her ear? Was she walking funny? Could they smell semen on her? "Just taking care of some business. I'll go change and we can go to dinner. I made a reservation at a wonderful place."

She escaped as quickly as possible, and locked herself in the bathroom, staring at her face. There was a sparkle there, a sparkle that hadn't been there for years. Was it love? Did she love Stefano? But even if she did, it could go no place.

The next morning she was at his hotel by nine. And by noon they were out at the beach, eating at a restaurant that overlooked the water. It was beautiful and romantic, and she didn't even notice what she was eating, and then after, they took off their shoes and walked along the sand for what must have been two miles, and then back, holding their shoes in one hand, their other hands entwined. They were like two young lovers, except he was 34, she was 40, and both of them were married.

They went back to the hotel, and as the elevator doors opened, there was Frank, Cookie and their two children. Edie wished the floor would open and swallow her up, but it didn't. "Frank, Cookie, Stuart, Sheryl," she said as cheerily as she could, "this is Janet's cousin, Stefano, from Florence. I've just been taking him to see some sights in L.A."

"I thought you were working today," Frank said.

"Yes, I was, and then I bumped into Stefano."

Frank looked skeptical, but shook Stefano's hand, as Edie continued breathlessly, "I lived at his parents' home in Italy." After Frank and his family had gone, and she and Stefano were alone in the elevator, she fell apart. "They know," she said.

Stefano wrapped his arms around her, "How can they know?"

"Because they've always known and now I've confirmed how right they were about me."

"Well I don't care if they know. I want the whole world to know."

"Oh, Stefano, it's not that simple."

Back inside his room, he kissed away her anxiety and then they made love, and after, lay wrapped in each other's arms until it was time for Edie to go.

As she was buttoning her blouse, he said, "I'm leaving tomorrow. What are we going to do?"

"Nothing," she said. "You're going back to your life; I'm going back to mine."

"But I can't do that, Edie. I want you to come to Italy with me."

"With or without my three children?"

"Bring them all," he said.

"And what about Luisa?"

"I will divorce her."

"And your two little boys?"

"I will support them, I will be a father to them, but I want to live with you."

And for a fleeting moment, Edie considered it, running off to Italy with him, taking the three children, leaving Janet and the restaurants...what did anything else matter if you were with the man you love? If she were 18, dreaming of New York Penthouses, she might have done it. If she were 21, pregnant with Wendy, she might have done it. And if she were 28 and there was just Wendy and Brian, she might have done it. But she was 40, and Wendy was in college, and she couldn't take Brian away from his father or Missy away from hers. And there were the two restaurants she had given birth to, and Janet depending on her. There was no way she could leave. "I can't do it, Stefano."

He thought for a moment. "Maybe I should move here." But he said the words without conviction.

"Give up your profession, your family, your sons?" she asked.

He was silent for a moment. "You are my dream come true," he said.

"And you are mine," she said, "but maybe sometimes it's better to keep dreams as dreams. That way they can never be ruined."

"I just can't accept that we can't be together."

"Someday the children will be grown. Someday our circumstances will change."

"You mean in another 15 years?"

"Yes," she said, smiling.

"I don't know if I can't wait that long," he said.

"I hear the second 15 are easier than the first," she said.

He took her in his arms. "You will always be my dearest love."

"I will miss you more than you know," she said.

He walked her to the door, "Will you take me to the airport tomorrow?"

"Of course. What time does your plane leave?"

"Noon," he said. "It'll take us 40 minutes to get there, so be here at eight."

"Is that enough time?" she asked, a twinkle in her eye.

"Make it seven," he said.

That night, Edie's parents, Frank, Cookie and their two children came to dinner, and as the 11 of them sat around the dining room table passing the turkey, stuffing, mashed potatoes, green peas, Edie realized how much all of this meant to her, the warmth of her family, all of them joking, laughing, having fun together. She looked at her mom and dad, her brother, Wendy, Brian, and Melissa. How innocent they all were. How shocked they would be if they knew what had been going on the past few days; if they knew how easily she could have destroyed their world. Thank God, she had not done it.

The next morning at seven, Edie was at Stefano's hotel, and they held each other, talked, and made love until it was time to leave for the airport.

She drove slowly, wanting to savor every minute of their time together.

And then they were there, his baggage was checked, they walked to the gate his arm around her shoulder, hers around his waist, and when his flight was called, he drew her to him and they stood clinging together as if they could not part.

"We will meet again," he said.

"I know," she said."

"Remember me," he said.

"How could I forget?" she said.

And then he pulled away and was gone.

She stood at the great picture window watching until his plane took off, looking at all the little windows in the plane, trying to decipher which one was his, and the tears streamed down her face. Had she screwed up her life by not marrying him 15 years ago? And was she screwing it up again by not running off with him now?

Chapter Thirty-Six

Life must go on, I forget just why.

It was a line from a poem she had read in high school, and Edie found herself thinking it as the days passed. She thought of Stefano constantly, reliving every moment of their three glorious days together, and wondering where she had gotten the courage to let him go.

Because there had been no choice. Was no choice. There were all those other people to consider: his family, her family. She often looked at Ken and thought, why can't I love him? Because it would make life too easy?

Even the restaurants had lost their appeal. But she went through the motions. She had to. Janet was pregnant and it fell to Edie during the early months of Janet's pregnancy and then during the later months to run both restaurants. She tried to be happy for Janet, but Janet being pregnant only added to her gloom. Now Mike Kelly had finished the job he had started so long ago in Paris. He had impregnated both of them. The bastard.

Nine months after her wedding, Janet gave birth to a baby boy, naming him Ernesto after her father.

"Now, Ernesto," she said to her baby, "my family will live on in you."

Both Janet and Mike were ecstatic about the baby, and Brian was excited, too. "At last I have a brother."

"You already had a brother," Edie reminded him. "Josh."

"Yeah, but I didn't grow up with him."

"Was it so bad growing up with sisters?" Edie teased.

"No, but somehow this feels different. Maybe because I never had a dad before. Or maybe because Aunt Janet's more like a mom to me than an aunt."

Edie's stomach did a turn. She didn't think it was jealousy--that Brian loved Janet more than he loved Edie. Perhaps it was anger that he loved Mike so much. Perhaps remorse that she hadn't married someone who would have been a better father to Brian than Ken had been.

In June, Missy was playing in a tournament in Long Beach. She was very excited about it because it was her first national tournament and if she won, she would be ranked nationally. There was no way Edie was going to miss this tournament, no matter what Ken said.

Missy won all four of her matches the first weekend, and if she won two the following Saturday, she would be in the finals on Sunday.

That Saturday, Ken drove the whole family, including Grandma Liz, down to Long Beach to see Missy play. Wendy and Brian, who hadn't been that close to Missy over the years--probably because Ken had kept her from them--had insisted on coming along "to root for their little sister."

Although Missy was 11, she had to compete against 11 and 12-year-olds. Still she won her morning match easily, 6-2, 6-1. The afternoon match, however, was not so easy. The other girl was good. Maybe as good as Missy; maybe better. The first two sets went on forever, long, hard rallies that could have gone either way. Missy lost the first set, 6-4, and won the second, 7-5 in a tie-breaker. Then in the third set, the other girl folded. She was tired and Missy kept bringing her up to the net, then lobbing the ball over her head, part of the strategy Ken had taught her, so that Missy won the third set, 6-3, and the match.

Everyone was elated--Missy was in the finals! And Edie realized that this was the first time since Stefano had left that she felt any positive emotion. She was so happy for Missy, and so happy to have the whole family involved--all of them pulling for a common goal--to have Missy win.

On the drive back home, Edie insisted that Missy sit up front with Ken. It seemed only right that the star get to sit with her coach. All the way home, Missy kept thanking Ken for all the hours he had spent with her.

"It wasn't me, kitten, it was you. You're the one who did it," Ken said.

"But you're the one who taught me how."

And Edie sitting behind them felt so grateful to Ken. No matter how belligerent he'd been to Edie, he'd been a good father to Missy. No, a great father to Missy.

As for Ken, it had been a glorious day. More important than anything that could have happened at the office, more fulfilling than passing the CPA exam, more exciting than the day Missy was born. He had put all of his energy into his daughter and she had come through for him. No, not for him, for herself, he corrected. Nothing he did for her was for himself, but so that she could fulfill her potential. If he couldn't have the dainty, delicate daughter he had envisioned for himself, he would accept her as she was and make her the best that she could be.

Ken even felt loving toward Edie today. There was a spirit of camaraderie between them that had not existed for a long time. Maybe never. If only things had always been like this. Maybe then he wouldn't have needed Maria. But he couldn't think of Maria today. Today was Missy's day.

As soon as Edie got home, she thought about calling Janet. She wanted Janet to come to the match tomorrow, but she didn't want Janet to bring Mike. His presence would only put a damper on things. She looked at the phone on and off for an hour, and then blocking out her thoughts, dialed Janet's number. "Janet, Missy won today. She's in the finals!"

"Oh, Edie, how exciting."

Edie paused. "I thought maybe you'd want to come tomorrow."

"Of course I'll come. Is it all right if I bring Mike and the baby?"

Exactly what Edie didn't want. "Couldn't you leave Ernesto with Mike and come with us?"

"Edie," Janet said, annoyance in her voice, "Mike is my husband."

As if Edie didn't know that. Edie wanted to say, "Forget it, I'm sorry I called," but she couldn't do that to Janet. "Okay, sure, bring Mike and the baby."

She gave Janet directions and then called Gordon and asked if he wanted to come tomorrow.

"I wouldn't miss it for the world," Gordon said.

So on Sunday, Ken again drove Edie's station wagon down to Long Beach, taking the same people as yesterday, *and* Gordon; while Janet, three-month old Ernesto and Mike Kelly drove down in Mike's Jaguar.

They all met in the stands and Brian insisted on holding Ernesto on his lap, another twinge in Edie's stomach, which was already doing somersaults. Edie didn't know if she could watch Missy play, she was too nervous. And Ken wasn't doing much better. He kept getting up, walking around the bleachers, hanging onto the 12 foot high wire fence. It was as if everything was at stake.

Everything.

Missy's opponent was 12 and the first game was a struggle, but Missy broke the other girl's serve and won 6-4. Then in the next set, the other girl came to life. Every time Missy came to the net, the other girl passed her, and every time Missy brought her up to the net, she put the ball away. Missy lost the second set 6-3. In the final set, Missy's opponent was just too tough, and while Missy played valiantly, she lost 6-4.

It was a dejected group of people in the stands, it was as if something in each of them had died. And maybe it had--their dream for Missy. But they all came off the stands cheerful, surrounding her with compliments, "You played beautifully, you were great," but it was her dad she turned to. "I tried my best."

"I know you did, kitten," he said, wrapping his arms around her. "Don't forget that other girl is 12; you're only 11. In another year, you'll beat the pants off her."

"Well I want to see that," Gordon said, in his snide way. "Be sure to invite me."

"You were terrific," Janet said.

"Second place is nothing to be ashamed of," Wendy said.

"That other girl was just too tough," Brian said.

Missy turned to them, "Thanks for coming."

Edie put her arms around her daughter, "I'm so sorry, sweetheart."

But Missy was less friendly to Edie than she had been to anyone else, and Edie wondered if Missy thought this loss was also Edie's fault.

Brian decided to go home with Janet and Mike, so Edie headed to the car, arm and arm with Wendy, watching Missy, Ken and Liz walking ahead of them, and wondering why it was that she felt so left out of Ken and Missy's life.

Chapter Thirty-Seven

In April of l979, Edie began planning Missy's Bat Mitzvah. It was going to take place in June.

Brian was now in his junior year of high school and spending most weekends with his father and Janet. He still wanted to be an artist, but was also considering becoming an architect. And the child who wouldn't play baseball, was now jogging with Mike, working out at his gym, and going golfing with him. It just galled Ken that Brian now loved sports, and Ken wanted to say to Brian on more than one occasion, "How come all of a sudden you're such a big athlete, and I couldn't even get you to play Little League." But he kept silent.

Edie was happy that Brian had such a good relationship with his father, but sometimes it seemed too good. Sometimes it seemed he preferred to be with Janet and Mike than at home with her. She knew she was being petty, but she couldn't help how she was feeling. She just mustn't let it show.

As for Wendy, she was in her third year at U.C.L.A. with a 3.9 average. She was still waitressing at Trattoria Mia, and she was in love. Her boyfriend's name was Mitchell Hollander. His family was from Hungary, but he was born in California, and like all good Californians, he wanted to become an actor. He worked part time in a shoe store and spent the rest of his time getting publicity shots, going for interviews, trying out for parts, trying to get a manager and an agent.

So it was on a Wednesday afternoon, when Edie returned home after dropping Missy at Hebrew school, that Edie's beautiful and brilliant daughter, Wendy, came to her and said, "Mom, there's something I have to tell you."

Edie shuddered. Did she know what was coming? "What is it, Wendy?"

"Mom, I don't know how to tell you this, but I'm pregnant."

Edie felt her body go numb. It was like she was suspended in time. She felt herself a young girl again, coming out of the bathroom, facing her mother. "Mother, I'm pregnant."

And then the adrenaline began to flow and her body turned hot. She needed a place to sit down. "Wendy, Wendy, how could this have happened?"

"The usual way."

"But weren't you using something?"

"I ran out of pills, and we didn't think anything would happen."

Again, Edie thought of herself, so young, so romantic, not realizing the consequences of her actions. "You're my daughter. You should have known something would happen."

"I'm sorry, mom. What else can I say?"

Edie didn't know what to do, yell at her daughter, chastise her, or take her in her arms and comfort her? She saw Wendy's life stretching before her--an unmarried mother, an outcast, never finding love, struggling to survive, and yet Edie could not tell her to have an abortion. What if Edie had had an abortion?

"What are you going to do?" Edie asked.

"I'm going to have the baby. Mitch and I love each other. We want to get married. We've already got it figured out. We're going to get married as soon as possible, move to New York, and then I'm going to get a job waitressing until the baby is born, while Mitch looks for work as an actor."

Edie heard nothing after the words, "move to New York." "New York!" Edie said.

"Yes. That's where all the theaters are."

"But here's where all the movies are."

"But Mitch says it's easier to get started in the theater than in the movies."

Edie didn't know if she was more upset about Wendy being pregnant or about Wendy moving to New York. "But what about school? What about your PHD? What about your becoming a college professor?"

"I can always go back to school later, after Mitch is rich and famous."

Edie felt like a popped balloon, all the air rushing out of her. "I don't know what to say."

"Say you're happy for me."

Again, Edie felt the connection to that day so many years ago, how ashamed she felt, how humiliated, and she determined she would not do to Wendy what her mother had done to her. "It's not what I would have chosen for you, but I know it'll all work out."

Tears came to Wendy's eyes as she put her arms around her mother, "Thanks mom. I'd knew you'd understand."

"I love you, Wendy."

"I'm sorry if I've disappointed you."

Edie looked into her daughter's black eyes, Zola's eyes, and said, "Never. Never for one moment have you ever disappointed me."

Edie dreaded telling Ken about Wendy. She knew she was handing him a knife and giving him the excuse to plunge it into her heart. But whatever he was thinking, his words were kinder than she expected.

"What's she going to do?" he asked.

"She's going to marry the boy," Edie answered, relieved.

On Friday afternoon, Edie and Wendy got together to plan the wedding. Missy's Bat Mitzvah was going to be the second Saturday in June, and Mitch and Wendy decided to have the wedding as close to that date as possible, so that the out-of-towners could be at both affairs without making two trips.

"The first thing we have to do," Edie said, "is get a place."

And Wendy sitting on Edie's floral print sofa with the yellow pages open on her lap, said, "You know where I'd like to get married?"

"Where?"

"Where Janet and Mike got married. Outdoors at the Calabasas Inn."

"Then we'd better not have candles, my pet."

"Why?"

"Don't you remember at Janet's wedding how all the candles kept blowing out?"

"Maybe we should have it at lunchtime. I'd really like to be married in the sunlight."

"That would be lovely," Edie said. "If only the place is available."

Wendy read the number to Edie, and Edie dialed the phone. Yes, the Calabasas Inn was available for lunch the week after Missy's Bat Mitzvah.

"Now," Edie said, hanging up the phone, "I think it's time I talked to the Hollanders."

"They're not going to be very friendly," Wendy said. "Mitch has two teen-age sisters and his parents think I'm a bad influence on them."

"And is Mitch a bad influence too?"

"No, because they think it's all my fault."

"Right," Edie said, "Mitch had nothing to do with it."

Edie called them the following Monday morning, and Mrs. Hollander agreed to come over that night to discuss wedding plans.

Ken called to say he had a meeting and wouldn't be home until late, Brian was out with friends, and Edie told Wendy and Mitch not to show up, so that except for Missy who was in her room studying, Edie was alone in the house. The doorbell rang, and with some trepidation, Edie opened the door to Ruth and Milton Hollander.

Edie knew that Milton had make a fortune in the clothing business, that they had a beautiful home, and that they belonged to the Hillcrest Country Club. Ruth was in her early forties, well dressed, with a stylish hair-do, a large diamond ring on her finger, and bright red manicured nails. Milton looked about the same, except for the manicured nails.

The three of them sat sipping coffee in the living room, and Edie put out cookies, but no one touched them.

"About the wedding," Edie said.

"That's what we want to talk to you about," Ruth Hollander said. "We don't think there should be a wedding. We came to appeal to you to talk your daughter into having an abortion."

"But Wendy doesn't want an abortion."

"Do you know how old our son is? He's 21. He wants to be an actor. He wants a career. What's he going to do with a wife and baby?"

"The same thing my daughter is going to do. Take care of it."

"But he wants to be a movie star. How is he going to do that with a wife and baby."

"He should have thought of that before he.....made love to my daughter."

"Your daughter should have been using something."

"Your son could have used something, too."

"Ladies, ladies," Milton interrupted, "we're not going to get anywhere like this." Then, turning to Edie, "The fact is we like Wendy. She's a lovely girl. And what we're proposing is what's best for her, too. She's a bright girl. She should finish school. She should have a career. She shouldn't be burdened with a baby." And then, in an especially appealing voice, "Tell her to have an abortion."

Edie: "I don't tell my daughter what to do."

"Well maybe you should have," Ruth said, and turning to her husband, exasperated, "I told you it would be useless talking to her. Like mother, like daughter."

Edie's heart began to race, "And what's that supposed to mean?"

"We know all about Wendy," Mrs. Hollander said with a sneer.

"All about what?" the tension building in Edie's chest.

"All about that she's a bastard."

And Edie reeling back, feeling the blood rushing to her head, "Who told you that?"

"Wendy told Mitch and Mitch told us."

Edie was boiling. "You can say anything you want about me, but don't ever, ever insult my daughter again."

Ruth Hollander set her coffee cup down and stood up. "Come on, Milt, there's no point to this conversation."

Milt, whose face had turned red, set his cup down, and followed his wife to the door. And then Ruth turned to Edie, "As for the wedding, you can forget it. There's not going to be a wedding. There's no way my son is going to marry your daughter." And with that they were out the door.

Edie stood shaking for several minutes, and then she walked into the kitchen and poured herself a glass of white wine. The Bible was right--the sins of the mother shall be visited upon the daughter.

Later that night, she told Wendy part of the conversation, but not all of it, and Wendy put her arms around her mother and tried to comfort her.

"Don't worry, mom, there will be a wedding and if they don't want to come, that's their loss."

"You're sure Mitch wants to go through with this?"

"Don't worry, mom, he'll be there."

"I want to talk to him."

"Now?"

"Yes."

"I'll phone him to come over."

In 15 minutes, Mitch, the blond-haired blue-eyed would-be star of stage, screen and radio appeared. Edie could not help thinking as she looked at him, "What a little boy." And yet Edie had been in love with Stanley, Zola, Stefano, when they were no older than Mitch.

"I just feel a little uncomfortable," Edie said to Mitch, who had his arm around her daughter, "about this problem with your parents."

"Oh, don't worry about them," Mitch said. "They'll come around. I told them that unless they let Wendy in the house, I'm moving out."

"They won't let Wendy in the house?"

And Mitch looked at Wendy as if he'd let something out he shouldn't have. "They're just worried about my sisters, you know that somehow Wendy's going to corrupt them."

Edie tried to calm herself. "Mitch, if Wendy weren't pregnant, would you still marry her?"

"Maybe not right now. I'd wait until I could support her. But I love Wendy, Mrs. Rosenberg. I want to spend the rest of my life with her."

And seeing the look of love in his teary blue eyes, what else could Edie do but believe him?

Chapter Thirty-Eight

When Ken arrived at the Mexican restaurant, Maria was already waiting for him. She had ordered a Strawberry Marguerita and was sipping her drink as she perused the menu.

He did not kiss her. He never kissed her in public, but he took her hand under the table and rested it on his thigh. She looked particularly gorgeous today. She had grown in beauty over the years, learning how to wear make-up, how to dress. But she didn't need to do much to excite him, just those short skirts and high heels were enough.

Now, she pulled her hand away. "Ken, there's something I have to tell you."

She was no longer working for him. Between the other employees and his partners, it had become too awkward. One of his partners had practically insisted that Maria leave. But Ken knew it was best, too. Better to separate his business life from his personal life. Besides it made their time together even more precious.

"What?" picking up a menu.

"Ken, I think we should stop seeing each other."

"What?" he said, still distracted. It wasn't the first time she had said this.

She lowered her eyes, "Ken, I've met someone, someone who wants to marry me."

He was stunned. "What do you mean?"

"I mean, I've met someone."

"But how could that happen? How could you meet someone?"

"I don't spend all my time with you, you know. Only your leftovers."

"That's not true," Ken said. "I spend more time with you than with my wife."

"Oh yeah? You don't sleep with me every night, all night."

"All we do is sleep."

"Well, I don't care." She began to cry, "I can't go on like this any longer. I want my own home. I want babies."

Ken stared at her. When did she have time for another man? "Have you been sleeping with him?"

She dabbed at her eyes with a tissue, "What difference does it make?"

"It makes a helluva difference to me."

"What did you expect me to do? What am I supposed to do? You're off every weekend with your daughter, you're home every night with your wife. What am I supposed to do?"

"You're supposed to be faithful to me."

"Oh that's a laugh," she said. "You're the married man and I'm supposed to be faithful to you."

He turned away from her, terribly hurt. "How could you do this to me?"

She sighed, frustrated. "Ken, I love you very much. You're my whole life. I'd do anything for you, you know that, but I can't go on like this. I have a man who wants to marry me, who wants to give me babies."

Oh God. That last killed him. He could not stand the thought of her having another man's babies. "I want you to have my babies," he said.

"But when?" she said. "By the time you get around to leaving your wife, we'll both be too old."

He knew the moment had come; the moment he had been trying to stave off for six years. He had to make a decision; he had to choose. But, of course, there was no choice. He could not give up Maria. The thing he dreaded most was telling Missy and his mother.

"All right," he said. "I'll tell her."

But Maria wasn't giving in so easily. "When?"

"Right after Wendy's wedding."

"That's still a month away."

"Give me a break," he said. "I can't tell her now, before Missy's Bat Mitzvah and Wendy's wedding. It wouldn't be fair."

"And have you been fair to me all these years?"

"No, I haven't. I admit it. But you've waited all these years. Wait one more month."

She thought it over. "All right," she said. "One more month. The week after Wendy's wedding. But if you don't leave her then, then...." She didn't need to finish the sentence.

"As for this other man..." he said.

"I won't break it off with him," Maria said. "Not until you're free."

"Please Maria. I can't bear the thought of it," he said, again taking her hand.

And Maria leaning forward, "How do you think I've felt all these years?"

"I'm sorry. I'm really sorry, but I beg you, don't see him again."

"All right," she sighed. "But you better not disappoint me."

"I won't," he said, and kissed her hand, there in public, for all the world to see.

Chapter Thirty-Nine

The week of Missy's Bat Mitzvah and Wendy's wedding was probably the most hectic of Edie's life. There were going to be 120 people at the Bat Mitzvah; 80 at the wedding.

Edie took two weeks off from the restaurants, the longest she had ever left them, and if she didn't waste a minute, hopefully, she could get it all done.

"I'm so confused," she told Wendy. "The chupa will probably show up at the Bat Mitzvah and the Menorah for the candle lighting will probably show up at the wedding."

Edie's parents, and Frank, Cookie and all four of their children came out the day before the Bat Mitzvah and would be staying until after the wedding. Edie's aunts and uncles from Cleveland and Chicago also came out for the week, but Edie's Grandma Rose, whose husband had passed away the year before, was too weak to travel.

Edie was struck by how much everyone had aged since she had last seen them. Everyone seemed shorter, heavier, more wrinkled, with more gray hair, and her father was almost completely bald. Even Cookie, who had always looked so elegant, had gained weight, and now looked like a middle-aged matron.

On the morning of the Bat Mitzvah, as Edie was getting dressed, she looked at herself in the mirror, critically. Was she, also, looking middle-aged? Fortunately, she was still slim, her brown hair cut short, showed no signs of gray--thanks to Ms. Clairol--and her skin was still smooth and luminous. There was a certain weariness in her eyes, but inside, she still felt vigorous, young, no more than 24. It was hard to believe she was already 42, that she would soon have a married daughter and soon after that be a grandmother! She smiled at the thought, then stepped into her high heels, added a little more blush to her cheeks, and went to see how Missy was doing.

Missy was standing in front of her dresser mirror, putting Acnomel on a pimple on her chin. (Thank goodness, Edie thought, that none of her children had inherited her teen-age acne--probably because they all took after their fathers!) Missy's room was all pink ruffles and tennis trophies.

"How's my baby-girl doing?" Edie asked.

"I would have to get a pimple today of all days."

"Don't worry, darling, no one can see it but you."

"Are your sure?" Missy asked, turning to face Edie so that Edie could look at it.

"Positive." And then taking in the whole picture of Missy, she said, "You look gorgeous."

Missy was wearing a short white dress with a print of tiny pink and purple flowers, a jacket to match, and white pumps. Edie had taken her to the beauty shop the day before, and her hair, fluffed about her face, softened her features and made her look entirely feminine. "Gorgeous," Edie repeated.

"Mom, one thing," Missy said, "I'm thirteen. I think it's time you stopped calling me your baby girl."

"All right, sweetheart, if that's what you want, but you always will be my baby girl." Edie gave her daughter a hug and said, "Time to go."

The religious service began at 10 o'clock and sitting in the synagogue, surrounded by all her loved ones, watching her daughter, her baby, up on the bimah, looking so sweet and grown up, Edie thought her chest would burst with happiness. She felt overwhelmed with love for Missy, and for Wendy and Brian, and for everyone in her family. How lucky she was. Perhaps here, perhaps through the love of their daughter, she and Ken could regain all they had lost. She reached for Ken's hand and felt the love flowing between them.

That evening, at the dinner, Janet came up to her. "Edie, I know it's not the time or place, but could I talk to you?"

"What about?"

"About Mike."

"There's nothing to talk about."

"Yes, there is. I can't stand the tension between us. Aren't you ever going to forgive him?"

"I'm sorry, Janet. I can't help how I feel."

"What does he have to do?"

"I don't know, Janet. I'll always love you, but as for Mike, I don't think I can ever forgive him."

"I never thought you would be like this," Janet said.

The band was playing a "hora" and someone grabbed Edie's arms and whisked her to the center of the wild, unruly circle, and in the abandon of the dance, Edie lost sight of Janet's unhappy face.

That night, when Edie came to bed, she was hoping that Ken was still awake. She wanted to lie in his arms and talk about all that had happened today. She wanted to share with him the pride she felt toward Melissa: how bright she was, how beautiful, how much she loved her. And she wanted to make love. To express with her body, all she could not express in words. But he was turned away from her, and when she leaned over and kissed his cheek, he did not move, so she lay beside him, feeling more alone than if he had not been there.

On Thursday, Zola, his wife, Bobbie, and her three children arrived from Palo Alto. Wendy picked them up at the airport and brought them over to Edie's house. Edie had not seen Zola for 15 years, and when she opened the door to him, she was stunned. He had no beard, he was overweight, and his beautiful thick black hair was streaked with gray. "Zola," she said, and without any hesitation on either part, they embraced. It seemed so natural to her. He was a dear old friend. When he let her go, she turned her attention to Bobbie.

Bobbie also had graying black hair, but still she was attractive. She wore no makeup, but she had an open face and happy eyes. She seemed full of energy, and took Edie's hand firmly in hers. "I'm so happy to meet you," she said. "I've been wanting to meet you ever since I met Wendy. She's a super gal." And Edie was immediately enamored with Bobbie. Bobbie's three children, two boys and a girl, were rambunctious, bordering on obnoxious, and romped through the house freely. "Oh, a pool," the older boy, said. "Can we go swimming?"

"If it's all right with your mom," Edie said.

"Please, mom, please," they all clamored around Bobbie.

"You're sure it's okay with you?" Bobbie asked.

"Let them have fun," Edie said. "That's why they're here."

Later that day, Olga Bitterman arrived from Detroit (Yuri had passed away the year before) and Edie was busy for the next few days with breakfasts, lunches, and dinners for all the out-of-towners.

And then it was the morning of the wedding.

Wendy was still hoping that Mitch's parents would show up; Edie was just hoping that Mitch would show up.

"I can't believe they'd let their son get married and not be at the wedding," Wendy said.

"As long as Mitch is at the wedding," Edie said.

"Mom, you can't really still doubt him."

"Of course not," Edie said, but Wendy didn't hear her, because overcome with nausea, she had run to the bathroom.

By the time they got to the Calabasas Inn, Mitch was already there waiting for them, looking very handsome in his white tuxedo, and Edie relaxed.

The weather had been cloudy all morning, but now the haze had burned off, and the sun was shining brightly.

Edie, sequestered with the bride and her bridesmaids in the bride's dressing room, came out every few minutes to look for Mitch's parents, and then reported back to Wendy.

After her third trip out, she told Wendy, "Sorry, honey, no sign of them yet."

"I'm feeling so sick right now, I don't think I even care."

"Here's two Pepto Bismo."

"I just hope I don't throw up all over my wedding dress."

"Maybe take four."

And Wendy chewing and swallowing, and then looking up at her mother, "Would you mind checking one more time?"

"Of course not."

And Edie, outside again, perused the crowd, all her relatives, friends, loved ones, but no Ruth and Milton. And then a flute started playing; it was time for the ceremony.

Edie rushed back to Wendy. "It's time," she said.

And the procession began: the four ushers and four bridesmaids including Melissa; Brian as best man; Wendy's best friend as maid of honor; Edie's parents; Olga Bitterman; and finally Edie and Zola walking down the aisle together, one on each side of their love-child, Wendy.

When all of them were under the Chupa, the Rabbi began speaking his magic words, "And do you Wendy Bitterman promise to love, honor and respect Mitchell Hollander, for better or worse, in sickness and in health, for all the days of your life?"

And Edie was terribly touched. So much emotion this past week. She looked at Ken and was overcome by a great sense of remorse. She had made this same promise to him and yet how unfair she'd been to him all these years. She had put everything and everyone else ahead of him. She had never given him that part of herself she had given to Zola, Stefano, Stanley, even Mike Kelly. And yet he had been a good man, a good father, a good husband, had gone along with all her schemes, all her ventures, even though he was opposed to all of them. Perhaps it was time to do something for Ken. Now, after 14 years of marriage, perhaps it was time to give him her love.

And standing under the Chupa, listening to her daughter's vows, Edie vowed she would make it up to Ken. They could start anew. They could be happy together.

Chapter Forty

Within a week after the wedding, all of the relatives had left, and then Wendy and Mitchell left. That was the hardest parting of Edie's life. She had been so close to Wendy, saw her every day, worked with her, shared almost all her feelings and thoughts with her. And now Wendy was gone, 3000 miles away, and Edie felt this great emptiness in her life, this great hole.

She was determined to make good on all the promises she had made about Ken standing under the chupa at Wendy's wedding, and on a Thursday night, as they were dressing to meet friends for dinner, she turned to him. "Ken, I've been thinking, perhaps we could go on vacation together. Just you and I. We've never really done that."

"You mean you'd leave the restaurants?"

"Yes."

"I don't believe it."

"Well, it's true. I've been handling most of the responsibility since Janet had Ernesto. I think she can manage without me for a few weeks. And I'd like to go away with you. I think it'd be good for us."

"Where would we go?" he asked.

"Europe, Hawaii, wherever you want. We could even rent a cottage somewhere, or a condominium and I'll do all the cooking and we won't go out to one restaurant."

"Now you're going too far," he joked.

"I mean it, Ken, really I do. We've never had a proper honeymoon, why not have one now?"

"Well, let me think about it," he said.

That Sunday, Edie took the whole day off, and during the next week came home early every evening to be with Ken. But he was seldom there. There was always some business he had to attend to, a meeting he had to go to. Had he always spent so much time away from home, and she too busy to notice?

The following Sunday, after dinner, when Brian and Melissa were out visiting friends, and Edie and Ken were alone in the house, Edie decided to bring up the idea of the vacation again. She was standing at the sink, washing the dishes, when she said, "Ken, have you given any thought to our vacation?"

He was wiping the pine table with a sponge. He walked over to the sink, set the sponge on the counter, and said, "Edie, there's something I have to talk to you about."

She turned the water off and turned to face him. "What is it?"

He knew what he was going to say. He had written it down and memorized it. "Edie, when we first got married, I told you it didn't matter that you didn't love me, that I had enough love for both of us. But I was wrong. It does matter. It isn't enough."

Edie felt her knees weaken. "What are you trying to say, Ken?"

"Edie," a pause, "I want a divorce."

It was worse. Worse than anything she could have expected. And yet she should have expected it. Things hadn't been good between them for years. But why did he have to decide this now, just when she had made up her mind to make the marriage work? "Ken, I know I haven't been the best wife to you, but I can change. Give me a chance, that's all I ask."

"It isn't that simple, Edie."

And then she knew. "Is there someone else, Ken?"

"It's not that," he said. "I'm just not happy. I don't think you're happy either. I think we should both be free to find someone else."

"But," she persisted, "have you found someone else?"

He looked down, unable to meet her eyes. "Yes."

She needed to sit down. She needed a moment to think. She needed to figure out what was happening. "How long has this been going on?" she asked.

"What difference does it make?"

"I want to know."

"For some time," he said.

"And how long is that?"

"Do you want weeks, months?"

"I want to know how long."

Looking totally miserable, "A few years."

"A few years!" She was appalled. "How many?"

"Six," he said.

"Six years," she repeated. All those years of her feeling guilty about working, about purchasing Edie's Cafe and Trattoria Mia, and all his complaints about Wendy and Brian -- through all of that he had been carrying on an affair with another woman. It was more than she could hold. "How could you have done such a thing?" she asked.

"It just happened."

"And all this time I thought it was my fault--something I'd done, when all the time we were doomed. We were doomed, weren't we?"

"I think we were doomed from the day we got married. But I take full responsibility. You told me when we got married how you felt about me. I just thought things would change."

And now her hurt turned to anger. Anger at him for cheating, anger at herself for being such a fool. "Who is she?" she demanded.

"It's not important."

"It is to me."

He looked down at his feet. "Just a girl I met at the office."

"What's her name?"

Meeting her gaze, "Why is this so important to you?"

"Because it is."

"Maria Kent," he said.

"Maria Kent," she repeated, trying to place her, but she couldn't.

"I should have told you sooner," he said. "I hated cheating on you."

"Then why didn't you tell me?"

"I didn't want to hurt you."

"And you think cheating on me wasn't hurting me?" She looked at this man she had been living with for l4 years, this man whom she had thought was so honest and ethical, and realized she didn't know him at all. "If only you had told me when it first started, I would have some respect for you."

"Would you?"

"I wouldn't have wasted six years of my life on you."

"You didn't waste a day of your life on me. You were never here."

"I was here emotionally. I thought I belonged to you."

"You belonged to Wendy and Brian. Not me. And not to Melissa either."

"How can you say such a thing?"

"Admit it. You always loved Wendy and Brian more than you loved Melissa." His eyes were glaring.

"That's ridiculous. Utterly ridiculous."

He turned away from her. She thought of her three days with Stefano. She could tell him about Stefano. But telling him about Stefano would only tarnish her memory of that beautiful interlude. "When do you plan to move out?" she asked.

"Immediately," he answered. "I've already consulted an attorney. I think you should see one, too."

Again the rage was rising in her chest, "You already consulted an attorney?"

"Yes. I felt I had to. There's a lot to consider."

"Like what?"

"Like our child," he said. "The attorney and I agreed it would be best for Melissa and most fair to us to have joint custody. You get her for the school year; I get her every weekend and all vacations."

Now she was furious. He was dividing their daughter up as if she were a sack of potatoes. "Anything else I should know?"

"Look, Edie, these are things we're going to have to face. Things we're going to have to work out."

"But you have a little advantage over me. You knew about all this; I didn't."

"I just thought it would make it easier if I understood everything involved ahead of time."

"Practical to the end," she said. And then wanting to hurt him. "Now I know why I could never love you, Ken. You're just too damn practical."

"I'm not going to get into an argument with you. I did whatever I did so that we could avoid arguing."

"Fine," she said, "we won't argue. Everything is fine. Yes, I agree to the custody, and what else? Have you figured out who gets the house, who gets the furniture, who gets the restaurants?"

He stood up. "I didn't think you'd react this way."

"How did you think I'd react? Accept it all with a smile and a handshake?"

"Frankly, yes."

"Then that shows how little you know me. I think you'd better leave tonight. I don't really think I want to spend the night with you."

"That's fine with me," he said. "I'll come back in the morning for my things."

"If they're still here," she said.

Ken walked out of the blue and yellow kitchen, to the front door, and sighed with relief. Thank God it was over. He had done it. He didn't think he'd ever be able to do it--face her, tell her the truth, but now it was over. And it had been horrible, worse than he could have imagined--and the worst part of all was admitting that it had gone on for six years. He shivered. How could he have kept such a secret for six years? Because dammit, she had driven him to it. She and her restaurants. Now he was free. Free to go to Maria. He pulled the door open and slammed it behind him.

Edie sat at the kitchen table for several minutes unable to move. She was in a state of shock. She felt that her world had shattered like a piece of glass, and there was no way to put it back together. And yet, why should she feel so devastated? She didn't love Ken; had never loved him. Still there was this terrible pain in her head. She was a failure. A total failure.

She thought of Stefano again. She could go to him. Go to Italy. Destroy his happy home. But there were still the children to think of. His and hers.

She looked at the telephone. There was only one person who could help her now. Only one person in the world she wanted to talk to. But that person was married to the one person in the world she hated most, next to Ken. No, she would not confide her misery in Janet. She would carry it alone.

Chapter Forty-One

Missy was devastated by the news of the divorce. She didn't want her father to leave. She didn't want to see him just on the weekends and holidays. She needed to see him every day. They needed to practice her tennis. And of course Missy knew it wasn't his fault. It was her mother's fault. Her mother had driven her father away with all that restaurant stuff. How was Missy going to live without him, her father, her coach, her best buddy?

Ken got an apartment in town, and Missy moved in with him for the rest of the summer. It was part of the agreement, and then, in September, when school started, she moved back home with Edie.

It was terrible for both of them. Missy didn't want anything to do with her mother. She avoided Edie whenever possible, and if she couldn't avoid her, she was belligerent, monosyllabic. Edie kept trying to talk to Missy, but every time Edie approached her, Missy had a tennis practice, a match, a friend she had to meet, some homework to do.

In time, Edie kept telling herself. In time.

And then in January, Wendy gave birth to a son, and Edie left Missy with Ken and flew back to New York for a few weeks to take care of her daughter and her new grandchild.

Edie couldn't wait to see Wendy, but it was the baby, little Jason Yuri Hollander who captivated her heart. From the moment, Edie took her grandchild in her arms, she was overwhelmed with love for him. She wondered how it was possible to love anyone as she loved this little person.

"Wendy, he's gorgeous."

"Isn't he though."

Wendy was still a little plump, and Mitch, who was working as a house painter, until his big break came, was just as handsome as Edie remembered him. They were living in a tiny one bedroom walk-up apartment in Greenwich Village. The walls, freshly painted by Mitch, were covered with posters from current and past Broadway shows, and a couple of Brian's paintings. In spite of how small the place was, it was charming.

"Tell me," Edie asked, "have you heard from the Hollanders?"

"Not a word since the night they talked to you."

"Sure," Edie jibed, "blame it all on me."

"You'd think," Wendy said, "their only grandchild, they'd want to see him."

"I'm sure they'll come around. Just be patient."

Edie spent the next few days cleaning the apartment, shopping for food, cooking, and taking care of Jason.

Wendy and Mitch had already made arrangements for a briss, and at 9 a.m., eight days after the baby's birth, as Edie was scurrying about the apartment trying to get the place neatened up and the food set out before the Mohel and the guests arrived, the doorbell rang. Edie hoped, prayed, it would be the Hollanders, realizing the error of their ways, and surprising Wendy and Mitch by coming to the briss.

But when she opened the door, it was Zola.

"Hi," he said, "am I on time?"

"Yes," she hugged him. "I wasn't expecting you."

"I decided I couldn't miss my grandson's briss."

"So you hitched all the way to New York?" a twinkle in her eyes.

"I'm afraid those days are gone forever," he said.

"Sad," she said. "In a way I miss the old Zola."

"I'm still here," he said, "somewhere under this clean shaven skin."

And later, that evening, as Edie and Zola stood by the baby's crib admiring their grandchild, Edie said to Zola, "Who would have thought back there in Ann Arbor, it would have ended like this."

"Why, is this the end?"

"No," she said, "you're right. It's the beginning." And then looking down at little Jason Yuri Hollander, with his soft brown hair and blue eyes, Edie asked, half-joking, half-serious, "Do you think the baby looks like me?"

And Zola looking from the baby to her said, "Yes. He looks exactly like you."

Zola stayed another few days, and Edie stayed another week and then it was back to Los Angeles and all the problems that awaited her there.

The morning after Edie returned, she called Ken to tell him she was back and that he could drop Melissa off that evening.

"Edie," he said, "I'm sorry but I'm not bringing Missy home."

Panic grabbed her throat, "What do you mean?"

"Edie, Missy has decided that she wants to stay with me."

"But I don't understand. We have an agreement."

"Missy's 13. She doesn't have to abide by any agreement. She can choose who she wants to live with. And she wants to live with me."

"I don't believe you."

"Check with your attorney."

"But we agreed to joint custody. You're the one who suggested it."

"But that was before I knew how much she wants to live with me."

"You mean before you poisoned her mind against me." Edie sank into a chair. She felt dizzy, breathless. "And what about Maria? Is she going to want Missy to live with her?"

"Maria loves Missy as much as I do."

"I don't believe that," Edie said.

"Well then at least as much as you do."

Another blow beneath the belt. How could she ever have thought this man was good and kind. "What did I ever do to you?"

"Don't take this personally. It's what Missy wants. I just wanted you to know my lawyer has already filed the papers."

"I can't believe you're doing this. Trying to take my baby away from me."

"She's not your baby. She's never been your baby. Edie's Cafe and Trattoria Mia are your babies."

"That isn't fair, Ken."

"Fair or not, it's the truth."

"Well, I'm not going to let it happen. I'm going to fight you all the way."

"You're just going to be wasting a lot of your money, and mine. There's no way you can win this, Edie. Missy has the right to choose who she wants to live with."

"We'll see," she said.

The minute she hung up on Ken, Edie called her attorney, Bob Rogers, and told him what Ken had said.

"We'll do what we can," Bob said, "but I think he's got a good shot at getting her."

"But how can the court take a child away from her mother?"

"She's not a child anymore, Edie."

"Oh God, this can't be happening. You've got to help me, Bob."

"I'll do everything I can, but the only sure thing is your talking to Melissa, convincing her that she'd be better off with you."

"How can I talk to her? He's got her."

"Well then, we'll just have to do the best we can do."

She hung up the phone and aloud she said, "I'm not going to give up my baby girl. I'm not."

Chapter Forty-Two

A hearing was scheduled for the first Tuesday in June. Ken, Missy, Maria, Ken's attorney and Liz were all waiting in the hall of the courthouse when Edie and her attorney, Bob Rogers, arrived. Edie, alternately sweating and shivering, walked over to Missy. "Missy, can I talk to you for a minute?"

Missy clung to her father, "I have nothing to say."

Tears formed in Edie's eyes. "Please."

Missy looked at her father, who nodded "Yes." Grudgingly, she pulled away from her father, and trailed her mother down the hall.

When they were several yards from the others, Edie turned to Missy, "Missy, this is very hard for me. Please, just tell me what I did to make you so angry with me?"

Missy glared at her. "You sent my dad away."

"I didn't send him away. He chose to go."

"Because you weren't a good wife to him."

"Missy, your father is the one who was cheating on me."

"Because you never gave him any time, any attention."

"Is that what he told you?"

"He didn't have to tell me. I can see. I have eyes."

"Missy, I know it's hard for you to understand, but I did care for your father."

"No you didn't," Missy snapped. "You never cared for him. Or me. All you ever cared about was your precious Wendy and your precious Brian. They're the only ones you ever loved."

Edie felt the blood rushing to her head. "That's not true. I always loved you."

Missy's eyes were red and glassy. "No, you didn't. You never loved me." And she turned and ran back down the hall to her father's waiting arms.

Edie stood, unable to move for several minutes. Her insides were in a scramble, she was shaking. How could Missy believe that Edie never loved her? It wasn't true, it wasn't.

The bailiff came out to get them and they followed him through an empty courtroom to the judge's chambers, where they all took seats at a long table before the judge's desk. Liz, Maria, Missy, Ken and Ken's attorney were at one end of the table; Edie and Bob were at the other end.

The judge, Judge Goren, was a woman who looked to be about Edie's age. Bob was happy about that. A woman, especially one Edie's age, was bound to be more sympathetic to her. It was a good sign, he told Edie.

Two file folders filled with papers were on the desk in front of Judge Goren, and after shuffling through them a bit, she looked up at the people in front of her.

"I've read all of your declarations and I have a few questions I'd like to ask each of you." Looking at Edie, "Mr. Rosenberg states that you were never home."

"I was home, your honor. Maybe not as much as some mothers, but I was there every afternoon between 3 and 5, and I was there for the important things. When the children needed me."

"You hardly ever came to Missy's tennis matches," Ken said.

Edie addressed Missy, not Ken. "Missy, if I didn't come to your matches, it wasn't because I didn't want to be there, it was because your father didn't want me there."

And Liz, raising her hand, "I'd like to say something, judge. Even when Missy was a little baby, Edie was off working at the restaurants and Ken had to feed Missy breakfast and drive her to nursery school."

"Yes," the judge said to Liz, "I read your declaration. And I must ask you not to speak out unless you're called on."

"Sorry, Judge," Liz said, looking triumphant. She had said what she wanted to say.

The judge again focused on Edie, "Tell me, Mrs. Rosenberg, if Melissa stays with you, what are your plans?"

"I plan to cut down on my hours. The restaurants are doing fine without me. I plan to spend as much time with Missy as she wants."

Now the judge looked at Maria. "Mrs. Rosenberg, I understand you're a newlywed. How do you feel about having Melissa live with you?"

"Oh, I'd love it," Maria said. And then deciding to add something on her own, "I've heard all about Melissa for the six years I've known Ken, so I feel very close to her."

Ken and his attorney winced.

The judge: "Well, I'd like to speak with Melissa alone, but before I do that," looking from Edie to Ken, "do either of you have anything to add?"

"Yes," Ken said. "I'd just like to say that ever since Missy was born, we've been kind of a twosome. I'm the one who takes her to all her tennis lessons and to all her tennis tournaments. Before I moved out of the house, I used to go out and hit balls with her just about every day. And in the winter, we'd go skiing together, either for the weekend, or up to Mammoth for a whole week. Just the two of us." He took a breath. "As I stated in my declaration, your honor, my former wife has two children from previous liaisons, and I really believe her feelings for Missy were never what they were for those two previous children."

"Your honor," Edie said, interrupting, "I'm sorry, but I can't sit here and listen to this. It's true that Ken and Missy have a special relationship, but that's because that's how Ken arranged it. As for my "previous children", yes, I have a special place in my heart for them, but I also have a special place in my heart for Missy. I don't deny that Ken's been a good father to Missy, a great father, but I've also been a good mother. I'm not asking that you take Missy away from Ken, I'm only asking that you give me an equal chance to be a parent to her. Please, your honor, don't take my child away from me."

A moment of silence.

"All right," the judge said, "I'll see Melissa alone, now."

Edie, her attorney, Ken, his attorney, Liz and Maria all rose and returned to the courtroom.

Edie could not look at Ken. She had never hated anyone as much she hated him at this moment. How could he have said all those things? How could he have intimated that Edie did not love Missy?

Bob put his hand on her arm. "Calm down," he said.

"I can't," she said.

After what seemed like an interminable amount of time, the judge summoned them back into her chambers. A court reporter was now seated at a small table beside the judge and began typing as the judge began to speak.

"As you know, these are very difficult cases, and there usually isn't a right way. But a choice has to be made, and it has fallen to me to make that choice. In this case I find that both homes are suitable environments for the child, and that both parents are suitable parents. And in most cases, I do favor joint custody. However, in this instance, since there seems to be such a great amount of hostility from the child toward her mother, I feel that at this time, it would benefit the child to be placed with her father."

Ken hugged Missy, and then hugged Maria and his mother.

The judge continued, "I therefore award sole physical and legal custody of Melissa Rosenberg to her father." And then looking at Edie, "This doesn't mean that at some later date, things cannot change, that at some later date, joint custody cannot be restored. I think it's a matter of you working on your relationship with your daughter, Mrs. Rosenberg."

The court reporter finished typing, and the judge banged her gavel, "Court is adjourned."

Edie felt she could not stand, that she had been thrust into a deep, dark pit, and there was no way out. She wanted to scream, "This is not fair," but no words came out. Bob pulled her to her feet, and while the people at the other end of the table were celebrating, Bob led her out of the chambers, and there waiting alone in the empty courtroom was Janet. Janet, her dearest and truest friend.

Janet could see from the expression on Edie's face what had happened, and came to her and cradled her in her arms. "Oh, Edie, I'm so sorry."

"Janet, they're taking my baby from me. What am I going to do?"

And Janet smoothing Edie's hair, "You'll get her back. Don't worry. One day you'll get her back."

And Edie sobbing, "Oh, Janet, I'm so miserable."

"I know. I know."

Gently, Janet led Edie out of the courtroom, out of the courthouse, down the steps, and into Janet's waiting car.

As they drove through the congested streets, onto the crowded freeway, Edie wondered what had she done wrong? Why was God punishing her like this? And then she looked at Janet sitting beside her. Janet, who had been so loyal and faithful since the day they met, and she so cruel and unforgiving since Janet married Mike. Maybe God was punishing her for that. She turned to her friend. "Janet, I've treated you so badly. Can you ever forgive me?"

"Of course, I forgive you."

"I've been so mean to you."

"It's okay," Janet said.

And then Edie, recalling Missy's words in the hallway, knew that she would have to face the fear that had been gnawing at her stomach ever since Missy had spoken them. "Maybe Missy's right," she said, almost to herself. "Maybe they're all right. Maybe I did favor Wendy and Brian over Missy." And then, turning to Janet, looking for some solace, "But if I did, Janet, it wasn't intentional. I always thought I loved Missy as much as I loved Wendy and Brian."

"Don't be ridiculous," Janet said. "You adored Missy. Always. From the day she was born."

"Then why do I feel so guilty?"

"Edie, you've got to learn to stop blaming yourself for every bad thing that happens in your life."

And Edie and Janet looked at each other and smiled. How often had Edie said that to Janet.

"What you need," Janet said, "is something to get your mind off of all this. How about us opening a new restaurant?"

"A new restaurant? When did you come up with that idea?"

"It's something I've been thinking about for awhile. Now that we've got Edie's Cafe and Trattoria Mia pretty much under control, why not open another restaurant?"

"But where? How?"

"We'd have to find a good location and it shouldn't be Italian. It should be something new and trendy, like all the other restaurants opening around town."

"You mean with a Far Eastern influence?"

"Yes, but we should still serve pastas," Janet said. "Pastas are in."

"And pizzas," Edie said. "People love pizzas."

"We'll have to come up with a good name for it," Janet said. "Something that will carry over our image but won't tie us to Italian. You're good at names. Think of something."

And Edie thought for a moment, "How about Mia, Too?"

"I like it," Janet said. "It's perfect."

"But if we're going to do Asian," Edie said, "we should go to China, Japan, Thailand."

"Well there's no reason you can't go," Janet said, thinking that Brian would be starting college in the fall, and Edie no longer had Missy to take care of.

"I don't know," Edie said. "I don't know if I'm ready to take all this on. Not after what just happened in that courtroom."

"That's exactly why you should take it on. There's nothing you can do about Missy in the immediate future. You've got to do something, keep busy with something. It'd be good for you to get away for awhile, and when you come back, who knows? Maybe Missy will be more receptive to seeing you."

Janet was right, Edie thought. There was nothing she could do in the immediate future to win Missy back. Maybe it would be a good idea to focus on a new restaurant, to get away from Los Angeles for awhile. She pictured herself stepping off a plane in China, Japan, Thailand, as she once pictured herself as an archaeologist. Only now instead of hunting for fossils, she would be hunting for new ideas, new ingredients. But Janet should go with her. "But Janet, if I go, then you should go, too. It'll be like old times."

"I'd love to go. Of course, I'd love to go, but how can I, with the baby and all?"

"You could leave Ernesto with Mike," Edie ventured.

"After I waited 40 years to have him? Would you?"

"No," Edie said without hesitation. And then, pleased with herself for thinking of it, "But I would take him with."

"And what about Mike?"

Ah, that was the problem. What to do about Mike? Perhaps Edie had carried this grudge long enough. Perhaps it was time to let go of her anger toward Mike. "I guess Mike could come too."

"You mean it, Edie?"

And Edie feeling the dark shadow that had been following her for the last few years, evaporate, said, "Yes. Yes, I mean it."

"Well in that case...," Janet said, "let me talk to Mike about it."

Edie leaned back on the soft leather of Janet's new Volvo and felt the warmth of the sunlight on her face. If she decided to go, she was sure Janet would go with her, with or without Ernesto, with or without Mike, and even if Janet wouldn't go, Edie could find someone who would. She had met a lot of chefs and restaurateurs over the past few years; people who loved the world of food as much as she did. Perhaps Gordon would go. He was always ready to move on a whim, and he was as interested in new trends as anyone.

She was feeling stronger now, more confident. She would win Missy back, she would, and in the meantime, she would begin scouting for a new location. Santa Monica, perhaps. Or Venice Beach. The future was wide open.